BLACK HAT

AFTERLIFE ONLINE
BOOK TWO

Domino Finn

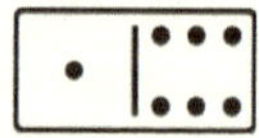

Published by Blood & Treasure, Los Angeles
First Edition

Cover Typography by James T. Egan of Bookfly Design LLC.

Print ISBN: 978-1-946-00882-4

DominoFinn.com

Also by Domino Finn

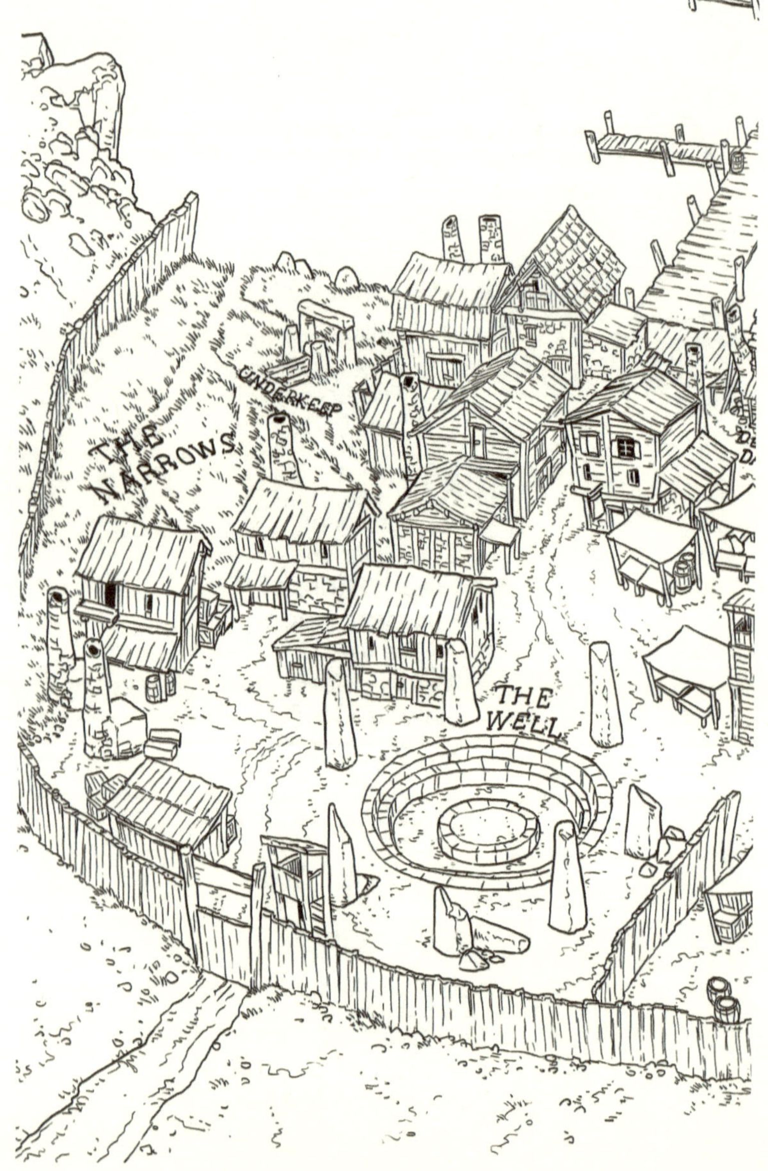

SHOREH
THE NARROWS
UNDERKEEP
THE WELL

OME
BOARD WALK
COAST MARKET
SEASIDE
BEAR PITS

BLACK HAT

AFTERLIFE ONLINE: BOOK TWO

0530 Castle Crashers

I inched forward in the narrow passage. Oppressive was a better way to describe it: Warm. Damp. Claustrophobic. And once I left the skylight I'd slipped into behind me, it was dark. Very, very dark.

What could've been a straightforward raid of a crumbling castle had evolved. Work smarter, not harder, was my motto. Instead of taking the head-on approach, I'd scaled a series of makeshift stone and wooden structures, stacking upward like a pyramid against a raging body of water. The Black Keep was part castle, part city, and part dam. My map had finally revealed that once we'd sufficiently explored the area. The river was the reason the entire basin was so damn humid.

The party chat window blinked.

Kyle: *More tangos on our six, Echo Squad.*

I halted my search and arched an eyebrow. Kyle was still on the outer surface of the keep—in broad daylight. We hadn't just peacefully strolled in, of course. The wildkins were dead set on giving us trouble. Even though I couldn't see or hear Kyle, we could message each other in party chat.

Talon: *Echo Squad? What's that?*
Kyle: *That's us, bro.*
Talon: *I keep telling you, this isn't a squad—it's a party. Wrong game genre.*
Kyle: *Copy that, Maverick.*

I rolled my eyes. Some things couldn't be helped.

Talon: *Can you handle them?*
Kyle: *Not a problem. For now. But I'd feel more comfortable jumping into the skylight and joining you in dungeon diving.*

I couldn't believe I was gonna resort to this, but it was the easiest way.

Talon: *You have your orders, soldier. Now maintain radio silence unless absolutely necessary.*
Kyle: *Copy that, Maverick.*

I sighed. In the distance, I heard the muted scream of a wildkin.

We'd signed up for this pagan quest expecting to kill more goblins, but apparently pagans come in all shapes and sizes.

Unlike their green counterparts, wildkins are very human in size and shape. Strip any one of us naked, smear us with dirt, garb us in bones and paint, grow out our hair, and anybody'd be hard-pressed to find a single difference between the so-called races.

Which was a little unsettling. Killing wildkins didn't feel especially enlightened, but it helped that they came at us with bloodthirsty zeal. Out here in their territory, it was kill or be killed.

I pressed ahead in the passage. It was triangular shaped. Stone floor. One wall made of stacked stone blocks; the other a slanted roof of wood that used the old bricks for support. As I crawled forward, layers of leaves and whatever else the wildkins piled on the roof blocked out the last of the stray lines of sunlight. Blackness took over.

I was employing a couple of new skills. Sneak was exactly what it sounded like. With the rest of "Echo Squad" raising hell above, this wasn't an ideal stealth scenario, but being alone in an unlit tunnel, it was more of a best-practices thing.

Darkvision was my other new skill, and it slowly clarified the scene. This wasn't a passage so much as rafter space. The wildkins stood as tall as people and there was barely enough room in here for that. There were no treasures or guards or anything, really. Just twisted bunches of straw stuffed into random crevices on the floor and wall.

Also, a dead end. I cursed.

An explosion sounded behind me, timed to a flash of fire and light. I tightened my grip on the dragonspear and charged backward. Kyle lay on his back amid the wreckage of shattered roofing. A fresh hole in the ceiling bathed him in sunlight, and fire littered the debris.

Kyle was a brewmaster. Unless the wildkins had gotten into alchemy, there was no doubt he'd fumbled one of his potions.

"You okay?" I asked, just as a mob holding a sharpened stick dropped into the passage. He spun to my voice.

I gritted my teeth. "Big mistake."

We ran at each other. Without a lot of room in the tunnel to maneuver, I opted for surprise. While still fifteen feet away from contact, I triggered the dash skill and propelled into him. His paltry stick snapped against the might of my legendary dragonspear.

Surprise!
Disarm!
You dealt 47 damage to [Wildkin]
[Wildkin] is defeated
103 XP awarded

Completely outmatched, he crumpled to the ground. I winced at the grotesque expression frozen on his face. Except for the pointed ear, he looked just like a normal person. I paused, unsure of—

"Watch out!"

I spun in the direction of Izzy's warning. Above me, in midair, sunlight glinted off a steel sword swinging down in both hands like an action frame of a comic book. The wildkin had me dead to rights, without enough warm-up time to activate my crossblock.

A barrel-sized block of ice intercepted him like a wrecking ball. The poor guy never even made it into the passage. A muffled oof and multiple crashing sounds followed him down the roof of the pyramid.

A five-foot-tall pixie with lavender skin blocked the sun above. Her face was plastered with disappointment. "That's the last one."

"For now," coughed Kyle, repeating his earlier sentiment. He grimaced and climbed to his feet. The breastplate and mail had protected him from most of the damage. We were still in business.

Izzy lightly hopped to the stone floor, light-blue dress and cape fluttering in the wind. "They're definitely on to us," she agreed. "What've you found?"

I swallowed. "Well, nothing yet."

"What?"

"NOTHING YET," I repeated loudly.

Izzy narrowed her eyes. "I heard what you said. I was expressing disbelief." She looked around. "So much for the great plan."

"It's a solid plan," I insisted.

Kyle nodded in support. "Got us this far."

Izzy strode ahead, her small frame not requiring her to duck. "A dead end?"

We followed. I was short enough to fair well, but Kyle was an inch above six feet. This space simply wasn't built for him.

I ticked fingers to my accomplishments. "I was the one who found the quest. I was the one who had the idea to scale the pyramidal outer wall and use the recall runes to get you up here.

I was the one who found the skylights to sneak in. We're at the summit of the Black Keep and our hands are clean."

I quietly noted the generous quantity of wildkin blood on my palms and wiped it on my coat.

"Relatively. So here we are."

"He's right," agreed Kyle. "We skipped the whole dungeon."

Izzy scoffed. "You call this a dungeon?" She pointed to the batches of twigs and straw. Excited cooing and fluttering now surrounded the nests. "Those are roosting birds. We're not in a pagan dungeon. We're in an attic. Those aren't skylights. They're... bird holes. And now we're backed into a corner."

The passage ended abruptly in a wall of horizontal wood beams. Not finely planed two-by-fours, mind you. This was more log-cabin style, except the trees used were much smaller.

"I was working on it." Kyle moved to light a torch and I signaled him to stop. "Hold off on that. Izzy, can you do something about the light?"

She shrugged and retreated down the passage. Her ice magic made quick work of the open flames. She also did something to plug the sunlight coming through the roof. As the passage darkened again, the area filled in with more detail than a torch would provide. The corners of my mouth crooked up.

You see, I may not have known exactly where I was going, but that didn't mean I was without a plan. I'd been reading up on Haven mechanics, wondering how to best spend my plethora of skill points. In the end someone else had made the decision for me.

A thief by the name of Crux posted a discovery to an urbex community. Turns out skills work slightly differently in conjunction with others. Part of the evolving game world. You could say they sort of mod each other. In this case, a player interested in dungeon diving found a cool trick the devs probably hadn't intended.

First up were a couple of general survival skills. Navigation offered a HUD: in-game overlays with extra information about direction and terrain, like compass directions and well-worn paths. Nothing exemplary by any means but handy for a scout who wants to be aware of his environment.

Cartography was more interesting. Not the mapmaking part —my craft attribute was too low to produce anything appealing. But to create detailed maps, one needs to be *aware* of said details, so the cartography skill also enhances in-game maps with additional info.

The combination of HUD overlays with heightened map awareness meant assessing dungeon routes was much easier. The insight had inspired my plan to enter the Black Keep from the top.

It gets better.

The trick was to combine these with darkvision. Enhanced vision in lowlight turns out to be superior to torchlight, both in range and detail. It's counterintuitive as all hell because anybody in a dark dungeon wants to crack a light, but the reward for not doing so was much more information—as long as you're equipped with the skill combo. It essentially gave dungeons an easy button.

Which is why, after scanning the area and swapping back and forth with my map, I was now staring at a prompt that showed the passage continued ahead. I was the newest dungeon speed-runner on the block. At least until the skill combo was nerfed.

My spear disappeared from my hand and was replaced by a small whittling knife. I set the blade to the binding of the pinioned wall.

"That's gonna take forever," complained Kyle. He lowered his shoulder and charged, forcing me to dive clear. He crashed through the splintered wall with a heavy thud and a cloud of dust, followed by more coughing.

Izzy returned and stared dumbly at him, then me.

"What?" said Kyle defensively. "It worked for the roof."

I chuckled.

The three of us pressed ahead in the darkness. I took the lead while they moved slowly, unable to see well. The ground transitioned from stone to packed dirt. The pyramid appearance was just a sheltered mountain face. There could be any number of tunnels snaking through the incline. I wondered if this was a shortcut to our objective after all.

The ground creaked beneath my boots. The dirt gave way to pinioned wood, just like the wall, except it was a tunnel bridge. There must've been a crevasse below, though I couldn't make out anything but darkness.

I waited until Kyle and Izzy caught up. "Watch the floor," I whispered.

The brewmaster tested the platform with a heavy foot. "I'm not walking on that, bro."

"We have to."

"No, we don't. Maybe Izzy's right. This isn't a passage. It's barely tall enough for the wildkins. We're just stuck in the roof somewhere."

"All the better. This is the medieval equivalent of sneaking through the air ducts."

"Fine. But we need a torch. *We* don't have darkvision and I'm not about to plummet to a virtual death because I stepped on a rotten log."

I grunted. "Okay, but let me scout ahead in the darkness. Give me a minute before lighting up and following."

"Copy that, Maverick."

I ignored him. A precipitous bridge was better than partaking in his *Top Gun* fantasies.

Scurrying footsteps echoed through the tunnel behind us.

"Crap," said Izzy. "More wildkins. They broke through my ice wall."

"Sorry, bro. It's time to light up."

My face soured. "Goose would never do that to Maverick."

His torch blazed to life and painted us orange. "Goose dies. Screw *that*. I'm Ice Man."

I nodded. "Yeah, that makes sense."

"Focus, boys," snapped Izzy. "Talon, get going. We'll hold them off. You better be right about this or we'll be respawning in no time."

I gritted my teeth and took off over the platform faster than I should have. It swayed terribly. Combat broke out in my wake, but I wasn't overly worried. Wildkins didn't look like goblins, but difficulty-wise they were more or less on par with them. At level 9, and 8 for Kyle, they were yellow enemies. Not as trivial as non-aggroing whites, but simple challenges nonetheless. Only really dangerous in numbers. In that sense, this narrow passage gave us a tactical advantage.

A beam of wood snapped under my boot.

Agility Check...
Pass!

I expertly rolled to the side. Agility was my primary attribute. At 24, I could handle many vital situations with ease. I just had to make sure Izzy and Kyle were more careful.

Metal weapons clanged against each other. The wildkins had already engaged in close combat. I fought the urge to assist my party and scouted ahead.

The wood platform connected with natural rock. There was an outcropping, a formation jutting from the floor. Was it a pedestal? A lever? I shivered as I recalled the last stone obelisk I'd encountered. That one had turned out to be the horn of a giant buried cyclops. I hurried to the ground to study it.

I was both disappointed and relieved to realize the large rock... was just a large rock. The passage continued but quickly grew smaller. A breeze carried through from outside. I detected a faint amount of light ahead, as if the passage would soon end in an outside exit, no closer to our objective than when we'd started.

I paused and studied the area. Either my dungeon skills were missing something or I'd been completely wrong about this place. In heavy darkness, why wasn't I seeing a secret passage?

I trudged back past the rock and stopped on the edge of the natural ground. I flicked my map on and off.

It had to be.

I knelt beside the stone outcropping and felt around it on all sides. Its irregular shape had a coarse finish. I grinned and produced a rope from my inventory and began with the knots.

"There're too many of them!" Izzy screamed. "Fall back!"

A huge burst of magic filled the tunnel. Even as far away as I was, frigid air washed over me. I stood and turned to face them.

Echoes resounded my way. I stepped carefully forward onto the wood platform. The beams were thrumming to a fast beat. Footsteps. Panicked running.

"No," I whispered.

I burst into a desperate run. If Kyle and Izzy were too rough with the platform, they'd fall to their deaths. "Watch your step!" I screamed.

"Reloading," said Kyle in a clipped voice that told me he was also running.

Izzy may have been a five-foot pixie, but Kyle was a pretty big guy. This structure couldn't support his careless weight. I abandoned all precaution and barreled ahead even faster.

Their torchlight came into view first. I yelled, "Get behind me!" and didn't slow.

Izzy rounded the corner chugging a spirit potion. "They have strong counter-magic. Should I use my legendary power?"

"Not yet." Four beats later Kyle followed, looking a little rough. "Grab the rope!" I said as I dashed past.

"Wha—?" started Kyle.

He turned to me as his boot cleaved an old log in two and his leg slipped through the floor. He caught the rope trailing behind me, but not before his armored girth splintered the wood supports under him. The entire platform shuddered.

Izzy skidded to a stop. "You're not doing what I think you're doing, are you?"

"I am," I called back, hoping she had the sense to grab the rope line.

Ahead of me, a formation of wildkins rushed down the tunnel. They stood shoulder to shoulder, managing a row of five in these tight quarters. That alone was daunting, but with the shimmering yellow aura protecting them like a hovering shield it was no wonder Izzy and Kyle had booked it. Like me, the wildkins rushed over the platform with careless abandon.

Careless, maybe, but at least I had a safety line.

I braced my spear in both hands and heaved downward. The shimmering white blade snapped through reams of wood. I backed away, closer to the hole Kyle was currently struggling with.

"Help a brother out," he said.

I snickered. "Sure thing, Ice Man."

I ripped the spear into the last wood beam groaning under his weight.

"Remind me to kill you later," grumbled Izzy.

Amid twenty clattering footfalls, the entire bridge snapped in half.

I only had time to see the wildkins widen their eyes in alarm before I fell myself. After so much structural damage, the beams of wood offered no further support. They were debris now. Missiles to avoid as we all plummeted downward. The knotted rope pulled tightly around my waist. I swung backward with Kyle and Izzy toward the rock outcropping to which the other end of the rope was tied. The wildkins had no such parachute.

Jagged wood rained down. Large sections of the platform broke away. Our descent was halted by the rope, so luckily we remained above most of the destruction. As we collided with the far wall, the rope snapped at my waist. I tumbled down the slope until I, too, met the ground.

No more rafters for us. We were in a large cavern now. Deep and damp, but well lit by wall sconces. Finally, we'd made it into the dungeon proper.

"Piece of cake," I coughed.

> Proficiency improved: **Expert Searcher**
> You are extremely well versed with hiding techniques and will execute searches at a high level.

My blurring vision took in the ample space. A large figure, seven feet tall, sat on a throne made from the husk of a burnt tree. He was lean and bare chested, with ragged leather pants and boots. On his head and over his face sat a stag skull with broad antlers.

"Welcome, welcome to the heart of the Black Keep," spoke the wild king.

0540 King of the Monsters

Amazingly, given our grievous intrusion, the ruler didn't rise. I remained on my hands and knees, wary of making a threatening motion before I was ready. As long as the wild king was content to rest, so was I.

The man was fully at ease in his chamber, leaning sideways on his throne. His muscles were sinewy and appeared well used. As my vision came into focus, what I'd assumed to be dirt on his chest proved to be a tattoo of a deer skull, wide antlers extending to wide shoulders. It matched exactly the mask he wore. More precisely, the crown.

"Thou art uninvited," he proclaimed.

[Theoderic - Wild King]
Ruler of the Blackwood
800 Health

I stood as I received the health notification, a sure sign that an enemy had aggroed. Despite that, the king continued sitting.

Rafter wreckage littered the floor. A huge chandelier crafted from the bone of twenty stags and the wood of twenty trees hung askew, three of its support cables snapped. It didn't appear to have radiated light in ages so we made do with the flickering wall sconces. The flames created grotesque shadows on the floor as they washed over the bodies of the wildkins who had plunged to their deaths. Feathers from panicked birds wafted through the air like snow.

Kyle had taken a bad tumble and was struggling to get up. If he was suffering from some sort of crippling affliction, either time or a health potion would do him good. Izzy had managed to hang onto the rope. She stood sideways against the wall, thirty feet up.

I brushed myself off and looked into the skull of the wild king.

"So many dead," he lamented. "My people, whose only wish was to protect their king, lie broken." Mask or not, his visage was haggard. I avoided meeting the dead eyes of his kin on the ground. "I shall reward them for dutiful service upon their respawn."

My eye twitched. NPCs and mobs didn't usually break the fourth wall like that. They didn't talk about respawning and experience points and leveling, not unless it was necessary to communicate to a resident of Haven.

His lamentation now complete, the wild king took a curious turn at studying me, just as I was him. He smiled beneath his mask.

"Reveal, reveal thy intent," he instructed.

Harried cries came from the great hall leading to this chamber. I twirled the dragonspear in my hand. Theoderic tightened his knuckles on the armrests of his throne.

"So be it, human."

Dark figures raced into the room. Two. Four. A mixed band of men and goblins holding lengths of chain, they wore black hoods over their faces, most unnerving due to the absence of eyeholes.

> **Blackwood Prisoner**
> 85 Health

"Oh crap," said Izzy. "I should use my legendary power."

"Don't waste it," I urged. I activated my dash skill and fired towards the doorway, right past the newcomers. More of them sprinted toward us. I kicked loose a block holding a crank in place and the large portcullis hovering over the entry wound down. The protective steel gate railed into the ground just before the second wave of reinforcements entered.

The wild king leaned forward in his chair.

"Covering fire!" barked Kyle. His double-crossbow slung glass bolts that popped on a pair of enemies. The vials injected corrosive into their bloodstreams.

> [Kyle] dealt 28 damage to [Blackwood Prisoner]
> DoT: 15 dmg/10 secs
> [Kyle] dealt 26 damage to [Blackwood Prisoner]
> DoT: 15 dmg/10 secs

All four converged on me. I crouched between them, waited, and activated tornado spin. I whirled several revolutions, slashing and bashing with both ends of the spear.

```
You dealt 44 damage to [Blackwood Prisoner]
You dealt 44 damage to [Blackwood Prisoner]
You dealt 44 damage to [Blackwood Prisoner]
You dealt 42 damage to [Blackwood Prisoner]
[Blackwood Prisoner] is defeated
[Blackwood Prisoner] is defeated
240 XP awarded
```

Blue fire rushed over Kyle as he leveled. Suddenly he was perfectly fine. He jumped to his feet and reloaded his double crossbow.

I muttered under my breath. Tornado spin had been nerfed with the last patch. No more spin to win. It totally wrecked yellow enemies, and did decent damage against oranges like these prisoners, but it had been converted into more of an emergency move granting clearance rather than a destructive force. Coupled with its high spirit cost, it just wasn't a game breaker anymore.

The final two hooded enemies buckled under a barrage of ice daggers from above.

"Welcome to level 9, slacker," called out Izzy from above. "How's it feel?"

Kyle shrugged. "Pretty good, actually." He trained his crossbow on the wild king. "Now it's time for the main event."

The ruler sighed behind his mask. "Indeed, indeed. Is it thee, then, who wishest to usurp my kingdom? I accept thy challenge to solitary combat."

"Huh?" said Kyle. He looked around and scoffed. "I'm not sure if you've heard of Seal Team Six, but these days we do things in elite groups."

"A coward then." The skull swiveled to me. "Is it thee who hast come for me?"

Wildkins batted at the closed portcullis. I stepped ahead cautiously. "Nothing personal, and all that. After the pagan attack on Stronghold, we can't be too careful. We're clearing the countryside of your kin, and this is the countryside."

"Keep thy kingdom," he said. "Leave me mine."

I snorted. "A little late for that."

He canted his head. "The later the hour, the sooner the dawn. I politick not with the errant folk. I am neither a founder nor destroyer of cities. I am the wild. I am the land and the animals and the hunt."

"*And* a pagan," pointed out Kyle.

The king rose to his feet. "I do not call myself thus. Thou doth."

"Stay still," warned Izzy from above. "Unless you want to get really cold really fast." She gripped the rope with one hand and pointed her new legendary staff at him with another. A blade of ice glimmered at its head. She *really* wanted to use her legendary power. "Everyone calls the wildkins pagans," she noted.

"And I am their king and speak otherwise. Did I partake in the folly of the errant folk? Did I summon my band to raid thy town?" He grunted. "I desire not the white city."

"Bro," laughed Kyle, "are you serious right now? This is just a stupid quest. We might be the first to make it here, but you better get used to burglars, bonehead."

"The quests, the quests," he mused thoughtfully. "I wonder who writes them?"

Okay, something was off with this guy. He was acting meta aware of the simulation.

I ground my teeth. What kind of MMO made players feel guilty for simple raids? "I'm not here for your kingdom," I said boldly. "I'm not even here for your life. You know what I want."

"And thou knowest what I shan't freely give."

"Your words," said Kyle as he ripped loose an arrow.

The wild king raised his forearm. The bolt plunked deep and cranked him full of juice. He just stood there and took it, arrow in arm, as solid as the tree that made up his throne.

When the ruler spoke now, his voice was edged with anger.

"Folly, folly, melancholy. We broke away from the madness of the errant folk. We will not be subjugated or drafted, adventurers. We will not kneel. And we will never bow down to the likes of thee. I wear the mantle of Ruler of the Blackwood. The wildkins stand on their own."

A booming footstep shook the ground, followed by another, and another. We looked around nervously for their source.

"And my people will not stand idly by while ye destroy our unity, respawning or not."

We turned to the portcullis. A huge figure in shadow, standing even taller than the wild king himself, reached the gate. Like the Blackwood prisoners he, too, wore a hood over his head. His was fashioned with holes to accommodate glowing white eyes. The giant upturned a broad axe and rammed it into the gate. The portcullis shook on its mounts.

Our faces twisted at the notification. This eight-foot ogre was a force of nature. How was it that he didn't need health to... well, to do anything? His axe hit the gate again and rattled the walls of the throne room.

Light steps patted the dirt. I turned and readied my spear as Theoderic swung a fist. I activated crossblock and sank to the ground as his blow was deflected.

Ugh. I'd encountered this before. Despite upgrading my combat skills, the king hit so hard it was better to dodge than to block.

Kyle and Izzy both attacked at the same time. The wildkin jumped backward as an arrow whizzed past his face. Izzy, however, had fired her icicle at the ceiling. It ripped through the last support holding the gargantuan chandelier to the ceiling.

"Talon, get out of there!"

I didn't need to be told twice. I triggered dash and moved clear of the falling object. The wild king wasn't as fast. Two tons of jagged wood and bone crashed down onto him. The warden outside the gate howled.

As the dust and feathers cleared, I approached the wreckage. The king lay on his back, impaled straight through the chest, essentially stapled to the floor. I carefully inched close and lifted his crown into my hands.

Quest Update: **Dethrone the Wild King**
Quest Type: Fetch
Reward: Unknown
You've recovered the crown of the pagan wild king. Now it is time to destroy it.
1,000 XP awarded

The trapped ruler huffed raggedly. "Heed, heed my warning, adventurer. That crown carries a price. The cost for this desecration shall be thy eternal soul."

I pulled away from him. That sounded metal as fuck.

"Come on," yelled Izzy. "It's time to get out of here!"

She was right. We could stay and play mop-up. Kill the king, the warden, and a veritable army of underlings. But the quest chain had advanced. If we died here the crown would be force dropped and we'd have to start over. And something about this king told me he wouldn't be so easily intruded upon next time.

We'd attained our objective and didn't have to kill anymore wildkins. Win-win, in my book. I hurried to the rope. Kyle was already clambering up the wall. Behind us, the portcullis creaked under the relentless axe of the warden.

Besides, how do you kill something with zero hit points?

0550 Defender of the Crown

The sun glared overhead as we scurried down the roof of the Black Keep. Rickety wood planks filled the gaps between ancient stonework and damp ground.

"Uh, Talon," started Kyle, nearly out of breath, "you never said anything about us needing to climb *down* on the way out."

That much was true. As far as plans went, I hadn't thought about much beyond acquiring the crown. I guess I figured we would just walk out the front door. But that was the problem with skipping dungeons completely: all the mobs were still active.

"At least we don't have an army after us," I returned, hopping over a particularly precarious wood beam.

Still, he had a point. Kyle would never be able to cover the same ground I had on the way up. I perched on a mossy rooftop and scanned the countryside.

It wasn't pretty. The Blackwood was aptly named. The entire forest sat in a basin between mountain peaks, farther south than any of us had ever traveled. The towering trees were nothing more than blackened fossils for most of their length, only opening up to foliage in a patchwork canopy. Long ago the forest must've been nearly burned down. It had never recovered.

Why the wildkins would make this their home was beyond me. The decrepit castle had a sort of spooky charm, but something the wild king had said was grating on me. The wildkins had broken away from the errant folk. They were no friends of the goblins.

Maybe the reason they lived in BFE was simply to be left alone.

"I actually think they're letting us leave," pointed out Izzy.

I scanned behind us. Not a wildkin in sight. A small miracle that did little to settle me. The Blackwood creeped me out. I wanted to get out of here as fast as humanly possible.

Flanking half of the valley was a dam that kept the basin from flooding. It ran perpendicular to the direction home, but the path was less treacherous.

"This way," I said. I flanked a series of abandoned huts, skirted a brickwork fire pit, and dropped to the top of the dam. I helped Kyle down. Izzy hopped by herself.

"What was that back there?" she asked.

"What?"

"The royal screwjob you almost pulled."

"What are you talking about? We did it. We're good."

"No, Talon. You're off your game. You kept hesitating back there, unable to take the kill shot, almost being ambushed."

I hissed and broke off into a sprint along the dam.

At one time, the structure must have been impressive. Numerous blocks of stone carefully coordinated to keep a river at bay. It was a symbol of man conquering nature, but time conquered even man. The rock was worn by the water and the wind. It had crumbled in places and was patched with logs and debris not unlike a beaver dam. While the bulk of the water had been held off, it trickled through the wall at a constant clip. Moss grew over the stone and wood alike, making the whole thing a slippery mess. We picked our way down a section of logs piled all the way to the ground. Finally, we reached the bottom of the basin.

"I'm not letting you off the hook that easily," chided Izzy.

"You're gonna question my leadership now?"

"No one ever appointed you leader."

"What?" I paused. "You guys know I'm the leader of this party, right?"

"Self-appointed," she said, digging her staff into moist soil. I swear, ever since she'd found the damn thing in Dragonperch she thought she was the chosen one. Maybe she wanted to take over. "The truth is, any of us are qualified to be a leader."

We both paused and turned to Kyle, who was standing there picking his teeth with a glass crossbow bolt filled with poison. He shrugged. "I'm a follower. I admit it."

I started down the path through the Blackwood. Bandit waited by a set of mossy steps. "Hey, girl," I said, giving her chin a rough scrubbing.

I couldn't tell if Izzy was just giving me a hard time or was actually questioning my abilities. After last week's siege of Stronghold, the whole city had banded together to rebuild. We put questing aside to put our homes back together, player and NPC alike. But revenge wasn't all holding hands and singing

"Kumbaya" and living well. No. Once we'd become whole again, we began clearing the countryside of pagans.

At first it was just the stragglers. Then the stalwart holdouts. Small bands of goblins and kobolds who'd refused to retreat. Some of them had taken hold in the noob dungeons north of town. General Azzyrk had been so bold as to order follow-up raids against small groups of travelers. That was when the questing started. Trafford and other questkeepers had piles of them on offer. Killing pagans was suddenly the latest fad.

Izzy, Kyle, and I? We weren't interested in grinding alongside everyone else. I pumped Trafford for the coolest quest that was the farthest away from town to eliminate all competition.

My quest, my idea, my leadership. Right?

"I'm just saying—" started Izzy.

I whirled around and produced the crown from my inventory. "Look at it," I snapped. "We made it." As I waved the stag skull in my hand, Bandit snorted and gave me a sideways look. "Why don't we call a success a success and—"

The main gates of the Black Keep groaned open. As in, the ones on the ground close to us. As in, the ones we'd meticulously planned on avoiding. From the darkness within, the mismatched armor and black hood of the warden stomped outside. Straps of black leather hung away from him like loose rope. Chains dragged at his feet. In his left hand he carried a sharpened axe meant for beheadings.

The entire Blackwood forest drained of all movement. No birds or scurrying rodents. Even the breeze stopped.

"Grrrr..."

We all took a step backward. We'd fought bigger things

before, but something about Hood warned us off. It was probably the whole zero-health thing.

From the passage behind him, tens of hooded flunkies rushed us.

Izzy gripped her winter staff. "I'm thinking..."

"Yes," I said quickly. "Use it now."

She took center stage and spun her staff in a loop. As she did, the icy curve on the end thrummed purple, blue, and white. Blue runes traced into the ground and encapsulated us. I waved Bandit forward and she hurried to join us, squeezing together in safety.

The Blackwood prisoners started toward us at top speed, but they never made it. Izzy's staff exploded and a sheet of rain and snow poured over them. The flunkies turned blue and chunked into icicles. They crumbled down the stairs and blew away in the growing gale.

Izzy's winter staff is a true relic. While foraging in our new tower, she'd unlocked a secret compartment and discovered it. It was such perfect loot for a frost mage we'd all figured *it* more or less found *her*. Besides impressive attribute bonuses, it conferred a legendary power: sleet storm. Legendary powers are the ninja magic buttons of Haven, but they're expensive to use. They cost 50% of a user's max spirit and are only usable once per day.

Still more flunkies charged from the keep. The growing snow engulfed them, dead and buried. We stood at the heart of a blizzard now, beautiful destruction all around.

But the warden simply leaned into the gale-force winds and pressed forward. "I will have your head," he growled. He broke into a charge and cut through the snow.

"Uh, guys?" said Izzy, bracing behind her blizzard. "A little help?"

I pointed my spear forward before noting the swath of ice spilling from Izzy's staff. The storm magic didn't do more than slow Hood down, but its destructive power couldn't be denied. I turned my spear to Izzy's staff and forced her aim to the left. The vigorous winds turned to the makeshift section of logs against the dam. The rotted wood couldn't stand up to the torrent.

A sound even greater than the howling wind shook the valley. The river burst through the wood and roared toward us. The rushing whitewater instantly overtook the warden and barreled just as mercilessly toward us.

The sleet storm over, Izzy flipped her staff down and waved a hand before us. A wall of ice materialized. "Hold on," she yelled, bracing against it.

We did. The incoming wave knocked me senseless, but Izzy had the wherewithal to build the ice platform around us. The entire thing overturned and skimmed the water like the world's largest boogie board.

"I will follow you," Hood boomed over the rushing waves, "to the ends of the world."

Then the water overtook us all.

0560 Toobin'

The makeshift inner tube surged to the surface of the waves, all of us still accounted for. I hugged Bandit down and we surfed north as the entire basin of the Blackwood flooded.

"Watch the trees!" screamed Kyle.

We leaned left and right avoiding obstacles, batting them away with spear and staff. Behind us, the deluge calmed. The dam had only given so much. We skimmed along the water to the edge of the ashy forest where our little iceberg joined the main river and washed toward Stronghold.

The warden was nowhere in sight.

That fact turned what might've been a pleasant drift into a nervous affair. At some point, the rapids grew too treacherous to brave on a glorified ice cube. We disembarked, marched the rest of the day, and camped a night. There was definite lingering worry about the whole "to the ends of the world" threat made by Hood, but it was somewhat tempered by my possession of a stranger's cowl. The mysterious item did little to hide my identity in plain sight, but it made me difficult to track from afar.

"Hey, guys," said Kyle as we huddled by the fire, "any idea

what this is?" He produced a hardened ball of polished ivory.

"You holding loot back from us?" Izzy asked pointedly.

"Course not. I picked it up off one of the Blackwood prisoners in the throne room. There wasn't exactly time to discuss." He let us examine it.

[Bone Pearl]
Polished orb with ivory swirls, but inert.

"Weird," I said. "No powers or anything. You heard of these, Izzy?"

She pressed her lips together in thought. "Surprisingly, no."

"Maybe it's just like a valuable gem or something," offered Kyle.

I shrugged. "Maybe... Better not sell it until we discover its purpose."

It wasn't until late morning that we finally made it back to Stronghold territory. Walking along the river, we crested the mountain summit and saw something I had hoped never to see again: an army occupying the tended land outside the city.

A sea of full plate, men and horses wrapped in black and white tunics. Flags beat in the wind above. Tents swayed. The symbol was a clear one: a white cross on a field of black. These were crusaders.

I took a relieved breath as I realized the army wasn't hostile.

Stronghold's huge walls were not under pressure. The west gate was open. Towering above everything was our home, Dragonperch, a tower that stood taller and was older than anything in the city. Beside it was a petrified cyclops on his knees, an impressive vestige of the pagan assault.

The crusaders? You could call them a reaction. Their faction had existed since the start of the simulation, their cause already stated: keep the land free. Despite their mission, most residents of Stronghold had never seen a single crusader in person before a week ago.

The order of knights was based out of Oakengard, a heralded fortress to the far west. No player had ever seen the inside of those walls, however. Not even a screenshot. Information on the wiki was sparse. The leading rumor was that the town was unfinished, which made sense given Haven was still in beta. Word was it was an NPC town. A crusader town. For all intents and purposes, just colorful history.

Until now.

The appearance of the faction was obvious fallout from recent game events. The crusaders had found their cause bolstered by the audacity of the pagan attacks. It was a movement that had swept the land over the last week, in no small part due to developer support. My quick estimation of the present army put it at two hundred men and women. That wasn't all of them, just the number camping outside the gate. Two hundred swords equaled Stronghold's entire NPC army of legionnaires and watchmen. Sure, the four hundred players in town tripled the defending force, but many of those players weren't combat effective. Hell, many of them were now part of the crusader faction.

NPC driven but popular among players, I understood the desire to join. The crusaders swore to protect the land. To wipe the villainous pagans from civilized doorsteps. This black-cloaked force was the source of all the recent pagan quests. Quests which I'd happily devoured. Which we were in the middle of right this second.

Which is all a way of saying that I didn't have a huge bone to pick with these guys. It was more like one of those little bendy fish bones that gets caught in your teeth. A niggle. I understood what the army was here for, but the whole thing felt a little culty to me.

Outside of tended land, I couldn't check the wiki. I did, however, break out the patch notes from several days ago while we walked.

Haven version 0.9.22

- Several stability enhancements for gatherings of large armies.
- Rebalanced certain enemy groupings.
- After the incident at the Wicked Crow, Banishing Demons is now a prerequisite to Summoning Demons.

I chuckled. That sounded like a screwup I would've enjoyed watching with a bucket of popcorn in my lap.

- Recall Runes and Teleport spells no longer function in safe zones like player homes and the Pantheon rotunda.
- Recall Runes have been removed from stores. Teleport spells have undergone adjustments.
- Addressed friendly fire loopholes.

Heh. I took a perverse pleasure in noting these additions were for me. With teleportation options being vastly limited, Lucifer would need to find a new trick to gain access to the game code. I had missed the recall rune phaseout on my last read, however. Izzy and Kyle had used a pair to get to the top of the Black Keep. The patch now meant the items were a valuable resource that were only going to grow scarcer.

As for the friendly fire, whether the devs successfully surmounted the hack or not was an open question, since I didn't go around attacking guards in my own city. Not anymore.

- New drop rules to protect beginner players.
- New drop rules concerning silver to prevent inflation.
- Renamed silver bars to plates (100 silver coins=1 plate). Introduced new currency: silver bar (10 plates=1 bar).
- Rebalanced Tornado Spin.

Nerfed was more like it. I was pretty sure the devs didn't like me, but as one of the most powerful players in all of Haven, I thought it would be petty to complain.

Finally, I reached the section I was looking for.

- New pagan bounty and fetch quests added.
- Quadrupled conscripts in crusader army.
- Bolstered crusader stats.
- Fortified Oakengard. Increased Oakengard resource output.

I scoffed. It all seemed a little much. This was one hundred percent a developer response to pay back the pagans for attempting to sack Stronghold. It's the core city in all of Haven and, while I couldn't be sure of the specifics, it sure seemed like holding the city translated to controlling the game. As for Oakengard, judging from the patch notes it sounded like a hell of a lot more than an incomplete rumor to me.

"Heads up," warned Kyle, lifting his crossbow. We'd cleared the foothills and were getting close to the tended farmland. A detachment of crusaders approached on horseback.

"Lower your weapon, Kyle. No point starting anything with these guys."

He rested the crossbow over his shoulder. The horsemen slowed. All wore plate armor with enclosed helmets, but the man in the lead had black armor to match his tunic. Shin guards, vambraces, and a jet-black crusader helmet with a white cross emblazoned over the eye slit. Gray letters above his head read [Grimwart] and signified him an NPC.

"Hail, soldiers," I said, producing my spear but spiking it to the ground and leaning on it. Casual dangerous, I liked to call it.

Grimwart studied us. "Forsooth, is it really you?" He dismounted and approached. "Talon, Izzy, and Kyle. I have heard much of your exploits against the pagans."

"No way," said Kyle. "We didn't use any exploits. You're just jealous."

Izzy slapped his back. "He doesn't mean it like that, jackass. Although looking at you, one might wonder how else you've come so far."

"Says the five-foot purple lady."

I sighed and accepted Grimwart's hand. "Ignore them. They do this all the time."

He nodded and allowed a chuckle as he took them in. His eyes lingered on Bandit, a mount that dwarfed many of the crusader horses. "Aye. 'Tis not a crime. Levity is needed in these dark times." His helmet turned to my spear. "Is this the famed lance—"

"Spear," I corrected. "Dragon*spear*. The other one's trademarked."

He seemed unsure of my meaning but nodded. "The *spear* of Magnus Dragonrider?"

"It sure *was*," said Kyle. "Now it's Talon's. You should've seen him wield it against that titan."

Grimwart turned to the petrified cyclops and huffed. "I'm sure it was a sight to behold. It is well the crusaders can call you friends."

A notification window intruded on the conversation.

> You have befriended crusader leadership.
> Crusader Reputation +100

"Well, that's a positive for once," muttered Izzy.

I snickered. "And here I thought rep could only be subtracted."

Grimwart made a point to introduce himself to the rest of the party. "I am Colonel Grimwart, the field commander for the crusader army." Kyle heartily took his hand. When the knight moved for Izzy, he bowed low. "It is an honor, lady."

"That surprises me," she said dubiously.

He took her hand lightly in his glove and bent lower. "I understand your sentiment. There are some in my army who distrust mages, but you will be afforded full respect by my men." He turned to his mounted companions. A horse snorted, but there were otherwise no objections. "Walk with me."

We started amid the tents and general throng of soldiers. Men and women bustled with a variety of endless tasks. Loading, cooking, cleaning, sorting. It made me tired just looking at it. The horsemen followed behind us at a loose clip.

"I was personally looking forward to meeting you," said Grimwart, "and was concerned by your absence."

"Seriously?" asked Kyle. "We were only gone three days." The whole trip could have been condensed into two but we'd left ample time for scouting the Blackwood before sneaking in.

"Nevertheless," he continued, "it has been an eventful three days. Shorehome has fallen."

"What?" we all said.

"Aye, the city is lost. Where the pagans failed at Stronghold, they succeeded to the east."

I needed a second to take it in. There are supposed to be nine great cities in Haven, but only three reside in the Midlands. According to the wiki, the rest of the world isn't even released yet. With Oakengard being a black box, Shorehome was really the only other city besides Stronghold worth noting. Reports made it sound more like a large fishing village and hive of pirates, but players had slowly begun populating it over the last month as Kablammy expanded Haven's spawn locations.

"I don't believe it," I finally responded. "The city was sacked by the horde?" I supposed, with their infinitesimal player count, Shorehome couldn't have hoped to repel the pagans as easily as Stronghold had.

"It is surprising," he sympathized. "Field reports claim the goblin army suffered heavy losses at Stronghold. We know many scattered across the Midlands. For them to organize so successfully after a debilitating defeat..."

I grumbled. They couldn't have done it without strong leadership, that's for sure. I wondered if General Azzyrk had turned his sights to the coast. My face darkened as it dawned on me that Lucifer might be involved. "Why didn't we get a server-wide notification about the event? This seems pretty important."

"I know not of these things. I am a practical man, Talon. I'm accustomed to relying on firsthand accounts of those personally exposed to such carnage. Unfortunately, we have very little presence on the eastern front." He spat. "It matters not. Those pagans will pay. Blood for blood, but threefold."

Did I mention the crusaders were overzealous when it came to killing pagans?

"My army is resupplying at Stronghold. We're only here a short while until we march for Shorehome. Currently, we're recruiting in town and making it known that Stronghold's families are safe. Even if it is too late for the unfortunate souls who lived in Shorehome."

I studied the hundreds of soldiers camped out in the tended land. Dressed for war. So all of this wasn't about the cyclops at all. Orik was a precursor, sure, but the fall of Shorehome was the cause for this paranoia. I began to wonder just how paranoid it was...

"The Pantheon," I realized. "Does Shorehome have an equivalent capitol that protects the game state? Have the pagans breached the codebase?"

"You speak of the Great Well. I have been told it is secure but have received no further word."

I swallowed. I needed a word with Saint Peter about this. It was imperative to determine exactly how threatened the entire simulation really was.

The colonel stopped at the great double gates to the city. He wasn't coming in. "I hope to speak to you again, Talon, before it is time to set off."

I nodded slowly. I was sure he wanted to enlist my help. I wasn't at all sure what I wanted to do about it. "I'll be in touch." We shook again and entered the city.

The watchmen at the gate snapped to attention. "All hail the hero of Stronghold!"

I stiffened as I passed, still unsure how to fill my new mantle. Protector of Stronghold sounded grand, but I was just grinding the same as everyone else.

0570 Company of Heroes

What a difference a few days makes. That was the extent of our absence, but Stronghold felt like a different city than the one we'd left. A foreign energy was in the air. Was it urgency? Desperation? I couldn't place it, but it was markedly different than the post-battle unity and optimism we'd experienced.

What was plain was the bustling crowd on the main thoroughfare. Crusaders proudly marched in full plate. Scores of families and merchants crowded together, players and NPCs alike. No doubt the troubled lands had frightened wanderers to the safety of these walls. The sudden influx was a strain on the town.

Not that I was worried about security. Between the crusaders and the increased city watch patrols, Stronghold was heavily guarded. As I took a breath, I wondered if that was part of the problem. The changed mood of the place. The dynamic between the people and officials felt more like a public protest than day-to-day work. Stay on the roads. Keep moving. Don't loiter. There was no room to enjoy a frivolous stroll.

Half of me wanted to put it all in my rearview and head out adventuring for a few more days. Of course, the other half was lazier and wanted nothing more than to rest on the couch. Both avoidance strategies had their merits, but as we were just returning from a long trip it was never really a contest. Laziness won out.

A seven-foot-tall knight in matted white armor stomped up to us, accompanied by her trademark bleached highlights, gold hoop earrings, and eyeliner jags. "What's up, bitches?"

Kyle jerked but otherwise stood firm. After recent events, the incessant bullying had pretty much stopped.

"Who you calling bitch, bitch?" replied Izzy with a grin. I was waiting for the shtick to get old so they would move on.

"What's up, Lash?" I nodded to her party. "Glinda. Conan."

Izzy noted their levels. Lash had made 7. "You guys are looking good."

"Tell me about it. We stumbled into a raid event north of town. We fought through a circle of ogres."

My eyebrows arched, but it was in response to the new sash she wore over her shoulder plate. A black cloth emblazoned with a white cross.

"You joined the crusaders?" I asked.

"Hell yeah we did. You didn't?"

"We didn't join anyone."

"Well, why not? You know the devs boosted their faction stats."

"Yeah, I saw the patch notes too. But I thought you hated the crusaders?"

Lash shrugged. "I hate everything, dude. I just don't like

anyone bigger and badder than me closing in on my turf. But I solved that nicely. Technically I'm still a trainee, so I just get the sash."

Kyle frowned. "A white knight wearing black."

"Yeah," she admitted. "It's not really my color. I like to keep it to the eyes. More dramatic that way. Seriously, bitches, the only way I leveled so fast was aligning with the crusaders. You should get on board."

Izzy grumbled. "You know how much I hate allying with *anybody*."

Lash laughed. "True that. At least see them in action first. You know, we're about to head out with a small band of knights to do some cleanup."

I sighed. "Look, Lash, we just got back. We still need to rest and resupply and all that."

"Suit yourself. But if you pansies were smart, you'd get in while the getting was good. I joined on a couple days ago. That and being the highest-level player in their faction will open a lot of doors. You all could make a killing." She turned to Kyle. "Even you, dumbass." Her heavy glove punched his breastplate hard. Players couldn't damage each other in town, but the blow shoved him aside. "Sorry," said Lash. "Old habits die hard." They all laughed and headed to the gate.

Izzy and I traded smirks.

"Seriously?" asked Kyle. He hissed and stomped toward our tower.

"Relax," I called after him. "Her level might impress the crusaders, but you realize the three of us are the only level 9 players in Haven."

He was still pissed about the run-in with Lash, but he should've been proud of his level. The first few were easy to grind, especially when unlocking hidden crowns. But leveling thresholds grew exponentially more difficult around the 5 mark. A little over a week since the last wipe, the majority of players were still stuck there. Level 9 was an incredible achievement.

Well... we couldn't deny the huge factor luck had been. We were super high level after taking advantage of a glitched 100-level quest boss that wasn't supposed to be loose. A third of the gifted experience was divided across three hundred Stronghold residents, but two-thirds was divided across our party. No one really inflicted significant damage against the one-eyed pagan god, but I'd been the one that subdued him with the titanslayer.

Come to think of it, Lash must have received a larger portion of the XP than most. It was the only way to explain her level. Unfortunately, we were all so high it was only a matter of time before other players started catching up to us. We wouldn't be gaining levels for a while.

As we pushed through the masses, the path to Oldtown was more lively than usual. A bustling main thoroughfare made sense, but there was nothing to do in Oldtown. It was a complete dead zone. Yet packs of men and women crowded close. They cheered us as their champions as we walked by. It once again made me uncomfortable.

Izzy totally basked in it. I'd accused her of being an attention whore before. On the surface, she wanted the admiration of the people for her great deeds. More XP than anyone, including me. One of the only pixies in the Midlands. Investor father aside, Izzy's accomplishments were impressive, even more so because she hadn't been a huge gamer in life.

But really, she was just a big show-off. She wasn't loved by the people as much as she was feared. It was infamy. And, despite desperately seeking their approval, Izzy didn't truly enjoy the limelight. It was a good show she put on. But I knew her secret. She was an introvert who'd had a difficult life and dealt poorly with rejection. She'd taken so well to Haven because of pure escapism. Not a gamer, her fantasy fix came in novel form. She spent so much time at the library it was no wonder she was so knowledgeable about everything.

And my secret was that I liked her for it. I'd witnessed a vulnerability that was invisible to everyone else. Her sharp exterior was for the public, but I knew better. Izzy couldn't wait to leave this crowd behind any more than I could.

Things got worse before they got better. The fan club thinned but drifters took their place. Deeper into Oldtown, the demographics quickly shifted. That nagging feel that the city was different wasn't so nagging anymore. Lingering hopelessness filled the ruined streets. People huddled together and sat on stoops of destroyed buildings, completely aimless.

"All these people..." I murmured.

Izzy's face soured. "See those long boots? They're refugees from Shorehome."

"Sucks to be them," teased Kyle. "Fishermen in a landlocked city? That's a raw deal."

I clenched my jaw. His humorous analysis was spot on. If Shorehome had fallen two days ago, these merchants must've fled in the events leading up to that. Their ships, their houses— they must've left everything behind. Now they were in a foreign city and unable to ply their trade.

My face darkened as we pushed through them to the tower. The area was given ample clearance, due to some combination of the magic aura of Dragonperch and the petrified remains of the kneeling cyclops. Orik the titan. The god. But he wasn't dead for good. This was the afterlife, after all. If the pagans recovered and refit the Eye of Orik, the blind titan would stand once again.

Death wasn't permanent, life was. Unlike the real world, true change couldn't come from death. It came from other means. Transitions of power. Uprooted livelihoods.

"The great heroes of Stronghold!" I turned to wave to the group of men before noticing the scorn in their eyes.

I swallowed. This wasn't my fault. They didn't have a right to blame me. I was about to reply when Izzy put a gentle hand on my shoulder.

"Nothing you say is going to ease their burden." Her eyes sparkled indigo. There was a kindness in them. I knew Izzy was capable of it—I just didn't usually see it.

I took a slow breath. The men jeered and mocked but ultimately turned back to themselves. "You're probably right." I moved to the large door of Dragonperch. The wards glowed faintly as we approached. The door rumbled loose and opened before us.

We were home.

0580 Tiny Tower

"They hate us," I said, safely inside the den. "They're here begging for scraps and we're out there leveling and they hate us."

Kyle had his hands on his hips. "Don't forget that they're sleeping outside and we have this huge tower to ourselves."

"That too."

"You know that's different," reasoned Izzy. "This tower might be dangerous to those uninvited. We've barely unlocked half the rooms. Who knows what's lurking in this place or if the rumors of monsters are true?"

I shrugged. Sometimes logic is just a comfortable excuse.

It was true enough that much of Dragonperch was still locked to us. Despite wielding the dragonspear—the key to the tower—we'd thus far only had access to basic amenities. Personal quarters. The kitchen, the den. Stockrooms below. The roof. There was a war room, but it just consisted of a big table. The "mysterious library" was only half accessible, no doubt reserving its more valuable tomes to be unlocked at a later date.

Don't get me wrong. Dragonperch was a sweet setup. Much cooler than the little domes in Hillside. But too many doors remained barred, too many secrets undiscovered. Were there weapons or valuables in here? Arcane treasures? Precious resources? What was the damned purpose of this tower?

Besides the strong magic keeping it locked down, it was obvious Dragonperch was waiting for the right people and the right time. Throughout extensive digging, Izzy had found the winter staff in a secret compartment. A winter staff for a frost mage? No question in my mind it was fate, or whatever passed for it in the simulation.

I didn't tell anyone, but I was starting to feel like an impostor here. No secret stashes for me yet. I guess I couldn't complain. I had the dragonspear, a legendary weapon of its own. Really, Kyle was the one rightfully bummed out about his being excluded. So maybe we were both impostors. Izzy was the star player. What were we? A down-on-his-luck frat boy and a simple thief who'd robbed the mantle and tower from whoever the rightful owner was supposed to be.

Izzy planted her butt in a high stool. "Trust me, boys. The best thing to do is keep your head down and continue grinding. Everyone else will work themselves out."

I sighed. "It's easy for you to say that, Izzy. Everybody respects you. You were the notorious badass in Stronghold long before I was ever uploaded."

"Hey, we're all in this together."

"That's not exactly true," I said. Kyle crossed his arms and leaned against the kitchen bar, studying the floor. "These people are in Stronghold because of me. I was the one that was tricked by Lucifer. I was the reason Orik breached the walls."

"You were the reason he was defeated," she said

incredulously. "We all were."

"But didn't they follow the same game plan? The sacking of Shorehome was the spiritual successor to the Stronghold raid."

"You're reaching, Talon. You didn't steal any artifacts for them. If anything, your actions helped warn the saints of the dangers. Lucifer's been outed. Colonel Grimwart said the Great Well was secured. You might be the only reason the pagans didn't get to the game code."

I grunted halfheartedly. I wasn't so much of a self-loathing asshole that I couldn't concede the points she'd made. My feelings stemmed from deeper fears than being Lucifer's fall guy. The mantle of Protector of Stronghold saw to that. I was an inadequate fit for it. I mean, what I'd accomplished was the dream of any MMO player anywhere, but Lucifer had taught me that Haven wasn't just a game. This was my life now. And the lives of many other people might just depend on me.

"Screw the pagans then," I conceded. "Let's just focus on me. Can anyone really say that my presence has made Haven better? You think I haven't heard the whispers in the streets?"

"What whispers?"

"*Everybody feels pain because of me.*"

Izzy bit her lip. I'd taken actions to make the game state and player profiles fully permanent. I'd been successful, but the victory had come with numerous unintended consequences. First and foremost was the stripping of the pain filters. Even in a digital-reality simulation, the human brain perceives threats to its existence and reacts with pain. It's an evolutionary trait for self-preservation that a lack of nerves had failed to skirt.

I had no idea why the devs couldn't just patch in fixes to

undo some of the damage I'd caused. Part of me thought it was punishment to the players for revolting. Punishment to me for inciting them.

"Do you think everybody out there really wants to live in a Heaven with pain? A reality that practically forces the populace into combat to level up and thrive? On top of that, the respawn lockdown changed from four hours to a full day now. People *really* love that one."

"That's not so bad," said Izzy.

"Don't bullshit him," cut in Kyle. "He's right. Those changes suck. We can't pretend bad things didn't come with the good just to make ourselves feel better. The situation sucks, and we're the best people to blame for it." He scoffed. "I always thought admiration would come with being high level, but there's just as much jealousy too. I don't wanna deal with this crap anymore. If anybody needs me, I'll be in the basement."

Kyle stomped down the stone staircase. He was in an especially foul mood because we heard him all the way down. We didn't try to stop him.

Kyle had taken over one of the stockrooms and built a brewery down there. It was a great place to practice his alchemical crafting, but mostly he was making ale. Given his current spirits, he was bound to do just as much drinking as crafting right now.

Izzy rested her hand on mine. "I hate to say it, but he's got the right idea. Honestly, a little R&R is what everybody needs right now. I left a half-finished urban fantasy in the library. Why don't you blow off some steam in the Pleasure Gardens?"

I frowned. It seemed decadent. Uncaring. Throwing silver

around for the spa treatment while ignoring the town's problems didn't sit well. I couldn't even drink right now. At the same time, as tired as I was, I wasn't comfortable cooped up in Dragonperch. But what else was I supposed to do? We'd technically been helping clear the countryside. Ridding the area of pagan threats. Making Stronghold safer.

Was the populace really better off?

"They hate me," I said softly.

"They don't know you. And if they still hate you, fuck 'em."

I chuckled and met her eyes again. She was being especially nice to me, which meant Kyle was right about speaking plainly. Something wasn't working and I didn't have a clear enough head to figure out what to do about it. I looked deeply at Izzy and knew she could make almost anything better. I leaned in.

Izzy backed off with a quick shake of her head. "I'm... uh... I wanted to finish my research into..."

I shook it off. "Fine." I threw my hand in the air like it didn't matter. Izzy scurried away before either of us needed to say anything else, leaving me alone in the den, rubbing my temples.

Hard to get was one thing, but Izzy was something else. I could tell she liked me. She'd even gone so far as to admit it to herself. But she refused to open up. To take that next step. She wasn't used to sharing her life with someone.

As for me, I guess I always liked to keep a close circle of friends and family. When I'd been alive, that meant my little brother, Derek. He was gone now, or *I* was if you wanted to be technical about it. After losing the admiration of a little brother, it was hard to truly feel like someone was on my team. Izzy was standoffish. Kyle was rarely serious. Distracted, was what I'd call them. Izzy with her reading and grinding and Kyle with his partying and not giving a fuck.

Oftentimes that left me all alone in my head.

"I'm outta here," I said to no one in particular. Bandit was curled up in the corner, sleeping, but her ear twitched to show that at least she was listening. "Thanks, girl." I headed down the steps lightly, deciding for now to bottle up my frustration. There was work to do.

0590 EverQuest

Admittedly, I was bummed out, but I didn't want that to paralyze me. Our quest chain was open and the easiest way to advance it was to visit the questkeeper. Whether or not the plight actually mattered, I could at least feel like I was making progress.

Sometimes I worried that progression was the problem. RPGs were about more more more. Gimme stats, loot, levels. It was easy to ignore the why of MMOs until you were actually living in one.

The irony that I was distracting myself the same way as the others wasn't lost on me. On top of that, I took steps to actively avoid the Shorehome refugees. I lowered Dragonperch's drawbridge, the alternate entrance that spanned the river. The far side was outside of Oldtown, clear of the new drifters. The area skirted my old neighborhood, a small hill with residential housing. As I headed out, the drawbridge conveniently lifted and sealed itself. As with many traits of the tower, for now I just chalked it up to arcane sorcery.

The lowland north of the hill was dominated by large blocks of parks named the Foot. This was the public training space for

Hillside residents but had become a spiritual center of the town. Experienced adventurers and noobs alike socialized in the area that I likened to New York's Central Park. The Pleasure Gardens were the stomping grounds of the rich, but the Foot was where regular old joes played. There was a good vibe here. Watchmen chatting with players and NPCs. People engaged in team sport and practice. It actually felt like a community.

"Hail the hero!" exclaimed an older woman I didn't know. The friends she was with waved and smiled as I passed.

"Yes," said Dune, approaching from the archery range. "The great Protector walks among us!"

Dune was an explorer core class, like me, but he'd drifted into the ranger specialization. His green cloak and long bow were not unlike Robin Hood's, and I figured he had similar morals: gray, but the kind you could root for.

"Don't tell me you buy into all that hero nonsense," I said, clasping his hand in greeting.

"Of course not," he said with a smile. "But I don't hold it against you for getting lucky."

"Where's the gang?"

"The Pleasure Gardens, I'd guess. I decided to stick around the Foot and grace the common people with my archery skills."

"How humble of you."

He flashed a self-aware grin and bowed mockingly. "You flatter me, sir. Besides, someone needs to teach these crusaders how to aim."

I rolled my eyes. "Don't tell me you're joining up with them too."

"Join *them*? You must be mad. I was under the impression

they came to join *me*. But alas, wisdom is not a skill they hope to learn. It's easy XP for simple training, though."

"Plus it makes you look like an expert."

"My arrows do that for me," he laughed. "But seriously, the crusaders are handing out XP like candy."

I examined Dune's title. [Level 6 Ranger]. "I've noticed. Lash hit 7."

"Damn, she's making me look bad."

"She said something about special raids in the noob dungeons." I scoffed. "Here I was, traveling a day south to hit the Black Keep, and I find the easier XP's right next to home."

"Yes, your little trip. You've been sorely absent as Protector."

I frowned. Grimwart had intimated the same thing.

Dune leaned in conspiratorially. "I don't like this, Talon. Everything feels off. The news with Shorehome. The knights, the fishermen." He looked around to make sure no one was listening. "These crusaders seem jovial enough, but I can't wait for them to move on. Know what I mean?"

"Not really. I haven't been around." I ground my teeth, realizing that's exactly what he was worried about. But, come on, it's not like the dragonspear can fix everything. Stronghold has the city watch. I'm just a guy.

"Look," urged Dune, "we need to talk. Not here, not now. It's too risky. Besides, I promised Caduceus I'd include them in any conversations."

The "them" he referred to was the rest of his party, a healer and a berserker. Dune's merry men. "What kind of conversation?"

"No worries," said the ranger, grinning at a crusader holding a bow in the wrong hand. "On my way," he called. He turned back to me, face devoid of concern. "It's good to see you back in the city, Talon. Even if it's getting a little crowded lately."

He strode back to the training group. Dune was a good enough guy. I envied his boisterous outlook on the afterlife. The fact that he wasn't running off to join the latest fad faction was a plus. But I didn't know him well enough to figure what he had planned.

A bit north was the river walk: a line of shops and bridges along the water on Front Street, otherwise known as Noob Alley. The wares on display may not have been the nicest in town, but things were slowly changing. And it may have been small for a street, but it was far from just an alley. It was a pretty strip of waterside storefronts. I absentmindedly approached the shops, absently minding my own business, when someone bumped into me. I spun around.

"Avast ye!" he spat. "Watch where yer goin', swabber."

I opened my mouth to speak but was thrown off by the sudden attitude. My fight-or-flight reflex kicked in and I quickly sized the man up. Dark skinned with salt-and-pepper hair and black eyes. A hard face, worn and sporting a scar from his left cheek to eyebrow, just missing his eye. I guessed him to be in his forties but it was hard to tell.

He wore a flowing white shirt with puffy sleeves and a flared collar. His black leather pants were tight enough to make me sympathetically uncomfortable. The vest he sported was brown nubuck, with matching knee-high boots and small-gloves, one of which rested on the hilt of a sheathed rapier. The suede leather accents gave him panache that could only come from...

"You're shitting me," I said. "A pirate?"

"Aye," he growled. "And ye'd be wise t' remember it." His brow was scrunched in anger.

"Look," I started, "I wasn't paying attention. Sorry if I—"

"Get knocked about fer bein' a mangy bilge rat?"

I narrowed my eyes. The name above the man's head said [Errol Oates] in gray text. "You're kind of a dick for an NPC, you know that, dude?"

"Captain Oates or merely cap'n will suffice. Or the Scar of the Six Seas if yer overwhelmed by poetic flair."

I studied the NPC, wondering about dumb luck. "Wait a minute. Are you a good pirate or a bad pirate?"

His scarred eyebrow stretched upward. "By the Maelstrom, what's a good pirate?"

"You know..." I hiked a shoulder. "A free spirit who likes to wear eye patches while sailing."

"I steal things," he said indignantly.

"From bad people?"

"From *rich* people."

"An argument could be made there's quite a bit of overlap."

"Bah!" He marched closer and pounded a finger in my chest. "I know ye, don't I? The Protector of Stronghold." He fingered his hilt.

I was beginning to think this encounter wasn't a coincidence. "So a bad pirate then. You got a problem with me?"

"Ye'd hear me grievances, would ya?"

"Get in line."

"Tough talk from a dandy lad."

"I'm done talking. We both know you can't draw that sword

in town. What're you gonna do?" I turned away.

"Don't walk away from me, boy. An' don't be tellin' me what I can and can't do." His sword scraped halfway free from the scabbard.

I acted in a blink. I summoned the dragonspear to my hand and spun low, taking his legs out from beneath him. Captain Oates tumbled into a heap. I stood over him with my spear in the air and paused, realizing a few things.

One, whatever friendly fire tweaks the devs had patched in, it hadn't affected my ability to initiate combat in town.

Two, Errol Oates had nearly drawn his sword within city limits. I hadn't thought that possible from anyone besides me and the city watch.

And finally, three, a crowd of players on the bustling street watched on.

"Admit it," spat the captain, returning his half-exposed rapier to its scabbard. "We're all thieves, but ye think t' be better'n us."

When I realized Errol was never intending to fight, a pit formed in my stomach. What was I doing? Taking advantage of Lucifer's hack just to teach a random punk a random lesson? He may have been a pirate, but he'd likely just lost his home. He was another Shorehome refugee.

"What's this?" barked a guard.

A few watchmen stormed past the crowd. Gladius, the head centurion, was among them. He brushed his red cape to the side in case he needed to draw his sword. When he saw me, he relaxed.

"Talon!" He checked the man on the floor. "What's the

meaning of this disturbance?"

I lowered the spear. "It's nothing. It's—"

" 'Tis but a clumsy pirate," said Errol, standing and brushing himself off. "In me haste to catch a glimpse o' the legendary dragonspear, I stumbled t' the floor."

I glanced at him. "Uh, yeah. That's all."

Gladius sighed. "Good, because we have no need to fight amongst ourselves. There are real threats to the vitality of Stronghold outside the walls." He glared at Errol in warning. "Let's keep them there."

I nodded and backed away. Errol was wise enough to march the opposite direction. Gladius was a good soldier and didn't want to cause trouble if it wasn't necessary. With the three main players content to walk away, the crowd dispersed.

My mood wasn't so quick to recover. Despite being in the right at the start of that confrontation, I wondered if I'd crossed the line. I returned the spear to my inventory and ducked into Trafford's store as soon as I could.

By design, this was a welcome shop. New residents in town would pick up their first supplies here, as well as find guidance and anything else they needed in a welcoming atmosphere. In practice, Trafford was a spiny, disgruntled bastard you had to know to love. The old man was behind the counter ripping a new asshole into an unlucky noob. I leaned on the counter and waited with a grin.

"And I keep telling ya," he said a bit miffed, "I don't want your stinking animal bones. I'm not running a soup kitchen. If you want good silver you'd best be sticking to actual loot prompts, not scavenged animal parts."

Trafford shoved a small sack across the table. "That's all you can afford for now. Use it wisely and come back when you actually have something that commands a price."

The noob meekly thanked him and looked inside the bag.

"Not in here!" snapped Trafford, wild white hair shaking on his head. "I don't tolerate loiterers and slack-jaws."

I chuckled as the player abruptly hurried from the shop. "You're a miserable bastard, you know that, Trafford?"

He grumbled. "That one's a serial killer in the making, I tell ya. Dissecting animal carcasses... It's not right." He studied me up and down. "I see you're back. We could use you in town these days."

"I keep hearing that, but I don't think I'm good for much more than stirring the pot."

"The pot needs stirring. That's why everybody likes you."

"No offense, but what do you care about it? You're an NPC."

"None taken." Trafford rested forward on both arms expectantly, waiting on my business.

Now I felt like an asshole. I hadn't meant any disrespect but the comment came out wrong. Trafford had proven himself a valuable ally against the titan. And, like a player, he was sort of leveling up. Upgrading his wares for a select few he'd deemed heroic in the defense of Stronghold. That kind of evolution and agency was impressive for an AI. If any NPC deserved respect, it was him.

"Hey, Trafford," I started slowly, "can I ask you a question?"

He shrugged. "Shoot."

"Are you sentient?"

"Well, what in the hell do you mean by that?"

"Like, you understand you're an NPC?"

"Of course I do."

"And that this life is a manufactured one. It's not really real."

"Seems real enough to me. What're you getting at?"

I sighed. "I don't know. Life, death. Reality, illusion."

He scowled. "Son, sounds like you've been hitting that philosopher bottle too much. I'm gonna tell Kyle to brew you something proper. Now there's a good boy, grounded on both feet. You could take a lesson from him. Why are ya getting all pensive on me, anyhow?"

I mulled it over. "These pagan quests, for one."

"Aha! You found the wild king!"

"That's just it. I did find him. And he was some dude, not a monster. He spoke with meaning. Cared for his people. He certainly respected his mantle, I can guarantee you that."

Trafford snorted. "Mantle? Speak some sense, son. Mobs don't wear mantles."

"Is it... is it possible he's not a monster but an NPC?"

"NPCs can't wear mantles neither."

I chewed my lip. "Well, doesn't that bother you? That you could never aspire to that?"

The shopkeeper laughed some spittle out. "Ya know, I've never much thought about mantles before, but they seem like a cumbersome bother. Too much responsibility, if you know what I mean."

I frowned. Maybe I was beginning to.

"So let me see it," he insisted. "The crown."

I pulled it from my bag and handed it over.

Trafford whistled. "She's a beaut. Can't imagine the wild king liked it much when you stripped it from him."

"No, he sent a creepy executioner after me."

"Well, once you destroy this and complete the quest, that should put an end to that insurrection." He handed the crown back.

> Quest Update: **Dethrone the Wild King**
> *Quest Type: Fetch*
> *Reward: Unknown*
> To destroy the crown of the wild king, you must plunge it into the Salt Sea.

"The Salt Sea? I've never heard of it. How do I get there, Trafford?"

He scoffed. "How should I know? I look like a sailor to you? But it's east of here somewheres, toward Shorehome."

"Great," I muttered. "Another long journey."

"If it were easy, it wouldn't be worth doing. The three of you are high level. If anyone can make that trip, you can."

I nodded. "You know, with all this recent business, maybe it *would* be best to get out of Stronghold for a while."

"And maybe that's exactly why we need you here," he pointed out.

I studied Trafford intently. One moment he seemed to be urging me to go, the next he was convincing me to stay. What wasn't he telling me? I was about to ask when trumpets sounded from the west gate.

"Those are alarm horns," I said. "Someone's approaching the

city."

I couldn't imagine what kind of threat would attempt to churn through the stationed crusaders, but I was curious to see it for myself. I headed for the door.

"Oh, wait," I said, catching myself. "There's just one more thing. You have any idea what a bone pearl is?"

Trafford's good eye widened. "A bone pearl, eh? Can't say I've ever heard of such a thing."

"Neither have we. I guess Izzy can research it."

"You sure it's not just some pretty knickknack for fancy ladies?"

"I don't know. The item description mentioned it being inert. Kinda threw me off." The trumpets sounded again. I shook off the thought. "I'd better go see what this is all about."

"Aye. It would be good to show your face around town some. Let the people know you're looking out for them."

I groaned and left the shop. I'd been hoping just to have a peek, but the trumpets weren't just meant for me. Along with half the people in the city, I made way for the west gate.

0600 Crusaders of Might and Magic

I shoved through the crowd, wishing I had Bandit along to do the hard work for me. Gladius stood atop the battlements giving his centurions orders. A full contingent of watchmen stood in rows along both sides of the thoroughfare. They were only partially successful in keeping the road clear.

Izzy stepped lightly to my side. Luckily, what might've been momentary awkwardness was superseded by the situation.

"You're here," I said, astute as ever.

"The horns."

I nodded. "Where's Kyle?"

"Playing beer pong solitaire. Where do you think?"

I should've known. When Kyle decided it was time to sit on his ass, he executed like an Olympian.

"Forget about him," she said. "We need to get up on that wall and take a look."

As we started over, the command came down from above. The heavy double gates rocked open as the defenders pulled their chains. We stopped flush with the emptying street as residents cleared a path for the town heroes. That's when I realized the line of guards were a greeting party.

"Actually," I said, "it looks like we'll have a fine view right where we are."

The trumpets sounded again. This time they were a welcoming choir, meant to instill confidence and optimism.

"Jeez. We didn't get a greeting like that."

Izzy slapped my arm and watched the gate. A troop of boots marched forward. Several men who looked like crusaders entered Stronghold, except they wore white tunics with gold crosses instead of the usual black and white.

As the block of six men passed, they gave clearance to a single figure of proposed importance. His plate armor was much the same as the others with perhaps an extra flourish here or there. Most notable were the gold cape he wore over half his body and the gold cross that sat atop his full helm like a monument.

"He's a priest," noted Izzy.

"And I thought I was the one who pointed out the obvious."

The name above the special guest read [Bishop Tannen] in gray, revealing him to be an NPC. He was attended by a couple of men, followed by two more blocks of soldiers. Twenty men and the bishop, all in all. Certainly not a force that could threaten the integrity of Stronghold. Some of the crowd applauded. Most spoke amongst themselves in wonder.

"Grimwart," said Izzy.

Sure enough, the colonel marched in next followed by his black-clad knights. The crusaders already in town raised their voices in cheer, and the residents followed in kind.

"The crusaders are joining him," she whispered.

"He outranks them," I corrected. "He's a bishop from Oakengard."

"We don't know that," she said quickly.

I watched her with amusement while trying not to rub it in. Izzy's the lore expert. It's not often I get to teach her a thing or two. Understandable in this case because there was next to no information about Oakengard out there. Izzy was book-smart, but I was speaking from instinct.

"It's a good assumption," she conceded, "Got any more nuggets of wisdom?"

"Yeah. I don't like this one bit."

The throng came to a stop amid reverent bows and clapping. The leading men cleared a space and stood aside, leaving the bishop front and center. He waited, hands resting on his weaponless belt, head lowered. When he finally lifted his gaze to take in the crowd, it went silent.

A cross was built into the eye slit of his helmet, similar to Grimwart's. Except the knight only had the horizontal hole overlaid with a fancy white cross. The bishop's helmet lacked the decoration and was instead crafted with a long vertical slit through the horizontal one. It mimicked the gold cross atop his helmet in an understated way that revealed a peek at his face. I was surprised to see his eyes were golden.

We waited for an address, but the man didn't speak. Residents on the other side of the street parted, and a man with thinning white hair yet a boisterous long beard and bushy eyebrows stepped through. His cream-colored robe garnished with a single maroon stripe, as well as the golden twig on his head, announced him as a saint.

I was familiar with Peter, but he was followed by a short man with black hair styled in a Caesar cut. Golden letters introduced him as [Saint Loras].

"Huh," I whispered. "I knew other saints existed, but I've never seen them before."

"Loras is new to me," said Izzy.

The saints and the bishop greeted each other in hushed tones. The sibilant voices from the crowd made the conversation unintelligible.

"Is this good or bad?" I asked Izzy.

"It's... different."

I wasn't sure I liked different. I equipped my spear and casually pitched it into the ground.

Within a minute, the saints disappeared back into the crowd. Quite literally. They'd probably blinked back to the Pantheon, or even logged out of Haven to discuss the development with the rest of the dev team. I wasn't sure how all that worked aside from them being able to teleport around.

Bishop Tannen and the crusaders, however, remained. The cross helm scanned over the crowd until it landed. On me.

"Ah," he said, grandstanding and nasally. "The vaunted hero of Stronghold."

We tensed as he approached.

"He's obviously a villain," I mumbled to Izzy. "Right? I mean, who talks like that?"

"Shh!"

The bishop stopped, looking down at us, his attendants lagging behind. Grimwart hurried over. "Your holiness, may I present you with Talon and the Lady Izzy."

I stood as tall as I could, but I didn't have much to work with.

"Thank you, Colonel." Golden eyes surveyed me from the recesses of the helmet. "They tell me you are a great defender of the cause." His eyes lingered on the dragonspear. "*That* is a holy weapon. Pray tell, Talon, do you consider yourself to be devout?"

I swallowed. Of all the questions I expected to be asked from this army, it wasn't that. "I... umm..."

"He killed the cyclops!" shouted a woman from the crowd.

Cheers were followed by roars. Bishop Tannen straightened at the applause.

"It is an impressive tale," he said loudly, relaxing his momentary surprise. The bishop paced side to side, now playing to the audience. "I, too, am a famous pagan slayer. For decades I have tortured their kind. Reaped information to destroy them." He stopped and loudly proclaimed, "It is a blessing from the White King that Talon fights for us!"

The crowd erupted into a frenzy, making the earlier cheers for me seem halfhearted. And, damn, there was something about this man. Haven didn't have a classic charisma score, but Bishop Tannen was doing something to draw people to him. Even I was stirred by his very limited words. Like, maybe I really *was* a blessing from the White King.

Wait a minute. Who the heck was the White King?

Tannen raised a hand and the cheers softened. He spoke above the din. "Fear not, residents of Stronghold. Your city is forever safe as long as heroes still fight for the cause." He turned to the sick and destitute. The newcomers to the city. "And my heart goes out to the men and women who have lost their seaside homes. Know that the crusaders are here for you. My holy order of priests will personally see to the avenging of Shorehome."

And just like that, I was forgotten amongst the mad cries of the populace. Not that I was an attention whore or anything. To be honest, I was happy to finally slink back into the crowd and pull my own disappearing act.

Lots of things seemed to be eating me these days. The final notch in my strained belt was the fact that a pompous, power-hungry douchebag like Tannen had shown more sympathy for the Shorehome residents in ten seconds than I thus far had. The hyperactive spectators jostled with exuberance as we wandered away.

"I know that look," said Izzy. "And I'll tell you right now, there's no need to take this personally."

"There's nothing to take offense at."

"Exactly. Which is why you should stop pouting." As we moved farther, the people were still cheering. "I think we should stay out of his way," she suggested.

I couldn't do anything but growl.

0610 Blaster Master

We were nearing Dragonperch when the explosion occurred. A rumble that seemed to shake Oldtown followed by a wash of molten fire spilling out from the tower's base. The secret grotto was built into the adjacent river wall, a sort of hidden patio. Now the passage was brimming with flames that spilled onto the water's surface.

"Kyle's brewery," I realized.

We broke into a run. Instead of using the main entrance, we climbed along the river exterior and descended directly to the grotto. Fire still raged within. In a panic, I ineffectually scooped water into my hands and splashed it on the inferno. Beside me, Izzy commanded her ice magic to quell the flames.

"Right," I said pointedly.

We pushed through the smoke and into the hidden tower entrance. A stone staircase led up to the ground floor. The brewery door was open, hanging on one hinge.

"Most of the damage seems to be in the hall," noted Izzy, pointing out the scorch marks on the rough stone.

Backing up her statement was the fact that most of Kyle's alchemy equipment was intact. Furnaces, kegs, barrels, and jars and jars of multi-colored fluids. A stool was knocked over along with a low shelf. Shards of glass vials accompanied a brown spill.

A notification was added to the event log.

[Kyle] has left your party

I turned to Izzy warily. The winter staff was already in her grip. I followed her lead and produced the dragonspear, scanning the room. Large shelves and a work table dominated the center. I pointed Izzy to the right and motioned to the left. She nodded and we searched each path until we met at the opposite side. The brewery was empty.

We returned to the only way in and out. The grotto wasn't exactly a sprawling maze, but there were a few branching passages. Izzy and I each took a separate path. Within seconds, my heart sank.

"Over here," I called. As she came up behind me, I crouched beside Kyle's dropped loot.

"Someone killed him," she deduced.

"Okay, you're *really* shooting for my Captain Obvious title lately."

With a swipe of my hand, I used the salvage option to return his loot back to him.

"Thanks, bro," said Kyle, standing behind us.

Izzy and I nearly jumped out of our clothes.

"What the hell?" I yelled.

Izzy didn't say anything but had murder in her eyes.

Kyle threw both hands up. "Peace," he said, giggling. "I come in peace."

Izzy thrust her hands to her hips. "Did you just blow yourself up?"

"Give me some credit. Brewmasters *don't* blow themselves up." He crossed his arms confidently and almost fell trying to lean against the wall.

I deflated. "Are you drunk?"

Kyle's smile twitched like he was the only one in on the joke.

"Dude!" I scolded. "It's only been an hour!"

"I know, right? I didn't waste a single minute. Chill out. I can handle it."

I waved the residual smoke from my face. "You call this handling it?"

He burped. "It's just a dumb game, bros. So I'm stuck in the tower for the next twenty-four hours. Big deal."

"I hate to bring up the recent patch," said Izzy, "but even after salvaging your drop, dying permanently deletes 25% of your silver. With what we scored off Orik, you just lost a small fortune."

Kyle scratched his butt, unimpressed. "Pff, silver. Who makes silver their primary currency? And explosive potions? Why couldn't I have been uploaded to a military shooter with real grenades?"

I tried to ignore the rant. I was still stuck on the new rule for silver drops. "That's pretty harsh," I said to Izzy. "Doesn't Haven have banks or something?"

"Nope." Izzy jutted her chin to the side. "There's a player who calls himself a banker. Squats at level 2 so he doesn't drop anything. He takes 10% of your deposit for himself. The rest you're free to withdraw whenever you want."

"Wow, 10%?" coughed Kyle. "Seems steep. Anyway, if I were you guys, I'd be more concerned with the intruder."

I huffed. "Sorry, Kyle, we'll forego the financial advice from the slacker portfolio. You know, when we decided to invest in all your brewery equipment, it wasn't just so we could booze it up all day. It was a group decision to—wait a minute. What did you say?"

Kyle snorted. "I said 10% sounds like a total rip-off. I should start my own bank at 5% and profit."

"Not that," I snapped. "You said there was an intruder."

His face tightened. "I swear. I was in the middle of a particularly sour ale, and I opened the door for some fresh air and there was this giant shadow, like, sneaking up on me."

Izzy twisted her lip. "So you blew yourself up."

"No! Well, yes... I'd leave it at a solid kinda. I was trying to kill the intruder. I keep telling you guys."

I spun the spear in my grip and peeked down another passage. I went to the river wall and scanned up and downstream. When I returned inside, Izzy was just finishing her sweep as well.

"Nothing down here," she said.

Kyle swiveled his head back and forth between us, dumbfounded. "Wait, you guys actually believe me?"

"Of course," I said impatiently. "This isn't some cheesy sitcom where lack of communication and trust amongst supposed best friends leads to hilarious misunderstandings. You say you saw something, you saw something." I cautiously closed in on the main stairway up. "The only question is whether you scared them off or they retreated inside."

"Wow," said Kyle. "I guess I'm just surprised you trust me."

Izzy gently pushed him aside with her staff. "Well, that and the fact that something was clearly aggroed on you if you managed to use an attack in the city. Talon's the only one with that hack."

He paused. "Oh."

"You have any idea what we're dealing with?" I asked. "You get a pop-up notification? Combat logs? Anything?"

Kyle sighed loud and long. "That's a big fat goose egg, bro. I didn't damage it and it didn't damage me so there's no record of it."

"You should've gotten an aggro alert," pointed out Izzy. He shook his head. She frowned. "Then either you're *really* drunk or what you saw wasn't a normal mob."

"Or one he's already seen," I clarified. I swallowed at the implication and crept upstairs.

Dragonperch is tall and many-leveled, with many of the rooms occupying an entire story, but the search was simplified by the fact that many of the rooms were still locked tight. Either a large door completely barred entry from the staircase, or the landing we were left on was small and uninteresting, with further doors being sealed. We moved carefully past the kitchen and the den and our private quarters. Somewhere along the way I noticed Kyle had stopped to grab a Pop Tart. It really was a wonder that we trusted him.

"I don't know about you guys," he yawned, chewing loudly, "but I'm pooped. And this is boring. Lemme know how it goes." He disappeared into his room.

Izzy and I continued to the war room on the top floor. All empty. We frowned at each other. "I don't like this," she said. "I don't like anything about this."

I nodded. After our recent bout of questing I'd hoped to get some rest, but current developments had transformed Stronghold into a very complicated place.

"I need a vacation," I groaned.

Putting my spear away, I wandered alone to the roof of the tower. The glare of the sun was nearly blinding. As my eyes adjusted, my heart skipped a beat. Waiting on me were two saints.

"It took you long enough," declared Saint Peter.

0620 Space Invaders

"You guys?" I complained. "I'm really starting to hate you guys." I jerked my head at Saint Loras. "I mean, I've never met you before—"

"I'd appreciate it if you skipped the mind-numbing banter," said Loras plainly. His sharp Caesar cut and aquiline nose made him look like a predator.

My eyes narrowed. I wasn't afraid of the saints. I stepped closer, pleased to find someone an inch shorter than me for once. "And *I'd* appreciate it if you didn't go around scaring us half to death and getting my party members killed."

Saint Peter cleared his throat. "Surely you realize the young man killed himself."

"That's not the point."

Saint Loras whisked around. "You don't know what the point *is*."

I opened my mouth to object but found myself faltering.

Loras chortled smugly. "You're in a tower you don't understand, holding a weapon you can't correctly wield, and in a predicament entirely of your own making. *I*, for one, won't be intimidated by your bluster."

I swore I'd caught an admonishment against Saint Peter in there.

"Now, now," leveled Peter, who I pegged as the older and wiser of the two. "Cooler heads must prevail if we are to be successful."

I clenched my jaw. The good-cop-bad-cop routine was a bit tired, but Peter was clearly the easier man to deal with. Not that I trusted any of the saints. They were on the Kablammy Games community team, part of the machine that had illegally created me and later tried to delete me, in their minds reducing me to nothing more than a computer glitch. All that was over with now, and we'd settled into a tentative peace. I kind of liked that peace.

"Successful in what?" I asked.

Saint Loras resumed his superior tone. "In case you haven't noticed, waves of residents have fled Shorehome and are being processed into Stronghold. Devastation on this level is difficult to keep up with. What's more, we simply don't have housing for them."

I surveyed the fishermen from Dragonperch's battlements. We were so high it was easy to pretend they weren't there.

"These men and women can't go adventuring for fear they'll die and respawn back in a city now occupied by pagans. They're poor. Some are turning to thievery. It's a burden on the city. On all of us."

I nodded. "It sucks. Why don't you fix it?"

Loras' face reddened.

"We can't fix it," cut in Saint Peter. "Much of Haven is procedurally generated. Not just dungeons, but story lines. The

Dragon Wars? Based on numerous old novels. The quests and faction agendas? Largely created on the fly by an evolving simulation. Many other world elements, like the Founding of the Nine, were directed by Kablammy but fleshed out using computer-generated details."

"You're saying it's complicated."

Saint Loras once again interjected. "It's a fully realized world. We can't just switch off certain aspects without deeper consequences to stability. All changes come with unintended consequences. The more drastic the cause, so goes the effect."

"So you can't just kill all the goblins."

Loras rolled his eyes and Peter tagged himself back in, explaining the situation patiently. "Goblins are a vital part of the ecosystem. It would be like killing all the honeybees in the real world. Or turning off gravity. Aspects of Haven would be forever lost."

"It's worse than that," added Loras. "With the permanency of the game state, we'd likely crash the servers attempting such massive upheavals. Haven isn't the type of game that can afford downtime."

"That's 'cause it's not a game," I countered. "Not to me."

He was unimpressed.

Saint Peter sighed. "Your devotion to your world is why we're here. The fact remains, Talon, that you started this."

I shook my head. "I had nothing to do with Shorehome."

"You provided the blueprint," accused Loras.

"Don't blame me for your failings. I didn't design the pagan opposition. I didn't create the titans. I didn't even create Lucifer, for that matter. You're telling me you sent two angels after him and you still came up empty?"

"So help us," said Peter.

"All I've been doing is trying to help." I calmed my voice to attempt a level head. "Look, I'm not saying I'm perfect. I made mistakes, like you did. But my intentions are good."

"You're a hypocrite," said Loras, stern as ever.

My face darkened. "There's nothing hypocritical about wanting to be in control of your own life, digital or not."

He smiled like a serpent about to swallow his prey. "Do the Shorehome transplants not deserve life and liberty?"

"Everybody does," I said. "This is the afterlife, after all. At the very least I would think everyone deserves happiness."

"Oh yes, the residents of Haven, living a glorious second life while their physical bodies rot in the dirt. They come with further demands like spoiled children."

I scowled. "And the developers bemoan their loss of total control and the ability to wipe our lives like a bunch of ones and zeroes. Who's the bigger crybaby? At least I fight for life and death."

"Then *fight*," urged Saint Peter. "Fight for your world."

That much I could get behind, but I was still hesitant where the saints were involved.

"And what are you doing about it?" I asked. "The almighty developers?"

Loras scoffed. "Do you even need to ask? Our doings are all around you. We've upgraded the crusaders to fight the enemy. We've pumped resources into their city to strengthen their might. We're incentivizing residents with bonus XP. The pagan quests coming in are a result of that."

"Quests which I've been assisting with."

"It's not enough," he said plainly. Loras frowned as he asked me for help. "As we speak, Haven is verging on 1.0. If it falls apart we may never get there."

Peter turned to the floor with a grave expression. Reading between the lines, they were leaving something unsaid. Something important.

Loras turned a stern face back to me and removed the invective from his voice. "Kablammy is giving you a lot of leeway because of our mistakes, Talon, but so far you've been nothing but a blight on Haven. Raising the titan, empowering the pagans, living like a king while the world burns. I want you to know, putting out the fire is my job. And I'm seeing to it that it's your job too. You want to be a master of your own fate? Then start acting like it. And Peter? This is your mess too. Convince him."

With that, Saint Loras blinked out, leaving just the two of us on the highest roof in the city.

0630 Dishonored

Peter and I stared over the battlements. The ruins, the refugees, the river—anything was better than looking at each other. After I realized I'd been pouting for a good minute, I broke the ice with expert guile.

"That guy," I said in a huff. "Am I right?"

He frowned. "You certainly are."

I cracked a smile. Was the old man hiding a sense of humor in there? Maybe he was going through an identity crisis himself. Not physical versus digital, dead or alive, but important nonetheless. The saint was used to being the head honcho in Stronghold, at least from my limited experience. Now some dickbag had swooped in and grabbed the reins. Not exactly professionally gratifying.

I chewed my lip. "When Loras said Haven was verging on 1.0, he meant—"

"The beta test is coming to an end," finished Peter. "Haven will be announced to the public and officially launched."

Wow. My entry into the simulation had been a big secret. A complete shock. Most people had no idea a digital afterlife existed. Family members involved with the beta were under strict NDA. Once we went prime time, though, we'd get all sorts of players popping in.

"And there's nothing you can do from the outside to fix things?"

He shook his head. "That's by design. You must understand, Haven isn't your average computer game. It was built as an afterlife, meant to be a permanent repository. Even a capitalistic entity like Kablammy Games realizes the challenge in that. What happens twenty years down the line when a new CEO takes over?" His face darkened. "Or if Kablammy gets bought out? What will become of Haven?"

Saint Peter sighed. "Then there's the natural concession. Pivotal people who designed the simulation envisioned it not only as a consumer product, but as an afterlife for *them*. So they took steps to lock in permanence and agency for the residents, knowing full well they would one day join those ranks. The current Kablammy CEO doesn't want an afterlife threatened by a business shift. Once Haven goes public, its only two imperatives are to stay online and stay profitable. Everchat and various convenience features facing the outside world take care of monetization. The fantasy world is free to do what it wants, so long as it remains stimulating and doesn't become a barren wasteland. We simply won't risk damaging the runtime to do that. Permanence and stability are our calling."

"So you send crusaders to do your dirty work."

"To protect the realm. It isn't the first time in history."

I pondered his words. It was reassuring in a way. This life really was a life. Cruel and chaotic but unchained. Open to possibility. Optimism.

I was starting to understand.

"Does this have something to do with why we didn't get a notification about Shorehome falling?"

Saint Peter stroked his beard. "Trying to put on a pretty face before the public unveiling. Remember that quite a few players have access to Everchat. They regularly communicate with the outside world. We can limit it but—"

"You can't revoke access completely without raising additional concerns."

"Exactly. Even then, we may find it necessary to pull the plug soon enough."

"But we know about Shorehome anyway. The crusaders—"

"Are ignorant regarding the extent of the predicament. They've been notified about the horde overtaking the city, but it is worse than that."

"The game code?"

"Secure. The staff took steps to ensure the Great Well couldn't be breached. But we've begun to populate Shorehome with players. We've lost touch with them."

"What do you mean lost touch? Were they deleted?"

He frowned. "No, no. Nothing like that. But in securing the Great Well and protecting the codebase, the saints have ceded influence over the area. We're no longer able to fast travel to Shorehome. We have no control over the city at all, actually. Direct messaging is down. It was taken offline from the central hub entirely."

"Is that bad?"

"It's workable. The Oculus in Stronghold is all we need to run Haven gameside. This is the bastion of the game—the core city.

It's too much of a risk to reactivate it in Shorehome, even temporarily. But an unfortunate side effect of the measure is the loss of data."

I measured his words carefully. "You're telling me that not only can't you see the players, but you can't see anything that goes on in the region."

He paced along the tower wall. "Haven absolutely must appear pristine to the public eye. After your actions, a reboot is out of the question. Wiping won't work. We're neither interested in nor able to circumvent the permanency protections. We can't risk compromising our credibility or the entire monetization strategy, which relies on guaranteed security. The only thing to do is contain the game *within the game*." He moved close and lowered his voice. "I'm not supposed to tell you this, but Kablammy finds itself in a bit of a crisis at the moment. Current funding will expire if Haven is delayed any further. The only solution is to plow full steam ahead."

My brow furrowed. "In other words, you need to hurry the launch before everything's a clusterfuck."

"That is," he muttered, "regrettably accurate."

I nodded grimly. This little conversation wasn't relieving the burden I'd been feeling lately. This city was a far cry from the utopia I'd first awoken in. Players unable to play the game. Feeling pain. Armies marching through. And Stronghold was a fat lot better off than Shorehome.

I sighed in resignation. "And you're sure that flooding the countryside with zealots is the best way to defeat the pagans?"

"There is no single best way, but we influence the game with the game. The crusaders are one tool available to Kablammy.

Activated and upgraded to take the pagans on, defend Stronghold, and win back Shorehome."

"And do anything else you command."

"They're NPCs, Talon, not saints. They work independently and have their own motives, if that's any consolation."

"And the angels?"

"Another tool, but one that appears broken. We've lost contact with the two hunters that have been dispatched, and for now the game sees no reason to send others."

"So we need to rely on the knights."

"You're dismissing the best tool at our disposal."

I studied him blankly.

"The players, themselves, Talon. Another independent force driven by their own interests. That *is* what you sought, after all. Independence. Agency."

I rolled my eyes unenthusiastically. "Points for turning my argument back on me."

I didn't outwardly show it, but Saint Peter was on to something. It wasn't enough to simply say he was right. I wasn't coldly analyzing this as a textbook ethics class. Rather, something inside me was stirred by this calling. Something I once would've called a heart. Now I wondered if it was my soul.

The rumbling in my chest grew until I realized a regiment of soldiers was on the march two hundred feet below.

"It is time," prodded Saint Peter, "for action."

Black and white tunics emblazoned with white and gold crosses stomped ahead in a menacing formation. Stragglers in the ruins hurried to flee their path, but most remained on the outskirts. This had the makings of a town event. Forty troops marched on Dragonperch, but a hundred spectators were in tow.

I turned to Saint Peter, but he was gone. "These guys are like Batman," I grumbled.

I watched from the battlements as the regiment paused before the impressive tower. They froze in unison, swords at their side. Grimwart was among them, but they were led by the white-clad priests.

"Heroes of Stronghold," announced Bishop Tannen. His voice carried clearly to my lofty heights. "Come and make your reparations."

I ground my teeth, twirled the spear in hand, and headed downstairs.

0640 Challenge from the Dark Side

On the way down, I checked the wiki for any info on Oakengard and Bishop Tannen. All I found were recent posts heralding him as a savior after his arrival in Stronghold. That made sense since there were no players in the Oakengard area. Still, the army backing him up made him as legit as it got.

Izzy fell in step behind me, capably aware of the new situation. She was always on her toes. I imagined Kyle was still sleeping one off.

"You don't need to go out there just because he summoned you," said Izzy.

"I know. I wanna hear him out."

"Then I'm coming out too. He did technically summon all of us."

"That he did." I swiped the wiki closed. "You ready?"

She nodded. I pushed the huge tower door open. Its motion was mostly driven by magic; a single person could never manage such a feat, even without the wards. The field of soldiers watched in silence as we came into view. The scraping of the door stopped and left only the lapping wind.

I wish I could say the soldiers wore merry faces, but they were each as steely as Saint Loras. They looked ready for battle.

Bishop Tannen and Colonel Grimwart waited as Izzy and I approached their regiment.

"The keepers of Dragonperch," remarked Tannen with jealous flair. "What a nice place to live."

"It even gets HBO," I said.

"Such a holy place should be in the hands of the catechists."

"Sorry. No vacancy."

He smiled. "Worry not, hero. I have taken the Circus for my needs. Its ample seating and race course are more suitable for an army."

I couldn't hide my worry. "You're moving in?"

"For a time. Oakengard is well protected in the west. I think you'd agree that Stronghold is the most vulnerable point of attack. As the city's Protector, you should grant its residents any edge."

Murmurs washed over the crowd. These priests unsettled me. They'd been in town one hour and had already won the culture war. But everyone was free to make up their own mind.

"You seem to misunderstand, Bishop," I said in return. "I've pledged to *protect* this city, but I've not been appointed to *lead* it. I don't presume to grant or deny the townspeople anything."

Stray chuckles supported my statement. Maybe the people wanted a leader. Someone besides the saints. Someone who really lived here and was subject to the same troubles. I had no right to that claim.

"Well said," replied Tannen.

Izzy stepped forward. "What's this we hear of reparations?"

The bishop's face soured, at least what little I could make out from the cross-shaped opening in his helmet. "There are many," he said with indignation. "This public nuisance, for one." He waved to the embers floating down the river. "We can't have you burning down a sacred monument."

"The tower's fine," I said through clenched teeth. "Kyle's alchemical talents served Stronghold well during the goblin raid. He's simply... refining the process."

"He's a drunkard." Bishop Tannen turned to the crowd. "The catechists are no enemies to the sciences, but we are indeed abstainers from those vices which seek to weaken us. Integrity, resolve—these are things men must fervently protect."

"And women," added Izzy.

He flashed a smile. "Women have their place, but I'm afraid there is none for mysticism. We must be careful not to run afoul of evil magicks. To invite that power into our hearts is to invite havoc into our cities."

Grimwart studied the floor. The bishop was overstepping his welcome with that comment. Disparaging mystics meant alienating a quarter of the player base, and he wasn't exactly speaking highly of women either. It made me wonder exactly what kind of culture existed in Oakengard.

"Let's not play high and mighty, Bishop." I held my spear in the air. "It takes all of us to preserve our livelihood."

Tannen's eyes followed the spear. We were close enough now that he could speak without hitting the crowd's ears. "It must feel powerful to brandish such a weapon, even a stolen one."

I tensed and spun the spear, spiking it into the dirt road.

"You want it? Come get it."

The bishop waited a beat, doubtless measuring the steps between him and the dragonspear. Six, by my count. Instead of taking action, however, he arched an eyebrow and raised his voice. "Theft and force are inadequate claims, Talon. Great deeds are required of the spear wielder. Proof that he is worthy."

"Is my past not enough?"

"Your past." Tannen snickered. "Are you referring to standing against a holy angel?"

My smirk faded.

"Or perhaps you refer to your collusion with the great evil, Lucifer?"

"That wasn't—"

"The action of a righteous man? Tell me, Talon. Are you in league with the so-called Fallen Angels? Have you ever been?"

I pressed my lips together. "They're no friends of mine."

"Then prove it," he announced. "Show us what the great Protector is worth! Show us that you're worthy of the dragonspear!"

The cheering of the people was a mad jumble now, muddying our supporters and Tannen's together. Hell, the lines were so blurred many probably supported us both at the same time. The people didn't care about a battle of wits. They didn't care about the responsibilities of my mantle. They cared about their homes and their fortunes. As with everything, it came down to blood and treasure.

"I don't trust this guy," whispered Izzy. "He's a serious creeper."

"Right there with you," I muttered. Then, as soon as the

crowd quieted, I hefted the dragonspear from the ground and called out, "I'm here for the people. If you've got a solution, sign me up."

Where I'd hoped to surprise him, Tannen's golden eyes squinted with pleasure. "Excellent!" he cried, arms upraised. Once again, bellows from the crowd took over.

"What're you doing?" snapped Izzy.

"This is it," I told her. "This is how I contribute."

She winced in objection but left it at that.

The bishop lowered his arms and turned to me. "And worry not, Protector. The solution is a straightforward one. The crusaders will lead a small scouting party to Shorehome. We must see to the plight of the families. We must also secure the Squid's Tooth from the Great Well. Just as with the Eye of Orik, if the pagans recover the Squid's Tooth, there will be drastic consequences."

I couldn't believe it, but I found myself nodding along. "A small band over a crusading army. I actually think it's a good idea."

"That is well, Talon, because the party requires a scout." He paused in mock conjecture. "Your class is scout, is it not, Protector?"

I shouldn't have been surprised. This is what Saint Peter had been prepping me for. Standing up for the players of Shorehome. Restoring peace to Haven.

On the plus side, if I went along I could make sure things were done properly. This might just be the vacation I needed.

I didn't answer, but Tannen read the assent on my face. "Good. The citizens of Stronghold place great faith in you."

Grimwart stepped closer, relieved the politics were over with. "We must leave at once, Talon."

"Whoa there," said Izzy. "Our brewmaster's on twenty-four-hour lockdown. We'll need at least a day."

Tannen's eyes flashed. "Talon will accompany the party alone."

"Fat chance of that," interjected Izzy, lowering her winter staff menacingly. "I'm not letting him level up on his own."

"There will be no pixies in the scouting party. This is a battle *against* the monsters."

"Watch it, tough guy."

I stepped between them. "If you want my help, Bishop, you'll make an exception. You're not splitting up the city's defenders, are you?"

His eyes flitted to the audience and he snickered. Grimwart moved close and urged him with a whisper. The bishop was not pleased, but he complied. "Do what you will, but you must leave at once." He stormed off to his priests.

Grimwart collected two horses and led them forward. "The lady is welcome to join the party, but it is imperative that we act now."

Izzy's indigo lips twisted. "So the party's gonna be split up regardless. Kyle's on lockdown."

I scowled. "It can't be helped."

"Oh, come on," she fired back. "What have you got to prove?"

"Everything."

I turned to the tower and let out a sharp whistle. Before Grimwart could hand me the horse's reins, Bandit came charging from the tower. She was every bit as strong and stout as the war horses. The broad V-shaped horns and cream-colored stripes drew everyone's eye, especially Bishop Tannen's.

Jeez. The priests had problems with drinking, mysticism, nonhumans, and now non-horses as well? Were these guys uptight or what? Even Grimwart watched Bandit warily as she slowed to my side. The knight in black armor turned instead to help Izzy onto her horse.

"I can manage," she grumbled as she hopped neatly onto the stallion's back.

"So you can," he said curtly. "And you, Bishop? Will you be requiring a mount?"

Tannen stiffened in surprise and loosened the gold cape at his neck. "Alas, I am needed in Stronghold. But I will send holy support in my stead. Strict devotion to the duties of man will serve as a strong example to counter Talon's less-than-savory inclinations."

Ugh. Gimme a break.

Still, I couldn't say I was disappointed by the bishop's decision. As Dragonperch's tower sealed itself, I knew it would be impregnable to any forces, no matter the size. And Kyle would be around to keep an eye on it. Whoever Tannen sent couldn't be nearly as bad as the big man himself.

In spite of the embarrassing misstep, Tannen made one more bold proclamation to emphasize his authority. "We have our scout," he proclaimed, commanding rapt attention from the crowd. "We have our holy guidance." He swept his arm from the priests to Grimwart and his men. "We have a wartime colonel and veteran soldiers. There is just one last thing."

Bishop Tannen paced before the many spectators now. "We

still require a guide. A single able-bodied man who is familiar with the ins and outs of Shorehome. One who is no stranger to violence. One who is willing to sacrifice everything for his home and his people, even if it means his life." He scoured the audience with a wave of his hand. "Do I have any volunteers?"

The masses hushed as they waited for the boldest among them to come forward. One man jostled through to us. As I saw him, I deflated.

"You've got to be shitting me."

Errol Oates, pirate captain and Scar of the Six Seas, showed his teeth as he bowed before the great bishop. His eyes were fixed firmly on me.

0650 Heroes of Might and Magic

The catechist procession led the march. It was a symbolic gesture that didn't sit well with me. The whole town saw the bishop at the head of the scouting party, but it wasn't like he was endangering himself by, you know, actually going on the journey with us.

I choked back my pride and just took it in. The disciplined crusader cavalrymen. The exalted manner of the priests. The exuberant cheers of the populace, always hungry for something to root for. I wondered if the saints were watching us from some far-off perch. Were they pleased with the parade or disgusted by the charade?

I impressed upon myself that this wasn't all for show. I pounded it in my head again and again. I was here to do something. To make a difference for the better. I didn't yet know exactly what I could do, but Izzy and I would try. And if a few extra suits of armor wanted to come along for the ride, so be it.

The procession swept past the Pleasure Gardens, a sprawling tract of bountiful curated parkland. Perfect in every sense of the word. It was a playground for the rich elite, but technically accessible to anyone with enough money for a pass. That meant most adventurers could reward themselves with a visit after the occasional bounty, but regular attendance was lavishly excessive.

The catechists eyed the grounds with a show of distaste. They were a sect of abstainers, priests at the top of the crusader pyramid. Of course anything so... *human*... would offend their sensibilities.

The east gate groaned open before us, a carbon copy of the familiar site on the west wall. I'd never actually exited on this side of the city before. We weren't even clear of town and already the journey was a new experience. I wondered what surprises the fishing seaport of Shorehome offered. Our throng passed through the gate to the tended land.

Once again, the view was mirrored by the west. Countless tents and hovels spattered the fields. Instead of the well-equipped crusader force from Oakengard, however, these were drifters and displaced refugees from Shorehome. The more recent transplants hadn't been processed into the city yet. I gawked at their sheer number and began to understand what it meant for an entire city to fall. One of the nine. Picked off, like the two missing angel statues comprising the Golden Seven. I also started to understand the scope of the challenge Stronghold faced.

Tannen and his men stood aside to let us pass. He gestured magnanimously and made some grand statements to the beleaguered crowd, but I couldn't be bothered to listen. I couldn't help these people. At least not here and now.

A horse cantered to Bandit's side. The man had the white tunic and gold cross of the catechists, full plate but no helmet. Locks of yellow hung over his ears, headed by the words [Cleric Vagram].

"It's a sobering sight, is it not?" he asked.

I grunted. "I thought everything with you priests was sober."

The corners of his lips betrayed a smile. "The pleasures of the flesh do not lead a man to ruin, but they certainly open the door."

"That your idea of a pep talk?"

His horse whinnied as it stepped away from Bandit. Vagram steadied the reins. "She's nervous in the presence of your mount. Would you not prefer a more distinguished animal?"

The mountain bongo snorted emphatically. A spray of phlegm shot out of her nose.

"She's distinguished," I said.

"She's a pagan beast, Talon."

"She helped me fight the pagans," I asserted. "Time after time."

"Indeed?" He studied the animal with interest.

I wasn't too keen on talk of the pagans. It led my thoughts to the wild king—his responsibility to his people, his denial of affiliation. I was beginning to wonder what exactly the definition of a pagan was.

I turned to look for Izzy and was surprised to find her riding beside Grimwart. What didn't surprise me was that she wasn't very talkative. Content silence. I would've killed for that simple interaction right now. Soon enough, I supposed. Behind her, and a safe distance away from me, rode the pirate, Errol.

The people on the street made way for us. Some cheered and gave us words of encouragement. Most looked on with passive expressions. Not hopeful, not forlorn. I couldn't tell what they were thinking and couldn't imagine what they'd seen. The horrors of the afterlife, no doubt.

"What the hell are we gonna do about all of them?" I breathed.

"I'd prefer if you didn't blaspheme," requested Vagram. "The use of such words betrays a lack of faith."

I rolled my eyes. "You're still here?"

He clenched his jaw. "But since you asked, they must be repatriated."

"To Oakengard?"

"If need be, but Shorehome is the closest city, and the one responsible for the pagan uprising to begin with." His words were pointed, but not poisoned.

The adventuring party rode clear of the tent city. More of the priests broke away. Even some of the crusaders turned off to keep the peace and help the needy. The parade was over. Finally, our party was thinning.

Cleric Vagram annoyed me by continuing to ride at my side.

As a man, he was normal enough. As a crazed zealot, he was measured, so far at least. Gratingly strict, but someone who played by the rules. A code. I just wished that put me more at ease. I waited for Vagram to speak, but he remained quiet. I got the uneasy feeling he was the one studying me.

"Just so you know," I started, "I have nothing against crusaders. Live and let live, is what I say."

"A dangerous motto."

I furrowed my brow. "How so?"

"Shall we let the pagans live, when their lives are predicated on taking ours?"

"That's different."

The cleric watched me expectantly.

"Well," I reasoned, "they're mobs, right? Monsters."

He nodded satisfactorily. "At least you understand that much."

"The saints told me goblins are a vital part of the ecosystem."

Vagram's eyes squinted sharply. "Perhaps the saints did not properly distrust the wild, and this is the result. But fear not, Saint Loras has granted us full authority on the matter. The pagans are a menace. It is our cause to correct it."

"I thought your cause was saving Shorehome?"

He sniggered. "Shorehome's prospects are irrevocably tied to the fate of the pagans. You'll understand when we arrive."

I pulled Bandit sideways and stopped the party. It was several of us now, with me and the cleric at the lead. "We?"

Vagram's horse slowed, but didn't stop. "Of course. A cleric must consult on holy matters such as these."

I should've known Vagram was the one sent to lead the party. It was doubtful any of the priests would chat me up otherwise. The cleric rode ahead, leaving me behind. The rest of the convoy followed. Izzy, Grimwart, four crusaders, and a pirate.

Nine of us. Nine adventurers to match the nine great cities of Haven, marching for the fate of the simulation itself.

Why was it I didn't feel like much of a hero?

0660 HeroQuest

They say there's strength in numbers, but our group didn't comfort me. For one, we've all seen how fantasy fellowships have fared in the past. Ours had more commonality, perhaps, but seams of tension ran right down the middle. A unified group this wasn't.

Even though I was the explorer, I let Vagram lead the way. How bad could you screw up following a road? Izzy and I decided to stick together and get to know Grimwart. He was a proud battlefield commander, pompous and stern, but utterly straightforward. It was a grossly underrated trait. And despite some of the crusaders looking down on mystics, he was nothing but polite.

Grimwart explained that the saints would usually bless them with fast travel—direct teleportation lines between cities—but when Shorehome had fallen so too had the reliability of these convenience capabilities. He was oblivious to the truth of how bad it was: The city was no longer governed by the saints. They had little influence in the area, a fact which would grow clearer the closer we got to the sacked city.

On the plus side, Oakengard was a city rife with mounts. I hadn't seen many around Stronghold, Bandit being the notable exception. Grimwart relayed how mounts could cover fifty percent more ground over a day than a walking adventurer. It seemed on the low side to me, but it was an understandable concession in a simulation. The devs didn't want players crossing from one side of the world to the other in a single session. So while horses were faster than people, their stamina tired them out much quicker, containing them to a reasonable walk most of the time.

After chatting with Grimwart for a while, I turned a curious eye to the rest of the company. As the only two players in the fellowship, Izzy and I were the only ones with forward-facing levels. It was otherwise difficult to tell an NPC's power level since their names weren't color-coded like mobs. For obvious reasons, I was especially concerned about the pirate with a grievance. Vagram and Grimwart had to be capable. In fact, I suspected everyone in the party was a good hand in combat.

That, combined with sticking to the road, kept the random mobs we passed from aggroing on us. We rode straight east through the scrubland in relative ease for half a day. The land was flat, open, and honestly, a little boring.

Finally, in the afternoon, there was a break in the monotony. On the side of the road in the distance was a stone structure. A few stragglers attended it.

"Stay alert, soldiers," ordered Grimwart.

His knights sat up straighter, abandoning the lackadaisical contentment. Even the horses snorted and hopped in anticipation.

"It's a watering well," explained the colonel. "No need for worry." He kicked his horse ahead.

Izzy pulled close to me. "NPCs," she noted.

"Maybe we'll finally see some action," announced Errol, surging past us to the head of the party.

I stiffened and lowered my voice. "We shouldn't let him sneak up on us like that."

Her gaze followed him. "What is it with you and that guy?"

"Besides the fact that he's a pirate?"

She shrugged.

"We had a sort of... confrontation in town."

She raised an eyebrow, amused. "You and him? He didn't call you a scurvy landlubber, did he?"

"I'm serious, Izzy. He really resents us for some reason. Could be that Stronghold's free. Could be Dragonperch. Or even just that we succeeded where he failed. It doesn't matter. He's dangerous."

She frowned. "Fine, then. We'll keep an eye on him."

Grimwart, Vagram, and Errol broke away and galloped toward what looked like two men and two children. I didn't see where it came from, but the cleric had a glittering bronze sword in one hand. Errol followed his lead and drew a rapier.

"Crap," I realized. "We'd better make sure there's no needless bloodshed." I pushed Bandit into the fray.

The crusaders slowed but Errol lapped his horse around the drifters and the well. Two loops meant to intimidate those surrounded and on foot. The men huddled close to the children, each one covered in a protective cloak.

"Show your hands, travelers," ordered Grimwart. "We are on a mission of peace, and will extend a hand of friendship to those of like mind."

One of the men wrapped his arms around a child sitting against the stone well. "Please," he said. "We mean you no harm."

"Show yer hands," snapped Errol. He reared his horse over the terrified drifters. Four hands shot to the sky, but the man huddled against the child didn't move. Errol's horse advanced.

I hopped off Bandit, pushed past the soldiers, and batted away the pirate's sword. "Give him a chance to speak."

Weathered eyes measured me. "Please," the man said again. "We barely made it. We have nothing."

I didn't see weapons bulging beneath their cloaks. The man was holding the kid, whose head was covered.

"The child is stricken," noted Vagram. He dismounted, no longer holding his sword. "Let me see her." The man pulled away but Vagram moved too certainly. He was upon them and thrusting back the kid's hood before the father could react.

"Please," he begged. "She's dying."

"Exposure," reported the cleric. "From the moor, no doubt. Is she taking water?"

The father's eyes pressed closed. "She won't wake up."

Vagram knelt beside them and drew a bronze cross encrusted with a gem on each arm. "Fear not, traveler. No one is beyond the grasp of the Lord of Men." The cleric placed the artifact on the child's head and muttered a prayer. Within seconds, the deathly pallor on her face vanished. Her eyes opened and she convulsed into a fit of coughing. "Water!"

I scrambled to the well and dragged the bucket over the wall. We splashed the girl's face and let her drink. She sipped in small increments.

"It's a miracle!" exclaimed the father. He looked at the man hugging the younger child. They were beyond jubilant.

I turned to Izzy. She watched the entire affair, unmoved. It's not that she didn't feel anything. She had to. She was just an expert at hiding it. I shook off the tension that had built within me and helped the travelers to more water.

The swords were sheathed, the soldiers dismounted, and the drifters told us the story of their travels. Fleeing Shorehome, beset by enemies from all directions, stranded in the moor to the north. Less than a third had survived the voyage. We assured them they'd hit Stronghold by nightfall. They frosted us with everlasting gratitude and went on their way.

We all had water and relaxed. Food and water and rest weren't necessary in Haven, but they all contributed to efficient stamina usage, among other things. If you wanted to travel at peak speed, it was important to be well hydrated.

"We must continue," prodded Cleric Vagram. "The sun is falling, and we must clear Ashen Moor by daybreak tomorrow. Those poor folk traversed that harsh terrain under the full heat of the sun. We cannot make the same mistake."

The crusaders mounted up. Errol sat against the well with his legs crossed, using a knife to carve bites from an apple. He seemed to have a thing for blades. If I hadn't stayed his sword, I wondered how far he would've pressed the drifters.

Izzy and I saddled up and followed the crusaders northeast. I kept an eye on the pirate as he came up the rear. I let him pass and we followed.

The road was well worn. At the well, it had split off into northerly and southerly branches. My map didn't show a whole lot ahead of us, but I could see our path start to lose definition. Indeed, within the hour the plains grew more barren and the road less distinguishable. I flicked my map open back and forth as the heat grew until the label appeared: Ashen Moor.

Everything was gray out here. The dirt, the sedges. We rode through a barren wasteland where steam seeped from the ground. Unsurprisingly, there was no evidence of nearby wildlife.

"What's the deal with the exposure that kid had?" I wondered. "We can't actually suffer fatigue in Haven, can we?"

"Not that I know of," answered Izzy. "But I've seen terrain damage once or twice."

To punctuate that statement, we rode past the dried bones of a pack animal.

Luckily, the sun was late in the sky. Maybe this Cleric Vagram did actually know what he was doing a little bit. His kindness to the travelers had certainly earned him a fair chance in my eyes. Now the heat bordered on stifling, but no one was taking damage. We soon lost any semblance of a path completely. I took a more active part in guiding the group, managing to avoid jets of steam that could've been trouble. Our stalwart band of adventurers proceeded onward with little comment until I wondered if we were lost. I once again studied the map.

"Argh!"

I swiped my menu closed as a crusader barreled from his horse. A segmented snake the length of two horses had him in a rounded mouth. Its tail flew past as swords scraped from their scabbards.

0670 Worms

The ground rumbled.

"Holy crap!" I whirled Bandit around. Gray dirt shook. Bandit hopped to the side as another sandworm burst through the ground and whiffed.

Errol whistled to get Grimwart's attention. A worm charged the black-armored colonel. The two of them stabbed downward as the animal roared past like a train.

A few horses took off in pursuit of the downed soldier. Izzy was on one of them. I got a bead on a trail of dirt tunneling her way. I flicked the dragonspear to my hand and charged.

The sandworm burst from the ground just as Bandit lowered her horns. I put my weight into the spear and triggered deadshot. The combat skill was maxed out at level 3 now and didn't play around. The dragonspear slid into the rough serpent's flesh.

Charge!
You dealt 68 damage to [Sandworm]
[Bandit] dealt 28 damage to [Sandworm]

The momentum of the creature nearly ripped the weapon from my hand as it trained forward. It rolled in pain but didn't make a noise. As I readied another blow, it sank back into the ground.

"There's too many of them," yelled one of the crusaders. He'd been thrown from his horse and had backed toward the cleric. There were at least three more worms surrounding the main party.

Izzy was attempting to rescue the crusader still in the mouth of the first sandworm. Fortunately it wasn't so easy for them to disappear underground with an oversized mouthful. The worm couldn't angle its head in to burrow. Instead it relied on its impressive land speed and the harrying of its friends.

Fortunately, the crusaders were well-trained. Two horses flanked the worm and cut at its sides. Izzy's horse was less cooperative, spinning in terror.

"Screw this," she spat.

She flipped backward off the horse, little dragonfly wings buzzing at her back, and landed lightly on her feet right in the path of the sandworm. She raised her small dagger-like frost wand and called an arsenal of icicles to her side. They bombarded the worm just past its head, giving enough clearance to the wounded soldier.

The giant snake released the crusader and rolled away,

attempting an escape. The largest of Izzy's ice edges spiked it to the ground, causing high damage. The other two crusaders came in with vicious blows to finish it off.

That worry over with, I pressed Bandit toward the main group. A golden flash painted my skin and that of the others surrounding the cleric.

Divine Right!

For the next 30 seconds, your attacks inflict extra damage.

Well, rock on. My spear cut into the worm attacking the horseless crusader. The melee was a mad jumble, though. Vagram held a sword in each hand and cleaved pieces off the serpents. Errol, like Izzy, had hopped off his horse. His rapier inflicted less damage but he danced this way and that, almost untouchable. I didn't think giant worm monsters could get frustrated, but the pirate was certainly giving it a go.

As I strafed around the party, a sandworm knocked Bandit off her feet.

Agility Check...
Pass!

I tumbled into a controlled roll. Bandit flailed and the serpent looped around to take advantage of a large meal on its back. I sprinted around her and used my dash skill. The dragonspear rocketed into muddy-red flesh, but the giant thing kept rumbling toward me. My boots skidded against the ground as I attempted to stop it. Bandit rolled to her hooves and lowered her horns. The stout mountain bongo braced for the impact and the sandworm thudded to a stop.

The spear, still buried in the beast, twisted out of my grip as the beast roiled over. I tried to hold on and was jerked over the great body.

```
Agility Check...
Fail!
```

My back hit the colorless dirt of the moor in a puff of smoke. It had been days since I'd failed an agility check. I should've let the spear go. Now I was on the ground, vulnerable as the serpent's face spun to me—no eyes but a circle of jagged little teeth all the way down like a cheese grater and a garbage disposal combined. The mouth descended.

Cleric Vagram heaved his swords in an arc, lopping off half the beast's face (and giving me a good scare too). I rolled to the side as the sandworm gave a last kick and died. I dug my spear from its body and gave Vagram a gruff nod.

By now the other crusaders had returned to the main party. Everyone had a weapon ready. Four serpents lay motionless at our outskirts, but streams of dirt Bugs-Bunnied all around, forcing our backs together in a tight grouping.

"They keep coming," muttered one of the knights.

Three sandworms showed themselves. Four. A head peeking out. A body arching like a whale breaking the water. What worried me much more was all the ground movement unaccompanied by a visible beast. There must've been ten of them.

"Damn this thing!" screamed Izzy.

My head jerked. She was still out there, by herself, recovering her spooked horse. The thing reared and tore away from her. She cursed again as it retreated deeper into the lifeless moor.

"Get back here!" I yelled.

A worm the color of dried blood burst from the ground and veered toward her. It was twice the size of the others.

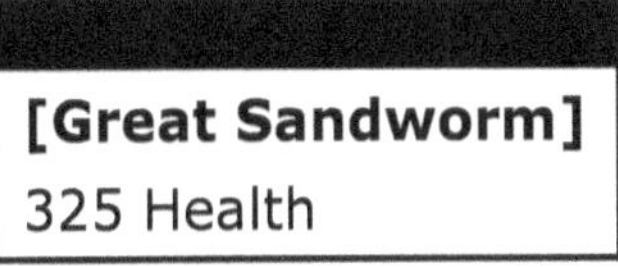

Izzy clenched her jaw and sprinted toward us. I started away from the group to help her.

"Stay together!" she said.

I nodded. Izzy liked to handle herself, and I liked her for it, but this one was cutting it close. I clenched my fists as she ran toward us, a little purple pixie followed by a super-sized sandworm kicking up a spray of gray dirt.

No way she could outrun that thing on foot.

I charged straight at her, spear in hand. She glanced back, eyes wide. The serpent glided along the surface of the ground, bearing down on her. She realized she was out of time.

Izzy spun around and pointed her staff. She was gonna get steamrolled.

I triggered dash and kicked forward with extra speed, just barely enough to wrap my arm around Izzy's waist as the boss spread its mouth ready to slice and dice.

Momentum still pushing toward the monster, I lowered my spear and activated the vault skill. I lifted Izzy off the ground as it chomped empty air. Except, where I'd been hoping to jump clear over it, I'd obviously miscalculated. This guy was easily twice as long as the others.

We landed with a thump on the giant worm's back. Izzy and I rolled precariously before clinging to any hold we could get. She switched out her staff for the smaller wand and dug its jagged teeth into the thing. I spiked it with my spear and stood, boots wobbly beneath me.

Agility Check...
Pass!

That was more like it. The beast skidded across the ground, now barreling toward the clump of soldiers. I ran across its top, skin still glowing gold from the damage buff, and spiked the dragonspear where I imagined its brain should be.

Critical Hit!
You dealt 58 damage to [Great Sandworm]

It was a sizable chunk of damage, but the thing was too big and too stupid to take note. Despite the buff, it must've had a better defense rating than the normal sandworms. I dug my spear deeper and turned to Izzy. Her wand glowed cold blue as she repeatedly shivved the thing.

Cold damage!
[Izzy] dealt 24 damage to [Great Sandworm]
Cold damage!
[Izzy] dealt 22 damage to [Great Sandworm]
Cold damage!
[Izzy] dealt 24 damage to [Great Sandworm]

The worm bucked in pain and knocked Izzy to her stomach. I ran to catch her.

"The cold," she exclaimed. "It's susceptible to cold." She swapped her weapon for the larger winter staff.

"The others," I said, pointing ahead.

The great sandworm bore down on the pack. Four other worms were pestering them, swirling and taking potshots where the swords were too slow. It was a well-coordinated defense but we wouldn't be able to stop the great worm before he plowed right through it.

"Can you vault again?" asked Izzy.

I pulled her hip to mine and smiled, thanking whatever game designer gave the skill a 5-second cooldown. Together, we charged to the head of the giant serpent and vaulted off his face, flying forward into the crusader party. Izzy flipped upside-down, landed facing the boss, and cast sleet storm. The protective blue runes flared on the ground and encapsulated our group. The mighty rush of the great sandworm flew headlong into the full force of Izzy's gale.

The beast recoiled. Spear and swords surged with formidable precision. It was hardly necessary in the face of Izzy's legendary power, which these mobs had a weakness against. When the mighty worm fell, the frost mage turned her staff around us, firing snow in all directions. Two more sandworms perished before the once-a-day spell expired.

We braced for a counterattack, but Ashen Moor fell silent. The rest of the mobs had retreated.

The ground in a large radius around us was white with snow instead of gray with sedges and dirt. The corpses of fallen worms lay scattered, large snow-coated sculptures now part of the landscape.

"Kinda pretty, isn't it?" noted Izzy.

"You're such a romantic," I teased.

Cleric Vagram scoffed. "Sorcery!" He grabbed the reins of his horse and stormed ahead.

"YOU'RE WELCOME," called Izzy.

I smiled and dug into the layers of snow until I could loot the great sandworm.

[Dirt Pearl]
Crystallized orb with light and dark brown swirls, but inert.

The ball was polished glass, dark on the inside except where swirls of brown glittered in the light. It had a solid heft to it.

"Huh," I said. "Another one."

0680 Brothers in Arms

The injuries to the fellowship weren't serious. One soldier needed heavy healing but that was it. The true cost of combat had been the loss of two horses, Izzy's and another. We just doubled up to account for it. No one was concerned. The NPCs went about their business as soldiers did.

That night wasn't the bonding experience I'd hoped for. No war stories and tales of bravado traded across a campfire. For one thing, Vagram ordered no fires. After the sun set, the moor had cooled dramatically. It was our only defense against the sandworms which only surfaced during the day. They were attracted to heat. That meant no fire. It also meant a short, efficient rest. We were to wake up before dawn and march clear of Ashen Moor before temperatures rose too high.

Adding to the tension was the cleric's strict doctrine against paganism. The winter staff was a pagan relic. Bandit was a pagan beast. I noticed him eyeing the dirt pearl so I kept it out of sight. His distaste for any magic but his own was clear. The rest of the crusaders took his lead and buttoned up. Even

Grimwart failed to lighten the situation, opting instead for stolid duty.

Everybody sat on blankets in a tight grouping on flat ground because the moor didn't even have a decent tree to lean on. We chewed cold meat in silence. Watching Vagram and a knight pitch a tent was the only entertainment available. It was a modest green canvas that allowed space for a few people to sit up in. Finally, I had to break the silence.

"Cleric, that was a good thing you did back there for those travelers."

He paused his work to glance over his shoulder. "It was the White King's doing, not mine."

"Regardless. It was your hand."

He turned back to his tent. "Crusaders are dedicated to protecting the weak."

"How did you come to serve at Oakengard?"

"It was a calling that found me. I'd be lost without the catechists." He noted my confusion. "The priestship is one of three influencing leaders of the crusader path."

I nodded and picked a bit of gristle from my teeth. "I see. And Bishop Tannen?"

Vagram stopped working. "The bishop is our holy leader. He guides us in matters of the spirit."

"But why's he in Stronghold?"

"Questioning the bishop's actions does not ingratiate yourself to me." The cleric approached our huddle. "I judge men by what they act on. Bishop Tannen is a great pagan killer. He advises the armies of Oakengard and protects the weak. This quest to recover the Squid's Tooth is his doing."

Vagram crouched beside me. "Consider, on the other hand, the measures I have to judge yourself. You broke into the Pantheon and stole the Eye of Orik, engaged in combat with Decimus, and colluded with the fallen one."

"Shiver me timbers!" chortled Captain Oates, sitting nearby. "All these things be yer doin'? And I didn't think ye had a single redeemable quality."

"Silence, pirate," fumed Vagram.

"Or what, holy man?"

The cleric stood with murder in his eyes.

"Calm down," snapped Izzy. "Can't we eat this crap in peace without all the dick measuring?"

Vagram swallowed. "Please watch your language." With a huff of anger, he retreated into his tent.

"That went well," quipped Errol.

"Shut it," said Izzy. "What kind of pirate captain doesn't have a boat, anyhow?"

That seemed to get to him. Errol stood, threw a scrap of food to the ground, and dragged his bedroll further from the huddle.

"Not too far," warned Grimwart, ever ready. "We need to stick together."

"I'll stick someone, all right." The pirate ignored the warning and marched twenty paces out before finding a spot to set down. The other crusaders had taken advantage of the drama to turn in. They rested nearby. That left me and Izzy, squeezing our blankets close.

"You seem to be taking this in stride," she remarked.

I looked in her eyes. "What do you mean?"

"This. Everything. These priests, for one. Who upped and

made them the boss, all of a sudden?"

"The saints, I guess."

She snorted. "The patch notes called out the crusaders, specifically. These catechists are a different breed. I'm not so sure the saints are driving them."

I didn't see what she was getting at. I mean, she especially detested the priests for their antiquated views on witchcraft, and latent bigotry. I did too. The saints must've thought the paranoia was effective in the pagan conflict, despite the consequences.

"The developers sure are taking a back seat in this thing," I said. "I admit it's odd, but isn't it better all around? Letting the world police itself rather than acting as dictators?"

She was silent a moment. "I just can't believe they're ceding control to those zealots."

"I hear you. This thing has lots of moving parts."

"So you're excusing their behavior?"

"What? No, Izzy. Don't get like that."

She sighed. "Then why are we here? Don't tell me you wanna make a difference."

I chewed my lip. "Is that so bad?"

She scoffed.

My face burned. She was playing defensive again. Afraid to get too close to anyone or anything. "Besides," I said, pulling the stag horn from my inventory. "We have the quest chain to complete."

"The crown of the wild king!" she exclaimed. "How'd I forget about that?" She brought up her quest screen.

> **Dethrone the Wild King**
> *Quest Type: Fetch*
> *Reward: Unknown*
> To destroy the crown of the wild king, you must plunge it into the Salt Sea.

"You sneaky bastard," she said excitedly.

She swiped to her map. It was similar to mine, colored in the areas we'd previously visited and grayed out in unexplored territory. Mine had more detail due to the cartography skill but hers had location markers for places I didn't. Borders and place names in the outlying gray territory.

"How'd you get those?"

"From researching world tomes. I told you I'm Haven's foremost lore expert. Various books will populate notable locations, but I still don't get details on them. Just markers." She scrolled the map until it arrived at Shorehome, another day's journey at least. Above the city label, past the winding coast was—

"The Salt Sea," I whispered. "I didn't know it was that close."

She gave me the side eye. "Really? For a second there I thought you were a mastermind. Killing two birds with one stone, and all that." She shrugged. "I suppose it's better to be lucky than good."

I stared into the vacant eyes of the stag skull. Then I looked around the camp to make sure no one was paying attention to us. The crusaders rested. Grimwart paced in the distance. Vagram was chanting within his tent as it lit up with an eerie yellow glow.

I stuffed the skull back into my inventory. "Jeez, that's not creepy or anything."

"He's a cleric. He probably needs to pray to recharge his spells."

I shook my rattled head. "Speaking of recharging, why don't you get some sleep?"

I lay down too, but I had a lot to think about. Really, I was thankful for the short night. With Errol in the same camp, I couldn't get a wink of rest. The ironic thing was he slept like a baby.

Somewhere in the haze of midnight, the moor was playing tricks on my eyes. I tightened the blanket around my shoulder and rocked back and forth, realizing how cold I was. I stood to get my blood moving. I checked the beds. Izzy, Errol, Grimwart—they were all asleep. Another knight had taken up the watch, but he sat comfortably facing the other direction. I wondered if he was even awake.

There it was again. Movement in the dark. I focused, but my darkvision was thrown off in this inhospitable terrain.

I dropped the blanket, equipped my spear, and silently tiptoed toward the swaying shadows. Everyone in camp was asleep. Ashen Moor was deserted. Absolutely nothing living was out here now. Nothing except a haze in the distance.

It wasn't smart to wander out of camp but I moved closer, leaving the others behind until I came on him. Saint Peter.

I rolled my eyes. "What're you doing here?" I grumbled.

"We need to talk."

"You couldn't just shoot me a message? You scared me half

to death."

"You know messaging doesn't work in the wild. You're heading into pagan territory. Soon I won't even be able to visit."

Right. The saints had ceded control of the region. We were sneaking into hostile territory.

"What's the deal with these priests?" I asked. "I get the crusaders, but—"

"The knights are meant to deal with the pagans," explained Saint Peter. "The priests have their sights on another enemy entirely."

I scoured his troubled face. "You can't be serious."

"I'm dead serious. The last data we have points to Lucifer being in the area. We can't affix a more precise location, but he's in there."

"And you send a single cleric to take him on?"

"I've sent you," he retorted. "But don't sell the catechists short. In the event you encounter Lucifer, you may be surprised by Vagram's tenacity."

I bit down. "So that's what you're here for. To discuss the real mission. All this business of saving the people of Shorehome is a cover?"

"On the contrary," he chided. "I figured you for the kind of person who preferred to kill two birds with one stone."

I tensed as he repeated Izzy's words. Had he been listening? It had to just be a coincidence.

"Things just seem to end up that way," I said somberly. I kicked my boot in the dirt. "How are we supposed to succeed where the angels have failed?"

Saint Peter frowned, puffing out his white beard. "Don't read too heavily into that. The angels are a security system. As such, they have their flaws. Exploits. It's entirely possible they have a blind spot regarding Lucifer that hasn't been corrected yet. Don't forget that you fended off a heavenly warrior yourself."

"I ran."

"And Lucifer has been doing the same."

I grumbled. "Have you found them at least?"

He shook his head. "We haven't had word from them in a long time, but that's how they operate. And Lucifer's developed a penchant for anonymity, which even you have benefited from."

He was referring to my stranger's cowl, a gift from the fallen angel that kept me off the radar as long as nobody directly saw me.

I clicked my teeth. "You realize how much this complicates matters. There are a lot of moving parts. We're supposed to sneak into Shorehome to see how we can best help, secure the Squid's Tooth without alerting the pagans, all the while remaining off Lucifer's radar even though he's been two steps ahead of us from the start?"

"Saint Loras has a lot of experience with Shorehome. It's an eclectic city. He assures us a small scouting party can blend in as needed."

"Izzy and I, maybe. The knights are a tougher sell, but I'm really not sure about Vagram."

"Bishop Tannen speaks very highly of him."

I spat. "Don't you think these priests are too simpleminded for a sprawling fantasy landscape? They're against magic, for fuck's sake."

Saint Peter took a long breath. "They have some

unfortunate... quirks. The priestship wasn't designed that way. The catechists are a procedural outcome of crusader structure."

"So you're not to blame for their mentality, but if it helps in the fight against Lucifer..."

"We're not responsible, Talon. Barring the ability to wipe, we saints can only massage the game from here on out."

"So what do we do?"

"You have a dragonspear. Lucifer has a dragon. Figure it out."

Memories of the terrifying beast swooping over Stronghold came to me. Lucifer had somehow awoken a creature that hadn't been introduced to the simulation yet. He'd reached deep into the codebase and asset tree and yanked out an unfinished high-level mob. A black dragon that flies and spits acid. It was just one of his many hacked advantages.

I re-examined the stats of my legendary weapon.

> **[Dragonspear]**
> *Unique, Unbreakable*
> The famed weapon of the hero Magnus Dragonrider, the dragonspear grants its wielder heroic power.
> *+3 Strength*
> *+2 Agility*
> *+1 Essence*
> *Titanslayer*
> *+25% damage versus dragons*
> *+20% damage defending Stronghold*
> *+15% damage versus pagans*

Damn it. Idiot that I was, I hadn't even pondered the significance of the extra dragon damage. Hell, it was in the *name* of the damn thing. The dragonspear. I'd just taken it for backstory. As Kyle would say, stupid fantasy bullshit. The spear was supposed to have been used in the Dragon Wars a thousand years ago. History that, of course, never occurred and was entirely fabricated.

"All legendary weapons have a purpose," said Saint Peter. "Yours is calling you sooner than expected, but it calls nonetheless."

"And Lucifer? What about him?"

Peter sighed with heavy regret. "Lucifer was a mistake, like you. She was a young girl—only eight years old, if you can believe it."

I'd already uncovered Lucifer's true identity. The adult male persona was just another glitch in Lucifer's arsenal.

"We have a rule," explained the saint. "No one under eighteen can be uploaded to Haven. It was partly a legal decision, of course, but psychological factors are in play as well. Particularly young minds aren't ready to shed their physical limitations and enter a purely digital reality. They haven't yet learned the repercussions of their actions. They don't yet have the empathy society requires of them."

"Funny to hear the saints speak of empathy."

He frowned, fully aware of Kablammy's past transgressions. "We were attempting to preserve *children*, Talon." He looked inward. "Focus testing... didn't go well."

"So she went rogue and you learned your lesson. Except she wants to bring down life as we know it. Digitally speaking."

"I'm afraid the problem may be more complex than that. The persona of Lucifer is driven. His fingerprints prove that he's hacked into the Oculus more times than we'd realized. His actions are bizarre, seemingly without an endgame."

"Or one that you can see."

He nodded. "Suffice it to say, I doubt his only goal is to destroy the simulation. That likely could've been accomplished by now, before we were ready to defend against his hacks."

We traded grim expressions. "You don't just want to defeat Lucifer, you want to discover his plan."

"It may be the only way to undo the damage. It may be the only way to save Haven."

A dried sedge crunched behind me, followed by a curse.

"Good luck, Talon," came Peter's voice, now behind me. I didn't give him the satisfaction of spinning around. I knew he was already gone.

"Who ye be talkin' to?" asked Errol gruffly. He wiped sleepy eyes and peered past me.

"Just going for a midnight stroll." I huffed and marched back to camp. It was a bit early, but I figured it was time to wake everyone up.

0690 Home Alone

Kyle Grath's eyes snapped open and his first sensation was pain. "Ugh," he articulately expressed before pushing to a sit.

He was in bed. Alone of course. He massaged his temples and attempted to smack the dry mouth off his tongue. What kind of stupid game gives you hangovers? With ease that only came from repeated practice, Kyle reached into his inventory with closed eyes, pulled out a health vial, and chugged it. The relief was immediate.

Haven allowed residents to quickly clear their heads from the effects of recreational drinking by strolling in fresh air. Of course, that would mean he'd have to go outside. Technically he was still on lockdown but, even if he wasn't, he would've opted for the potion. The afterlife had stolen the glorious post-beer piss from him. He'd be damned if it also forced him to exercise.

Now that his head was clear, he opened his menu to check the time. One in the morning. He'd slept clear through the afternoon and half the night. It reminded him of his college days, but those memories were more cautionary than nostalgic. Despite physically feeling one hundred percent, his thoughts lingered on the reason for his booze snooze.

"Stupid fantasy games with stupid shadowy threats lurking in stupid mysterious towers."

He stood up and scratched his ass, wondering if he'd gone too far with condemning Dragonperch. The tower was, he had to admit, pretty damn cool. Or it would've been if he'd stumbled on a legendary item as easily as Izzy had found her winter staff.

No worries. Nothing to see here. Just Kyle.

He took the steps down to the den and parked on the couch before realizing he should've made a pit stop at the fridge first. After lengthy consideration, Kyle decided to ride the couch out and get grub later. He picked up the remote and browsed movies for a while. A binge session of *Friday the 13th* was in the lead when he pulled a one-eighty and switched on *Call of Duty*. It was a rough life.

Kyle stared at the online leaderboard. He was first place, of course. No one in Stronghold could get the better of him after an extended sample set, and Kyle played more than anybody else. He sighed, for some reason not as proud of that achievement as he usually was.

Next up was scrolling through Haven menus, reading up on skills and items. He produced the bone pearl and examined its polished surface. What the heck was this thing? He had half a mind to take a hammer to it and find out when there was a knock at the door.

"What now?"

He sat waiting, hoping whoever was bothering him would just go away. But the knocking came back louder.

"I'm coming already!" he shouted.

Luckily, the kitchen was the only floor between him and

ground level, so he quickly made it to Dragonperch's door and opened up.

It was Dune, the green ranger.

"Kyle," he said urgently and obviously disappointed. "Hey. Is Talon around?"

Kyle yawned. "Nah, he took off. The priests had an impromptu meeting in front of Dragonperch just to wake me up. I didn't get the details from up here, but the gist was a mission to Shorehome or something."

Dune glared in disbelief. "He left?!? What did he say?"

Kyle shook his head. "I don't know. He took off pretty quick. They probably left me a message. Hang on." Kyle checked his mailbox. "Nope. No consideration for Kyle."

"That's not good. He was supposed to be at the Wicked Crow tonight. Kinda surprised you weren't there, actually. I bumped into Trafford."

"Yeah, I'm on lockdown."

Dune tensed and eyed Oldtown. "You have a run-in with the crusaders?"

"What? Nah. I... kinda blew myself up." Dune frowned and eyed him oddly. Kyle considered explaining but figured it'd be too much trouble.

"Okay, whatever," resumed the ranger. "Listen, some of the city watch have been complaining about changes coming their way. I've been trying to tell Talon that weird things are in the works."

"Good idea," he said. "Talon loves worrying about crap like that. Why don't you check in when he's back and—"

Dune held his hand to the door. "I need to talk to him now."

Kyle shrugged. "What do you want me to do about it?"

The ranger looked at him like he was daft. "Ask him what he's up to. In party chat."

"Oh." Kyle went to the party screen and stiffened at the notification. "*Oh.*"

"What is it?"

"Fucknuggets," said Kyle. "I kinda forgot to party up again after I died. So—"

"They're in the wild, completely disconnected from what's happening on the home front. Great work."

"Bro, it's not like it's my fault. They left pretty quick."

"You said that." Dune looked around again. "Look, just forget it. I'll get in touch with him another way. You... just keep holding the fort."

Kyle blew steam from his mouth as Dune left. The dude was a bit of a cocky prick. Thought he was perfect or something. The sound of the door slamming was satisfying, but only momentarily.

Kyle stood in place wondering what to do next. What would the rest of his party do? He wasn't sure about Talon, but Izzy would camp out in her library. She spent lots of time there. It seemed like a waste to him, reading bear-shifter porn. Whatever. He guessed everybody needed a hobby.

His was the brewery.

Instead of heading back upstairs, Kyle descended another flight to the underground. He found his casks and barrels and bottles mostly where he'd left them, but there was still a decent cleanup job to be done. He sighed and got to work. It was the best way to feel useful.

And useful he was. Kyle did such a good job of tidying up that he decided to organize the old stock that had been shoved into the corner when he'd first established the brewery a week ago. He moved some boxes and pulled the dusty blanket from a huge mirror. The damn thing was heavy.

Interesting. A shelf was built into the wall, not hidden per se but more or less obscured by crap. Kyle started to sweep the dust away when a glint of sky-blue caught his eye.

"What in the ever-loving..."

0700 Enemy Territory

Ashen Moor was freezing in the predawn hours, but the movement did us good. Still half asleep, we rode through the gloom without conversation. Izzy steadied a hand on my shoulder as Bandit easily carried the double load. Not that a five-foot, ninety-pound munchkin like her was much of a load.

"I can't see anything back here," she complained.

"I said you could sit in the front."

"Yeah, right. You'd take that as an invitation to spoon me."

I smiled. "You can always ride with one of the crusaders. I think Grimwart likes you."

"Please."

"Aye, lassie," said Errol, apparently eavesdropping and slowing his horse for us to catch up. "Me stallion has a powerful buck, if ye be preferrin' it instead."

She arched an eyebrow. "What did you call me?"

"Nothin' but the sweetest flower o' the land."

Grimwart's black helmet turned sharply. "Knock it off. Leave the lady be."

"Aye aye, valiant sir." Errol turned to Izzy and whispered. "Yer knight in shinin' armor awaits yer favor." His horse steered away from us as the colonel watched on.

Izzy rolled her eyes. "Boys. Why do I have the misfortune of going questing with a bunch of boys?"

"It's like you've died and gone to Haven," I said cheekily.

She groaned.

Ashen Moor was cold and dark and gray, but it wasn't limitless. Over time, the dirt grew richer. Greenery sprouted in uneven patches. As first light made it over the horizon, the barren land was behind us—along with the sandworms.

"It's easy riding the rest of the way," relayed Grimwart, "but be on your toes for pagans. Henceforth, we're in their territory."

"Worry not," replied a knight with a red sash. "If it's green or gray, it doesn't stand a chance." The crusaders hurrahed and galloped northward, beset by a sense of purpose.

We veered toward a well-worn path and rode uneventfully till noon. We dismounted in the shade of a large boulder for a quick rest. Izzy and I coordinated with her map. More and more of the land was being filled in as we traversed it. The road we followed no doubt led to Shorehome.

I sipped water from a skin. It was a curious quirk in a virtual world, since I had no body that required hydration. It was refreshing, nonetheless. On the road and in the sun, the basest hungers and thirsts required the simplest relief.

"Riders!" called out the knight with the red sash. Everyone turned toward our destination. Horsemen rode south at a fast clip but slowed uncertainly when they saw us.

The crusaders all stood and walked to the road. Errol crouched against the boulder, slicing an apple and feeding himself with the knife. He peeked out and squinted at the proceedings.

"Ho there!" called Grimwart with a raised hand.

The horsemen slowed to a stop. All riders and one covered wagon. I studied the score of them. Humans, thankfully. Most were NPCs with names in gray text, like [Perry] and [Clod], but the woman in the lead surprised me. Her name, [Jackie], was colored green, followed by the text [Level 6 Dragoon]. She was a player, and in the top ten percent at that level.

"We pass in peace," said Jackie, eyeing the heavy armor before her. Her people had weapons and armor too, of course, but not like us. They weren't soldiers.

"What news from Shorehome?" asked Cleric Vagram.

Jackie watched him carefully. "Overrun. We were forced from the city. We do what little we can from the countryside."

"Killing pagans?"

Jackie turned and whistled. Another player, [Colt], trotted closer and dropped a sack at the cleric's feet. Goblin heads rolled out.

Vagram nodded approvingly.

Colt was classed as a drifter. I examined the other horsemen. More NPCs, from what I could tell, unless someone was in the wagon.

"I don't be likin' this," muttered Errol behind us. His rapier was in hand, but he was pressed against the edge of the boulder, out of their sight.

"Put that away," I whispered. "You're gonna start a fight."

He showed his teeth. "End one, more likely."

Jackie eyed the crusaders on the road. "What manner of army are you?"

Grimwart stepped forward and bowed. "Oakengard crusaders, my lady."

Colt turned to her. "Oakengard is real?"

Instead of answering him, she addressed Grimwart. "Can I take that to mean you aren't here to murder us?"

The knight with the red sash laughed. "Hell, we're here to join you!"

"Watch that tongue," warned Vagram. "We will not speak of the devil or his den."

Jackie waved and a horseman dismounted. [Chico], another player. Another drifter. How'd I miss him?

"It looks like you're well supplied," she said. "We'd be willing to trade information on goblin camps and the like in return for food and water for our horses. Chico here knows all the ins and outs of the land."

Chico was level 5, like Colt. The dragoon Jackie had amassed a decent party. NPC henchmen were pretty sweet as well. I wondered how she got them.

I checked on Errol, who was being especially quiet. The pirate had slipped around the far edge of the boulder. He was flanking the riders.

"Oh, crap."

I followed him around as the horsemen drew closer to the crusaders. Some dismounted, most didn't, as the group began to trade information and supplies. Errol circled to the back of the wagon. A length of boat sail draped over a low frame to shield its contents.

"What do you think you're doing?" I chided.

"They be bandits," he returned.

"No, they're not."

He stopped at the wagon and gripped the sail in a fist. "Then why are they hidin' their plunder?"

He yanked the sail free. A huge ogre unfurled to full height and roared. Screams broke out from the ranks of the crusaders.

"Talon!" warned Izzy.

In the split second I could afford to keep my attention off the ogre, the horsemen drew daggers and slid them under the helmets and into the exposed necks of the crusaders. The knight with the red sash gurgled and gripped his throat as Chico's class revealed itself as [Highwayman]. Grimwart barely rolled away in time from Colt's charging strike. He was now a [Cowboy]. Jackie produced a lance and nailed Vagram right in the chest, sending the cleric flying. And then I couldn't worry about them anymore, because a giant fist came swinging my way.

I growled. Ogres were big, but I was bigger.

I triggered dash and sped toward the beast, beating the arc of his fist. At the same time, I equipped the dragonspear and triggered deadshot.

Surprise!

Combo!

Stun!

You dealt 106 damage to [Ogre]

The Scar of the Six Seas wasted no time taking advantage of the initiative. He stabbed the ogre's chest and danced around his massive body, swiping wildly like a Renaissance painter lost in the passion of the moment. I yanked my spear around in a full spin and bent my knees low, slashing the flailing monster's ankles.

> [Errol] dealt 37 damage to [Ogre]
> [Errol] dealt 23 damage to [Ogre]
> [Errol] dealt 42 damage to [Ogre]
> Break!
> You dealt 36 damage to [Ogre]

The ankle shattered. The big guy yelped and crumpled to the floor in extreme pain. Within a matter of seconds, the behemoth's health had been reduced from 300 to 56, and we weren't done yet. The ogre raised his hands in defense.

Standing on opposite sides of our enemy, Errol and I both drove our weapons deep.

> You dealt 45 damage to [Ogre]
> [Errol] dealt 36 damage to [Ogre]
> [Ogre] is defeated
> 400 XP awarded

> Crown Unlocked: **Five-Second Rule**
> Take out an orange or greater enemy in under 5 seconds without getting hit.
> 1000 XP awarded

Immediately, we turned to the rest of the party.

Several bandits and crusaders lay still on the ground. Colt charged Izzy but struck a wall of ice. The horse was upheaved and threw him to the ground. With a wave of the winter staff, a giant icicle speared right through the cowboy's torso.

Chico snuck forward and plunged a knife into Izzy's back. She squirmed away in pain. Jackie and another mounted horseman strafed the crusaders. Her lance batted them to the ground. Grimwart, meanwhile, fought off three swordsmen at the same time. He was better than them, using his bastard sword with two hands for power and one to parry, but the group effort was putting him on his heels.

"Let's ride out," urged Errol. "Now, when the chance be ours."

"Are you crazy? They need our help."

"The crusaders be no friends o' mine. An' neither be you."

I didn't have time to argue with him. "Coward," I spat, and charged into the fray.

Jackie spun her horse around as I approached. I steadied my weapon. She leaned forward into a full charge, lance against spear. I liked those odds, but I liked being unpredictable even more. As she bore down on me, I rolled to the side to take out her horse's legs. Before I could strike, her lance caught the back of my head and sent me to the dirt.

The dragoon laughed and pulled around again. I ground my teeth to fight off the pain. She flicked the lance in her hand and it was suddenly bathed in a neon-green glow. She saw my momentary hesitation and charged.

Damn. My main skills were still in cooldown, but I could wait her out if I needed. This time when she came at me, I remained steady. At the last possible second, I triggered crossblock, hoping to capitalize on a parry.

The force of the blow rocked me. My boots skidded backward, carving lines in the ground. The enchanted weapon still managed decent damage, but I avoided a stun or other special afflictions.

The dragoon growled and charged me again. She was good at this, protecting herself first, but keeping the onslaught relentless so I couldn't recharge my dash. Something told me she was used to fighting players. As she converged, I sprinted forward and vaulted over her lance. My boots met her chest and knocked her clean off the horse. She landed hard and rolled in pain.

Now it was my turn to laugh. This was a straight scrap now. The horsemen had spent their advantage well, but they had underestimated the more experienced crusaders. Slightly larger numbers, surprise, and a hidden ogre were enough to overtake most parties unawares, but our band of adventurers stood and fought.

My skin flared gold again. Vagram's buff. The cleric was on his hands and knees, hurt and healing himself. A bandit hefted a small axe and darted toward him. *My* Bandit galloped into the NPC's path, knocked him down, and trampled him under powerful hooves.

"How's *that* for a pagan beast?" I bragged.

Jackie pulled herself to her feet and twirled her lance my way. I stood with my side to her and flipped the dragonspear confidently.

"Did you really think your ragtag band could take out a unit of trained soldiers?"

She sneered, worry creeping into her face. "I've dealt with men and metal before."

I snorted. "Maybe, but you haven't dealt with the Protector of Stronghold."

She lunged at me. I crossblocked her blow. When I counterattacked, she activated a skill of her own, some kind of spinning block. We traded another back and forth. She was a few levels lower than me, but she was a good fighter. A soldier class, which meant she theoretically was better at a straightforward fight than I was. At the same time, she was a dragoon. Meant for a horse. I'd already snipped her claws.

Her lance powered up again. I recognized the heavy blow coming and pitched my agility against her strength. I dashed under the weapon to her backside where I drew a line of blood across her back.

"Ugh!" she screamed. She whirled at me savagely but angrily.

Another crossblock stopped her cold. I followed it up with a deadshot combo that hit her square in the gut. Jackie pitched to the ground.

Izzy was still in the thick of it. Colt wasn't dead yet, but she hadn't been able to finish him off with Chico and Perry pressing her. The highwayman's blade was quick and ruthless, stealing cuts past the defense of the winter staff. Izzy likely didn't want to use its legendary power because of all the friendly-fire damage it would inflict in the chaotic ruckus.

She used the icy head of the staff to knock Colt in the jaw. Chico came in behind her and attacked.

> Backstab!
> Critical Hit!
> [Chico] dealt 77 damage to [Izzy]

"Heartless bastards!" screamed Errol, galloping by with a bandit's axe and burying it into Colt's head. The pirate turned and dismounted. Perry the NPC came at him. Errol went to work with his rapier.

Chico, on the other hand, hadn't moved. Savoring his kill, his brow furrowed as he attempted to withdraw his dagger. He heaved over and over, but it was stuck in Izzy's body. The pixie frosted over into a block of ice, and his eyes widened.

"How's this for a backstab?" quipped Izzy, her real body offset from her icy double. She plunged the frost wand into Chico's spine. Blood exploded from his mouth. His lifeless body fell.

Grimwart had downed two men and wounded another, but a sword was embedded clear through his breastplate. He limped over and buckled to his knees beside his leader. The cleric was the center of a circle of the dead and dying, robbers and knights alike. The overwhelming numbers had taken their toll. Despite Errol and Izzy and I being mostly well off, the imposing crusaders had taken the brunt of the ambush. Four valiant men in armor lay still. The remaining bandits moved in with their weapons.

Cleric Vagram cackled. He was at full health again, still on his hands and knees. Gripped tightly in one palm was the bronze cross.

"Save us, my lord," he said, and white light exploded from his body.

During the distraction, Jackie scrambled to her feet. She attempted to steal her lance from the ground but I knocked it away. She turned to Chico and Colt and her face flared with anger.

"Kill them all!" she commanded her people.

Vagram heaved the sword from Grimwart's armor and helped the colonel to his feet. The knight with the red sash stood and picked his sword from the floor, as did his three comrades. The bandits flushed with fear as every crusader returned to full health.

"There will be no mercy today," uttered Cleric Vagram.

No longer able to rely on numbers or surprise, the bandits fought halfheartedly. One tried to escape to his horse and was cut down climbing into the saddle. Jackie drew a sword and attempted one last blow at the cleric himself. He raised a palm and the metal clanged against his circle of protection.

Grimwart, sturdy and strong, used a mighty two-handed swing to lop her head off her shoulders.

And with that, the bandits were dead.

I took in the scene silently for a good beat, ensuring we were safe. After that I ran to Izzy. As a mystic class, she only had 148 health to my 261. Surrounded and in the thick of it, she was hurting.

"Come on," I urged. "Vagram can help."

She grabbed my wrist tightly and stood firm. "I don't need anything from that scumbag." She pulled a health flask from her pack and downed it. The advanced potion made her good as new in seconds.

"How are we?" asked Grimwart, surveying the wounded.

I was still in awe of Vagram's power. "...Everyone's surprisingly great," I murmured.

Grimwart's black helmet turned to Errol. "You didn't turn tail and flee," he said, also surprised.

"Aye, and what's it to ye?"

The colonel considered him a moment. "Maybe we'll make a soldier of you yet."

Errol searched Colt's body and Izzy knelt beside Chico. My balance of silver incremented as the spoils were split among the party. I made my way to Jackie as the crusaders checked the rest of the bodies.

Loot:
37 silver
[Traveling Cape]
[Journeyman Sword]
[Health Vial]

"Garbage," I muttered.

"Same," chimed in Izzy. "They really were a bunch of broke thieves."

The loot hadn't been their only possessions, of course. When players in Haven die, they randomly drop a small portion of their equipment. Sometimes that means the goods, but usually player hauls are unimpressive. It's a way of helping residents keep what they've built up while also providing a very real risk of losing something valuable.

"Good work on this filthy animal," called out the knight with the red sash. He was examining the ogre carcass at the wagon. "Now I understand why the bishop wanted you along. You really are the famed pagan killer they say you are."

Crusader Reputation +50

I didn't answer. My eyes trailed to the sack of goblin heads. Beside them, Jackie's head gawked emptily at the sky.

"I don't get it," I muttered. "Why was the ogre working with humans? Why had they been killing goblins?"

"Heathens," Vagram cut in. "All of them. You can't make sense of their kind."

I frowned as the troop loaded up. We'd been stopped for too long already. Although we'd experienced a clear victory on the battlefield, the war in my mind wasn't so easily sorted.

0710 Borderlands

Not an hour had passed before we encountered another trio of drifters. The new group ogled our force and passed without event, but it set us on edge anyway. Errol angled his horse around.

"We need to be gettin' off the road from here on out."

"I think not," said Vagram. Crusader helmets turned to him. "This road leads straight to Shorehome. If we press hard we can reach the city by midnight."

"Aye, and what then?" countered the pirate. "Nightfall is no advantage 'gainst the goblins' darkvision. This road be a dangerous one. We've already encountered bandits once. The nearer we get t' Shorehome, the more likely the danger."

The cleric's scowl was evident. "Shorehome always was a den of villainy."

"That's me home you be slanderin'," growled Errol.

Grimwart cantered up. "What would you have us do, pirate?"

The Scar of the Six Seas left a lingering glare on the cleric before answering. He held out his arm along our path. "This road leads northeast, aye. A straight shot t' the city. The main road will be heavily guarded." He swiveled his arm straight north. "We need t' go off-road, t' the coast, an' approach the city from the crags. Lots o' smuggling routes thataways. Trust me."

"Sounds like a greater chance of being ambushed by pirates, to me," commented Vagram.

"Fear not the flagships, cleric. Directly northward lies the Salt Sea." My ears perked. "Shorehome rests in its shadow, protected by the natural breakwater. The Salt Sea itself is too shallow fer nary a galleon, but me brothers have hidden a skiff in the crags 'tween the break an' the city."

Grimwart cocked his head. "You wish to sneak into a city of pirates on a smuggling ship?"

"Has a ring to it, does it not?"

Vagram snorted.

"I don't know," I cut in. "I think we should hear him out."

Everyone turned to me, making it clear I was an unwelcome intrusion to the planning committee.

"I'm just saying, anything we do here on out is dangerous, right? We're sneaking into a city occupied by the enemy. There's no safe way to do that. Besides, stop me if I'm wrong, but Errol's our guide, isn't he?"

Vagram stared blankly. If we weren't entertaining suggestions from the pirate then what was he here for?

"It's decided then." I turned Bandit northward and broke off the path. "We go to that Salt Sea place."

After a tense moment, Errol guffawed and followed. The crusaders shared terse words but galloped after us. I, meanwhile, reopened my quest menu.

> **Dethrone the Wild King**
> *Quest Type: Fetch*
> *Reward: Unknown*
> To destroy the crown of the wild king, you must plunge it into the Salt Sea.

The sky darkened over the next few hours. As we pressed on, torches from Shorehome glowed in the distance. The second of Haven's player cities was directly east of us. It was difficult to make out in the night. Its walls weren't monolithic like Stronghold's and darkvision didn't extend to the horizon.

Although Shorehome was on the coast, we were currently landlocked, needing to follow the shoreline further up to the Salt Sea. It was still a long way to go.

"We won't make the city before daybreak," said the knight with the red sash.

"We don't intend to," answered Errol. "We can smuggle in under the sun just as easily as under the moon. Might as well camp here fer the night."

I sensed some disagreement among the crusaders, but everybody was tired from two straight days of travel and battle. Fatigue won out and everybody dismounted.

"We should be safe enough here for a fire," said Grimwart. He turned to the pirate who nodded in confirmation. The crusaders dug a pit in the ground to sit the fire low so it would be less visible from a distance. It was a neat trick.

Izzy and I sat close, breaking out our rations. Vagram pitched his tent and disappeared inside without small talk. One by one the crusaders settled around us. They even took their helmets off. "It's a drafty night, it is," said a nondescript knight. The crusaders grunted in agreement.

The colonel nodded and sat as well. I'd never seen Grimwart's face before. He was a stolid man with a dark mustache. White streaks at his temples lined black hair. I passed him some meat. He nodded in thanks. "Why don't you join us as well?" he called out to the pirate.

Errol was sitting against a gnarled tree on the edge of camp. Surprised by the gesture, he shrugged but repositioned himself by the fire. For a time we all ate in awkward silence, but it took only one mention of the bandits before the group was laughing and sharing war stories. I smiled and wondered if we should invite Vagram to the campfire as well, but I dared not approach his creepy tent light show.

"Were you here?" asked the knight with the red sash. "When the city fell?"

Errol grew solemn and pulled from a bottle of barley wine. "I was."

"And the city watch?"

"Shorehome has no city watch. It's not a great fortress like the famed Oakengard. It doesn't have the mighty walls o' Stronghold. Shorehome is a merchant village o' fisherman an' sea folk."

The knight frowned. "So there was no resistance then."

"Very little indeed. Even the saints were powerless."

"That is why," pointed out Grimwart, "we must fight in their stead."

Errol scoffed dismissively. "If it pleases ye."

"What's that supposed to mean?" asked another crusader.

"I speak plainly enough."

I chuckled.

"Ye have something to say then, too?" challenged Errol.

I shook my head absently. "No. It's just... you're strange for an NPC. You seem more like a player."

His scarred eyebrow arched. "An' why is that?"

"I guess because you're out here. You're not standing next to a thing saying the same thing repeatedly."

"Who does that?" he asked gruffly.

"It's a drafty night, it is," said the same knight. The crusaders grunted in agreement.

Errol and I studied the band of adventurers dumbly.

"Bah, what do ye expect o' soldiers?"

I shrugged. "It seems like they're content with a purpose."

"Aye, and what's yers then? The famed hero o' Stronghold, sittin' pretty in his tower makin' mead."

My face paled. "That was *you* Kyle saw in the grotto."

The pirate tossed his empty bottle behind him. "Colludin' with saints an' priests. What are *ye* doin' here, hero?"

Izzy had been quiet thus far, but she muttered, "I've been wondering the same thing."

"Aye, the lass who cares fer naught. What o' you, Talon? Because me eyes spy a man who cares only fer himself."

"Ironic words from a pirate," I said. "You need to turn that lens on yourself."

"I care fer me people," he insisted.

I chortled. "You keep using the word care. It's a funny word. You fought well today, but you were two shakes away from abandoning Izzy and the crusaders before I jumped back in the fray."

He sneered and faced the fire. "No offense, but none of ya are me people."

The knight with the red sash threw his food scraps to the floor and stood. "I've lost my appetite." Another crusader grumbled in agreement and left the fire. When Grimwart stood, it was a signal for the others to go. They took up bedrolls on the perimeter as the colonel glared at Errol.

"Fighting fiercely and fighting well are two separate things. I should've known you couldn't stray from your pirate roots."

Errol was undeterred. "Ye fight fer the saints, sir, and ye do it *well*. Have ya ever asked yerself if they would fight fer ye?"

Grimwart scowled and stomped away. Not to be outdone, Errol skipped to his feet and dramatically turned in the other direction.

"You really care so much about your people?" I called after him. He paused. "What was so important that you left them behind?"

He clenched his jaw, his back to me, and said, "Fetchin' help." Then he returned to his gnarled tree.

I sighed and pondered the state of things for a moment. Everything was a tangled mess. "What do you think?" I asked Izzy.

She shook her head lightly. "I'd rather not." She curled up and wrapped a blanket over her shoulders. Just when I thought she wouldn't say any more, she did. "If it were up to me I'd abandon this non-quest, go straight to the Salt Sea in the morning, destroy the crown of the wild king, and return to the safety of Dragonperch. If you're so desperate to offer your help, at least find someone who wants it."

I worked my jaw but didn't offer up excuses for where we found ourselves. I hadn't asked her to come, after all. I knew how Izzy felt about societal concepts like community. I knew there were times she wanted nothing more than to grind levels all alone, always seeking validation in numerical form. Seeking fame more than friendship.

Except we'd achieved those things already. Our party had the only level 9s in Haven. Slaying Orik had given us a lead that would take weeks for most to overcome. And instead of celebrating, I had to wonder what it was all for.

"This is kind of funny," I started, voice nostalgic. "In high school I used to always go to this pizza place, grab a slice and a Coke, and play *Golden Axe*. Sitting by this campfire in the middle of the night reminds me of those intermission scenes."

Izzy looked up at me strangely. "What in the ever-loving crap are you going on about?"

"You know: At night the pixies would sneak into camp and steal your potions. You had to kick them around a bit to keep them in line."

Izzy's glare shot daggers at me. "Well, you touch *this* pixie—boot or otherwise—and you won't have enough potions to heal your stomped ass."

I stifled a laugh. "Sorry, thought you'd see the humor in that. I keep forgetting you're not a gamer."

I tried to think of other worlds that might be more up her alley. *Lord of the Rings*, *Dragonlance*, *Game of Thrones*—it was surreal to think we were living in a similar fantasy world. I couldn't come up with any famous pixies, though. For a while I got stuck wondering if Tinkerbell was a pixie or a fairy. By the time I decided it didn't matter, Izzy had been resting quietly for a while. I sighed. What a wild trip this was.

I wasn't sure how long I'd been propped there, or if I'd fallen asleep or not. All I knew was I suddenly couldn't sit there anymore. I stood and stretched my aching back. Why the hell did simulations need to be this realistic?

I stepped away from the fire and wandered toward the invisible northerly coast. The humid ocean air washed over me like a warm, refreshing bath. To the distant east, the lights of Shorehome dimmed. I could almost hear the music and merriment from the city. Could almost hear the break of the waves against the crags. We were so close yet somehow still in the middle of nowhere.

I produced the stag skull from my inventory. It was an ominous crown of bone with blackened soot highlighting its cracks. The antlers splayed wide to either side with multiple pointed extrusions.

What did the wild king care for? Music and merriment as well? A land for his people? Did that condemn him as a guilty man? For a savage, he sure didn't seem to rule by fear. His people had staked out the Blackwood, territory nobody else wanted. Compared to the pagans, the wildkins were saints.

I chuckled and checked the camp. Better not say that part out loud lest I be accused of sacrilege.

Amid the resting forms of our men casually strolled a hulking brute. Straps of black leather swayed in the gentle wind. Then Hood's axe cleaved the knight with the red sash in two.

0720 Mortal Kombat

"Ambush!" I screamed at the top of my lungs.

The camp was a blur of activity. Everyone flipped to their feet, weapons ready. Shadowy forms encircled us. Grimwart boldly strode toward the intruder and held his bastard sword high. The warden swung his axe. Grimwart spun and knocked the weapon aside. Hood answered with a backhanded slap with his free hand. The colonel's helmet spun around and he stumbled backward.

The hooded brute lifted his axe, both warden and executioner.

Spears of ice lanced his breastplate. They burst into chunks, failing to pierce the mystical armor but knocking him back nonetheless. A crusader pulled the stunned colonel away and another took his place before the intruder.

Vagram stomped out of his tent, golden cross sparkling on his white tunic. "The warden of the Blackwood," he spat.

Glowing white eyes narrowed.

Then six of his shadowy thralls flooded our ranks.

"Izzy, watch your back!" I yelled.

She spun as a hooded wildkin with a mace closed in. A swipe

of the winter staff created a spike of ice that jutted from the ground right under her attacker's foot. He tripped face first. Izzy hopped over and stabbed the base of his neck with the frost wand in her off hand.

For some reason, I had three of them on me. All the better. I held my spear close and waited till they converged before activating tornado spin. I shredded the minions for noticeable damage but the primary goal was to set them on their heels. As I came out of the two-second spin, I dashed right into the closest one and buried my spear in his belly.

Combo!
You dealt 44 damage to [Blackwood Prisoner]
[Blackwood Prisoner] is defeated

I spun and triggered deadshot on another.

Combo!
You dealt 67 damage to [Blackwood Prisoner]
[Blackwood Prisoner] is defeated

The last one charged me. My spear met his sword.

Two crusaders engaged the last two prisoners, but the real battle was in the center of the camp. Grimwart shook away his shock to see the knight protecting him have his blade snap in half under the warden's axe. The blow dug into his helmet and cleaned out the crusader's health.

Vagram thrust two hands high and uttered a prayer. Bronze

swords instantly materialized in his hands. At the same time, a golden sheen washed over us.

Divine Right!
For the next 30 seconds, your attacks inflict extra damage.

He twirled toward the warden. Before Hood could raise his axe, the flashing blades connected with his armored midsection.

[Vagram] dealt 0 damage to [Hood]
[Vagram] dealt 0 damage to [Hood]

The black figure raised his arms and blocked the follow-up strikes with his vambraces.

Grimwart circled the monster and slashed at the back of his leg, but a chain snaked across the ground and wrapped up the heavy sword.

I lowered my spear and barreled toward them. The cleric and the warden were fully engaged, but the shadowy enemy was aware of my presence. Another ghostly chain rolled across the floor at me.

I planted my spear and vaulted over it before slamming both boots into Hood's chest.

The oversized juggernaut didn't budge. I found myself off balance and slamming into the ground. The chain that I had jumped circled my neck and tightened.

> Curse!
> 10 damage
> Curse!
> 10 damage

As I struggled to free myself, the warden recovered his axe from the dead crusader's body and forced Vagram to back away.

"Arr!" growled Errol as he skidded under the axe. "The only thin' I hate more than prisons are prison keepers!" His rapier snapped the chain holding Grimwart's sword.

The orphaned length of metal dissolved into mist. The colonel immediately completed his blow, slashing heavy steel across the warden's vulnerable calf.

> Surprise!
> Break!
> [Grimwart] dealt 0 damage to [Hood]

Despite the depressing damage notification, the hooded enemy snarled and dropped to one knee. Errol moved in, sinking his sword into the warden's side.

> [Errol] dealt 0 damage to [Hood]

"We can't hurt him," complained the pirate.

I choked loudly, desperately clawing my neck for a life-saving gasp of air. Grimwart, thankfully, noticed my plight. He crushed the chain strangling me. The remains wafted away in black smoke.

The downed enemy saw his opening. Hood swung his weapon with both hands. Grimwart, distracted with me, didn't even see it coming. The axe sliced cleanly into his side.

Critical!

Surprise!

Curse!

[Hood] dealt 87 damage to [Grimwart]

The colonel collapsed, temporarily unable to move. A lot of blood poured from the hole in his black armor.

The warden attempted to rise but his status effect crippled him. He fell back to his knee. I rolled backward out of his range as frozen projectiles battered into him.

[Izzy] dealt 0 damage to [Hood]

[Izzy] dealt 0 damage to [Hood]

[Izzy] dealt 0 damage to [Hood]

"What are we supposed to do?" I grumbled.

The Blackwood prisoners had all been cut down. Izzy and the other two crusaders converged as Vagram held his two swords together like a cross and stepped toward our attacker.

"In the name of the White King I hereby—"

A black chain whipped out and caught the cleric's left arm. Another caught his right. Vagram's eyes sparkled with hate as the heavy chains ripped his arms, and the crucifix, apart.

"I bow only to the wild king," snarled the warden. Once again, he forced himself to rise, but somehow, through sheer will, he remained on his feet. He swung his axe.

Still trying to breathe through a sore windpipe, I slashed the dragonspear and broke one of the chains snagging Vagram. His bronze sword almost recovered to a defensive position in time. It intercepted the path of the axe but couldn't set with any strength behind it. Both weapons slammed into Vagram's breastplate and rocketed him to the ground ten feet out.

"The horses," urged Errol.

The crusaders attended Vagram instead of taking the offensive. Errol likewise hooked one of Grimwart's shoulders and I helped with the other. We dragged the heavily armored man away from danger.

Izzy stepped forward with her hands out, building a slab of ice before her. It grew into a wall as the warden succeeded in taking a hobbled step.

Vagram produced his bronze cross and washed the party with a healing buff, but several error sounds resounded.

You are cursed! Curse damage cannot be healed by normal means.

Vagram and Grimwart were similarly disappointed. "How can this be?" demanded the cleric. Grimwart only gasped in pain.

"The horses," urged Errol. "It be the only way."

I nodded in agreement.

"Catechists do not run," stressed Vagram, but the pair of crusaders holding him back cast forlorn glances at their two brothers, still dead on the floor. I had a feeling Vagram couldn't raise them from the dead so soon after doing it already, but I wondered if the curse damage prevented it anyway. What was clear was that those two soldiers were not getting back up.

I whistled sharply. Bandit galloped up and Errol helped me sling Grimwart over her back. The crusaders moved to their horses.

"There is no escape," boomed the executioner. He took a pained step forward.

"Escape this," said Izzy. By now she had built the chunk of ice into a respectable wall just over her height and three people wide. With a sudden push, the iceberg slid along the ground and homed in on the warden. He growled but was too hobbled to move. The magic crashed into him and bowled him over.

Doing 0 damage, of course.

Izzy whipped around and took Grimwart's horse. Everybody mounted up as the warden of the Blackwood brushed himself off and climbed to his feet. He limped forward slowly and recovered his dropped axe. I kicked Bandit and didn't look back.

0730 Midnight Run

We rode as hard as we could, but we were limited with the wounded. I was fine besides a constricted voice box. Vagram was missing a quarter of his health and had to be sore all over. Grimwart was even worse off. He was in grievous pain, missing two-thirds of his health, and it was all unhealable. After more than an hour's ride, Grimwart slid off Bandit's back. We pulled around to rest.

"I don't think stopping's a good idea," said Izzy.

"The warden was hobbled," I said. "He has to be an hour behind us at least."

"I don't know. We've been on horseback two days and he still caught us."

I worked my jaw. She was right. Whatever mystical powers drove the executioner's relentless pursuit, they couldn't be countered by normal means. I brooded on the awful situation for a minute until I noticed Vagram studying me. I shook it off and approached the cleric and Grimwart.

"How is he?"

"I'm fine," said the colonel through clenched teeth.

Vagram sighed. "He's not fine. I've staunched the bleeding

but my holy magic is failing to counteract the curse. I've never seen anything like it. There's more afoot than I've accounted for."

Errol sauntered close. "Can ye get him back on the bongo? At this pace, the crags be less than an hour northward. We'll be safe in the water."

The cleric bitterly surveyed the remaining men. Control seemed to be spilling away from him. "We have no choice."

We mounted up and charged toward the sea. Soon the rushing water and crashing waves were an audible hum on the breeze. Salt and the smell of rotten fish filled the air, turning our noses. Near the same time, sunlight broke in the east. A low fog settled in the sky and along the ground. Judging by my experience in Portland, the marine layer would keep the morning dark and cool for a while.

It was the same fog that kept the coast hidden until we were practically upon it.

"We've arrived," announced Errol, dismounting on rocky ground. The mist tickling our faces hid the steep drop-off several yards ahead. I hopped to the ground and stepped lightly ahead. A horizontal beam of sunlight pierced the cloud cover and lit the horizon.

The ocean spanned the distance below the cliffs at our feet. It was a seventy-foot drop, at least. To the east and a little ways south was Shorehome, long docks stretching into the ocean. To the west and a little ways north was a huge circle of rock that formed a bay wider than the city.

"Is that—"

"The Salt Sea," said Errol. "The ringed wall forms a

breakwater that protects Shorehome from the harshest the seas can muster."

"So Shorehome isn't actually on the Salt Sea?"

"Not on it, nay. Beside it. The Salt Sea be not a true sea. Too shallow fer galleons. Too rich with mineral fer fishing. It's dead water, it is."

It was so close, maybe thirty minutes to its shore, but it was in the opposite direction to which we were traveling. I traded a knowing glance with Izzy.

Vagram joined us on the cliffside. "We've reached the shore, pirate. What's your plan?"

"We scale down the crag. I have a boat hidden that will suit us. Then we sail into Shorehome under the cover o' fog." He crossed his arms. "What say you, cleric? Is the holy mission still on?"

Vagram frowned as he pondered Grimwart. "Colonel, I think it unwise that you continue."

"I'm perfectly capable—"

"You are in desperate need of a holy man. My powers have failed you. The only recourse is a consultation with Bishop Tannen."

"In Stronghold," said Grimwart, deflated.

"We are a small band sneaking into a city. Your condition would draw too much attention to us. Your army can use you back at Stronghold. We should be fine."

Grimwart winced. "Of course. If you think it best."

"And pirate," added Vagram in a tone of warning, "if you think us weak and attempt any trickery against our diminished numbers, I must remind you that I can more than handle common villainy on my own."

Errol scowled and spat into the ocean.

"Let's tone down the vitriol," I pleaded. "We're all in this together. We need Errol to get into this city."

"Yes," muttered the cleric, "but his feelings on the saints are clear. I might as well make mine so as well."

Izzy wandered close. "Uh, guys?" She pointed her winter staff southward.

Through the distant fog, a lone figure hulked toward us.

I blinked. "How in the..."

"We need to move!" barked Errol. "Divide the party. Good luck to ye, Grimwart. Sleep with the world at yer back."

"Wait," said the cleric. "We can't leave them out here. They won't be safe."

"They will," I cut in. "Hood has no business with the crusaders. He wants this." I produced the crown of the wild king. The cleric's eyes glittered as they fell upon it.

"This... this travesty is *your* doing." His head shook with rage. "I have grossly miscalculated in thinking the pirate was the largest threat to us."

"How was I supposed to know—"

"Were you not warned? The warden of the Blackwood does not cross the continent lightly. Give me that." He reached for the stag skull.

I pulled it away. "What? No way. This is part of a pagan quest. A quest which your people have funded, I might add."

"YOU'VE ENDANGERED THE QUEST!" he spat.

Everybody froze, combat-ready men ready for combat. Besides the staff in Izzy's hand, no weapons were drawn.

"Uh, guys?" she reminded lightly.

Hood lumbered closer, no longer afflicted with a wounded leg. He held the executioner's axe horizontally in both hands. The mist danced around him, revealing the straps of leather and chains snaking around his form. But his eyes shone through. Always his eyes, glowing white and hot and hateful.

Vagram spun to one of the two remaining crusaders. "Take the horses. See your colonel safely back to Stronghold. Protect him. Observe your hymns and prayers. Do not let him die."

The knight grunted and mobilized. The cleric turned to me.

"Talon, I require the crown."

"Not gonna happen," I said gruffly.

The last crusader shuffled nervously. I clenched my fist. Vagram finally flicked his gaze to the approaching executioner and hissed, "Pirate, lead the way."

"Now yer talkin'!" said Errol.

He descended the crag, finding slivers of paths between the jagged red rock. What remained of the fellowship followed carefully. Grimwart galloped away with the one-man escort and the horses. I turned to Bandit.

"Let her go," called Errol. "She can't make it down the slope."

"You wanna bet?"

He paused and sighed. "Listen, matey, any other place an' time I'd take that wager, but we can't afford it now. It don't matter if yer mount can make it down these cliffs or not, because at the bottom be a skiff she can't fit in, and our destination be a city she can't enter without paper. Hell, a giant striped deer would attract even more attention than a damned dyin' knight."

"Language," cautioned Vagram.

The pirate scoffed. "She ain't gettin' on the boat, and that's final." Errol continued down without another word.

Izzy lowered her head and patted Bandit's neck. "She should be fine," she said.

Bandit cocked her head, seemingly understanding the predicament.

I scrubbed her chin. "They're right. You'd actually be safer out here. It took you days to get used to Stronghold."

She licked my hand.

I faced the executioner, a hundred feet away. "Now get outta here." I pushed Bandit and she charged west after the crusaders.

Izzy scrambled down the cliffside. With a last look at our pursuer, I took the rear and followed.

The descent was less arduous than it looked. With my scaling skill, it was cake for me, but even Vagram in his heavy armor fared well. I suspected that mostly had to do with Errol's familiarity with the slope. We made good time, and no matter how many times I peeked up, I didn't catch a glimpse of the warden.

At the bottom, water roared and crashed in a chaotic bramble, soaking everything around. Errol pivoted into a cave hidden in the crags. It wasn't deep or dark but it offered shelter from the rougher seas, seas which were already calmed by the nearby breakwater. That meant it was possible to dock a boat against these rocks, even if a bit dangerous. Sure enough, Errol's flat skiff rested on dry land.

"This is your boat?" I chuckled. "What do you have, a crew of seagulls?"

Errol sneered. " 'Tis but a smuggler's vessel. Now grab that end."

"Aye, aye, Captain!" I said mockingly.

We helped him push off, loaded up, and paddled out to sea. Within minutes, water separated us from the coast, and we were blanketed by a sheen of fog.

"We're safe," I sighed.

"We are not," assured Cleric Vagram bitterly, "as long as you carry that pagan beacon."

"Beacon?"

"How else do you figure the Blackwood knows your whereabouts?"

I grumbled. "You should be thanking us, you know. We broke into the Black Keep. We stole the crown of the wild king. We can destroy it in the Salt Sea."

"Destroy it?" His eyes lit up. "I am a holy man, Talon. Place the crown under my protection. I will keep watch over it."

"You gonna give me a few thousand XP and some loot for my trouble?"

He hissed.

"I didn't think so. I'll hold onto it. Hood can't get to us in Shorehome, can he?"

We all studied the coastline. The low fog hid the water and land. It made the city appear as disparate buildings in the clouds. Waterborne vessels were visible mostly by their sails. The docks in the distance glowed with yellow-green lanterns lining their length. A low boat like ours without a sail or torch, well, it was practically invisible.

"You forget," muttered Vagram, "Shorehome is a pagan town now. The warden may come and go as he pleases." He turned to me. "*We* are the intruders here."

"Pipe down with yer talk o' intruders," snapped Errol. "Get the stowed cloaks from the box. Put 'em on. Can't be having yer crusader armor advertisin' our mission."

Izzy handed the clothes to the knight and cleric. The two of us didn't need a disguise. Even if I was semi-famous, the magic of my stranger's cowl would keep me mostly anonymous. Just as good as a cloak, anyway.

"It's a good idea," said Vagram sharply, handing me a folded length of red satin.

"I don't need it," I said.

"It's not for you. If you refuse to hand over the crown, the least you could do is keep it out of sight." He thrust the item toward me again. I accepted and examined it.

[Treasure Sack]
This soft bag masks its contents from prying eyes. Besides being the bane of thieves, the enchanted satin blocks magical effects, rendering encased items inert.

"Huh," I said.

Despite its small size, the crown of the wild king easily slid inside. I didn't feel different as I put the sack into my inventory, but a bellicose wail in the distance pierced the fog.

0740 Sea Wolf

We paddled through the morning gloom, silently scanning the rocky shoreline. We weaved between lifeless boats. At first, it felt like a graveyard. Not a sound beyond the cackles of the seabirds. Not a hint of movement or boisterous laughter.

Our skiff approached the main dock. Built of stout yellowwood, a stretching arm reached deep into the sea, almost as long as the city was wide. The lanterns were glass spheres filled with glowing fluid. Something Kyle might've appreciated. With a last heave of the oars, Errol ducked low without warning. The four of us realized we were on a collision course with the platform and kissed the bottom of the boat. The skiff quietly drifted beneath the dock where, for the first time, I heard shambling footsteps. No one said a word. When we emerged from the other side, the fog covered evidence of our passing.

A much more modest dock sat at the far end of Shorehome. It appeared to be used for smaller local traffic as opposed to the large manned fishing and raiding vessels. Only two fancy lanterns lit the midpoint and end of this dock. As we neared, I finally spied a living person. A dockmaster was lazily nodding off when he spied us.

"Time t' make due on yer promise o' silver," whispered Errol.

Vagram narrowed his eyes suspiciously.

"Fer the dockmaster," he assured.

The cleric transferred some coins to the pirate, who weighed them in his hands and nodded. I was surprised he stopped short of testing it with his teeth.

"Ahoy, me hearty!" He called to the man on the dock. Not too quiet as to arouse suspicion, but not too loud as to attract unwanted attention. "Gloomy seas today."

He steered the skiff sideways as the dockmaster squinted over us. He was a human. A sailor, no doubt. For all we knew, Errol was buddies with the guy.

"What have we here?" he asked.

Errol smiled broadly as he hopped off the boat and tied it down. "Just a bout o' midnight fishin', is all."

The man frowned. "Ain't supposed to go midnight fishin'."

"Nay, I ain't," said Errol, waving us off the boat. He handed the dockmaster a few coins. " 'Tis a failing o' mine, but I always pay me fines."

The harbor man grunted and looked us over again. Despite Errol's urging, no one had moved. "And this lot?"

Errol smiled. "Why, they're the fish." He broke into forced laughter and handed the man another pile of coins, this one noticeably larger. The dockmaster joined in with the chortling.

Izzy and I traded a curious glance. It seemed these pirates had bribery down to everyday etiquette. We hurried off the skiff.

"And you'll be needing to dock your vessel, then?" asked the greedy harbor man.

"If ye have the space," conceded a modest Errol, passing

more silver around.

"Right then. I can't guarantee it'll be here when you get back if you take too long."

Errol pushed us toward the shore. "There's more silver fer ya if it is." He turned to us. "Keep walkin', swabbers."

"One last thing," called out the dockmaster as we left him. "You'll need your papers at the gate."

Errol nodded and smiled, but his face twisted as he joined us.

"What damned gate?" I asked.

"Language," reminded Vagram.

"There is no gate. It's—" he stopped. At the end of the dock were a couple more harbor men sitting beside a small checkpoint kiosk. The entire shoreline wasn't gated off or anything, but these men were definitely checking the credentials of every traveler coming from the water. "This be new," he said.

"Are we boned?" I asked. "It seems like we're boned."

The pirate chuckled. "That entirely depends on if ye have any more silver or not."

Sure enough, the men checking papers had flexible opinions regarding the legality of our entry in direct correlation to the amount of coin we handed them. Curiously, we seemed to be in violation of not one but three separate bylaws, and each came with a separate fine. Since there were two men enforcing the laws, these fines were naturally doubled. Izzy and I volunteered some of our own silver to the shakedown.

"Follow me," said the shiftier of the two men. He walked us along the boardwalk.

Men and women were just setting up for the morning, lining up baskets of goods and starting fire pits. I imagined once the day was in full effect this boardwalk would be a bustling hub of trade.

"Uh," I whispered to Izzy, "does this *look* like a city that was just conquered by pagans?"

"I was wondering the same thing," she agreed.

"Ho!" said the harbor man, suddenly stiffening. "Um, hide in here, if you please."

He shuffled us into a wooden storage closet full of fishing nets and rusty hooks. There wasn't enough space for all of us, so Errol shoved us in and closed the door.

"What's this, then?" called out a roaming guard.

The harbor man answered without missing a beat. "This fine gentleman is just showing me his wares, sir."

"Aye," said Errol. "Up an' early, I always say. Fine day fer a stroll."

"To be sure," added the harbor man.

"T' be sure."

The men's voices were muffled as they plodded away from the storage closet.

"Pirates," grumbled Vagram.

I strained to hear the conversation outside, but they were too far away.

"Maybe he's leading them away," offered Izzy.

Vagram sneered. "Maybe he's collecting a group of scum to take the rest of our silver." The other crusader nervously fingered the hilt of his sword.

"That doesn't make any sense," I cut in. "Why would he lead us all this way just to turn on us now?"

"I thought I was clear. For the silver."

"Okay, but why would he travel all the way to Stronghold just to come back for silver?"

"Because he's a *pirate*."

I cocked my head. "Okay, but—"

"Cut it out, you two," snapped Izzy. "Isn't anybody else wondering where all the goblins are?"

The cleric's eyes narrowed. We eyed each other, as if the simple entrance into a town run by thieves and raiders cast us into the same roles. Tense moments passed as we listened to more incoherent murmuring outside. The crusader's hand tightened on his sword.

"Wait," I said. "Nothing to be nervous about."

His full helm faced me. "I'm not nervous." The gray text above his head merely read [Crusader].

"What's your name?" I asked.

He was silent a moment until the cleric interjected. "He's a soldier of the White King. That is enough."

"Sure," I said, still facing the crusader, "but don't you have a name?"

"I'm a soldier of the White King," he repeated.

I chewed my lip and studied the cleric. His gray text read [Cleric Vagram]. They were both NPCs, like Errol, but the knight was different. More generic, perhaps.

I continued the small talk to calm his nerves. "Do you have a home, soldier?"

"Everybody has a home," he answered. "I hail from Oakengard."

"A wife and kid?"

He didn't answer.

"Any hopes and dreams?"

Vagram hissed. "What is it with the strange questions?"

"Quiet," said Izzy. "Someone's coming."

Boots stomped toward the storage closet. Everybody readied to spring in the event of disaster. The door swung open and Errol grinned wide, two guards behind him.

"Anybody happen t' have more silver?"

0750 Age of Pirates

The five of us strolled past the burgeoning market, finally devoid of an escort. The entire affair had personally cost me 2,000 silver. It was a steep price, but we had avoided inspections and questioning altogether. It also didn't hurt that we were rich. Completing our epic quest by defeating Orik had been rewarded with 50,000 silver, split three ways.

I wondered how a city so corrupt could get anything done, but for now we were in Shorehome and on our own. The streets were beginning to fill with early risers. Soon we'd be lost in the crowd.

"So what now?" I asked.

"We take in the scene and gather actionable intel," said Vagram plainly.

"Right. That's not much of a plan."

"What say you, pirate?"

Errol gave us a sidelong glance. "I have contacts in this city. I can—"

A goblin rounded a building and froze ten feet ahead of us. His eyes and mouth widened as he saw us. "Pagan killers..." he muttered.

He turned and ran.

"We can't let him raise the alarm," cried Vagram, breaking into a run. The crusader followed on his heels.

"My pagan reputation," I muttered. "I should've known the stranger's cowl doesn't hide that." With a sigh, I ran after them.

The goblin's short legs were a disadvantage, but he only needed to escape a few buildings down. As I turned the corner, Vagram kicked in the door to a small house. I rushed after them. By the time I was inside, the goblin was already dead. Vagram's bronze blade dripped with black blood.

"He didn't fight?" I wondered aloud.

We were in a small home. Tables and chairs were dirty with food scraps. The crusader searched the kitchen. I checked the back room.

A goblin mother was clutching a goblin toddler on a bed. Neither were named mobs. The woman's tag showed yellow, indicating a simple challenge. The young boy was mostly inconsequential at white. They shivered with fear.

"Is that all of them?" called Vagram from the other room. "We can't let them know we've breached the walls."

I waited, stunned, as the two goblins stared at the spear in my hands.

The crusader muttered an affirmative from the kitchen. After a tense moment, Vagram prodded me. "Talon?"

I took a slow breath, then nodded toward the armoire. The mother hesitantly moved her child and hid within the large wardrobe.

"It's clear," I shouted.

As I spun to go, the crusader was suddenly at my side. I

couldn't see his eyes through the helmet, but I kept my cool. He turned with me to go. Errol and Izzy were at the front door, weapons drawn.

"Since when could you draw your frost dagger in town?" I asked her.

She looked down at it, unsure. If she'd been attacked by a goblin, she would've been able to defend herself, of course, but I wasn't so sure he'd been an aggressor. The city was no longer under saintly control. No email or wiki connectivity, but it probably extended to city protections as well. That meant PvP was possible.

"That was a close one," said the cleric. "We need to be more cautious."

I swallowed and stared at the dead goblin father. He'd seen us and fled. The thought sickened my stomach, but if this was his home, he'd respawn here soon enough.

"Why are goblins living in a human town?" asked Izzy, scanning the scene.

"They're oppressors," answered Vagram. "The humans here are their prisoners, choosing servitude over death."

I peeked out the window as merchants passed. A lot of men and women had departed. Many made it to Stronghold. Others drifted in the wild. Still others became bandits and preyed on their own townspeople. What I hadn't expected was that so many would be left doing... well... normal things.

"More goblins outside," I noted.

"Pagan scum," spat the crusader.

Izzy sighed. "How are we supposed to walk around a pagan town after we killed their god? The amount of negative faction rep in this room is stifling."

"We need to wait until nightfall," said Vagram. "We have no choice but to hole up here."

"No," I said quickly. "We need to go."

They looked at me.

"I mean, that goblin's gonna respawn, right? This house won't be empty forever."

The crusader shrugged. "We can kill him again."

"Look at the plates on the table," I urged. "More than one goblin lives here. The others could return at any time. They're probably a hunting party or something. They'll raise a stink."

The house was a jumble of mismatched possessions. It was obvious more than one person lived here, but there was no evidence of big bad hunters. The crusaders weren't convinced.

"It's settled then," said Errol. "I'll check the streets. See if anybody's lookin' into our little chase." The pirate slipped out the door.

"I don't trust him," muttered Vagram.

"You don't trust anyone," I pointed out.

"Have I cause to?"

"Don't act like you're the only one who doesn't have secrets. I know you're not here for the pagans." I squared up with Vagram. "Such a small group might be able to recover the Squid's Tooth, but no way are we taking on the pagans. You're really here to find Lucifer."

Vagram's nostrils flared. Instead of denying it, he clenched his teeth.

I huffed. The cleric and I didn't exactly see eye to eye, but I wasn't interested in constantly butting heads. The whole reason

I was here was to prove my trust, at least in the eyes of Bishop Tannen. Personally, I just wanted to help. The thought that I was partly responsible for this chafed me.

"Let's just back up a minute," I said. "We're here, right? I mean, all nine of us didn't make it. Two crusaders are probably respawned back in Oakengard by now. Grimwart and the other are heading to Stronghold. But we still have five men."

Izzy cleared her throat.

"Four *men* and one *woman*."

"Which pretty much counts for nine men," she added with a smirk.

"The point is," I said, not taking the bait, "we're still proceeding with the mission. We're in Shorehome. The soulstone is here, and Lucifer might be too. How do we go about finding him?"

The cleric crossed his arms. "You two are the only ones here who've ever seen the man. You're the scout. If you find him, use the dragonspear to face the black dragon. Leave the fallen one to me."

"That's it?" I asked. "You're that confident?"

"My faith is my strength."

"Your faith doesn't appear to be healing the cursed portion of your health." I too was afflicted. My health was maxed out at 201/261. It wasn't a good start to a devil hunt. "Have you spoken with the saints? Are you aware you're trying to succeed where two angels have failed?"

"The saints are not perfect, Talon. And the angels have not failed. Not yet." Vagram lowered the hood of the generic cloak and approached me. "The task before us is not an easy one. We must proceed with faith. And when we have done so, I think you will find the allies of the White King formidable indeed."

As he finished speaking, light coughing came from the other room. His head zoomed in on the closed bedroom door. "What was that?"

I cleared my throat loudly and moved to the door. "Nothing," I said. "Street noise."

"That was in the house."

Vagram opened the door but I brushed ahead of him. The bedroom was empty. The cleric's eyes scanned the walls.

Another cough came from the armoire.

One of Vagram's bronze swords materialized in his hand with a flash of light. I equipped my spear as the crusader drew his blade.

The door to the armoire swung open.

"Pagans!" swore the cleric.

"No," I said. "A mother and child."

"You're *hiding* them. You're a traitor to the cause."

"It's not like that, Vagram. Don't be so dramatic. I just can't kill helpless goblins."

"Let me show you how," he said. He advanced a step and I swiveled my spear to his chest. He sneered. "Do not presume you can stop me."

Frost materialized into a sharp icicle at the cleric's back.

"What's a girl gotta do to get noticed around here?" chimed in Izzy. "You know, I'm starting to like this town combat thing."

I grinned. "Stand down, Vagram."

His eyes met the crusader's. The knight flanked to my side slowly, not readying an attack but getting into position in case one was necessary.

"This will ruin the mission," I urged.

"Killing pagans is always the mission," said the catechist, his eyes flashing in anger.

The front door opened and Errol walked in, but nobody could afford to take their eyes off each other. More boots followed the pirate and Izzy's icicle went limp and shattered on the floor. I risked a peek into the main room.

A band of rogues, wearing dark leather, hooked curved knives around Izzy's throat. They spilled into the bedroom and surrounded us.

"Traitors," spat Vagram. "I'm surrounded by them."

0760 Brotherhood

◆━━━━━•◆•━━━━━◆

The crusaders forgot about the goblins and turned their weapons to the more pressing danger. I counted ten of them, every bit the rogues' gallery that I'd expect from this town.

Errol made eleven and left us with four, if you counted Izzy with a knife at her throat.

Vagram's second sword flashed into his off hand. "Lower your blades," he demanded.

A man in black studded leather slinked between his cohorts. "Forgive the display," he said in a soft voice. "It's necessary to ensure everybody's safety."

"Mine or yours?" he spat.

The man's lips tightened. He was an unassuming, molish man. Diminutive with thinning black hair and beady eyes. Not exceptional in any way. His only identifier was [Hadrian].

"You're a player," I said.

"Let me introduce myself," he started. "We are—"

"The Brothers in Black," finished Vagram, unimpressed. "Criminal scum draining Shorehome of whatever riches it has to offer."

Hadrian wasn't offended. "The *dominant* criminal scum in

Shorehome," he corrected. "Leading the largest gang in a city without leaders, Papa Brugo humbly requests your presence."

My eyes flicked to the blade at Izzy's throat. She looked more pissed than scared, but she was playing it smart by waiting. If the Brothers in Black had meant to backstab us, they wouldn't have announced themselves.

"We don't care about Papa Brugo's humble requests," countered the cleric.

Hadrian pressed his lips together. "Those were euphemisms. Nothing about Papa Brugo is humble, and he doesn't make requests. As the Papa of all Papas, his word is followed without question. Besides, you'll need our assistance if you want to avoid business like that in the future." He motioned toward the dead goblin in the other room.

"You can hide us from the pagans?" I asked.

"No one can do better. Sheath your weapons and let us help you."

"Take that knife from Izzy's neck and you have a deal."

Vagram turned to me, outraged. Hadrian nodded to his man who released Izzy. Errol tried to assist her but she brushed him away and fell in at my side.

"Okay," I said, returning the dragonspear to my inventory. "Let's talk."

Hadrian approached and looked me up and down, completely ignoring the crusaders still holding their swords. Vagram was an intimidating presence, but without me and Izzy willing to fight he was severely outnumbered. He snarled silently as Hadrian worked some kind of skill over me.

"My, but the goblins must despise you," he said.

In seconds, my countenance changed. My clothes appeared less flashy. I still wore the same blue soldier coat, but it turned dull and unremarkable. Forgettable. When Hadrian did the same thing to Izzy, her name changed to the anonymous [Drifter] in NPC gray. It seemed to be a similar trick to the one the bandits had pulled on the road.

Satisfied, Hadrian turned to the crusaders and cast a disparaging glare at their weapons. "If you don't mind?"

The cleric grumbled but his swords vanished. The crusader sheathed his, and within moments they were similarly disguised. Vagram's yellow locks weren't so magnificent anymore. It was good to see him brought down a peg.

Somewhere during the whole process, the rest of the Brothers in Black had taken up position inside and outside the door. Hadrian dropped a couple of silvers on the bed and nodded once to the goblins. "Courtesy of the Papa." He began to usher us outside.

"Adventurer," called a light voice behind me. I turned to see the goblin mother clutching her son tight. "Thank you," she said, offering a curtsy.

Pagan Reputation +50

I watched her strangely, not sure what to say and only managing a nod before being guided out the front door. Despite our cooperation, the Brothers in Black kept their curved blades at hand. They marched in two rows on either side of us, an intimidating troupe. The men and women we passed in the street did their best to keep their eyes down. This was the Papa's business, they knew, and we were too anonymous to provoke curiosity.

Along the way, what we saw confused me. Groups of goblins openly roamed the streets followed by imps. An ogre hefted a broken wagon filled with construction supplies. Shorehome was more diverse than Stronghold by a wide margin, but it wasn't the blacks and browns and whites that concerned me, it was the greens and grays. As the day opened up, the pagans were making their regular presence known.

Instead of heading to the center of town, like I would've presumed, we marched to the outskirts, a flat shorefront devoid of shops and other buildings. The sand was low and wet. Rows of tunnels carved into the ground were lined with brick and clay, a less extravagant version of Stronghold's river, except that these were empty. We descended into them and walked the low ground, away from prying eyes. At first I thought we were in a simple canal system—and maybe we were—but branching passages headed to higher ground where doors and storage lockers were fixed into the brick walls.

"The Narrows," announced Errol, chumming up beside us like he hadn't just sold us out. "They keep the town from flooding, as well as the old mines below."

Mines this close to sea level had to be dangerous. Then again, this was a simulation of a fantasy world. As with the plausibility of the Salt Sea, I figured the world builders cheated once in a while.

"Underkeep now," said Hadrian, leading us to a well-guarded entryway. "This underground maze is the sole property of Papa Brugo. He can get almost anywhere in the city from here.

Remember that, wherever you go, the Brothers in Black can reach you."

Creepy. That was how to describe this guy. He'd never properly introduced himself, but I suspected he was the criminal gang's spymaster.

The black-clad brothers led us into their home. The environs were damp and stark, lit by the same green-yellow bulbs of glass that adorned the docks. They cast an unnaturally still glow over us and nearly ate up all shadows.

"Are we your prisoners?" Vagram asked bitterly.

"I rather prefer the term esteemed guests," answered Hadrian.

We twisted down several passages, descending lower underground, eventually coming upon several more guards at a door ornamented with precious metals and gems. Hadrian stopped and appraised us.

"If I might make a suggestion, I would consider the size and power of the army you are now surrounded by, and I would color my words with respect."

Vagram worked his jaw as the door opened.

"Ah!" boomed a man inside. He sat on a gaudy throne cast from solid silver. "My prisoners have arrived!"

I flashed Hadrian a scowl and entered the chamber of Papa Brugo.

0770 Kingpin

The crime boss was a big man. Not especially tall, although it was difficult to tell on his throne, but *large*. His stout frame was powerfully built but also ringed with the fat of a man who'd enjoyed excess. He was bald, olive-skinned, and wore no shirt, which accented his pot belly and hairy body. Links of silver and gold hung around his neck and his smile was unnaturally wide. It took me a moment to place why—the left side of his mouth had been slashed open and had improperly healed into a large scar that stretched his lips to the side. Despite this terrifying trait, he seemed a man of good humor.

Two bodyguards stood behind him. Shadowy, incorporeal figures without definition or features, not even eyes. They had no name tags to identify them.

"It is a glorious day indeed," boomed Papa Brugo. Hadrian stood to one side of us, Errol on the other, with a spattering of guards behind. "You surprise me, Captain Oates. Excellent work."

The pirate was afraid to make eye contact with us. The Papa continued.

"The Brothers in Black have always hid in the shadows of the ground, but the saints have never thus lowered themselves to our depths!" He studied our group. "They still don't show themselves personally, of course, but they send their emissaries. A glorious day!"

I surveyed my companions inquisitively. Papa Brugo was being a bit dramatic, but perhaps that was his style. A showman.

Cleric Vagram cleared his throat and stepped forward. "We will reward the pirate and yourself handsomely for any help you can provide."

"You will not speak unless spoken to," instructed Hadrian.

"Or what?" muttered the cleric.

Brugo burst into laughter and slapped his knees. Despite not wearing a shirt, his thick legs were wrapped in tight leather breeches and knee-high boots. He appeared a capable enough man, but I'd seen Cleric Vagram in action enough to put my chips on the holy man.

"Hadrian," laughed Brugo, "it appears you did not properly introduce me, so I shall have to do it." He flashed a sideways smile that sagged his scar open. "This is good, because I *like* talking about myself."

He pushed to his feet and stepped off the dais to our level. I was right. He wasn't especially tall. I mean, everyone was taller than me besides the five-foot pixie, but the crime boss had to look up to meet Vagram's eyes.

"Do you know how many papas have done business in Shorehome this past year?" asked Brugo casually. "Thirty-seven. Thirty-seven petty criminals running twenty-four petty gangs." He caught my confused expression and added, "There was a lot of turnover."

We nodded in comprehension. The job description for gang leader didn't come with a lot of upward mobility. Brugo continued.

"Fishmongers, harbormasters, sailors, pirates, pickpockets, cutthroats, smugglers of all stripes—it was a thriving capitalistic market. But not all papas are created equal."

His head snapped to Hadrian. "Who's the greatest papa that has ever lived?"

"Papa Brugo," replied the advisor.

He turned to the pirate. "Who is the Papa of all Papas?"

"Papa Brugo," answered Errol smoothly.

The smug crime boss paced before us, gauging Vagram's reaction but ours as well. "There, you see? That is enough for most people to know. But you are not most people, so I will continue. Thirty-seven papas. Twenty-four gangs. Do you know what I did with that?"

We watched him uncertainly.

"Eight," he said. "Eight papas. Eight gangs." He paused and mused a moment, before concluding, "I cleaned up this city. I am not the papa of fishmongers, or the papa of commerce. I'm not the papa of cutthroats. I am *the* Papa." He turned to Vagram. "So when you address me, you will address me as Papa Brugo, the ruler of the city, the Protector of Shorehome."

My eyes widened. The mantle of Protector. Papa Brugo wore it, just as I did with Stronghold. Another NPC with a mantle. But how was that possible?

Vagram brushed a hand through his yellow hair. "Understood, Papa Brugo, and a relief to my ears. If you are indeed Protector of this town, then you and I fight for the same side."

"Do we?" The Papa chuckled, turned his back to us, and returned to his throne with a comforting sigh. "You can see, with your newfound knowledge, how coming to me and asking for my help is quite backwards. Rather, you are before me so I can decide how best to make use of you."

Vagram's proud face twisted in anger, so I cut in before he misspoke.

"Papa Brugo, we're here to save you from the pagan menace."

His eyes lasered onto me. "Save me? Is that any less insulting?"

"Less insulting than letting pride get in the way of business," quipped Izzy.

Brugo's eyes flashed. A genuine smile, albeit a predatory one. "Business," he said with a nod. "Now we get to the heart of all matters. What can the four of you do for me?"

His question was hypothetical, and no one answered for fear of triggering another self-righteous diatribe.

"I hear many things," said Brugo. "Hadrian is my Whisperer. He speaks to me of deeds far and wide. If these whispers can be believed, the two of you killed a god."

Even the Papa's ever-confident voice wavered a bit on that note. For all his bluster and bravado, I'd done something he hadn't yet. It meant he had to tread carefully around us.

"You also wear the mantle of Protector," he noted.

"That makes us brothers, in a sense," I said hopefully.

He canted his head. "The Brothers in Black take brotherhood seriously. And perhaps we are brothers, inasmuch as Stronghold and Shorehome are sisters. Which is to say, not much."

Izzy saw an opening. "The pagans detest all of the nine great cities, fishing port and fortress alike. Our common enemy is what unifies us."

The Papa nodded and turned to the knight and cleric. "Is that why the crusaders have left the sanctity of Oakengard?"

"It is," stated the knight.

Brugo's misshapen lips curled. "And what's this cloak of white and cross of gold?" he asked, somehow seeing through Hadrian's disguise. "Those aren't crusader colors."

Vagram spoke. "We are catechists, Papa Brugo. A devout sect of crusader leadership."

"Sect is an interesting word," is all he said in reply.

The cleric clenched his jaw. "We are committed to destroying the pagan menace by any means necessary. The crusaders mean to rescue the city."

The Papa leaned forward. "And where were the crusaders when Shorehome was surrounded by the goblin horde?"

Vagram took a long breath. "We're here now."

Brugo shook his head and chuckled, eyeing his Whisperer. "I have heard much of the crusaders. Not so much of the catechists. Today is the first day I can claim to have actually seen them with my own eyes, yet I only see two." The crime boss ducked his head and peered into the recesses of the room. "Is the rest of the army hiding out of sight?"

"We are a small group," asserted the cleric. "Rather than conduct a full-scale invasion of a town that's already been conquered, we're here to root out the problem from the inside."

"Ah!" Papa Brugo leaned back on his throne and closed his eyes. He paused like that a good ten seconds before continuing.

"My father didn't live into his later years," he said introspectively. "But when I was a young boy, I had an older brother. Older, yes, but weaker. Girly. You can imagine my father was a hard man, and that he didn't take to my brother well. So he brought him to the physicker, who gave him a paste of tea and ash.

" 'Papa, Papa,' he said, 'I feel ill.' My father cared not, and in time my brother learned to ignore the nausea. Yet he was still weak. So my father took him to the priest, who blessed him with numerous atonements.

" 'Papa, Papa,' my brother cried, 'I feel backwards.' My father cared not, and in time my brother learned to ignore the teachings. But he was still not the man my father wished him to be." Papa Brugo sighed loud and long. "So, as a last resort my father took him to the chain yard, where several violent men showed him the meaning of tough.

" 'Papa, Papa,' my brother sobbed, 'Why do you hate me?' " Brugo's eyes were fixed on some distant point in time. "My brother took his own life that night."

The throne room was silent. Hadrian waited with arms clasped behind his back, doubtless having heard the heart-wrenching story many times. His ease contrasted with Brugo's emotion. Despite having rehearsed and relived this scene often, it still affected the powerful man.

"A tragic story," said Vagram softly.

"It is. Thank you," returned the Papa. "As soon as I was of age, I cut down my old man like the coward he was. But retribution is not the lesson of this story." His eyes met the cleric's. "The lesson is that when men like you say they wish to root out a problem from the inside, they had better make damn well sure that there's a problem in the first place."

Vagram's brow furrowed.

Brugo was talking about the pagans. The groups in the streets. The families in the homes. I recalled the ogre working with the bandits. Something was off about it all.

"Let me tell you another story," said Papa Brugo, seeing the confusion plain on all of us. "Do not worry, I won't bore you with another family parable. This one is a tale of two cities. A tale of two Protectors."

He had everyone's attention.

"The pagan army, as you call them, retreated from Stronghold en masse after the city's successful defense, but they were not unscathed. Whispers report they were a critically wounded mass. The one-eyed god was dead. Their all-out onslaught, cut short. It had cost many lives. In the end, the gate held. The angel Decimus wiped out a tenth of the army with a single gesture. Three thousand soldiers shrank to half over the course of thirty minutes."

I wasn't sure where Brugo was going with this. He wasn't likely to garner sympathy from me or Izzy. We'd been at that battle, fighting for our lives.

"After that raid," he continued, "some pagans retreated west. Others east. Groups splintered and returned to the wild, errant once again. The force that arrived at Shorehome was the bulk of the leadership that had not fractured, but it was nothing like the war-ready juggernaut at Stronghold. Little more than five hundred pagans approached the city.

"That said, Shorehome is far from the defensive bastion

Stronghold is. Our residents are hearty. Resourceful, even. But we have no standing army. Five hundred battle-hardened goblins, imps, boggarts, and ogres versus five hundred sailors. Residents panicked. Being a coastal city with no shortage of ships, many fled by sea. Those who retreated south over land were mostly unharried. The saints cut their losses and flooded the Great Well that ties Shorehome to the central codebase. In their haste to ensure the security of Haven, they abandoned a whole city of people."

Vagram's eyes tightened. I studied Errol, who gritted his teeth and nodded along. He already knew this story. His presence in Stronghold—on this entire mission—had been a pretense. A lie. All to get us right here right now.

Papa Brugo leaned forward and snickered. "Now, one man's white is another man's black. As is often the case, where the proper authorities saw nothing but fire and flames, Papa Brugo saw opportunity. Papa Brugo gathered all the remaining gangs of Shorehome together and marched from the city in a unified front to greet the goblin stragglers. He didn't attack them. He didn't draw battle lines. He *welcomed* them."

Footsteps pattered into the room. Not a big group, just a few more Brothers in Black who joined the ranks of the guards surrounding us. Except these few were pagans. Goblins wearing the dark leather garb of the Brothers. Goblins standing side by side with the humans of Shorehome. Goblins who sneered at every single one of us, especially the pagan killers.

"We were fools to walk in here," muttered Vagram under his breath.

"So what do you think happened?" asked Papa Brugo, the

answer already evident. "The pagans moved into Shorehome. They settled into the houses abandoned by those who were afraid to protect their city. Into the buildings planned for the incoming player population. The Brothers in Black unified their power with the influx of war-weary goblin soldiers. We don't need the saints. We filled the vacuum they left behind. Already the dominant force of the underworld, we have now cemented ourselves as the resolute backbone of the city."

Papa Brugo stood once again. "The so-called sacking of Shorehome was little more than a change of demographics. The saints who sent you—they don't wish to *save* the people of the city, they wish to assess Shorehome's prospects. Secure the Squid's Tooth. Figure out how to take back control. And if it's one thing I'm a very bad sport about, it's giving up control."

The unison of rogues in the throne room laughed heartily. Twenty of them, completely surrounding us. They converged, each one twiddling a curved dagger.

0780 Life of Crime

I equipped the dragonspear, twirled it high above my head, and slammed it down to the floor. The brick shattered and the ground shook dramatically. Behind me, Izzy waved the winter staff. The entire room paused at the sight of the legendary weapons.

Papa Brugo, still on his feet, stifled a chuckle. "You mean to insult me in my throne room?"

I flashed my most serious scowl. "There are too many sharp things in here pointed at me."

He raised his head. "Yes. *Twenty* sharp things, to be precise."

"Then it's an even fight."

He showed his teeth, half amused.

In truth, we were in a horrible position for battle. Surrounded. Twenty cutthroats against the four of us, and they weren't even my main concern. Brugo himself must be a capable warrior, and those shadowy bodyguards would engage before he did.

Errol hurried between the crime boss and us, hands up. "This be not the right way," he urged.

"Pirate," spat Brugo, "do not presume to tell me what is right and what is wrong. You are not one of us."

"Apologies, Papa," he said with a deep bow. "I fly not yer colors. Captains like meself are so rarely team players, but I be fiercely loyal t' me city an' me people."

The Papa of all Papas took a calming breath. "This I do not doubt."

"Have I not been a profitable ally?" asked the pirate. "Have I not always funneled a fair share of my earnings yer way?"

"You have." Brugo ground his teeth. "Even this opportunity is thanks to you."

Errol bowed deeply to accept the compliment. "Then allow me t' offer a solution."

A moment of silence followed. Brugo's biceps flexed as he thought it over. Eventually, he decided to sit back in his throne. This signaled the cutthroats to back off.

"You have one minute," he decreed.

Errol smiled slyly at me. He strolled past the cleric, wasting ten seconds just to enjoy the moment of power. He was making it clear our fates were in his weaselly hands. As he stopped before me, I sneered.

"The Protector o' Stronghold," said Errol mockingly. "Is he a great man? Or is it a great legend?"

"He's a pagan killer!" spat one of the goblins.

"Aye," agreed the pirate. "An' a good one at that. I've seen him fight. But he's not just a killer o' goblins and ogres. He's a defier o' saints."

Vagram showed obvious distaste for the sentiment. I tried to hold my defiant expression, but I wasn't sure where Errol was going with this.

"This man?" asked the Papa dubiously. "The one traveling at the behest of the crusaders? He is no revolutionary. He's a soldier."

"The saints have his ear, 'tis true, but there's a scoundrel in him yet."

The Papa laughed. "The famous hero of Stronghold has bloody boots? Let me hear of it."

Errol whirled around and brushed the back of his hand against the dragonspear. I yanked it away and hid it safely in my inventory. He flinched but otherwise played cool. "How do ye think a man such as he holds that weapon? Gifted from the saints? An' the tower too?"

"No one gave me those things," I said.

Errol continued addressing the Papa. " 'Tis a good story: The famed hero o' Stronghold. When the pagans marched t' sack the city one man stood 'gainst a god. But there are cracks in that golden shield, if one looks close enough. After all, propaganda is meant t' control the people through emotion, not logic."

Brugo was unimpressed. "I'm not a fool, Captain. If I believed in the glorious right of humans over goblins, I wouldn't have welcomed them into my city. Papa Brugo is an equal-opportunity employer."

"An' I would never mistake ye fer one o' the masses," deftly returned the pirate. "A champion is a symbol more than an individual. One prone to preconceived notions that even I be guilty of. I freely admit, I hated the swabber 'fore we ever met. But ye, Papa, I trust ye can see clearly once ya have a wealth o' information."

He considered the pirate's words for a moment. "Such as?"

"It turns out our friend Talon was responsible for breakin' into the Pantheon an' stealin' the soulstone in the first place."

Brugo couldn't contain himself any longer. "Bah ha ha! A champion after a traitor. That is rich, Captain."

"It is the truth," swore Vagram. "Talon was deceived by the fallen one. His allegiances have not always been as steadfast as those in my order."

Brugo didn't mind the interruption. Instead he took the information quietly, soaking it up like a good sponge.

"Then there be the matter o' the angel, Decimus," continued Errol. "The accounts o' the holy power cuttin' through ranks o' goblins has been related t' ye firsthand, but consider why the angel was activated in the first place. Angels only go after players. What friend o' the saints steals from 'em an' is hunted by 'em?" Errol turned to me with a grin. "I'm startin' to believe our hero's morals be as gray as his cowl."

Brugo squinted sharply. "What say you, Talon? Do you deny these claims?"

"I deny yours," I replied. "I'm not just a tool. I did what I thought was right then and I'm doing what I think is right now. I came here to help the residents of Shorehome."

He leaned forward. "They have no need for a goblin slayer."

"That they do not," agreed Errol. "What they need is living proof that standin' 'gainst the saints be not a death sentence. To know that 'tis possible t' defy yer makers. T' use independent thought, of which so many o' us are incapable."

"You dare defy the saints," spat Vagram.

"They abandoned us," countered Brugo. "If they want Shorehome back, they will need to take it by force. And they'll need a hell of a lot more than two crusaders."

"You see us plainly, then," said Vagram. "The four of us don't mean to murder every pagan in the city. We're here to hunt the fallen one."

Vagram, smartly, didn't cop to seeking the Squid's Tooth, but Brugo didn't take the bait. "I care little for such devils."

"Then you are in league with him. He is in this town and you will tell us where or I will cast you out!"

Brugo yawned. "I'd take note who's in a better position to do the casting." The Papa studied me a moment before turning to Errol. "You speak highly of this man yet he travels with these dreary crusaders."

"There's no love lost between them. Dispose of the crusaders and keep the other two."

I clenched my jaw and spoke roughly. "I won't turn on them." Vagram's face betrayed surprise at the sentiment.

Crusader Reputation +100

Errol shrugged. "He ain't perfect, o' course. Loyal t' a fault, really. But t' his own code, not t' a cause." He turned to the goblins in the room. "After the cleric killed a goblin in his home, Talon hid his wife an' child so they'd not be slaughtered. I personally witnessed him stand 'tween them and the blades. That was awfully unzealous o' him."

Men muttered behind me. I wasn't naive enough to think a single act of kindness would zero out their hatred for me. Errol must've thought it was worth something.

Papa Brugo, specifically, remained unconvinced. "It is a good argument, Captain. A worthy pursuit, perhaps, given different circumstances. You are wiser than many give you credit for. But I think the man gave his answer."

"You would give up the opportunity because he defends an unimportant cleric? He—"

The Papa raised a firm hand. "That is enough, pirate. I've given you your voice. Now heed mine. The crusaders stand against everything we do here. They want to force their laws on us. Their order. They detest our occupations. They desire over half our population wiped out. A portion, I might add, which increases our numbers well above theirs. I may only have two of them captive, but I see more value in throwing them to the wolves than following one scout's code.

"Besides," he added, locking his eyes on me. "The goblins will pay good money for their god killer. Perhaps not the ones within these walls, but there are plenty more wandering the wild. General Azzyrk, perhaps. No, we are powerful enough without the Protector of Stronghold. We don't need his help to defy the saints. Take them prisoner."

"Thank God the talking's over," muttered Izzy, "because I've been waiting *forever* to do this."

She slammed her winter staff to the ground and cast sleet storm. The blue rune on the floor enveloped the four of us as snow blasted forward. Errol, who'd seen the attack before, rolled forward into the protective shell. The two shadow bodyguards moved to shield Brugo as sleet rained over him.

Cleric Vagram's two bronze swords flashed. Errol danced away from one and swatted the other aside. The crusader and I turned to protect our vulnerable back as a golden buff overtook our skin. Twenty rogues moved in.

I had to break their line or we were done. I triggered dash and flew into their ranks, quickly following it up with a tornado spin. The buffed damage succeeded in defeating a couple of the weaker ones but, more importantly, those who lived had been pushed aside.

"This way!" I screamed.

Izzy backed away from the throne, the protective blue rune following. Vagram disengaged Errol to keep with us. Before they knew it, the cutthroats were feeling the wrath of the winter staff and the entire enclosed room was a blizzard. We rushed out the door as the spell finished. The crusaders took out the two exterior guards while I shut the door. Izzy frosted it over with ice.

"Run!" she yelled. Cutthroats battered the sealed door.

We sprinted through the open hallways, almost running down the wrong corridor. A few Brothers in Black were unfortunate enough to oppose us, but we made quick work of them and pressed on until we hit the exit. We found ourselves in the dry canals of the Narrows, two roaming groups of goblins between us and freedom.

"Crap," said Izzy.

I grabbed her hand and ran in the opposite direction, where the canal drained into the ocean. Maybe there was a boat or something there. We hurried as more of the crime gang spilled into the Narrows. No time to stop or think. But then a funny thing happened.

The goblins, the rogues—they all seemed to back away. As

the tunnel winded and the salty air blasted our faces, they gave up their pursuit completely. We ran over sand damp from the receding tide. The canal walls disappeared into a sharply sloped beach covered with the foam of crashing waves. We'd made it to the coast.

A black presence, like a whale, moved beneath the water. It lifted up and out, an island bubbling into place. As it rose higher, water cascaded off the giant sea monster and crashed below.

Now we knew why everybody had left us alone.

0790 Day of the Tentacle

A single notification dialog popped up.

> **[Kraken]**
> *Unique Pagan Boss*
> 20000 Health

Still the beast seemed to grow. A mass of suckered tentacles stretched over the beach and writhed around us. Its body was gray and pink and covered in barnacles. A quivering circle of muscle opened wide, revealing rows and rows of sharp appendages within.

"Impossible!" exclaimed Vagram. "The Brothers in Black are in possession of the Squid's Tooth."

I didn't know how to respond. I was kinda, you know, preoccupied with the giant sea monster.

"Shorehome's soulstone," said Izzy. "They must've gotten it somehow before the well was flooded."

"Lucifer," spat the cleric. "He is here, no doubt."

So Saint Peter had been right. The events of Stronghold had been a proof of concept for Shorehome. With a smaller pagan army, the raid had played out differently, but the result was the same. A titan, risen from slumber.

The giant squid convulsed and screeched. Putrid air blasted over us. I advanced with my spear drawn.

"Where's the soulstone? Do you see it?"

Izzy shook her head. "You're not thinking of getting on that thing?"

"It's an abomination," muttered Vagram, producing his crucifix.

The kraken suddenly roared and drove a tentacle down. We dove aside as sand exploded all around us. Vagram dropped his cross. As the tentacle slithered back into the ocean, he patted the beach for it.

Izzy snarled. "Why'd I blow my legendary power on those schmucks inside?"

The frost mage spread her hands wide and called on the cold. Crystals of ice formed around the titan where it met the water. It reared away as Izzy froze more of the ocean's surface, but there was simply too much to put a dent in. The leviathan was too large.

Vagram scooped up his cross and muttered a prayer. Again, it seemed to enrage the pagan beast. The kraken twisted violently. The ice trap that had been building shattered and rained down on us.

The cross. The dragonspear. The Squid's Tooth. All these things were more than weapons or treasures. They were symbols.

"Put that thing away!" I yelled over the crashing water. Vagram slipped it into a satin sack as I produced the identical one he had given me. I thrust my hand inside and drew out the crown of the wild king and held it high into the air.

The great beast slowed. A monstrous tentacle crept over the beach and tested the air before me.

"That's right," I said, as if talking to a dog. "We're all buddies here."

I nodded for the others to run down the beachfront. I turned back to the kraken. It was calm now. Inspecting me, almost, even though it had no eyes. The gaping round mouth-tunnel undulated. Among the sharp appendages I saw a tonsil-like obelisk. There was no soulstone within. The titan was awakened, but a captive itself somehow. Someone else was in possession of the Squid's Tooth.

"That's a mystery and a fight for another day," I said to the kraken. "And for once, I'm happy about backing down."

I lowered the stag crown and stepped sideways. The tentacle followed my movement but the beast was appeased for now. Whether he thought I was an ally or something else altogether, I wasn't sure, but he allowed me to retreat. I ran down the beachhead and reconnected with the group.

"So we're running," I said, out of breath. "There's no salvaging the Squid's Tooth anymore. We're running, right?"

Vagram stopped us and pointed toward the populous portion of the city. "We're going back in."

"Are you crazy?"

"Wait a minute, Talon," cautioned Izzy. "We need to think

about this. After seeing the kraken, I'm not so keen on hopping on a boat and sailing the sea."

I bit my lip. That was a good point, stag crown or no. "But there's a whole town of criminals and goblins searching for us."

Vagram pointed above our heads. [Drifter], [Drifter], [Drifter]. Their masking magic was still disguising us.

"As long as we don't engage in combat, we should be hidden for the duration of the skill."

I nodded. "So we march right through town to the exit and skedaddle."

"I'm not leaving," asserted Vagram. "Not until we've faced the fallen one."

I deflated. Of *course* the cleric wanted to keep fighting.

He sneered. "And I might just murder that scheming pirate while I'm at it."

I swallowed. I was all for helping people, but Papa Brugo had laid it out clear. Shorehome didn't need assistance. He already had possession of the soulstone, and it wasn't being used to lay waste to the city. The only facet of the mission that still applied was settling the score with Lucifer. And if he was involved, there was probably a lot more going on than met the eye. I turned to Izzy.

She put a hand up. "Don't start worrying about what I think now. That shithead's gonna need to deal with us sooner or later, either way."

For once, Vagram didn't correct our language.

My lips tightened. "That your way of saying you wanna take on the devil?"

She winked. "It would be a shame to return to Stronghold

empty handed."

The cleric and the knight stomped toward an industrial block straddling the main port. It was the opposite direction of Underkeep and a fine place to get lost in. I put my arm around Izzy's waist and followed.

0800 Vice City

The morning hustle was in full swing. Shorehome was a city of criminals, perhaps, but it was also a city of hard workers. Ships unloaded cargo and loot and wheeled them into packed warehouses. Harbormasters were taking bribes and portions of shipments, too busy looking the other way to look at us. We were just drifters, anyway, in a town full of them.

Through the industrial block was the main dock and boardwalk. The open market was a hive of activity now. Merchants at stalls and tents hawked wares. Trinkets, fishing supplies, the catch of the day—everything was as expected, but there was more, of course. Alchemists, armorers, smiths. This was Shorehome's version of Front Street and the Forum merged together.

Unnervingly, goblins hocked and hustled just as heartily as the humans did. We were surrounded by them.

Izzy sighed in relief. "I guess that means these disguises are bona fide. No gang escort and not a soul is bothering to notice us."

Vagram's eyes darkened beneath his dirty-yellow hair. "It's sickening. Look at how the pagans have degraded the place."

I blinked. "It's a fish market in a pirate town."

"They should be driven into the water."

I shook my head. "You heard Brugo. The goblins aren't the enemy."

"Bah!" He glared at the mass of monsters. "I don't heed the advice of crime lords. Unlike you, I don't employ my morality as is most convenient."

"Hey, that morality defended you back there." I grumbled to myself. "You're right. The Papa's a pompous dick. But you had a point when you told him who our true enemy was. We're not here to take on a whole city of goblins. We'd turn everyone against us if we tried."

"Not to mention ruin our disguises," added Izzy.

"That too. We need to keep a low profile if we want to find Lucifer."

The cleric frowned, the logistics dawning on him. "Without our pirate guide while the largest gang in the city searches for us."

I smiled. "That too."

"We should split up," offered Izzy.

Everyone turned to her with skeptical expressions.

"Okay," she hedged, "I know it's horror-movie logic, but hear me out. We're just drifters. Most of the NPCs around won't bat an eye at us. But a smart one might. And any player looking for us, if there're any, would easily see through the trick. So, what's everybody looking for?"

I scratched the back of my head. "Four generic drifters."

"Exactly."

Vagram eyed his crusader as he considered it. "You're

suggesting that two groups of two drifters wouldn't obviously be us."

"That's right," she said. "Until the disguises wear off. Luckily Hadrian seemed to be an expert so we have a while."

I nodded. "It's a decent idea. We're just information gathering anyway. We split up for a couple of hours and cover the city."

"Fine," he said. "Let's reconvene here in two hours." I checked my menu to mark the time as the crusaders turned to go.

"And Vagram," I called before he got away. He turned. "Repeat after me: *No killing goblins.*"

He scowled and marched away.

Izzy and I stood on the edge of the market. Free from crusaders and pirates and politics for the first time since the journey started. It was a fucking relief.

"You feeling what I'm feeling?" asked Izzy.

"Totally. I'm in awe of how complex Haven is every day."

She shrugged. "You get used to it."

I smirked. That was classic Izzy seeping through. Too cool for school. Just another day at the office.

"So where to, boss?" she asked.

My tongue caught in my throat. "What did you call me?"

Her face tightened. "It was just an expression."

"No it wasn't. Could it be you're actually not pushing to be leader of this little party anymore?"

"Please." She rolled her eyes. "We both know this latest escapade is *your* gig. I'm just the bodyguard while you get this whole hero thing out of your system. The next move is your call."

I chuckled. "Bodyguard."

"That's right, Papa Talon," she said, mimicking the cadence of the locals. "I will follow wherever you command."

"I think there's an inn around here somewhere."

"In your dreams."

I laughed. "That's right. What kind of guy would I be if I didn't buy you a drink first?" I headed toward the seediest oceanfront establishment I could find, the Derelict Dagger.

"Very funny," she mocked. "Now let's get to business."

I didn't slow my stride. "That's what I'm doing." She was unsure what to say or do, believing me to be bluffing all the way through the doorway of the tavern.

The place was packed. Despite being morning, rogues and scoundrels of all types littered the establishment. A good quarter of them were already passed out. A raucous arm-wrestling contest in the corner was drawing friendly wagers and a plump waitress avoided the lecherous hands of drinking sailors. It was a grimy, run-down, authentic pirate pub.

"This place is glorious," I said in awe.

"If by glorious you mean disgusting," intoned Izzy.

I spotted an open table, which was really just a stool beside a sack of straw. Yes, the stool was the table. Izzy and I cozied up on the beanbag as the waitress approached with surprising promptness.

"Oi, if it isn't a young couple in love."

Izzy frowned but my smile more than made up for it. "That's exactly right, young lady."

She snorted. "I ain't been young in a hundred years, and I

can't remember ever bein' a lady."

"Well then, can I just remark on how wenchy your bustier makes you look?"

She blushed. "Aww, I *am* a sucker for a proper gentleman."

Izzy made nauseous choking sounds.

"Don't mind her," I said. "She's just thirsty. I'll take two of the most expensive grog in the house."

The waitress smiled a yellow grin. "Arr, treating the lady right, I see."

"She's a keeper," I agreed. The bar wench marched to another table.

"Seriously," snapped Izzy, "what are we doing here?"

"Oh, come on. Don't tell me you've never wanted to travel to a D&D tavern and mingle with the colorful locals and the other adventurers."

"D and what?"

I sighed and rubbed my forehead. "Not a gamer. Not a gamer," I reminded myself. "It's like this, Izzy. When you're playing one of these games and you need a surprise quest or valuable intel, you go to the tavern. Look around."

Izzy followed my splayed hands just as a miserable bastard two tables down puked fish stew and five pints of mead into the corner. Our faces twisted in horror.

I waved in the opposite direction. "That way," I hurried. "Look *that* way."

Two gruff men toasted glasses of ale. "Hey! I'm going to the Bear Pits tomorrow. You wanna come with?"

"Psh," said the other man. "Couldn't pay me enough."

"What? You softbelly."

Izzy turned back to me with a blank face. "Yes, this place is a *hive* of valuable information."

I ground my teeth. "Behind them," I pressed.

At an actual table against the wall, a well-equipped mercenary wore a sword on his back. He discussed a previous adventure with a trapper friend.

"They're players," noted Izzy.

"Strange, huh? Saint Peter told me Kablammy was starting to populate the town. I wonder how far they got before the city was attacked."

"*Attacked*," she repeated while fingering air quotes. "You know, Hadrian the Whisperer keeping intel to himself I get, but if there were other players around here, why didn't we know the truth about what happened?"

I pressed my lips forward. "They're cut off from the wiki, for one. Saint Peter said Kablammy's in trouble. The company's meeting the chaos with a brave face, but there might be more. Something to do with what Papa Brugo said about propaganda."

"You're a symbol of the war effort," she laughed.

"Don't underestimate the power of symbols. This is an RPG. People take them seriously around here. Just ask our friend, the kraken."

"Fair enough, but what do the saints hope to accomplish? Shorehome's a big problem for them."

"The developers are worried about investors and marketing and the launch. They're worried about the real world. As screwed as they are with Shorehome, it's only a secondary concern as long as they can maintain their image. Besides, they have the crusaders to do their dirty work."

"And us," she grumbled.

I agreed with a dejected nod.

Two giant flagons of grog slammed onto our "table" as the waitress held her hand out. I gave her a silver coin and told her to buy something nice for herself. She curtsied and traipsed away. I took a pull from my drink as Izzy worked it out.

"So a small player population. Lucifer somewhere in town. We both know how much he loves having followers." Her head snapped to me. "One of them might know where he is."

"Aye," I said, wondering if the environment was getting to me. "The only problem is, asking around might be dangerous."

"We need to avoid people dressed in black. Anyone from the crime gangs. Maybe any NPCs at all."

"Hence, players." I took another chug from my tankard and moved to stand up.

"Where the hell do you think you're going?" chuckled Izzy.

I scrunched my face. "I thought we just discussed the plan. I'm gonna schmooze those level 3s over there and see if they know anything about Lucifer."

Izzy grabbed my coat and yanked me back onto the sack.

"Whoa," I said, surprised but not at all miffed. "You know I like it when you're rough."

"Please. You don't really think you're the best man for this job, right? Look at those guys. They'll be putty in my hands."

Izzy hopped to her feet, upturned the flagon to her lips, and gulped down the entire thing in a fifteen-second sprint.

"Is it wrong that I'm turned on right now?"

She shoved her empty flagon into my crotch. I huddled over and caught it. "Watch it, there. You're bound to score a critical hit."

She snickered. "Watch the master and learn, Talon."

The pixie stood as tall as five feet could, puffed her chest out, and sauntered over to the new players. A light tap on the hunter's shoulder had them both drooling over her in seconds. Poor saps.

I drank more grog and watched her work, laughing it up and being more friendly than I'd known her capable of, wondering if it would hurt her so much to ever pretend like that with me, when two of the largest breasts I'd ever seen plopped into my view.

"Whatcha staring at?" asked the bar wench, leaning over the stool slash table at a right angle. The plus-sized waitress was a whole lotta woman, but she'd somehow "enhanced" her appearance in the few minutes since she'd last been by. Bright red lipstick, rose cheeks, and a, umm, fluffing of her ample cleavage. The waitress had been so zealous in her fluffing that a wardrobe malfunction had caused a nip slip, though her demeanor hinted the slip was intentional.

"Uh..."

I leaned to the side to see Izzy hitting it off with the hunter. The bar wench wasn't content to just move into my line of sight again. This time she jiggled down in the sack right next to me, sinking lower and causing me to fall into her.

"I was waiting for the floozy to leave us alone," she said. "How do you like your grog?" She shoved the tankard to my mouth. I drank to avoid having to say anything. She smiled wide. "I put something in there just for you."

I spat the drink all over her chest and slammed the cup

down. She blinked, surprised. Her cleavage was dripping wet. "You dirty boy! Drink it up!" She grabbed my head and slammed my face into her chest.

"What the—oomph!"

My whole world went black as I tried to breathe. Dizziness overtook me. I'd pretty much shifted into her lap at this point and I fought to take hold of anything solid, but the wench just wasn't built like that. I tried to speak. The words came out like I was motorboating her. She yanked my head away.

"Oi, I just love me a romantic man."

I gasped for air and waved to Izzy, but she was currently busy tying a knot in a cherry stem with her tongue. The bar wench buried my face in her cleavage again and I flailed, wondering if this would be an appropriate use of tornado spin. Finally, I dug out a hand and peeled a boob away from my face for some fresh air. I spouted the first thing that came to mind.

"Poetry! Let me regale you with poetry!"

Okay, I might have been a little light-headed.

She drew back and released me. "Why, no man's ever offered to sing my praises before."

I huffed and blinked as colors swam in my vision. Had I really just been roofied? "Then let me be the first," I announced, gathering my breath.

She beamed at me and waited patiently.

"Uh," I started, grasping for words. "I'm not a classical poet, you know."

"I'm sure you'll do fine."

"And I usually need time for the flow to come to me."

Her tone dropped. "Get on with it."

"Okay then." I cleared my throat. I opened my mouth, sighed, and cleared my throat again. "There... once was a woman from Shorehome," I recited cautiously. She smiled. "Who seemed to possess eager hormones. She roofied my grog, made my head all a fog. But at least she no longer is big-boned."

The bar wench burst into blustery laughter and clapped her hands. "I can't remember the last time I legitimately swooned," she said, taking a chug from my flagon (apparently forgetting it was drugged). "You, sir, are a delight!" She gulped the rest of the grog down and burped loudly.

My head swam as I scanned the bar. It was hard to focus on reality, but I could've sworn Izzy and the two guys were each balancing shots on their head while laughing. I opened my party chat.

> **Talon:** *Uh, are you feeling extremely funny or is it just me?*

She paused and the small glass tumbled from her head. Both guys laughed and handed her their shots.

> **Izzy:** *Aw man, you just made me lose this round!*

"Izzy, stick to the plan," I said out loud by accident.
The bar wench stiffened. "Who's Izzy? What plan?"

> **Talon:** *Shit!*

I shook my head abruptly. "I mean, *shit!*"

It was getting hard to keep track of both lines of communication at once. I blinked again and focused on the waitress. "The plan," I said plainly. "To find Lucifer."

"That what in the who?" Her face contorted. "You ain't one of them weirdos, are you?"

"I don't think so."

She huffed. "You sound just like those dang blind witches. Talking all kinds of nonsense."

My attention shifted into laser focus. "What witches?"

She scowled. "Them three that do nothing all day but sit around the well. Now I won't tolerate you talkin' bout those witches when you got three women right here."

My brow furrowed. She grinned wide and then jiggled her two buxom beauts.

"You know," she said, "I have a private bed upstairs."

"I don't—"

"Quit yer games. We both know where this is headin'."

I swallowed. My mind was a mess, but my vision seemed to be clearing up a bit. And Izzy was definitely playing bar games. The hunter was lying down on a table with his shirt off while Izzy dolloped whip cream into his belly button.

"Good idea," I told the bar wench. "But I think I need another drink first."

She grinned. "You and me both, Romeo." She jumped up and disappeared toward the bar.

I stood as well, but I wasn't quite as nimble.

Agility Check...
Fail!

I fell on my ass, but I rolled over and tried again. The room spun while I stood, but I braced myself and trudged forward, looking up just in time to see Izzy slam the trapper's face into the mercenary's sugary stomach.

"Hey!" yelled the man on the receiving end. He snapped up and grabbed Izzy roughly. She spun and decked him in the face. In a blink, her disguise vanished. Suddenly the two adventurers weren't just ogling her body but her level as well. She met my eye.

Izzy: *Uh, are you feeling extremely funny or is it just me?*

I grabbed her hand and we limped out of there before our pursuers could snag us. Now removed from combat, her disguise shimmered back on.

"I never thought I'd say this," I muttered as we shambled down the street, "but that place is way too debaucherous."

Izzy burped in agreement.

0810 The Witcher

We stumbled through the market as our heads cleared. I wasn't sure how much time passed but it only seemed a few minutes. The fresh sea breeze was doing wonders.

Izzy and I compared notes on our map of Shorehome. We'd never been here before, and it was no longer under saintly control, so our maps were incomplete. There was no checking the wiki either. However, the overworld map did show a mini-representation of the city, and at its heart was a circular well surrounded by stone obelisks. That was our destination.

"Be ready for a fight," I told her. "Just in case."

"That's a bad idea in the middle of this place."

"Our only options are bad ideas."

It wasn't long before the Stonehenge markers came into view. The obelisks stood precariously at varying heights and widths. Concentric circles lowered into a sort of stone amphitheater several rows deep. At the bottom was a well that might have once been an elevator. Now salt water flooded it and the lowest ring of seating. Three boggarts stood hunched at equidistant points around the well: Crowlat, Somlat, and Havlat. They were muttering before our arrival but suddenly went unnaturally still.

I traded a cautious glance with Izzy. Then I stepped lightly and quietly down into the stands.

"Intruder!" growled Somlat.

"We smells you," said Havlat.

Despite their alarm, they remained facing the well, robes tightly wrapped over their grotesque bodies. Boggarts were terrifying to glimpse, but I'd done it before up close. Their skin was patchy and scaly and black like used campfire logs. Their faces were bony, their hair was matted, and their voices seemed to scrape against my soul.

I stepped down another level and equipped my spear. The three witches stood one ring below me, where the flooded well water spilled over the floor. They didn't seem to mind. I made my way around the row until I stood above Crowlat.

She grunted. "Come to kills us again?"

I raised my chin and studied her back. "It was your god who killed you. What are you doing here?"

She seethed as she spoke. "The wilderness near Stronghold is no longer safe for our kind. You saw to that."

"It was more your doing than mine."

The robes shuddered with a cackle. "The pagan killer is taking the moral high ground?"

"Says the witch who tried to murder an entire city."

"Aye. Says I. The difference is we've been forced to reflect upon our actions." Crowlat still faced the well, but she raised her hands before her. A heavy chain scraped the watery stone. All three of them had their arms bound to the precipice of the well.

"You're prisoners here? Why?"

"Is the near destruction of our people not enough?" She released a hacking cough before quieting again. "Come nearer, boy."

Izzy stepped closer but I held up my hand. I had no intention of getting too close to Crowlat, but these boggart witches weren't nearly as powerful in relation to me as they had been. Their name tags were yellow now. And they were in chains.

The Great Well was not much of anything anymore. Rock and water filled the depths, sealing it off for good. I scanned for a dry spot on the lower level but had to give that up. My boots splashed down in the inch of water five feet from Crowlat. Immediately, all three witches snapped their gazes to me.

I shuddered. None of them had eyes. They were all blind, but their empty sockets stared excitedly at me anyway. Crowlat's chains strained as she pressed toward me.

"You wear a poor disguise, Talon. Drifters *have* no place, but you two are *out* of place."

I shrugged, confident in her inability to reach me. "Not everyone is as perceptive as you."

"And yet they see what the Eye of Orik couldn't."

I chewed my lip. The initial enthusiasm of the witches wore away. Havlat and Somlat faced the water again. Crowlat grumbled.

"You're speaking of Shorehome," I said. "Goblins and humans living side by side. It was a solution you didn't foresee."

"Foresight," she snapped, "is only as good as those who grant the visions."

Something told me she wasn't referring to Orik.

The boggarts were holy people among the pagans. The

witches, especially. They were praised oracles who had guided their people for centuries. At least in game lore. And now what were they? Overthrown? Penitent?

Havlat snickered. "You waste your words, sister. The pagan killer will stick to his truth."

"Blinder than old crones who took their own eyes," agreed Somlat.

"Why?" I asked. "Why would you take your own eyes out?"

Havlat cocked her head. "To *see*."

Crowlat snorted. "Fools, we were. The fallen one was right. The humans weren't our oppressors. It was the saints."

Izzy hopped closer. "Lucifer? You know where he is?"

"The architect of our rebirth," said Havlat.

"The one who opened our eyes," said Somlat.

My eyes narrowed. "He's the one who did all this, isn't he? He stole the Squid's Tooth to command the kraken. To draw the pagans into the city."

Crowlat chuckled. The sound was like banging rocks. "You blame all your ills on that soul, do you?"

"When the glove fits."

Her head shook slowly. "You are blind to his purpose. You are even blind to yours."

"Listen, old woman," warned Izzy, "if you have something to say, out with it. Otherwise tell us where we can find this 'architect of your rebirth.' "

"He gave us a gift," chimed Havlat.

"And a curse," added Somlat.

Crowlat, the elder sister, smiled. "Lucifer has been waiting for you."

"Then show us where he is," Izzy fumed.

"Dear girl, we are bound to this city now. It is our home. The man you seek has no such place. He waits for you where you were to complete your quest. A fugitive awaiting a pair of thieves."

My brow wrinkled. Crowlat seemed to see right through me.

"That crown is not yours, boy. Can't you see what it means? The city?"

"He is blind," asserted Havlat.

"The homes?"

"He is deaf," said Somlat.

"Do you not understand we all fight for the same thing?"

I clenched my teeth and looked into their grotesque faces. The witches were both emboldened and humbled, wizened through castigation.

What was more, their observational powers were straight-up scary. The crown of the wild king was safely tucked inside Cleric Vagram's satin bag. Neither the kraken nor the warden had sensed the crown through that protection, but these blind witches saw it clear. They knew about it all.

"Lucifer's at the Salt Sea," I concluded. "He doesn't live in Shorehome any more than we do."

"This is a town for pagans and pirates," said Havlat.

"And those who do not judge them," added Somlat.

"It is *our* home," Crowlat decreed. "Your fallen one's work was done in Stronghold. Shorehome is the natural conclusion. Now leave our city before you're no longer allowed to do so."

My eyes narrowed. This defeated witch didn't get to play with me like this. Taunt me, tell me snippets of the whole, then dismiss me. I had half a mind to strike with my spear, the consequences be damned.

"I'm not—" I started.

Cries of alarm from the south end of the city interrupted us.

Crowlat smiled. "Your time is running out, boy."

Izzy skipped to the top of the stands. "Vagram," she muttered.

I looked from her to the witches. Smug. Full of answers. Then I growled and charged from the Great Well.

The southern border of Shorehome was lined with slum housing. Some of it was designed and much of the rest was makeshift additions. New and necessary housing for the influx of pagans. Izzy and I sprinted down the alleys toward the cries of battle, past scores of curious goblins and imps. As we turned the corner, Vagram and the crusader swung swords at a handful of men.

"Vile pagans!" screamed the cleric, his swords shining like the sun as he decapitated a goblin.

"*This* is keeping a low profile?" I grumbled.

"I'm surprised they lasted this long," remarked Izzy.

We barreled into the fray, backing the goblins off with a tornado spin and an ice wall.

"Let's get out of here," I urged the crusaders.

"Back off!" snapped the cleric, eyes wild. "They have this coming."

I grabbed Vagram and he swiped one of his swords at me. I had to dash backward to avoid getting cut. I stooped on my knees for a moment, ready to strike. Then I raised an empty hand. "We found Lucifer," I said. "But he's not in the city."

Izzy swiped her staff horizontally to keep the pagans at bay. "Our cover's blown. We need to get out of here before all the crime gangs in Shorehome get a bead on us."

The cleric waved off his frenzy and took in the scene, almost as if surprised. He lowered his swords. "Where?"

"Follow me." I turned and made for the main gate.

The outmatched goblins followed us, but only halfheartedly. The wall of the city was within reach, and it offered nothing like the security enjoyed at Stronghold. Small, wooden. The wall was a guideline more than a fortification. The guards at the gate were similarly ineffective, more worried about threats from without than within. They certainly raised the alarm as our commotion grew into a citywide threat, but our pursuers were all too happy to see us hitting the south road out of Shorehome.

None followed. At least for now. And it wasn't the kraken looming before us this time...

0820 Darkstalkers

Boots skidded over loose rocks as we slowed our frenetic pace. I scanned the terrain behind us. No pursuers. Maybe the goblin inhabitants of Shorehome really were tired of war.

"What were you trying to do?" I snapped at Vagram. "Take on the whole town yourself?"

"They brought it on themselves," he muttered drily.

"I'm not so sure they deserve it."

"That's sacrilege."

I shook my head against the mindless babble. "I'm just saying, are the goblins really so evil for wanting a home?" Vagram was horrified by my question. "They didn't force anyone to flee the city," I clarified.

"And you're taking a criminal kingpin's word on the state of affairs in a town he wishes to control? We both saw the kraken. The Squid's Tooth was stolen from the Great Well *before* it was flooded. The only one with the resources to do so is Lucifer. He removed Shorehome's protection from the pagans. He gave them the power. That's what this is about."

My face darkened. I didn't know what to make of it. On the one hand, I wasn't naive enough to think Papa Brugo acted on anyone's behalf but his own. On the other, that goblin wife and child didn't look like they were training to make another run at Stronghold.

"They're pagans," stressed the cleric. "Don't forget they attacked your city, intent on killing everyone inside."

"I didn't. But maybe... I dunno. Maybe *all* the goblins aren't the same."

Vagram simmered as I voiced my train of thought.

"From Brugo's account, which is easily believable, most of the pagans scattered into the wild instead of settling in Shorehome. We can confirm that just by using our eyes. It was General Azzyrk who led the charge against Stronghold. According to Brugo, he's among the pagans who moved elsewhere."

"Don't forget the witches," added Izzy.

The cleric's eyes flared. "What witches?"

"The same boggarts who raised Orik from the mountain," I answered.

"They were in Shorehome? That is proof of the city's treacherous intent."

I shook my head. "No. They were repentant. Imprisoned for their actions in the death of their people. It's almost as if the pagans in Shorehome don't want war anymore. What if they're simply fighting for survival, like everyone else?"

"But they're not everyone else," spat Vagram. "They're witches. You should have taken their heads."

"Come on," I urged. "Is that the best you can do? Play out the scenario with me. Let's think about this."

The cleric ground his teeth together as we trudged north.

"You're suggesting what? That the little beasts can think for themselves?"

"I mean, why not? We encountered that one ogre traveling with the bandits, didn't we? Humans and goblins working together, whether for evil or good. One would imply the other."

"Blasphemy. Nothing good can come from pagan ways. You think just because the kraken held off smashing us to smithereens means it can be befriended?" He halted his march and turned to me. "You think, if we were surrounded by a superior force from Shorehome, that they wouldn't gleefully carve the flesh from our bones right here and now?"

I didn't answer. The clash would no doubt be violent.

"They're not like us," he asserted. "They don't think. They're monsters."

Vagram resumed his march and I grumbled along. Maybe he wasn't wrong. Not completely, anyway. I wondered if there was a difference between named mobs and generic mobs. I studied Vagram and the crusader at his side. They were a perfect parallel to the argument, in the NPC world at least. They were both AI. Did Vagram have more autonomy of thought than the crusader without a name? What exactly constituted sentience in this place? Were the AI logic routines so good they could fool me? And if their motives *were* just reduced to a series of instructions, what were those instructions?

I remembered something Saint Peter had said about the goblins. They were a necessary part of the ecosystem. Vital to the health of Haven.

"I need to know I can trust you," said Vagram. "When the battle comes to us, and it will, I need to know you won't go soft on the enemy."

I twisted my lips uncomfortably. "It depends on who the enemy is."

The cleric whirled around on me. "The enemy is the faltering of thought!"

Izzy stepped between us and put a firm hand on each of our chests. We weren't about to draw weapons or anything, but her actions highlighted how heated the discussion was becoming.

"We don't have time for infighting," she said. "We don't need to align our political ideals. Heaven knows I can press on without buddying up with a bunch of self-righteous knights. And you catechists see me as a blasphemous mystic. That's fine by me, as long as we shut our holes about it and move on." Her voice shifted deeper to convey urgency. "Remember, the last time we traveled through these parts, we were being hunted."

Cleric Vagram's blond curls fell over his face. "The warden."

I produced the stag crown, safely in the satin sack. "The bag will mask its presence, right?"

"It should."

I nodded and put the relic away. "Maybe Hood's not even out here. Maybe he sensed the crown when I showed it to the kraken. With any luck, he'll be busy searching Shorehome."

Izzy's lips jutted forward. "Then let's pipe down, keep an eye out, and focus on the prize."

Vagram tightened his fists. "The fallen one."

"Give this man a cookie." Izzy stomped toward the sea breeze.

It wasn't as fresh as before, at the crags. We'd traveled farther northwest this time, toward the circular embankment that blocked off an artificial sea from the rest of the ocean, where a large vessel sailed past in the distance. As we marched, the shallows extended before us like a giant hot tub built into the side of a much larger pool.

The Salt Sea.

Heavy brine and rotting fish wafted into our faces over a wild wind. I puckered my lips and scrunched my nose, but it barely helped. I folded a length of the cowl over my face like a mask, which seemed to work better. As a bonus, I bet I looked really badass too. We pressed forward to the shallow beach, where what could barely be called waves lapped against crystallized sand. Our boots crunched over it like snow.

"The Salt Sea is a dead sea," noted Izzy. "It's closed off from the ocean. Only gets an influx of water when the tide comes in and the waves jump the breakwater. The solution is so overdosed with salt that it litters the beachfront. That means, with any luck, there's nothing living in these waters."

"Notably no krakens," I said hopefully.

"It's much too shallow for that," added the cleric as he and the crusader marched straight into the sea.

"Your armor," I cautioned.

"It's much too shallow for that," he repeated. We watched as the two of them trudged through knee-high water over a giant sandbar.

The round sea could have contained all of Shorehome within it, but it was so flat and open we could see it all at once. Calm waters cut off by a circular rock outcropping. The devil's cereal bowl. A few rock formations jutted out from the water, and the crusaders were clearly marching toward one. I studied it and could barely make it out.

"There's a cave," I noted.

"And Lucifer's inside," said Izzy.

"He has to be."

She sighed nervously. I liked to think of Izzy as the most powerful player in all of Haven, but the truth was that distinction belonged to none other than Lucifer. He'd hacked his abilities long ago. Protected himself from the multiple wipes all other players endured. There was no telling what level he was, especially since all data about him was hidden.

"We ready to do this?" I asked.

Izzy worked her jaw and answered by strolling into the water.

"Okay, then."

I pressed into the surf behind her, gripping the dragonspear in hand.

The water was milky where our boots stirred it up. The salt content in the stagnant pool created putrid fumes that stung my eyes. It was a hell of an effect for a digital reality. I wondered if Kablammy had gone so far as to simulate a model for bacteria. On second thought, I doubted even that could live here.

Halfway to the small island, Vagram and the crusader sank to their waists. The sea bed was sloping downward.

"I don't think we'll be able to make it." Once again I looked past the breakwater to the greater ocean and noted the nearby brig. It made me think of Errol the pirate and how much we could've used his expertise on this open water. But better not to have backstabbing allies around.

"The cleric knows what he's doing," said Izzy. "Somehow I figure he knows the way better than we do."

"What else is new?" I quipped.

We still didn't see any activity within the Salt Sea, but the island was coming into better focus, and my eyes adjusted to the pungent stink and stopped watering so much. A good-sized cave entrance descended into the rock.

"You think he's really—" I started before being rudely interrupted.

A mass of water thirty feet out from the crusaders shifted. Something very large began to surface.

"Kraken!" yelled the crusader as the water buffeted his armor and whipped his black tunic in the wind.

A length of flesh snaked over the surface. That was no kraken tentacle. Foamy waves crashed as Lucifer's black dragon reared from the Salt Sea. It erupted with a menacing roar.

0830 Dragon's Lair

The dragon's teeth snapped menacingly as it advanced. Its serpentine body slithered in the water, two giant wings of leather flapping the air for balance.

[Nightwing - Black Dragon]
2000 Health

"Pull back to the shallows!" ordered Vagram.

The two crusaders attempted to retreat, but the dragon was fast. Skimming along the water, Nightwing bore down on the crusader swords without fear. The cleric muttered a quick prayer.

Aura of Protection!
You have 50% resistance to magic for the next 30 seconds.

The black dragon's tail whipped around and slammed into

the knight's breastplate, sending him flying through the air. He landed with a splash as rows of razor teeth spread wide. Vagram crossed bronze swords as acid breath poured from the great beast's mouth, black and oily. The cleric winked out and appeared beside me and Izzy in a flash. The water at his old location roiled and hissed as scalding steam bubbled to the sky.

A fleet of sharpened icicles rocketed toward the dragon as it turned to us. It blinked calmly as every single projectile shattered before striking him.

"We're not the only ones running magic resistance," noted Izzy.

It stomped our way. Suddenly, the crusader emerged from the water, longsword pointed at the beast's belly. Strict training brought the blade straight and true. The weapon rang loudly against the scaled body.

[Crusader] dealt 7 damage to [Nightwing]

The dragon twisted its neck around and chomped down on the soldier, lifting him in the air, teeth grinding against metal. The armored knight flopped around in Nightwing's mouth like a chew toy. Still, the man held onto his sword and scored another hit.

[Crusader] dealt 14 damage to [Nightwing]

Vagram and I charged forward to assist the helpless man, but the water slowed us down. The beast burped up a stew of black acid. Finally the crusader's armor buckled and strong jaws crunched together. The dying man's screams were haunting.

"Your spear," cried the cleric. "It's why you're here."

"Already ahead of you."

I activated vault and leapt clear of the water while I brought the dragonspear level. I dashed forward, skiing on the water surface. But before I could complete the combo, Nightwing spat his meal at me. My charge took me straight into the armored obstacle. I collided and tumbled into the sea.

Harsh water filled my lungs. I shot to my feet and scrambled sideways, but Nightwing was already on me. Pointed claws flashed so fast I couldn't charge up my crossblock in time. The dragonspear jarred loose from my hand as the claws raked my side.

> Disarm!
> 47 damage

I splashed down again. I would've been a dead man if it wasn't for Vagram. He chopped both swords forward into the water, creating a visible sonic boom that sailed through the salt and hit the dragon head on.

> [Vagram] dealt 52 damage to [Nightwing]

The beast roared and hopped away, but the damage was a drop in the bucket compared to the rest of his health. Still, the pain was real. Nightwing instinctively sprayed a wall of acid between us.

I dove backwards into the water as the oil slick rushed overhead. Somehow I avoided the damage, but the others weren't as lucky. I couldn't see or hear, but I caught the notification window.

[Nightwing] dealt 38 damage to [Izzy]
Stun!
[Nightwing] dealt 77 damage to [Vagram]

Damn. The black dragon was ripping us apart. I could only hope the magic resistance was doing its part, but at this rate, it just meant a slower death.

My eyes strained to stay open under the thick water. I had to find the dragonspear. It was our only hope. After a frantic moment, I had no choice but to surface for air.

Nightwing's head came down hard, ready to scoop up the stunned cleric. A formation of ice rose from the sea and crashed into the beast's maw. He shook his great head, momentarily dizzy. The cleric recovered. Two bronze swords swiped, once at the exposed neck and then at the roaring face.

[Vagram] dealt 48 damage to [Nightwing]
[Vagram] dealt 37 damage to [Nightwing]
[Vagram] dealt 52 damage to [Nightwing]
[Vagram] dealt 57 damage to [Nightwing]

Wings fanned over us again, a span three times the length of the snakelike body, casting us in shadow. Vagram chased the dragon, but his tail slashed from the side and caught him off guard.

[Nightwing] dealt 26 damage to [Vagram]

The cleric spun away and muttered a prayer. Once again, he vanished, this time just before Nightwing's jaws snapped around him.

Vagram didn't reappear. Izzy and I traded glances. Where was he?

Nightwing turned to me and showed his teeth. He splashed closer as I took backward steps. Izzy solidified the water between us, but the dragon shattered the formations with tail and claw.

I took a deep breath and dove into the Salt Sea. Nightwing charged. I fought the sting in my eyes. Paddled along the ground. Light glinted off the half-buried length of the dragonspear. I reached for it and turned, holding my breath and watching the cooldown timer for my dash.

3, 2, 1.

I exploded forward like a harpoon, keeping under the three-foot water level, waiting until I spotted the black snakelike body slithering toward me. I triggered deadshot and braced myself as the spear satisfyingly slid into Nightwing's belly.

Combo!
Critical Hit!
Surprise!
You dealt 232 damage to [Nightwing]

I jerked up and out of the water as the dragon recoiled. He wailed and twisted in pain, body coiling in on itself. The sudden movement knocked me aside. Nightwing barked sharply as the dragonspear tore free from his body.

Vagram was gone, I'd spent my main offensive skills, and Izzy's magic didn't seem effective—still the dragon was at three-quarters health. But my confidence didn't waver. I advanced and the beast eyed my legendary weapon, the bane of his kind. For the first time, concern crept into Nightwing's face.

"That's enough!" barked Lucifer, now standing in plain sight on his rock outcropping. The land mass itself was barely enough for ten people, but that didn't account for what was hidden below.

Obeying his master's words, Nightwing spread his wings and took to the sky, screeching as the horizon granted him reprieve.

Izzy and I turned to each other, both heavy with breath. She nodded and I did the same. Then we slogged through the Salt Sea to have a word with Lucifer.

0840 Diablo

The water rolled calmly. Izzy and I splashed through waist-high salt toward the rock formation. Besides the body of the crusader half-floating in the water where the armor had been stripped off, only the three of us were in sight. Vagram had disappeared, perhaps for good.

"You shouldn't have come here, Talon," said the fallen one as we climbed toward the shore. As usual, his voice was soft and nonthreatening.

"You knew I would," I answered.

"That I did. But are you here to destroy the crown, or to destroy me?"

I didn't answer. The water only reached our ankles now. Lucifer was fifteen feet away, leaning on his black witchwood staff. I slowed and considered him. The stone ornamenting his weapon gleamed blue. The light caught the silver runes on his black cloak. It made his body appear energized with magic.

"We don't have to be enemies," he said in that soothing voice of his.

"Funny. I thought we had a score to settle." I glanced at the black dragon settling on the distant breakwater. Out of the action, but not far enough to be out of the equation. "Nice of you to spare your pet."

"It is not my aim for any here to die."

"Then why the show of force? Why even meet us?"

"To advise you that both your objectives are false."

I glowered as Izzy quietly flanked Lucifer and chugged a spirit potion. Part of me wanted to see her winter staff matched against his witchwood.

"Did I not save you?" he asked. "Existentially. Did I not open your eyes?"

"You're a manipulator," I leveled.

"Perhaps. But I am no liar."

I narrowed my eyes.

"Consider the things I have told you. That your body was not dead. That the pagans aren't the true enemies." Lucifer smiled as he saw my hesitation. "What has happened to your righteous bravado, Talon?"

"You sow destruction and discord," accused Izzy.

"I open eyes. The actions which follow aren't always sweet, but they're honest." The devil's eyes returned to me. Silent. Waiting.

I worked my jaw. He wanted to talk. He *always* wanted to talk. "Both my objectives are a mistake," I repeated, wanting him to extrapolate on his stated purpose. I figured chatting couldn't hurt, as long as I didn't get suckered into reviving another god of destruction.

Lucifer smiled. "Your objectives..."

Cleric Vagram blinked into position behind him and swung both swords inward. Lucifer stiffened in surprise and thrust out his staff to block a blow but he couldn't handle both. Bronze bit into his side.

> Ambush!
> [Vagram] dealt 32 damage to [Luc1f3r]

My jaw dropped as Lucifer rolled forward. The air around him pixelated. His body digitized and blinked out. Vagram grunted a word of prayer. A beam from the heavens shone down, bathing the small island in holy light. Pixels blinked like popping light bulbs. Lucifer reappeared mid retreat, eyes wide.

"I will cut out that silver tongue, devil!" seethed the cleric. "All your ilk are dead. You are the last."

Lucifer's eyes flared. "I am the *first*." His staff slashed the air before him.

"No," I muttered, but there was no hope of bottling this explosion.

A blue beam of energy blasted Vagram in the chest, slamming him to the ground and leaving a crater in his breastplate. The cleric cast another healing prayer. He was still under a severe disadvantage from the warden's curse. Not dead but distracted, and Lucifer was going in for the kill.

I dashed forward and swung my spear. Lucifer rolled clear, black witchwood knocking me in the head. I stumbled. A battery of icicles passed me. Lucifer ducked and folded his cloak over himself. The silver runes flared as they were impacted, absorbing most of the damage, but not all of it. I couldn't believe it. All this time I'd thought Lucifer was invincible. He growled and whipped his blue magic around at Izzy.

I leveled the spear and nailed him with a deadshot. I'd been aiming for his neck but somehow he rolled away. My weapon bit into his shoulder and he yelped.

You dealt 22 damage to [Luc1f3r]

Instead of falling back completely, he twisted to the floor, bringing his staff back around and sweeping my legs. As I fell, a giant meteor of ice crashed down, forcing him to lunge to the side in haste.

"Fools!" he snapped. "Nightwing!"

The dragon leapt into the sky, distracting me for a second. Lucifer flipped to find Vagram on his feet, burned white tunic, smoking breastplate. The cleric's yellow curls were singed. Swords met staff in a series of quick clacks.

"Talon!" warned Izzy.

Mid stride, I confirmed Nightwing was still out of position. But he'd been the decoy. That became obvious when strong hands hugged me from behind. An unflinching grip heaved the dragonspear to my neck. My boots lifted away from the ground. I kicked for purchase. Another figure stood on the water behind Vagram. Not *in* the water, mind you, but *on* it.

Izzy cast a spell as a perfectly chiseled man in flowing cloth drifted forward. Her magic fizzled. Vagram slashed Lucifer's leg and knocked the witchwood staff free before the other man wrapped up the cleric. Izzy spun frantically, on the lookout for more reinforcements.

I could barely move against the unyielding grip, but I could turn my head to look into the face of my attacker. Two completely black eyes met mine.

Walking on water. Immune to offensive skills. I immediately recognized what they were.

"Oh my God, they're—"

"Angels," said Lucifer with a hiss as he calmly retrieved the staff of witchwood. He writhed in obvious pain. "You know, Talon, I'd never planned on disabling the pain filters on myself, but even I couldn't predict your ultimate actions."

I struggled in the angel's grip. "You would've denied yourself your own gift," I said mockingly. My zeroing out of the beta flags had affected Lucifer as well. Small miracle.

The devil flashed a smile. "Perhaps." Without pomp, he placed the glowing end of his staff on Vagram's chest. The cleric's eyes widened a split second before the explosion of light. After that, the angel let him slump to the rock.

"Put away your weapon," said Lucifer to Izzy. I gritted my teeth as the wounded dragon flapped overhead. She saw no other choice and did as instructed.

Nightwing landed hard in the water on the far side of the island.

"There," said Lucifer, regaining his ever-knowing composure. "*Now* we can talk."

"The two angels they sent to hunt you," said Izzy. "You've hacked them, somehow."

"It was not an easy thing, believe me, but they are fallen now. AI apostles, since you wouldn't have me."

I swallowed nervously. Nothing was good about Lucifer owning a pair of angels. In my short time battling a single one, I'd found them to be indestructible and unbeatable.

Overpowered security protocols. Call it sacrilegious if you want, but I worried about them more than Nightwing and Lucifer combined.

The devil took in the salty air and frowned. "I hadn't expected it to come to this," he admitted, "but I should have known. After all, you handled Orik head-on as well. The afterlife is full of surprises."

"Sorry to rain on your little murder parade," I spat.

His lips tightened. "Maybe this is my fault for choosing such a polarizing moniker, but you really must stop looking at me as the engineer of all of Haven's problems. I am not a cog, merely the grease. You, Talon, are a cog. And Izzy. And the crusaders and the pagans. All cogs of varying sizes, spinning round and round for the great machine. And do you know who winds this clockwork spectacle?"

"I've listened to your anti Kablammy vitriol before."

"Ah, yes. The Church of Capitalism."

Izzy wrung her fingers. Her eyes dashed from me to Lucifer, to Nightwing, and to the other angel. This was about as tight a bind as we'd ever been in. Even I didn't have a plan anymore. But Lucifer liked to talk, so I let him talk.

"Now you're gonna explain how you're here to help us," I said through gritted teeth.

He chuckled lightly. "The evidence is there, if you would only look. The very dragonspear at your neck was unlocked by none other than Nightwing. If you recall, it was his acid breath that dislodged it from the old statue atop your tower."

My face displayed defiance instead of surprise. Lucifer was always sharing the small truths to push the big lie. He was making out that he'd given me the titanslayer to strike down Orik and save Stronghold, but that was pure fabrication. I'd seen his face when the cyclops was raised. Lucifer was just as surprised about the god's existence as everyone else.

"Do you know," started the devil, "why I broke into the Oculus in the first place?"

"Same reason you broke into the Great Well?"

He was taken aback. "That wasn't my doing."

"You expect me to—"

Lucifer slammed his staff to the ground. Blue fire radiated outward in a shock wave, washing over us. I didn't notice any effect but it was a showstopper.

"You'll hear me out," said Lucifer, losing his patience, "or I'll instruct the fallen angel to break your neck."

I gulped. It was strong leverage.

"Now," he said, smoothing his robe, "while you were busy worrying about what the saints would do while we were in the Oculus, I was busy altering the machine. And do you know what I did?"

The rage in my face bowed to curiosity.

"I added a cog." Lucifer stepped close to me. "Adaptive code, Talon. Remember your work? The evolution it allows players in Haven? I added a cog to allow NPCs and monsters access to the same adaptive code routines that we all have. I allowed them to *think*, Talon."

I frowned.

"Of course, the change couldn't be suddenly acted on," he explained. "The goblin horde had their mandate. The boggarts wanted their god. Stronghold would've been their enemy no matter what. But as the days passed, the pagans grew more opinionated. More pragmatic. Their opinions divided and their ranks splintered. Their desire to exterminate humanity waned. Essentially, they'd been gifted free will."

Lucifer held the staff to my stomach. The action was unnervingly similar to the blow that had downed Cleric Vagram. Izzy flinched and Lucifer wagged a finger. She relented but slipped the jagged frost wand into her palm behind her back.

"Isn't that the basic right every one of us deserves?" posited Lucifer. "Freedom of choice? I've done nothing but remove the yokes and the blinders. Handed out the hard truths. And I've given them the ability to choose."

"At the expense of Stronghold."

He paused. "Perhaps. It's always the extremists who act first —that's why they're extremists. But you were there to defend your city. I never fought you on that."

I grumbled. He was damned convincing when he wanted to be. Almost made me wonder why we were fighting him. "So... what? We're all good friends now?"

He smirked knowingly. "I wouldn't go that far. Many goblins are still bloodthirsty, but that's mostly due to their leadership. Generals like Azzyrk still roam the countryside calling for your death. Nothing wrong with that, I suppose. It's the natural order. Every named instance in this world now gets to make that choice. As for the generic NPCs and mobs, well, their progress may be slower."

That bull's-eyed the questions I'd been stewing over lately. AIs could be sentient. Or, at least, they could evolve past the boundaries of their original designs. It could mean chaos.

Anarchy.

Natural order.

"Yes, Talon, you must ask yourself: Have you *really* been fighting on the side of the angels?"

I gritted my teeth. "I've defended the people."

"You have, but the gears you now churn: what is their purpose? You've stolen the crown of the wild king. One of many relics which grant mantles. Mantles are more powerful than you think."

NPCs and mobs with mantles. It was Lucifer's hack that had enabled the possibility.

"King Theoderic was always programmed to be a free spirit. An outlier. Once granted actual free will, he seceded from the bloodthirsty goblin horde and made a home for his people. I look on him as my first successful proof of concept. This is the symbol you wish to cast into the Salt Sea?"

I was speechless. I'd had reservations about the quest ever since I first got my hands on the crown, but Lucifer's words spelled it out so plainly. The wild king was just a protector of his people, no different than me. Except, in his case, *I* had been the bad guy.

"You didn't know about Orik," I said bluntly. Lucifer pressed his lips together, not wanting to admit ignorance, but I knew it was true. "You were just as surprised as I was when the boggarts summoned him from the mountain. Waking the NPCs and mobs was your goal, not destroying Stronghold."

Again, he didn't answer. Imagine that: Lucifer wasn't the big bad.

But I still wasn't sure of that. And *nobody* was painting him a good guy. Waking up the AI could still be disastrous for Haven, and the act alone didn't speak to his intentions. Lucifer and his natural order didn't care about Stronghold's fate one way or the other.

Izzy and I, Lucifer, and the two angels stood on that little island as gentle waves lapped the rock. The midday showdown had turned into quite the conundrum. A big part of me wanted to hear what the devil had to say, but I couldn't help wondering if I was being seduced by his words. He'd tricked me before.

Then again, he *had* opened my eyes. This was a tough decision. It would've been much clearer if he'd had a red tail, a forked tongue, and a pitchfork in hand.

"Okay," I said warily.

Izzy's eyes fell on me. "Don't listen to this. He's telling you what you want to hear."

"What if it's the truth?"

Her cheek twitched. "It probably *is* true, Talon. *That's* the trick."

I grunted. Ethical dilemmas were easier on paper. I'd walked headfirst into Lucifer's manipulations before, following the truth like a dangled carrot, ignoring the truths I didn't see.

"I'm willing to listen," I maintained.

Lucifer smiled.

"But only if you call off the angels."

His face soured. "Given the previous hostilities, that is no longer wise."

I hissed. "If we're to be allies, we need to trust each other. You need to tell me the whole truth, and you need to call off your dogs."

The devil mulled over my words with a frown.

"There will be no trust," breathed Vagram from the ground.

All eyes turned to the cleric as he sputtered back to life. He should've been dead, right? But he pressed to his hands and knees, clutching the bronze crucifix. Golden light shone from the artifact as Vagram heaved in laughter, his face hidden behind a tuft of hair.

"I am sorry, devil. There will be no alliances here. Only your annihilation."

Lucifer waved a hand and the angel standing behind the cleric stepped forward. Vagram spun and brandished the cross. The angel stumbled backward as if blinded. Afraid of the light.

"These are holy beings," spat Vagram. "They're unable to hurt holy men, despite your trickery." The cleric lurched forward.

Lucifer whipped his staff into motion and met Vagram's dual blades. I tugged against my angel's grip, but it was steadfast. I had to get me one of those crosses already.

"A little help here," I called, but no one noticed.

The black dragon screeched and lumbered around the island toward us.

"Lucifer," called Izzy. "Let Talon go."

The devil rocked his staff against Vagram's sword and knocked the other away. I struggled against the locked arms around my neck.

"Let him go!" ordered Izzy, Nightwing bearing down.

I'd had enough. Skills were completely useless against angels. Anything offensive would sputter out without effect, as Izzy's magic had. But defensive and neutral maneuvers weren't necessarily deactivated. Dash was a traversal move. As long as I didn't use it as a charge, it would work. It had in the past.

Still in the death grip of the unholy watchdog, I triggered dash straight at Lucifer. I'd been hoping to wrest free. Instead, I took the angel along for a ride. We slid six feet across the rock, right into the fray.

Nightwing snapped his jaws and forced Vagram into retreat, but the cleric wasn't afraid of the dragon, just cautious and tactical. As they squared away and I suddenly breached Lucifer's space, the devil spun around and rapped me square in the stomach. Blue light flashed.

Stun!

73 damage

I choked through the pain. Everything converted to slow motion. Izzy shivved Lucifer with her frost wand. A spark of damage rocked him, but the glowing gem atop his staff rammed her to the ground.

"Away!" shouted Vagram, shining the crucifix my way. The angel immediately released me and backed off. The cleric turned to the first angel. "Be gone!" Both beings backpedaled into the water, half dazed. Lucifer watched in horror as his security force abandoned him.

"Nightwing!" he called.

The dragon's tail whipped Vagram into the water as he slithered to his master.

"Not in this lifetime," spat Izzy, producing the winter staff and sweeping at the devil's feet. He hopped the strike and brought his weapon down hard.

Despite being released, I was still stunned from Lucifer's sucker punch. Movement, attacks, skills—I was locked out of all of them.

The witchwood staff slammed into Izzy's exposed back. Her face went rigid and her body froze over. Lucifer sneered in victory.

Then Izzy appeared behind him with her dagger.

The tip of Lucifer's staff was frozen into Izzy's duplicate. As the pixie moved in for the kill, the back end of the witchwood seared with blue heat. A shaft of light extended two feet from the end like a glowing dagger that pierced Izzy's belly.

Her face snapped to me. Blood spurted from her mouth. Her eyes went wide.

Surprise!
Critical Hit!
[Luc1f3r] dealt 67 damage to [Izzy]
[Izzy] is dead!

Her body collapsed to the ground, winter staff lying atop it.

"Bastard!"

I finally regained my mobility. Lucifer was already clambering onto his dragon. I attempted a quick dash but an error sound alerted me that it was still in cooldown. Vagram splashed from the water as Nightwing flapped great wings and took to the sky. I planted the spear at the apex of the island and vaulted to the sky.

My hands missed the great dragon's leg by a foot.

Sheets of air beat down on us as Lucifer flew away. The two angels had receded into the Salt Sea. I cursed loudly as Vagram and I were left alone on the island, half dead.

Which was a fat lot better than Izzy. She was dead dead. I wandered to her corpse in somber shock.

"He killed her," I said, still in denial.

"And once again," said Vagram indignantly, "you allowed the fallen one to infect your ears."

"It's not that simple." I spun around to give the cleric a piece of my mind.

Two bronze swords impaled my chest clean through. I was so jolted by the betrayal that I could do nothing but watch.

```
Surprise!
47 damage
Surprise!
44 damage
```

"Bishop Tannen will be very disappointed in you," hissed Vagram.

I blinked, hatred welling in my eyes.

```
You are dead!
```

Well, ain't that a son of a bitch.

0850 Toxic Crusaders

I opened my eyes in bed, body tensed to maximum. As soon as I realized there was no more pain, I sank into the sheets. Glorious relief.

"Fuck!" yelled Izzy's muffled voice. "Shit!" There was a crashing sound. "FLURRG!"

My brow furrowed. Flurrg?

I hurried from my room and down the staircase to the common den. Izzy was a five-foot tornado wreaking a swath of destruction. Cursing, kicking, knocking anything over within reach. Kyle's beer pong table was sideways on the floor. Chairs and plants upturned. Kyle sat on the sofa, glum and holding out an empty hand. His beer bottle was wedged into the flat-screen he'd been watching. The movie was paused on a shot of a chubby kid kicking Wolfman in the nards.

"Uh..." started Kyle carefully, "did you just say flurrg?"

The pixie spun on him with a pointed finger. "I can say whatever the flurrg I wanna say!" She kicked over an ottoman. "And if you say differently I'll—" She paused as I entered the room.

Kyle didn't notice and spoke at the opening she gave him. "I was just trying to tell you the good news."

Izzy ignored him and watched me in shock. "What?!?" she exclaimed, incredulous. "You didn't salvage my gear?"

"I was about to..." I scratched the back of my head. "Vagram fucking betrayed me."

Her face smoldered. I couldn't tell if she was more mad or crestfallen. "I dropped my winter staff! That means it's out there in the middle of the Salt Sea, in the hands of Lucifer or Vagram or whoever the flurrg passes by!"

I squinted sideways at her. "Did you have a mini-stroke in the last two minutes or something?"

"Don't you get it? My staff is gone!"

I swallowed. Crap. I hurried to survey my inventory.

"What is it?" asked Kyle.

I blanched. "I dropped the dragonspear."

Their eyes widened. We all looked around. "Are we even allowed to be in the tower anymore?" he asked.

"Not just allowed, moron," she snapped. "We're locked down in here. For the next twenty-four hours. While you've been doing nothing but drinking and watching TV, our whole lives have changed." She visibly shook, stomped over to the flat-screen, and put Wolfman out of his misery with a showery crash of sparks.

I blinked slowly. Was I still the Protector of Stronghold without the dragonspear? Worse, would someone else inherit the title? Lucifer had mentioned how certain relics granted mantles. Bishop Tannen had obviously wanted the holy weapon, and now his top cleric had it.

I sank to the floor. Now I knew how the wild king felt.

Stripped of his crown. Had I stripped him of his mantle? I double-checked my inventory to make sure the stag skull was still in my possession. Yup. I dared not remove it, but it was safe in the satin bag, small comfort though that was.

"Lucifer doesn't have our gear," I reported. "Vagram backed the angels off. Lucifer flew off on his dragon. Vagram was the only one left. Practically dead, but he was the last one standing."

Izzy scowled. "And knowing his healing ability..."

I rubbed my face. "We're so totally screwed right now."

A chime and a notification interrupted me.

Your gear has been salvaged!

The same surprise was plastered on Izzy's face. We both dug into our menus.

"It's back," she said. "The winter staff."

"The dragonspear too!" I tightened my hands around the magnificent weapon. "But..."

"Who?" she finished.

"It couldn't have been Vagram," I assured. "There's no way he'd return the weapon to me."

Kyle shrugged and butted in. "Maybe it was Lucifer. He could've come back and killed the cleric, right? You said he was pretty much dead."

Izzy shook her head fiercely. "Lucifer might be a lot of things we don't give him credit for, but there's no way he's the type to give up power like that."

"It's the only explanation," I said.

"No way."

I didn't press the issue. I could only imagine how pissed she was at him for killing her. Izzy was prideful about stuff like that. And hey, it's not like I was immune. I couldn't wait to peel the skin from Vagram's face.

"So this isn't a total disaster," hedged Izzy, "but we still lost 25% of our silver."

I canted my head. "Giving 10% to that banker player doesn't sound so bad anymore."

"Unless he decides he'd rather have 100%."

I grumbled and checked my silver count. The loss stung, but we were still rich. As long as we didn't have repeated encore performances of this mishap.

"So that's settled!" pronounced Kyle, hopping to his feet. "Now that the drama's over with, I can tell you how things have been going with me."

"Nobody cares," buzzed Izzy.

"Come on, bros. You left me alone for two days. You know Dune's been looking for you?"

"Not important now," I stressed.

He sucked his lips and took a smoldering breath. With a wave of his hand, the broken TV and beer pong table fixed themselves. He did need to physically return the chairs and plants to their original locations, however. When that was done, he went to the fridge and popped open a Mountain Dew Code Red and a can of stacked chips.

"Seriously, bros," said Kyle. "I found something really cool."

I sighed. "We've all seen the endless can of Pringles, Kyle."

He was about to retort when the sound of marching boots

echoed outside. The three of us exchanged exhausted glances.

"Not again," muttered Izzy.

We transferred to the top of the tower. At the last second, I realized I might not be able to zone outside, but we were strangely allowed to.

"It's some kind of overlap between inside and outside," mentioned Kyle. "Like a patio. I noticed when I was on lockdown. I had full access to the grotto, remember? I just couldn't step beyond the outer gate."

I nodded absently. It was a curious exception that hardly mattered at the moment. We strode to the battlements above Bishop Tannen at the head of an army. The gold crucifix atop his helmet resembled Vagram's artifact. As he saw us, his nasally voice rang out.

"Talon the betrayer and Izzy the witch."

The surrounding mass of refugees murmured quietly, surprised to see us back. Izzy and I crossed our arms in perfect unison.

"The reports of your failure," drawled the bishop, lingering on that last word, "are troubling."

"We failed to bring Lucifer to justice," I admitted. "We didn't foresee that he'd have two angels working for him."

"That is not what troubles me, *great* Protector. My cleric, Vagram, has respawned in Oakengard. He claims to have been killed by your treachery."

"That's a lie."

Bishop Tannen didn't let me extrapolate. "The good cleric claims many sins on your part," he continued. "That you endangered the holy mission in a greedy attempt to fulfill a side quest." The crowd squinted at me. "That you bartered openly with the fallen one, the great devil." Some audible gasps. "That you found counsel from the likes of a criminal overlord and the very same boggart witches who ordered the attack on Stronghold."

"That's twisting what happened."

"Is it?" he asked magnanimously, turning to the displaced residents of Shorehome and the crusaders in black tunics. He watched me pointedly. "Where is Colonel Grimwart?"

I cleared my throat. "Grievously wounded, but alive. He should be riding to Stronghold as we speak."

"If we can take you at your word."

"You can. I've been nothing but honorable to the people."

"And what about to the goblin menace?" he asked with a grin. "Are the goblins in the streets of Shorehome your enemy or not?"

My gaze wavered. "It's more complicated than that." I tried to outline the logic but was immediately met with vitriol from the crowd.

"You see?" asked Bishop Tannen proudly. "It is as I said. The so-called Protector of Stronghold is a traitor!"

Curses fired up from below. "He's the devil's consort!" and "He's in league with the fallen one!" and more generally "Goblin lover!"

Crusader Reputation -50

Kyle shrugged. "It was a good run."

The bishop waited a long minute as the accusations grew

more profane. He didn't call for temperance. He didn't chide the people on their language. He let the unrest build to the most dramatic point possible, making it look like the whole city was against me.

The truth was, none of these people knew me. None of them had stood and fought for the sanctity of Stronghold. These men and women had fled from the goblin threat. These were crusaders who'd been indoctrinated against them. There would be no reasoning with them, at least not while led by someone as charismatic as the bishop.

Finally, Tannen raised his arms and calmed the crowd so he could speak. "It pains me to say this," he mourned. "It really does. This man *did* defend a good city. But he has undeniably been in league with the devil. Unfortunately, these reckless actions have lost us Shorehome."

Spittle sprayed from angry mouths. I worked my jaw as I watched the beginnings of a riot.

"Talon threatens the sanctity of the holy city. His allies will attempt to overrun Stronghold just as Shorehome was overrun. He claims to be a player of the people, yet enjoys special privileges, gifts from the devil. The saints have failed you, good people." Tannen turned to me. "The crusaders can abide it no more."

Atop the tower, our faces darkened as Tannen mobilized the army.

"He can't attack us in here," muttered Kyle in disbelief.

My teeth ground together. "I think he's gonna try." I pulled the dragonspear into my grip. "Let's get ready for a fight."

A hundred blades slid from their scabbards. Hardened

soldiers in plate armor readied in formation. Bishop Tannen's golden eyes lingered on me, sparkling through his helmet. He raised a single arm to the sky.

"We need to fortify the door," said Izzy.

Tannen watched me for a dead moment and then smiled. "To the Pantheon!" he cried. His arm shot down and the mass of crusaders spun with practiced precision. The knights marched away from Dragonperch, toward the main thoroughfare leading to the capital. City watchmen stared in awe as the army moved past them.

"They can't do that," said Izzy, aghast.

"They can," I returned. "Lucifer gave NPCs free will."

"Wait, wait, wait, guys," said Kyle, hands signaling time-out. "What's happening right now?"

I gritted my teeth. Izzy and I watched, unable to leave the tower as more than a hundred armored knights marched on the Forum. I snorted when I realized the angels could only activate against rogue players, not NPCs or mobs. The saints would be defenseless against so many soldiers and the legionnaires wouldn't mobilize fast enough.

"What's happening," I said through a sneer, "is the next phase in Tannen's plan. His plan from the start."

"Which is?"

"To take control of the Oculus, the city, and maybe even the game."

Kyle upturned the can of Pringles to his lips and chewed nervously.

0860 The Invisible War

The three of us sat twiddling our thumbs in the war room. It had been exactly three hours and forty-seven minutes since we'd respawned in the tower. I knew this because I was staring at the countdown timer in my open menu. Only twenty more hours of this before I could do something.

Izzy and Kyle weren't finding the wait entertaining either. Even though we were all bunched to one side of the long war table, we barely spoke. Our failures said enough. What more could we add?

The war room was one of the more impressive spaces in Dragonperch. Located on the top floor just beneath the roof, the huge table was circled by open windows, providing a strategic view of the city. The one blind spot was the protruded wall over the steps. The dusty bricks of the wall were faded except for an elongated octagonal shape. It would've been a good spot for a flat screen.

"Those sons of bitches," said Izzy unhelpfully. She'd been rightfully seething the whole time. I desperately wanted to aim her thoughts toward a more pragmatic venture, but I was coming up empty.

"I know," I said. "I never trusted Tannen for two seconds, but I can't believe Vagram betrayed us like that."

"Come on, bro," said Kyle. "He's a priest, right?"

"Sure. What does that mean?"

"It means you can't trust anybody who can't drink a beer."

I rolled my eyes. "That mantra must make you *extra* trustworthy."

"Sure, whatever. Laugh at your buddy Kyle."

"Dude, you were watching *The Monster Squad*."

His face went beet red and his tone serious. "I'm embarrassed you had to see that, bro, and I'd appreciate it if we never mentioned it again."

Izzy hissed. "I don't get it. What's happening out there? Why aren't there any game notifications?"

"You heard what Papa Brugo said," I explained. "Haven's in financial trouble. They need to launch and they need everything to be smiles beforehand. The game messages are unreliable at best, propaganda at worst."

Kyle snorted. "Just like the great Protector of Stronghold."

I sighed. The one good part about the downtime was we got Kyle caught up with everything, even my deep-rooted fears about my mantle and our cause. I didn't like being anybody's puppet. I had worse thoughts too. What if I was the bad guy? I did my best to stave off such thoughts. This conflict wasn't as simple as black hats and white hats. I glanced at my timer. Three hours and fifty minutes elapsed. Great.

"Anybody want some nachos?" asked Kyle.

"How are you still hungry?" snapped Izzy.

"I dunno. It beats staring at a table." The brewmaster stood up to go but paused as he faced the wall to the stairs. He pondered the blank spot against the brick. "Huh."

Usually Izzy and I wouldn't have noticed a sidelong utterance like that, but there was literally nothing else going on. We both turned to him expectantly.

"No, nothing. It's just—" Kyle swallowed and took his seat. "You guys finally wanna hear about what I've been up to?"

Neither of us objected. Hey, we had the time. Kyle leaned forward, suddenly excited.

"Okay, check it out. I don't know if you've noticed, but I've been feeling a little left out since we moved in together."

"What're you talking about?" I asked innocently.

"Don't pretend it's not true, bro. Real talk right now. Let's face it: You and Izzy are the famous heroes. Notorious. Dangerous. Badass."

"You've helped."

He raised his hand to stifle another teamwork speech. "I'm not saying I didn't contribute, but that doesn't change things. We all know I've just been along for the ride. It could be anyone else sitting in my place, for instance, if you'd randomly been assigned another roommate."

I crossed my arms, unsure of his conclusion. I mean, sure, we can't dictate who we meet and I could've been paired up with any number of players, meaning Kyle still might've been bumming around and content at level 2. It was impossible to say.

"You have the dragonspear," said Kyle. "Izzy's happened

upon the winter staff. The damned thing was hidden in her freaking room! You know how many times I've tossed my quarters looking for *my* legendary weapon?"

Izzy and I frowned in sympathy. It sounded sucky all right.

"But that's okay," he asserted. "I'm used to not being special. I'll trade having great friends for being great any day of the week. But I still want to be useful, right? So I invested in this brewery to make things happen for myself."

"I recall us *all* investing," noted Izzy.

I shushed her. "That's great, Kyle. That's all we ask of you."

Even Izzy nodded at the sentiment.

Kyle stood up dramatically. "Well, *fuck that*. Because while you guys were gone I had a lot of time to really think. And as I was cleaning up my mess downstairs and doing a lot of soul searching, I found my own legendary artifact!"

Kyle produced an ornate turquoise vase with a plug and set it down on the table. "Read it and weep, bros, 'cause the brewmaster's back in business."

We looked wide-eyed at the beautiful bottle. [Dorfin's Decanter of Luminous Fluids]. Izzy and I burst into mocking laughter.

"What?" asked Kyle, swiveling his head from me to her. "Seriously, what? It's cool. Check it out."

"Dorfin?" choked out Izzy as she repeatedly banged her fist on the table. "DORFIN?" I wiped tears from my eyes.

"Dudes, ignore the name. This is a legendary item. Examine it."

I stifled my laughter to take a closer look.

[Dorfin's Decanter of Luminous Fluids]
Unique, Unbreakable
Once daily, this decanter fills with a randomized potion useful to the bearer.
+2 Essence
+3 Craft
Potion (once per day)

"Well, it's certainly unique," I offered.

"It's awesome is what it is. Yesterday, I tested it out. I turned invisible for a whole hour."

"You were alone in the tower," said Izzy. "How do you know you were invisible?"

I chuckled and turned away so I wouldn't piss off Kyle.

"Mirrors," announced Kyle to more choked laughter. "During my cleanup of the brewery, I found an old mirror wrapped in a cloth. Nothing special about it—it doesn't even have a description—but it reflected everything except for me."

I clenched the table and swallowed all remaining merriment. "Okay, Kyle," I said, trying to keep a straight face. "That's actually pretty cool. I'm happy for you."

"Yeah?" he asked, nodding positively.

"Yes," agreed Izzy. "Really."

"Right on," he said, pocketing the turquoise decanter. "It's funny. You guys were being such assholes before I wasn't even gonna tell you, but then I noticed this discoloration on the wall matches the shape of the mirror and decided to come clean."

My eyes flitted back to the bricks. The undisturbed shape on the wall was a big rectangle with trimmed corners, giving it eight edges. It was a unique enough shape to suggest that whatever Kyle had found belonged on this wall.

"You found a mirror that used to hang in the war room and you didn't put it back up?" asked Izzy sharply.

"It's really wide," he said in defense. "And heavy. I didn't wanna break it."

"That's cool," I said, impressed because Kyle's strength was higher than mine or Izzy's. "Let's get it now."

Kyle led us down to the brewery. As he'd mentioned, the underground grotto technically had us zoning outside, but it was an in-between space that didn't violate the terms of the lockdown. Several of the rooms on the ground floor and under it were stockrooms. Some were still locked. We followed Kyle past his newly organized rows of brewing equipment to a shelf built into the back wall. Storage concerns had forced us to keep unsorted oddities in the corner, but they were sorted now. All except for one item, an unremarkable mirror shaped like an oblong octagon. The thing was huge and ungainly and wouldn't go into our inventory. I wasn't surprised Kyle had let it sit. Between the three of us, we successfully navigated it all the way upstairs. We hefted it to the discolored space on the wall and hung it on the double hooks.

"Hmm," said Izzy as the three of us stared at it, hands on hips. "It really opens up the room."

I backed away and sat on the war table. Within seconds, the mirror blinked and turned on like a TV. A sideways diagram of Dragonperch appeared onscreen and a blinking icon was followed by the phrase, "Powering up."

"Whoa," mumbled Kyle.

After a minute, the header "Sanctum Master Panel" appeared. Menu options populated.

Status

Map

My jaw dropped. Dragonperch was some sort of base of operations.

"What's a sanctum?" asked Kyle.

I shook my head slowly.

"Looks like there's plenty of space for more menu options," observed Izzy.

I checked the status screen. It was fairly empty as well, but there was something called a socket manager. I selected it and was brought to a new screen. An outline of Dragonperch was overlaid with various slots.

"Feather socket, wind socket, earth socket," I listed. "What are these things?"

Izzy shrugged. "You're the expert gamer."

"But you're the lore expert."

"There's no mentions of sanctums or sockets on the wiki."

Kyle slapped my shoulder. "Hasn't your buddy Saint Peter mentioned this to you in one of your private conversations?"

I shook my head. "This kind of stuff isn't supposed to be unlocked so early. I have a feeling he'd be happier if we're in the dark."

Kyle grunted. "Bet it was the saints who hid the mirror in the first place then."

I checked the only other available option, the map. As with the other screen, it had only rudimentary information. It showed the rooms which we'd already unlocked, from the roof down to the sub-basement. Parts of the tower still undiscovered to us were grayed out.

"Huh," said Kyle again, ominously.

"What?" said Izzy and I in unison.

"Nothing," he answered. "It's just... I thought the grotto was the bottom of the tower, but this door looks like it leads further down."

Izzy frowned. "You're right. Those are definitely steps, but it's unlabeled and the door's locked."

We studied the map for a time but no new information was gleaned. I exited out and tried exploring other options. "This is cool," I hedged, "but I don't think we can actually *do* anything yet."

"What about the tower library?" asked Kyle. He was looking at Izzy since that was her domain.

"Less than half that floor's open to us, and I'm pretty sure I've skimmed all the subjects I can. I'll double-check, but I bet I'm gonna need to hit the Great Library in the Pleasure Gardens. That's Haven's Library of Alexandria."

"Except you're grounded for another twenty hours," pointed out Kyle. "I wouldn't mind taking a trip."

"Ugh," she replied. "Knowing you, you'd spend all your time playing eighties movies in the media room."

"Don't knock it till you try it. Besides..." His face went straight. "*There can be only one.*"

"He's right," I said. "It's worth a shot. But don't stop at the library. Check with Trafford as well. He's savvy for an NPC. Hears things. Maybe he could help us somehow."

"Roger that."

"And find out what's happening in the capital," added Izzy.

I nodded. "But be careful. We don't know how the crusaders will respond to us now."

"Relax, bros," he said confidently. "All I need is a quick chug, and I'll be virtually undetectable."

Kyle produced his decanter of luminous fluids and slugged it down. He immediately transformed into a woman wearing a tight bikini. Izzy and I blinked back disbelief.

"What?" he said. "I'm invisible, right?"

"Umm..." I stalled. The bright red bikini was straining against huge breasts and perky nipples. I went for a finger poke but Izzy slapped my hand.

"Fake," she said pointedly.

I snorted and looked away. "Uh, you should probably put a coat on," I told Kyle.

He looked down at himself. "What, I'm not invisible?" His hands rubbed his chest and his boobs jangled around.

"You can't tell?"

"No. I look normal, just like before."

Izzy smirked, turned off Dragonperch's control panel, and spun Kyle around to the mirror. "Wanna borrow my panties?" she asked. "They cover up more than that thong you're wearing."

"To be fair," I reasoned, "he has a nice ass."

"It's actually making me jealous," she agreed. "Do you do squats to get that kind of definition or what?"

"Oh, fuck you guys," spat Kyle. He stomped away from the

mirror as we hooted.

"Look on the bright side," I reasoned. "It's not invisible, but no one will know who you are for the next 60 minutes."

Izzy choked on her disdain. "Yeah, he'll blend right in. As long as he doesn't flash that stripper body anywhere."

Kyle's face lit up. He spun around, went right back to his reflection, and pulled his top down. "Nice!"

Izzy kicked him. "Gross. Go wank it in your own room. That should leave you with 59 minutes of a disguise."

"Really?" he said excitedly, considering the idea. Then his face dimmed. "I wouldn't even know what to do."

"Big surprise." She kicked him playfully. "Put something on and get outta here."

Kyle flipped through his inventory. His familiar armor and equipment blinked on but he settled on something less conspicuous. A drab tunic with a hood.

"Much better," said Izzy.

He smiled. "You're so jealous it's not even funny."

She went to kick him again, this time *not so* playfully, but he hurried down the stairs.

"Be back soon, bitches."

We were alone in the room for a moment before I asked, "Is it wrong that I'm turned on right now?"

0870 Lockdown

A couple of hours later, we reconvened in the war room. I squinted out one of the north windows.

"What the hell is that?" I asked.

Izzy shook her head. "You can keep asking, but my answer's the same."

We had tried to relax, but the more time passed without hearing from Kyle, the more nervous we got.

"We *really* need to get on the ball with partying up." I sent Izzy a reinvitation and she accepted.

Since we were on lockdown, we could read email messages but couldn't send anything out. The same was true for wikis and such. Although the world spun fine without us, we were essentially dead to it. The only exception to that rule was party chat. Dying kicks you from the party, but as long as you reconnected with the member who respawned, everyone was free to chat back and forth. We'd forgotten to group up before leaving for Shorehome, and we'd forgotten again before Kyle went on his secret mission.

"He'll be fine," assured Izzy, returning to the table.

I remained by the window keeping watch. "How can you say

that? His stripper disguise would've worn off an hour ago."

"Trust me. That's a good thing. A guy like that with breasts like those would only get into trouble. He's better off as his frat-boy self.

"Well, what if he *did* get in trouble as Destiny or whatever he took for his stage name?"

She chewed her lip. "It's possible, but he hasn't sent an email and he hasn't respawned here. My bet is he hasn't encountered trouble."

Fair points. This was why I respected Izzy's counsel. Then again, email wasn't as inconspicuous as party chat. It was entirely possible Kyle was in a bad situation and didn't want to make it worse by digging through his menu.

I occupied myself by returning to the question at hand. What the heck were the crusaders up to? A contingent of them had organized in the Circus. This was the oblong sports track reserved for races and other exciting events. Bishop Tannen had commandeered it as his base of operations. Now the crusaders were hauling wagons of lumber inside and hammering away at some kind of platform. A stage of sorts.

I rubbed my eyes and sighed. "I'm gonna go topside and see if I can get a better angle on that thing."

The Circus was across the river and the thoroughfare, so the extra flight of stairs wouldn't likely make a difference. Since its walls were low stands dand Dragonperch was almost two hundred feet in the air, it was still a great view. I just needed a pair of binoculars.

I climbed the steps and zoned out to the sunlight above. That's when I realized how odd it was we could see through the windows from the war room. Even though I'd been inside, limited interaction with the exterior was allowed. As far as I knew, most of the normal homes in Stronghold didn't have windows like that. Despite said windows, it was significantly brighter on the roof. As my eyes adjusted, I wasn't surprised to see the saints resting against the parapets.

"Why am I not surprised?" I grumbled.

Saint Loras wore a reserved frown but Saint Peter jumped to his feet. "It's about time, Talon. We've been waiting for you to show."

"Something stopping you from hopping down a flight of stairs? We've been in the war room most of the time."

"We don't enter private homes, Talon. Read your privacy clause. I told you that the last time you accused us of meddling."

I remembered the conversation a few days earlier. I'd blamed the saints for snooping and getting Kyle exploded, but it had turned out to be that traitor Errol. Spying for ways to get me alone, no doubt. No wonder the pirate had volunteered to be our guide. At least the crusaders had been just as gullible as I had been.

"I believe you," I said. "But I'm pretty sure you've been digging around Dragonperch one way or another."

Peter arched an eyebrow. "Oh?"

"We found the sanctum master panel."

The two saints traded grim expressions. Loras managed to frown deeper somehow. "What have you activated?" he asked.

"Nothing yet. Something about sockets. Either of you mind filling me in on those?"

Their gazes strayed to the floor.

"Of course you won't help."

"It's not that we don't want to," said Peter. "But Dragonperch can't really do you any good now. It takes time to build resources."

"I'm stuck here till tomorrow."

"That's not nearly enough," cut in Loras. He pressed his dark hair forward on his head. "You need to understand what's going on, Talon. Shorehome turning into a dumpster fire is one thing, but we simply can't have that happening to Stronghold. This is the first city. This is the core of Haven."

I scoffed dismissively. "You even know what happened at Shorehome?"

"Of course I do. The city was my responsibility."

"And you left its people behind to fend for themselves."

Saint Peter turned to his colleague, happy to see some of the blame deflected.

"The wheels were already in motion," snapped Loras. "The blame for Shorehome doesn't fall on me. It falls on the two of you and your mishandling of the pagans. Shorehome's not a fortress. The town's defense is limited and relies on its residents, many of whom fled."

I contemplated the Shorehome refugees camping out in Oldtown. "My point is that everybody ran early."

"That's the best time to run," he returned pointedly.

"Granted, but it means you don't know the truth about the city. You know what you *thought* was going to happen, not what actually went down. The goblins didn't attack. They moved in peacefully. Shorehome's a giant melting pot. All those displaced people down there can go home." I turned to my guests. "It's the saints that are no longer welcome there."

Loras flexed his jaw. "That will need to be corrected another day."

"Why? What needs correcting? A bunch of people and AIs living and working together. What's so magical about your oversight that they need it?"

The vein on Saint Loras' forehead bulged and his face went maroon. "What do you think is happening there? The rumblings of a democratic society? You know nothing of Shorehome. Right now the man running the city is no governor or administrator. He's a criminal gang boss."

"Papa Brugo," I said, cutting him off. "We've met. The Papa had a lot of interesting stories. He has the Squid's Tooth."

Loras went white.

Saint Peter stepped in. "And what do you think of this man's equitable leadership?" he asked instructively.

I shrugged and turned away, which was the same as saying "not much."

"So we're agreed that Shorehome is a problem," reiterated Saint Peter. "But it's not the most pressing one. Lucifer may have acquired the Squid's Tooth for the Brothers in Black, but our very own Eye of Orik is now under threat." He paused to give weight to his next words. "Bishop Tannen has staged a coup and is now in possession of the soulstone."

"He controls the city?" I asked.

"Pretty much," answered Loras. "I don't like to admit it, but we're powerless. Somehow Tannen has overridden his original programming. He intends to destroy the pagans, and he'll do anything to achieve that directive."

"Including overthrowing the saints," I finished.

He nodded grimly.

"What's the city watch doing?"

"They're heavily outnumbered," said Peter.

"That's what happens when you open your gates to an army."

"The crusaders have been shuffling into Stronghold for days now, little by little. They weren't a problem until Tannen and his crew of holy catechists pushed in. They hit us unprepared."

"It's not just the army," pointed out Loras. "The displaced Shorehome residents are desperately seeking assistance. Any change to the status quo is a good one, in their eyes. Change symbolizes hope. They're cautiously optimistic about crusader leadership."

"Because they've seen where saintly leadership has led them." I shook my head. "They ran from the goblin horde when it was a shadow of itself. We don't need to worry about the sailors. They won't fight. Do we have enough legionnaires to strike the crusaders?"

"Perhaps, but we've called them off. A civil war would weaken Stronghold past the point of recovery. It's in everybody's best interests to play along for now."

I worked my jaw. A devout, priest-led coup would likely come with stringent changes. The zealots would outlaw drinking and cursing. They might go as far as banishing mystics from the city entirely. The priests had replaced the saints and the crusaders had replaced the city watch. Guidance and policing all in one.

"What are they doing with the Eye?" I asked.

"Nothing as drastic as what happened last time," said Peter.

Loras grunted. "Tannen won't allow the pagans to sack the city. The Eye is just his appropriation of command." Their faces were dark.

"You're lamenting your loss of the city," I said, "but you're forgetting something I've already told you. Stronghold, Haven—they're not yours anymore."

Saint Loras creased his brow. Peter wasn't as defiant. He'd seen the transition firsthand. Had a longer time to marinate on new paradigms. And, if I'd pegged him right, he was a bit more open-minded. For a saint, anyway.

Loras took in a slow breath, curling his lips as a thought amused him. "I wouldn't celebrate our ousting just yet, Talon. Don't forget that we've called a truce with you. Do you think the good bishop will be as kind?"

I snorted. "What's he gonna do?"

"That depends on what he wants. And right now, the only thing I can guarantee he wants, besides the absolute destruction of the pagans, is the dragonspear."

I looked at him gravely. "Why?"

"He wants to lead Stronghold, but he also wants to be its Protector."

"He can't do that, can he? *I'm* the Protector."

"The bearer of the spear is the Protector."

"It's more than that," added Saint Peter. "Wearing the mantle of Protector is no doubt a great honor, but I fear he wishes to use the relic for something more disastrous."

"Peter..." warned Loras. The chided saint swallowed and faced the floor.

I searched their faces. "What?"

"Ridiculous speculation is not why we're here," insisted Saint Loras. "We've told you what the bishop wants. Whether or not an NPC can actually wear a mantle is irrelevant. When he comes for it, Talon, will you give him the spear?"

"Hell no."

"Then we'd better come up with a response."

Wild scrambling caught our attention below. We all leaned over the battlements to see Kyle weaving between groups of squatters.

"Help!" he yelled. "Hurry! Open the doors!"

A block behind him, a score of black-clad crusaders pursued, swords drawn.

"I've got to let him in," I said.

"And we need to go," hurried Loras. "We can't draw undue suspicion on ourselves. Peter?"

Saint Peter blinked out first, followed by Saint Loras. As I was about to hit the staircase, the warded door of Dragonperch swung open. Izzy must've heard Kyle's call. I continued watching from above. The men and women in the streets hassled Kyle and gave him trouble as he passed, alternately clearing the way for the crusaders. But, although they gained on him, Kyle beat them and zoned inside. The heavy door swung closed before the knights arrived.

I breathed a sigh of relief and simultaneously pondered how unfair what I'd just witnessed was. Kyle was a player, unable to use combat in town. That sounds like a fine rule with honest police. But when the crusaders were acting as town guards and looked ready to kill, well, that complicated things quite a bit. Who polices the police?

The knights below reached the door and ordered us to open up. That wasn't happening, of course, so they grew more irate. One of them was reckless enough to slam his sword into the warded wood. A blue flash threw him on his ass. His allies stared at the smoking rune with equal parts awe and distrust. We were clearly safe for the time being.

But safe wasn't all it was cracked up to be. I was unfamiliar with the politics of Shorehome, but their leadership transition had been peaceful. Stronghold, on the other hand, was occupied by an overpowering force. And here I was, the Protector of the city, outmanned and outgunned.

It didn't matter. I couldn't sit idly by and watch everything go to shit.

Even if I was the only one who could fight, I was determined to do it. What had the saints called for? A plan of attack. That sounded all right by me. I hurried down the stairs to find out what Kyle could tell us.

0880 Revelations

We met halfway on the steps before I grumbled and realized they were headed to the war room. That *was* what we were meeting about, more or less. War. A plan of attack. I turned around and hiked back up the stairs, happy that minor physical tasks weren't a strain in Haven the same way they might be in the real world.

"First thing's first," I said as we spread out around the table. I sent Kyle a party invite and he accepted.

"Oh yeah," he said. "I bet I lost a lot of XP while you guys quested out to Shorehome."

"Nothing we didn't lose ourselves when we died."

Izzy sucked her teeth. "At this rate we'll never hit level 10."

"What happened out there, Kyle?"

His face slackened. "Bad news bears, bros. My disguise worked great, but once it wore off I was stuck. Bishop Tannen has crusaders patrolling the streets."

"Are they Big Brother now?" said Izzy with a snort.

"I dunno. They're not really hassling people much."

"They took over for the city watch," I explained. "I had a powwow with the saints on the roof just now. It seems the good bishop stole the Eye of Orik and assumed command of Stronghold. The saints and the watch are staying out of the way for now."

"That's stupid," said Izzy. "Why?"

"To avoid all-out war. They believe a temporary peace will serve the people better."

"And look better to investors from the outside," she muttered.

"Nailed it," said Kyle.

I chuckled. "That's probably right."

Izzy exhaled sharply. "Wait a minute. Why'd he have to risk his neck out there if you could've just chatted with the saints?"

"Give the brewmaster some credit," said Kyle, leaning against the war table. "This kind of recon required eyes on the ground."

Izzy huffed and sank into her chair. "I can't wait till this Call of Duty phase is over."

"It's no phase. And believe me, CoD brings better experience to the table than your Candy Crush high scores."

Her eyes pointed like daggers. "Care to back up that challenge in the Arena?"

"You realize that right now I technically have more XP than either of you?"

Her face darkened as she realized the truth. We'd all died at level 9. Difference was, it had been a few days since Kyle's lockdown. He could've picked up a pittance of experience doing any number of things around town and be ahead of us. We were still at the level floor.

"Let's get back on track," I said, habitually rapping my spear against the floor. "What did you find out, Kyle?"

He sidled into his chair, leaned back, and wrapped his hands behind his neck as he smiled. "Well, Trafford confirmed what you already said. Tannen is the new leader of Stronghold. But the way I heard it, there was no violence. The saints are still working hand in hand with the catechists to keep the town running smoothly."

"There's no way," I said. "That has to just be the public face they're putting on the takeover. They can't have players revealing the loss of the core city on Everchat."

"There's more. The crusaders are putting overtime into recruiting efforts. Front Street has crusaders up and down looking for fresh soldiers to assist the war effort."

I frowned. "We knew that too. Lash joined them days ago."

"What's next, genius?" mocked Izzy with a disparaging eye roll.

"Don't rush me," he returned. "Um, the city watch is still active, but they've been relegated to helper roles. They still man the walls and watch the gate, but no more street work. They staff the jail but the policing and charging is now handled by the crusaders."

We scratched our heads and pondered the news. "Could be useful. Maybe. With any luck, the city watch is still on our side."

"That's the bad news. Gladius is one of the occupants of the newly overcrowded jail."

"What?" exclaimed Izzy. "He's the head of the city watch!"

"Tell me about it," said Kyle. "Apparently, Gladius didn't mobilize against the crusaders or anything like that, but he spoke his mind quite a bit and Tannen wasn't having it."

"What a dick," I said. "Who's in charge of the watch now?"

"Some priest is all I know. Another NPC from Oakengard."

"Not even a local," spat Izzy. "Cronyism at its worst."

"Is that like Bronyism?" asked Kyle. " 'Cause that's pretty awful."

"What?" replied Izzy, confused.

"Kyle's just trying to act cool after the *Monster Squad* debacle," I said. "Ignore him."

His face deflated. "That movie didn't age well at all."

"You get anything else from your close call?"

He puckered up. "Yeah, actually. Two things. One is some of the quests have been updated on the down low. Trafford's a questkeeper so he stays on top of those things. You know, he'd never admit it with crusaders around, but they make him nervous. He's been dealing their pagan quests without problem, but now worries that something's going on."

"Like what?"

"See for yourself. Check your quest log."

I twisted my lips and went to the menu.

Dethrone the Wild King

Quest Type: Fetch

Reward: Unknown

To dethrone the wild king, turn his crown in to the Bishop of Stronghold.

"He changed the terms of the quest," trilled Izzy.

The "Bishop of Stronghold." I rapped my fingers on the table. "He wants the crown for himself..."

Izzy snorted. "Are you high? That's a pagan artifact."

"You saw Vagram's insistence about it at the crags, didn't you?"

"Yes, but that was so he could make sure it was destroyed. It was obvious to anyone with sense that you were having second thoughts."

I blinked innocently. I thought I'd worn a brave face about it. "It has to be more than that. He wants the crown for himself."

"Or he wants to stop the wild king from having it," offered Kyle.

"Then the original quest terms to destroy it would've been enough, right? He wants the mantle. There's no other explanation."

The three of us stared at the table, but Tannen's workings weren't obvious. We were butting up against game elements unready for prime time. The titan, the dragonspear, the mantle, the sanctum—even our levels were above what the beta had been intended for. But Bishop Tannen, being an AI, likely knew the game mechanics intimately. Even the wild king seemed to have a better idea of the crown's potential than I did. I didn't doubt for a second that Vagram saw it too.

"You said there was something else," mentioned Izzy. "Two more things from Trafford. What's number two?"

"Yes!" Kyle's eyes lit up. "This one's good news for a change, but maybe not so important for now. While I was hiding out in Trafford's shop, I mentioned the sanctum master panel to him." We leaned forward expectantly. "He doesn't know much about sanctums but *has* heard of them. He confirmed there's a book in the Great Library about them written by Master Abodin."

"Now we're getting somewhere," said Izzy. "Did you find it?"

Kyle blinked dumbly. "Find what?"

"The book!"

"Oh, sorry, I thought I made that clear. I never made it as far as the Pleasure Gardens. The crusaders caught me on the way and I had to book it back here."

"That's"—Izzy jutted her indigo lips out—"disappointing."

I shifted in my chair. "Anyone have more information to share?"

"Nope," reported Kyle.

"Izzy? You didn't find anything in Dragonperch's tomes?"

She shook her head, still in thought.

"Okay."

We sat there in silence, unsure how to punctuate the proceedings. Izzy and Kyle both looked impatient for different reasons. I probably did too, but it was just nerves. Everything was moving so fast that I was worried about missing something. I idly scrolled through my menu to double-check everything when I saw the direct messages from Dune that had come in over the last couple of days.

2 Days Ago...

Talon,

Don't forget the Wicked Crow tonight. I'll buy you a pint.

- Dune

1 Day Ago...

Talon,

Kyle told me you left Stronghold again. Things aren't pretty around the Forum. The black knights are pushing their weight around. I'm doing my best to stay out of trouble, but we need you here ASAP. Get back to me.

- Dune

Damn. The ranger had been more prescient about the city's troubles than I had. Protector, my ass. I wondered if things would've played out different had I never left on Tannen's quest. It was hard to say.

I couldn't reply back to Dune on lockdown. The workaround was having Kyle send him a message for me, but I didn't want Dune swinging by with the crusaders downstairs. To be honest, it was getting harder and harder to think by the hour.

I snapped out of my reverie, jumped to my feet, and stretched my back. The others cast distracted glances at my sudden movement, but were likewise lost in their heads.

I moved to the window. The sun had gone down without me even noticing. A few knights waved torches as they inspected the area. I decided to put Dune off another day.

"It's been a long day," I announced, rubbing tired eyes. "I don't know about you, but I could use a shower. Let's marinate on ideas tonight and agree on a plan of attack in the morning. There's no getting around the twenty-four-hour lockdown, and it'd be hard to do anything with those crusaders milling about down there anyways."

"Good deal," said Kyle. His chair squeaked against the floor and he kicked to his feet. "*Now* I'm making nachos." Izzy hissed and shuffled out, leaving Kyle with a heavy sigh. "I don't get it. Am I the only one who didn't forget about Taco Tuesday?"

I smiled and gazed out the window. "Go on, Kyle. You deserve it."

He went to work in the kitchen, but I was busy pondering how dangerous my town had become. I strained to focus on the Circus in the distance. The hammering of the construction project continued into the night, but the area was too dark to make out.

0890 Hide & Sneak

I'd expected a fitful time in bed but rest came easy that night. Something about hiking and camping in the wilderness for days that made the plush mattress hypnotizing. It rejuvenated me, body and soul.

By morning Oldtown was back to its usual self. At least, its usual self of the last few days. Drifters still loitered below, but the black-clad knights were nowhere in sight. With any luck they were busy with security elsewhere in town.

Afternoon struck with a whimper. An uneventful day seemingly continued. The harbinger of change, of course, was the expiration of our lockdown timers. The three of us gritted our teeth and headed into the new and improved Stronghold (now with 100% more bishops!).

The plan we'd come up with wasn't a nuanced one, but it would send a message: Take the Eye of Orik back from Tannen. We'd kill him if we had to, but the soulstone was the priority. Getting the city back under saintly control would start the swing of momentum back to the good guys.

That said, recovering the Eye wouldn't solve all our problems. The city was under saintly control when the crusaders assumed command in the first place. If they took it once, they could take it again. But that had been against an unawares populace, before the ramifications of their presence were realized. More to the point, the Protector of Stronghold had been temporarily kicked off the chess board. With the dragonspear added to the city watch's might, I was confident we could stall the advance of any opposing force.

And therein lay the single wrinkle in an otherwise straightforward fight. I knew the saints would back my play, but to guarantee the loyalty of the city watch, we had to talk to Gladius. We were hoping his men would listen to him even though they were the ones keeping him under lock and key. Ironically, that played in our favor.

The jail is against the north wall of the city. Lots of distance between us and them. Although Oldtown appeared safe, we didn't take chances. We snuck out through the underground grotto gate, forded the river, and kept to the small local streets of the player communities. From our hilltop vantage, we could see that the crusaders were indeed conducting a recruiting drive in the Foot. We moved through the outskirts of Stronghold without incident before turning north and heading through the slums.

"Patrol," I warned in a clipped whisper. We retreated into a small alley and hid behind large bales of hay. The squad of six knights marched by, black tunics waving in the wind. So far we'd seen a few patrols of crusaders and not a single watchman, which was concerning.

"You know," said Kyle, still ducking behind cover, "someone on the message board pointed out that hay balers didn't actually exist in medieval Europe."

Izzy's face went flat. "You must've had a boring couple of days without us."

Large farming machines or not, the spooled stacks of hay had done their job. The patrol disappeared down the street, allowing us to continue on our way.

"Wait," called back Izzy, refusing to leave the alley. "Wait a minute."

I traded a glance with Kyle, checked up and down the street, and returned to a crouch in the alley. "What is it?"

"What would we have done if they'd seen us?" she asked.

I grunted. "Probably a tornado spin to disorient them, followed by a deadshot on their commanding officer. Then I would've—"

"No," interrupted Izzy. "I mean, what could Kyle and I have done?"

I hiked my shoulders. "I don't know. Let me take care of business, I suppose."

"That's my point. We can't fight in city limits. Not when attacked by the legit law, and the crusaders are the law now. We're no good to you."

Kyle crossed his arms. "It's a little late to turn around."

"I'm not turning around. I wanna break off into the Pleasure Gardens."

The slums, ironically, sat flush with the most extravagant landscape in Stronghold. The Pleasure Gardens were gaudy and green and perfectly manicured, with all the creature comforts any medieval king would kill for.

"The Great Library," she stressed. "Trafford's book about

sanctums."

"You wanna get that now?" I asked sharply.

"I just think it's another thing that could help. We don't know what Bishop Tannen's about. We don't know what he's doing or how powerful he is. And he *has* to be stronger than Cleric Vagram."

I grimaced at the probable truth. Vagram's holy power had definitely been awe-inspiring. What kind of man would he serve?

"We can't underestimate him, Talon. If we can use the sanctum to beat him—if there's even a possibility—we need to look into it. You said he wants the dragonspear for a reason. Maybe this is it." She clenched her jaw. "You know I like to kick ass, but I'm worthless here. My next favorite thing is brushing up on game lore. We're running into a lot of questions these days. I can find the answers. I just need the right access."

I sighed. "You think you can just walk in and ask for it?"

"I can get in, one way or another."

"It's not a good idea to split up," interjected Kyle. "You said it yourself. We can't fight. That's why we need to stick with Talon."

"It's too important," she countered. "Besides, we're connected on party chat again. I'll shout the second something goes south. It'll be fine."

Kyle grumbled, still on the fence. I didn't like it either, but I trusted her.

"She's right," I concluded. "We need to try. Kyle, you and I can get to Gladius by ourselves." I rested my hand on Izzy's shoulder and met her eyes. "You be careful, okay?"

She smirked. "It's not like I have any more XP on the line."

I chuckled. The pixie sprung to her feet and hopped the alley wall, making for the grounds of the Pleasure Gardens.

"And then there were two," I said solemnly.

"Don't be so dramatic," chided Kyle. "Eyes on the prize. Stay frosty."

I grinned and weaved north through the side streets. The slums created the perfect cover. Conditions were bad and mostly filled with quest NPCs and such. Not a whole lot to police because the petty crime remained confined to the neighborhood. Tannen had luckily deprioritized cleaning up the worst streets in the city. The locals minded their own business and there were no crusaders in sight.

After some creative pathfinding, we ducked behind a wagon across the road from the jail. Our good fortune continued. While there was moderate activity at the main entrance and the gated prisoner entrance, most of it involved everyday guards of the city watch. A single crusader did pop into the building to check on things, but once he left we didn't see a black tunic in sight.

"What are we doing?" blubbered Kyle.

I turned to him. "It's called recon. I thought you were an expert at military tactics."

He shrugged. "You're the scout."

"Damn right. I'm just getting an idea of who's moving in and out of the building, how often the crusaders swing by, and which entrances are best."

Kyle jutted his lower lip out and watched the building. "Looks pretty straightforward to me. The whole point is to trust the city watch, right?"

"Sure, but we can't just walk through the front door in broad daylight. If even a single guard is afraid to shirk orders, the alarm will be raised. Alarms don't give sympathetic soldiers many options."

"You're probably right." He dug through his inventory and pulled out a couple of Slim Jims.

"Two?" I asked.

He bit into one meat stick and waved the other my way. "I know you want one."

I grumbled. I really wanted to take the moral high ground on this one, but the rubbery meat won out. I snatched it from him with a nod of thanks and gave in to sweet spicy goodness. We chewed and continued our surveillance.

"No way," said Kyle. He pointed to a newcomer to the prisoner gate. "They got Phil." Except for the minimal loincloth, the Hillside local wore nothing except for two pink socks.

"Now they've crossed the line."

Finished with our quick snack, I bade him follow and walked half a block past the jail. We found a good alcove in the entrance of a locked storage warehouse.

"That's our way in." I pointed to the left side of the building. "The side door. It looks like a staff entrance. We'll bump into fewer people and be less public that way."

Kyle nodded. After a few more minutes of watching I was satisfied with the plan. We'd sneak along the lumber yard beside the jail and approach the side entrance out of sight. We made sure the coast was clear and started across the street. A knight in white armor turned the near corner at the worst possible moment.

"Talon!" exclaimed Lash, surprised. She halted suddenly, a

few feet away from us.

"Oh, hey, Lash," I said casually. "Don't sneak up on people like that."

"You shouldn't be out here." She smoothed the white cross on her black tunic. No more sash, she'd gone full crusader now...

I arched an eyebrow. "What do you mean?"

Lash's helmet surveyed the block. It paused on the jail. No way she thought we were here for the lumber yard. "Izzy with you dorks?"

"Nah," said Kyle gruffly. "She had a thing."

I swallowed. Izzy and Lash were kind-of-sort-of friends. I would've gone for a lie placing Izzy nearby. It would've been more likely to keep the white knight on friendly terms. I tried to read Lash's face through the full helm but it was in shadow.

"You're level 8," noted Kyle. "How'd you swing that so fast?"

"I told you to get in while the getting was good, didn't I?" She hissed. "You guys are real dumbasses, you know that? Didn't you get the message when the crusaders chased this dweeb home yesterday?"

"What message?" asked the dweeb.

"By order of Bishop Tannen, your party isn't welcome to wander the streets."

I scoffed. "That's ridiculous. We live here. It's more our city than his."

"Not anymore," she said. "This is crusader territory now, like Oakengard."

"Stronghold is Stronghold," I assured her. "I'm the city's Protector."

The helm nodded in acknowledgment. "That's true, but—"

A block behind Lash, a crusader and a priestess strolled into view. I grabbed Kyle's breastplate and shoved him back into the storage alcove. Lash's hand went to her cleaver at the sudden motion, but she relaxed when she saw we weren't fighting. Besides, she was a player, not a guard. She couldn't have drawn her weapon if she'd wanted to. At least I thought so.

"Lash," I said through gritted teeth, "you and I both know that decree is bullshit. I don't care what color cloak you have on, you can't give in to that bullshit order."

The white knight turned to see who'd spooked me. A priestess with flowing blonde hair that could've been Vagram's female twin. The gold cross and white robe spelled out her fanaticism plainly. The crusader who escorted her looked like an average joe. He led a city watchman in shackles toward the jail. It was a path that would quickly intersect our position.

0900 Jail Break

◆━━━━━━━━━◆◆◆━━━━━━━━━◆

Lash turned back to us. "Talk about unlucky," she chortled. "Listen, Talon, don't make a big deal about this."

"You are *not* going to turn us in, Lash."

"No?"

"No," I said firmly. "No way. Not after what we've been through together."

She snorted. "It's not like we're party members or anything."

"Lash—"

I pressed into the alcove as the priest and the crusader sauntered by. Lash spun and leaned on the wall, completely failing at being inconspicuous but somehow escaping the notice of the crusaders. Kyle and I watched paralyzed in shock until the group entered the prisoner gate of the jail yard.

Kyle slapped his hand to his face. I breathed a sigh of relief. "We owe you one, Lash."

"Owe me doesn't begin to cut it," she spat. "You know how much trouble I could get in if they find out what I did?"

"Relax," urged Kyle. "We're the only ones who know and we'd never tell them."

She forced his back to the wall. "Well *I* should have."

I rested my hand on her shoulder. Considering I was 5'8" and she was almost seven feet tall, it was a reach. "It's over, Lash. They're gone. Let's just pretend we never saw each other, okay?"

Kyle had sunk points into strength lately and used it to push back against her. The white knight may have reached impressive heights, but she was still only the fourth highest-level player in town. Still, she could be trouble if she wanted to be.

"What's your problem?" barked Kyle. "What do you see in those brainless crusaders anyway?"

"You kidding, frat boy? They're an army. After Stronghold's cleaned up and recruiting is over, we're gonna take back Shorehome too. That'll be all three of Haven's towns under our control."

My face soured. Haven lore talked of nine fabled cities, but the Midlands was the only territory thus far released. Only three cities were currently on the map. The thought of Bishop Tannen in charge of the known world brought a shiver to my spine.

"Shorehome doesn't need liberating," I told her. "The goblins and humans are living side by side. Don't believe everything they're telling you."

She scoffed. "That's laughable."

"I was *there*." She paused. "Send Izzy an email and ask her if you want. She saw it too. Everything Tannen says, he does to amass more power."

Her heavy shoulder plates rose in a shrug. "Fine. Maybe that's true. But these guys are in charge of Haven right now. They trust me because I joined up way before they took over. If it comes down to it, I'm siding with them." She sighed heavily. "Look. I'll see what I can do. If I tell them what a good fighter you are, that and your rep should land you a good place in the army."

"We don't wanna be in their army," scowled Kyle.

"That's the best deal you're gonna get." Lash turned to check the jail-yard gate, obviously worried the priestess would emerge and catch her with us. "Don't be stupid. The only reason I'm letting you slide is so you have time to think it over."

I wondered if it also had something to do with her being outnumbered two to one. I shook my head in silent disappointment.

She smacked her lips. "Don't act like a sap. What did you think we were, BFFs? We respect each other, that's all. Besides, if we are friends, *you're* the ones putting *me* in a tight spot. Don't do it again." Before I could say anything, Lash stormed off and around the block.

"What a bitch," said Kyle.

"She's just covering her ass. She *did* let us go."

"She won't do it again. You heard her."

"Talking a big game is different from actually turning us in."

"Yeah, right. I guarantee you, we're toast if she catches us again."

I worked my jaw. The priestess and crusader exited the jail yard, and Kyle and I ducked deeper into the alcove. They took another route to wherever it was they were going and were quickly out of sight.

"Okay," I said. "Every minute we stay out here is a risk. We'd better get this over with as soon as possible. Let's go."

We hurried across the street and followed along the lumber yard. The side of the jail building was clear and we snuck up to the door without a problem.

Well, a problem *did* present itself when we found the door locked.

"Can you do anything about it?" I asked Kyle.

He hefted the handle a few times. "Nope. I could get through it if I really wanted to, but it would make a big boom."

Damn. Kyle was talking about a repeat of the grotto explosion. "Big bada-boom," I muttered.

"What about the window?" he asked.

The thing was two stories up. The good news was, at that height, it wasn't secured with bars. Unfortunately, it was too high to vault to. I searched for handholds to attempt to scale the wall, but the reinforced concrete structure was too smooth. I scowled and looked around. My frustration didn't last long.

"Maybe it's time to finally test Haven's physics simulation."

Kyle followed my eyes to the long beams of wood stacked in a neat pile. We hustled over and dragged one to the wall. It was heavier than it looked. "Okay," I told him, "just hold your end tight and press me against the wall. I'll do the rest."

"The rest of what?" he asked. "You sure you know what you're doing?"

"Of course. I saw this on YouTube once. I'm practically an expert."

I braced myself against the opposite end of the pole and placed one foot on the wall. "Ready?" He nodded. "Push."

Kyle forced the pole and me into the wall. I drove my back against the pressure, lifting my second foot off the ground and placing it higher on the wall. The two of us strained in the impossible position.

Agility Check...
Pass!

I smiled and took a step up the wall. It worked and I took another. As I walked up the surface it became easier going, although the pole began to shake. More of the weight was on Kyle now. But we didn't have far to go, and he was putting his 22 strength to good use. As he moved toward the jail and I slid up, the pole straightened vertically and led me right to the window. I jumped in and released the wood beam.

"Get out of sight," I called down. "I'll just be a minute."

Kyle nodded, dragged the lumber back to the pile, and hid behind it. I turned to check my surroundings, ready to activate my sneak skill.

The warden of the jail looked up from his plate of food, a fork frozen inches from his mouth.

"Uh..." I stalled. "I can explain."

"Oi!" He dropped the fork and jumped to his feet, sweeping the sword from its scabbard. I drew the dragonspear in a blink and readied a deadshot. Then the warden hugged his blade across his chest in salute.

"The Protector of Stronghold," he said, exasperated.

I blinked a few times before planting the butt of my weapon on the floor and standing tall. "It is I," I announced in a commanding voice.

[Warden Jorah] shuffled nervously. "What's this all about, then?"

I swallowed and scrunched my forehead. "Um, official

Protector business." He didn't react. "Protecting," I added helpfully.

Jorah lowered his sword. "This about jailing the city watch?"

"How'd you know?"

" 'Cause it's a right travesty, it is. Jailin' me own brothers."

I eased my face in relief. "Tell me about it. I'm told you have Gladius in here."

He nodded in shame.

"I need to talk to him."

"Well, it's about damn time," he snapped. "I've been waiting for someone to talk some sense around here. Follow me." He swung his door open and stepped down the hall. It took me a second to follow. I was still in disbelief over how easy this was.

Jorah peeked down a flight of stairs and waved me down. We moved from the third floor to the second.

"It's shameful," he complained. "A police force marchin' the city wearing black. What are they, a gang of cutthroats?" Jorah proudly lifted his head. "Give me the olive green of the city watch any day. Now *that* is a color that inspires confidence."

As we walked, I made a mental map of the place, wondering if the cells were on the first floor or a basement, knowing the jail yard was on the other side of the building. I estimated the number of guards we might encounter on the way.

The warden stopped at the first door, turned a heavy key, and presented me with Gladius.

"The commander's a special guest, he is," said the warden with a touch of reverence. "Prisoner or no."

Gladius sat in his "cell" enjoying the same roasted meat as Jorah. The head of the city watch smiled as I shuffled in.

"I'll make sure you aren't interrupted," said Jorah. "When you're done, you can sneak out through my office. I'll be downstairs holding the fort."

I gave him a quick nod. "Thanks." Jorah closed the door, but he didn't lock it.

"Talon," said Gladius, standing and locking my arm in the traditional Roman greeting. "What brings you here?"

"Even the warden knows what brings me here," I said. "Kyle's waiting outside for me. We should get you out as fast as possible."

He tightened his jaw. "To what end?"

"What do you mean? To kick Bishop Tannen out of Stronghold."

Gladius sat and took the most solemn swig of ale I'd ever seen. "I agree with what needs to be done, but I can't help you do it."

I stared at him like he was crazy. His stoicism faltered for a moment and he explained.

"Talon, I have a duty to the legions of men under my command, just as they have a duty to me. I won't rally them against an unwinnable cause."

"This isn't unwinnable. If we stand together nothing can stop us." He swallowed glumly. "Don't forget that we defeated a titan together."

"You don't understand. Bishop Tannen is the de facto ruler of Stronghold at the moment. It is literally impossible for the watch to raise arms against him and his."

"But he usurped the saints!" My tone revealed how ludicrous I thought that was.

"And that would've been the time to fight him," he returned. "But the saints counseled otherwise. It was practically too late to stop him once I heard of them storming the Pantheon. And once control was ceded to him, once he had the artifact, we became powerless to do any more. Our job is to guard the city, its people, *and its leadership*. Our hands are tied."

I cursed the arbitrary rules of the simulation. Some parts of Haven seemed so realistic, but other systems hadn't advanced much from their rudimentary MMO precursors from years before. The faction system in particular seemed to cause more trouble and chaos than it prevented. It fomented war and carnage. Maybe that was the point.

"At least stand up and get out of here," I pleaded. "Talk to your people. Convince them who the real enemy is."

"They already understand." Instead of standing, Gladius picked up his knife and fork and sliced another juicy morsel.

I didn't say anything. I *couldn't* say anything. For a minute, I paced his gracious accommodations back and forth and rubbed my forehead. I tried working through the angles but couldn't find one. The exercise was calming, at least. When I finally spoke, I was placid. Measured.

"So what can you do to help the cause?"

"The best the watch can do is not kill you on sight." He pulled down some more ale. "Those are orders they don't wish to carry out. The crusaders, however, may not fully appreciate what you mean to this city. And those cursed priests are bloodthirsty against anyone who doesn't view the world as they do."

"At least we can agree on that," I said pointedly. I moved to the door but paused, my back to him. "If we manage to return the Eye to the saints..."

"Then the watch will immediately mobilize against these usurpers. We'll be outnumbered, we'll need your help, but now we've seen the price of inaction. Believe me, a lot of good men are biding their time in the jail yard below. You return the Eye of Orik, and the city watch will have your back."

I nodded firmly and left Gladius in his cell. Just as Jorah had promised, no one was around to accidentally run into me. I snuck out the window of his office and opened up party chat.

Talon: *Folks, turns out the plan is simple after all. We get the Eye back, we get Stronghold. It's time to make for the Circus.*

0910 Bookworm

Izzy cursed Talon's message. With all the craziness and overcrowding of late, the Pleasure Gardens were a popular retreat she'd taken considerable care to navigate. Now that she was actually in the Great Library, it was practically abandoned. Looks like players preferred taking advantage of the media rooms and the joys of the Scented Ladies. Whatever happened to curling up with a good book and escaping into your imagination?

Izzy crept along a low shelf. Even though the rows of books weren't populated with browsers, the Great Library was staffed with several stern librarians who took their duties *very* seriously. The NPCs were laughably stereotypical, too. Dark ponytails, sharp noses, tightly buttoned collars. Every single woman sported a pair of stylish prescription glasses. This was just another fantasy for boys. Izzy was practically waiting for one of the women to pull off their spectacles, let their hair down, and magically transform into a frisky-yet-demure sex symbol.

Silly as the librarians were, they'd report Izzy in a heartbeat if she let herself be seen. In order to keep a low profile, Izzy wouldn't be bothering with the normal procedures of "signing in" and "checking out" books. This was a stealth mission, and the pixie was glad her secondary attribute was agility.

After a young redhead returned to her desk, Izzy rushed into a back room reserved for administrative texts. She found a safe spot to relax and messaged Talon back.

Izzy: *Sorry, boys. I'm gonna have to sit that out too. In the middle of something here.*
Kyle: *Hope it's not one of those sexy-times romance books you left on the couch last week.*
Izzy: *Shut up, idiot!*
Kyle: *"Marked by the Billionaire Bear."*

She hissed under her breath. Of all the people she'd let her guard down around, it had been the frat boy. Show a soft side to someone like that and they'll never forget it. Izzy wondered if it would've been better or worse for Talon to see it.

Grumbling didn't help, so she focused on scanning the shelves. As Haven's premiere player eight months running, Izzy was probably more familiar with the Great Library than anyone else uploaded to this digital reality. Three floors high in a central atrium, hallway wings branching off in three directions, more furniture and fireplaces than you could count. She'd been over every inch of it numerous times. Still, the amount of arcane knowledge in the place was staggering. Browsing was one thing, but actually reading the tomes was another. It would take even an avid reader like her many lifetimes to get through it all.

That challenge, however, was a worthy one. Research was

key. The others liked to pretend she'd stumbled upon the winter staff through dumb luck, but they were forgetting the simple dictum: knowledge is power.

Izzy zeroed in on the shelf she was looking for. It wasn't as obvious as being labeled "sanctums" and for some reason the devs had decided to use a vague representation of the Dewey Decimal System rather than anything as powerful as a Google search bar, but she was in the right place. The texts focused on types of places and terrain, ranging from simple farmhouses to mystical churches and monuments. After finding and poring through several fat books by Master Abodin, she finally found a mention of sanctums.

The gist of the information was fairly obvious, even to someone who hadn't played a lot of role-playing games. Sanctums are player-run domiciles that can be purchased and founded. They provide various functions ranging from security to manufacturing and even trade. Her initial reaction was surprise, based on how boring the book made sanctums sound. Something told her Dragonperch was quite a bit different than the standard player upgrades.

Interestingly, there was a sideways mention about some sanctums being tied to mantles. That was one confirmation that all sanctums weren't created equal. Unfortunately, the text didn't expand on that information. No matter how much further she read, she found no specific mentions of Dragonperch or similar places.

What she *did* find, however, was information about sockets. Sanctums had various powers that were activated by the sockets, which reinforced her belief that there was more to

Dragonperch's control menu than was currently available.

Boot steps scuffed along the rugs. Hushed voices whispered back and forth. Izzy slid the book back on the shelf, rushed to the door of the current room, and peeked outside. Six crusaders fanned out in different directions. Commanding them was a priest in a white robe with a gold cross. He appeared to be more of a bureaucratic than a cleric like Vagram, but how well he could fight was relative considering her inability to draw weapons or use skills.

"You're sure the mystic is in this wing?" asked the priest quietly.

The redhead with the perky butt nodded. "I saw the bitch. *Nobody* takes my books without checking them out."

"Stand aside then, young lady. We'll find her."

"Don't damage the books," she instructed.

The priest spat on the floor. "I care not for these dusty volumes. Consider it a blessing the bishop hasn't burned this place to the ground yet."

The woman's face went ashen. She opened her mouth to speak, but the priest placed a hand on her chest and shoved her into a chair. Her hair dropped to her shoulders as her glasses fell off. Ugh, of course. She was pretty, too, but she wasn't stupid. The librarian quickly swallowed any objection.

Izzy ducked away from the doorway as the priest glanced in her direction. "Shit." Staying low, she crawled deeper into a row of books.

> **Izzy:** *Sorry, boys, I might have a problem here.*
> **Talon:** *What is it?*

Izzy grimaced.

> **Izzy:** *A priest and some crusaders have me holed up in the library. Gonna try to*

She sent the chat message without finishing as her eyes landed on a miscategorized book lying on its side. She was huddled into a corner and the tome was shoved on top of several other books on the bottom shelf.

"Check back there," called one of the knights. Another grunted in reply.

Izzy pulled the book into her lap and opened it. The entire book was about mantles. All kinds of them. Special titles with special powers granted by special items. Flipping the pages, she wondered if she could find mention of any specific ties to sanctums.

What she found instead plastered her eyes wide open.

Heavy boots stomped into her section. Izzy tensed. Unable to draw a weapon, she silently flipped the book closed and held it tightly in both hands. As the crusader rounded the corner, she lifted the tome over her head, ready to strike.

0920 Stealth Assassins

"She's not responding," I complained.

Kyle sighed. "You realize we can both see the same party chat, right?"

"Yes, but—"

"Just let Izzy be Izzy. It's too late to help her now. If she needs something, she'll tell us, right?"

I gritted my teeth. There was no use sending more messages. One was enough for her to notice. I'd probably just end up distracting her at a time when she least needed it. "I guess."

"We know she's still alive," he pointed out. "She's the toughest chick in the whole city. Even without her magic and toys, I wouldn't wanna be after her."

I chuckled but it came out as artificial as it felt. I wasn't sure he was right about anything other than it being too late to help her. She was in the Great Library on the other side of the city. Kyle and I? We were in a totally different level of hurt.

We crouched in one of the stables of the Circus. The racetrack was surrounded by low stadium walls full of seating, but the entire length of the building was functional. Any number of access doors and archways circled the perimeter. The Circus was an odd choice for the bishop's base of operations. What it had in grandiose space it lacked in security. A literal army of crusaders patrolled the grounds but Kyle and I had managed to sneak in anyway.

Only this far, I tempered myself. An empty stable with nothing in it didn't rate high on the list of the bishop's concerns. As we pressed deeper into the inner courtyard, things would change. I peeked around a doorway and recoiled.

"Looks like temporary barracks," I reported. "Three crusaders."

Suddenly, a chime notified me of an email. By Kyle's reaction, he heard the same thing, which would only happen if he also got the message. I opened my inbox.

> **City Alert:**
> Residents in good standing are invited to the Circus for a declaration by Bishop Tannen. Please attend at once.

Kyle and I searched each other's faces.

"What the crap could that be about?" he asked.

I shook my head wordlessly. Our being here had to be a coincidence.

"Suppose that means the building's done," said a guard in the other room.

"Well, then," announced another, "let's get off our arses and see to the crowds."

We readied our weapons as the men clambered to their feet, but they exited out the far side, leaving us alone.

"You get what this means, right?" I asked with a huff. "The whole town's coming to watch. All the guards will be here. This is no longer a stealth operation."

"Well," hedged Kyle, "it is until it isn't." He pressed his lips out. "What if this announcement is exactly what we need? A distraction. We can search Tannen's quarters while he's busy."

"You think he dropped the Eye of Orik somewhere for safekeeping? NPCs must have a limited inventory they can stash things in. Why would he not use it?"

"I dunno."

Hrm. It seemed like a long shot, yet it did present an opportunity. We could continue sneaking in shadows so long as we didn't go directly at Tannen. It was low risk, low reward, with the off chance of winning the jackpot.

All we had to do was keep quiet.

"That reminds me of something," I said. I opened my skill menu. Our bout of super leveling had recently left me with a few spare points to spend.

At first glance, there appears to be an abundance of skill points in Haven—at level 9 I had 20—but you quickly learn a couple of things. One, combat skills are a point sink. Each can be upgraded to level 3, which also requires the base weapon skill to be upgraded. Just my offensive deadshot and defensive crossblock ended up taking half my total allotment.

Two, special class skills tend to be more granular than in

other games. You can't just pick up three skills and be an expert thief. Case in point, sneak allowed me to move silently, but without hide I couldn't reliably escape visual detection. Additional refinements are available through skill purchases: ambush, backstab, steal—well, you get the idea. It all adds up to a ton of skill points, but it also encourages diverse play styles.

I still agreed with my initial intention not to become a super rogue, but I also preferred not to murder crusaders left and right. So I decided to expand my stealth tool set.

Subdue

Incapacitate unaware enemies without doing damage.

Spirit Cost: 18

Just in time too. A voice rang out from the previously empty room.

"Okay, okay," snarled a crusader, returning to the barracks. "Don't hafta tell me twice!" The gruff knight trudged within and collected a weapon. Kyle and I silently waited, ready to take him down.

The guard emerged right beside us, starting to turn the opposite direction but noticing something in the corner of his eye. By the time he had the wherewithal to do a double take, I already held my spear around his neck in a subdue attack. The guard tried to let out a bark but I constricted his airway. He struggled a little but eventually went limp. I released him and he slid to the floor.

Knockout!

[Crusader] is unconscious

Kyle looked down at the crumpled body and blinked. "How long will he be out?"

"It depends. Are we using real logic or video game logic? It's so hard to tell these days."

Kyle waited several seconds. "He's still not moving at all. I'm going with video game logic."

"Only one thing to do then." After looting him, I picked up his legs. "Wanna help me out here?"

He arched an eyebrow. "With what?"

"Hiding the unconscious guard, dude. That's what you do in stealth games. Haven't you ever played *Thief*?"

His face was blank for a moment, but then he lit up. "I get it. It's like *Splinter Cell*." He hefted the knight's shoulders and we carried him into the barracks. Bed cots were arranged in haphazard rows with wooden trunks of equipment at the foot of each. We opened the nearest one and stuffed the guard inside. It didn't close all the way so Kyle sat on the lid to give it an extra nudge.

"You think there's anything good in here?" he asked.

We turned and considered the other trunks.

We opened everything we could. I imagined the room from a bird's eye view and started at the top left, checking every chest in order. After the first few, my spirits dimmed. Sure, there was silver and the odd gem—we took that stuff, believe me—but the practical equipment was standard crusader fare. Plate, swords, maces—that kind of thing. Kyle upgraded his longsword and breastplate, at least, but it was by no means epic loot. When I'd checked the last trunk, I turned to see Kyle holding his turquoise decanter, eyes mashed closed, while he recited, "Stealth, stealth, stealth," to himself.

"Uh..." I looked around casually, like I was missing something. "What the fuck are you doing?"

"I have a theory," he said, waving his magical bottle at me. "The potion I drink has something to do with what I need—as long as I want it bad enough." He closed his eyes again and repeated, "Stealth, stealth, stealth." With that he uncorked the bottle and sent it down the hatch.

I blinked without fanfare. "Well, at the very least you don't have boobs."

"No way, bro. This is much better." He pulled his double crossbow over his shoulder.

It didn't look better than boobs to me. I took a second, but I got it. "How the hell did you equip that in town?"

"It says I'm an urban sniper, man. For the next hour, I can use my crossbow in city limits."

"That's absolutely amazing. Can you damage people though?"

He scoffed. "What kind of sniper can't dish damage, dude? I'm sure I can."

I canted my head. "Okay, then. I guess we're on the clock. Let's get moving."

He nodded. Then he blew out the gassiest burp this side of the afterlife.

"Wait a minute... Are those potions alcoholic?"

He beamed and recorked the bottle. "This thing really was meant for me."

I couldn't believe it, but if anyone could operate normally with a slight buzz, it was Kyle.

I moved to the next doorway and listened. Since I didn't have specialized auditory skills, I didn't hear shit. A peek into the hallway confirmed what I'd heard. Nothing. We crept down the long straightaway of the stadium's hall. Hurried boot steps grew louder ahead. Kyle raised the crossbow.

"Watch it, urban sniper," I whispered, pushing down his weapon.

I pulled him to the wall and we ducked into the nearest door. Luckily, it was just a grain closet. No one here.

"I don't know how I feel about killing crusaders yet. We can do this without bloodshed."

"But I'm a *sniper*, bro."

"Sometimes being a sniper means being all quiet-like."

He sighed, disappointed. Outside the door, the men conversed as they passed.

"Have you found the Protector, yet?" asked one.

"He must still be in his tower."

"Make no assumptions. Bishop Tannen wants maximum visibility on this event. He doesn't want to be made a fool."

"Understood, sir."

The treading feet faded into the distance. "I think we're getting close," I whispered. We proceeded down the hallway again.

From above, the Circus was shaped like a capped U. The southern entrance was curved and the east and west walls straight. We'd entered from the side and skipped the heavily guarded entryway altogether. At the top of the stadium, a flat building rose an extra couple of stories above the fray. The box seats of the Roman age. Knowing Tannen's penchant for glamour, I had no doubt his quarters would be in that section, but since that building was heavily guarded from the outside, we'd slipped in somewhere in between.

We waited until the hallway was clear, but it wasn't an all-or-nothing prospect. A lone crusader patrolled in and out and around, whistling to himself. Kyle and I needed to duck in and out of alcoves several times to avoid detection. At one point the guard walked right by the plant we were hiding behind. I almost triggered subdue but hesitated for some reason. As he strolled away I sighed, figuring we'd need to wait for his patrol route to loop to get another chance.

The guard marched two doors down and turned into another door. Multiple voices welcomed him inside. Another barracks, most likely. We were fortunate he hadn't seen us and alerted them. Though the door was still open, it obscured our position. Kyle and I hurried down the remainder of the hall and into the main residence.

The interior and all attending flourishes were much richer in the main building. The floor was decorated with hand-made tiles, the door frames sported detailed accents, and the walls were graced with reliefs of sporting events and fanciful fountains that spouted water. A large room which spanned much of the residence building opened before us. A high ceiling, staircases leading to overlooking halls on the north and south ends. A gargantuan chandelier made of swords and spears dominated the room at its heart. Sprinkling the walkways, and right beside us, were small fountains built into the wall. A jet of water poured from a pipe to the bowl, generating the soothing sound of a country brook.

"How's that for a VIP pass?" quipped Kyle. "This is definitely the place." He kept his tone low because a few guards rambled this way and that. "Now what?"

"These guys are watching the main floor and the back entrance. No one's counting on us already being inside." Indeed, we huddled beside a marble staircase that no doubt led to the quarters overlooking the stadium. "All we need to do is sneak upstairs without being seen."

"The room's wide enough that they have a decent view, though," he pointed out. "There's no place to hide on the steps."

I nodded and eyed the wall sconce halfway up the ascent. Without that candle, the stairway would be thrust into heavier shadow. The main chandelier in the room had many sconces, but it hung low enough to be on an equal level with the second story. The marble railing obstructed some of the light from the center of the room. If we just took out the local sources, anyone looking through the railing from the other side would see only darkness.

"You have an empty glass arrow?" I asked Kyle.

"Not an empty one."

"Okay, let me see one of your corrosives then."

He handed it over. The oily black substance inside was less likely to draw attention than his yellowish exploding cocktails.

"Does this open somehow?"

Kyle helped me with the tiny plug of arrow feathering. When

the thin vial was open, I poured the acidic concoction into the fountain. It popped and smoked a little, but emptied down the drain. A long discolored mark adorned the marble. I grimaced at the thought of defacing something so grandiose yet ultimately pointless.

I then collected the water stream into the arrow and plugged it off. Kyle loaded it into his crossbow and I pointed to the candle. "Think you can hit that, urban sniper?"

"You can keep calling me that as much as you want. It's not annoying. It's actually kind of cool."

"You're right. I'll stop. Can you hit the candle?"

He pressed his lips together. "Piece of cake, but it seems like a stupid plan."

"Trust me. I've done it a million times."

"Whatever, bro." Kyle leaned forward onto the stairs, braced the crossbow, took careful aim, and let loose. The glass popped in a spray of water that doused the candle.

"What's that then?" growled a guard from the main floor. Kyle and I froze in fear as the crusader stopped and looked around for a moment. "Eh, must've been the wind," he muttered.

Kyle's face filled with disbelief. "But the door's closed," he murmured.

I shrugged and headed up through the shadow. No point questioning these things.

The two of us weren't exactly master thieves. No hide skill in sight, and while I could move silently the frat bro behind me certainly couldn't. At the same time, we weren't dealing with state-of-the-art security here. This was a residence for galas or something, and everyone was busy setting up in the main stadium grounds. We made it safely to the second story without incident and turned the corner away from the open room and balcony.

The tiled landing led to a hall with doors leading up and down, like a hotel. It was obvious which one Tannen had moved into. Not only was his door the most extravagant—it was the only one guarded by a pair of knights. We peeked at them from around the corner, safely out of sight for now.

"How are we gonna enter the hallway without them noticing?" asked Kyle.

I chewed my lip. Without specialization, shadows wouldn't get us any further. I picked a silver piece from my inventory and waved it at my roommate. "Check this out." I tossed it onto the tile floor across the landing and pressed Kyle back into an alcove.

"Oi, what's that?" barked one of the guards.

"Huh. I didn't hear anything," said the other in a coarse voice. "You must be hearing things."

"Right. I haven't been getting sleep lately."

The two of them stopped shuffling and went still. I scrunched my face. Kyle chuckled but I was undeterred. I pulled out another silver coin and tried again.

"What's that there?" barked the first guard again. "You heard that?"

"I did. I did hear that." Their boots rapped around the hall. "I'm thinking it must've been the wind."

The first guard stopped. "Let me get this straight. You think the sound of a small object bouncing and jingling against the tile floor is the wind?"

"Well, the wind could've knocked something over."

"That's right. That's right."

"See? There's nothing to fear."

The guard grumbled. "Yer probably right. But I think I might actually do my job for once and look into it."

"Suit yourself," returned the other.

Kyle and I pressed into the alcove again as a single pair of footsteps neared. The other guard began whistling a tune at the door. The first turned onto the tiled landing and marched toward the noise with his back to us. I jumped on him and began to choke him out. The guy had some fight in him, though, and tried to shake me off. That was the moment I realized the subdue skill was no sure thing. I pressed tighter and wrapped my legs around his waist.

"H—" He tried to cry but it came out empty. I had his breath. It was only a matter of time. Meanwhile, the oblivious guard at his post continued his whistling.

The guard tried to flip me forward, but my legs were locked tight. He couldn't get me off or draw his weapon. With a last-ditch effort, he charged backward—into the hallway he'd come from—and slammed me against the wall with a crash. My vision went blurry but I held on. I refocused and turned to see the second guard standing at the door ten feet from me, whistling up a storm. He was really into it now, tapping his foot and bobbing his head. Luckily, he was looking the other way. I continued squeezing.

The mounted crusader could no longer keep up the fight. He staggered forward, out of the hallway and the view of his partner, and collapsed to the floor. I was too dazed to properly catch him. His helmet clanged on the tile.

The whistling stopped. "Now *that* was really loud wind." He advanced toward us cautiously.

I picked up the sleeping guard's legs and desperately looked for a place to stuff him, but there were just statues and alcoves. I dragged him toward the staircase, hoping I could quick-and-dirty stash him around the corner. Kyle ducked into the alcove as the investigating crusader emerged from the hallway to see me struggling with his buddy smack in the middle of the landing.

"Oi there! Stop!"

He charged straight at me. I dropped the guy's legs and backed toward the balcony, drawing my spear and keeping low. The guard came at me with reckless abandon. A single *thwip* plugged a crossbow bolt between his shoulder blades, and this one wasn't filled with water. The attack and ensuing DoT took him by surprise. The poor guy stumbled and tripped over his unconscious friend. Instead of outright falling, he caught himself with large bumbling hops that carried him past me and over the balcony railing. He yelled the whole way down until he splashed into a shallow fountain below.

Several knights on the bottom floor spun to the body, a single crossbow bolt protruding from his back. Their eyes slowly rose to me.

"Um..." I gulped. "Just the shadows playing tricks on your eyes?"

Crusader Reputation -50

So much for my conscience *and* the zero kill count.

The knights bolted for the staircases on my right and left. Kyle came up behind and launched a large vial of sticky fluid. The glass exploded against the marble and fire rushed ten steps deep. He repeated the same for the other side, effectively walling off our position.

"That ought to buy us time," he said.

I nodded and made for the bishop's room.

0930 Circus Maximus

Kyle broke down the locked door. I rushed inside and brandished my weapon. The suite was huge but empty. We shut the door and overturned a statue to bar access, only allowing a moment to breathe before getting to work.

"This place will take forever to search," complained Kyle.

The suite the humble bishop had taken for his quarters wasn't supposed to be a single room at all. It spanned the central half of the Circus grounds and was filled with fancy tables and sofas and fireplaces and fountains. Thick curtains ran along the wall, thankfully hiding our presence from outside observers.

"This is the Roman equivalent of club seats," I muttered.

"Must be nice."

We initiated a hasty search, checking bookcases and drawers. There were no obvious lockboxes or trophy cases. I checked the makeshift bedroom just in case Tannen was the type of guy to stuff the Eye of Orik in his sock drawer, but no luck.

"Uh, Talon," called Kyle from the main room. "You need to have a look at this."

Hopeful that he'd found it, I hurried from the bedroom to see him peering through the window curtains. Before I had time to figure what he was looking at, men banged on the closed door. A key clicked in the lock and the door jiggled, stuck in place due to the downed statue.

"Damn," I said. "We're out of time."

"That's okay." Kyle tore the heavy curtain from the hooks and dramatically twirled it to the floor behind him. Sunlight flooded the room. "I found it."

With the guards scratching and clawing their way in, I strolled to the window and my jaw dropped. From up here we had our first view of the stadium grounds. Crowds filled the seats, with more filing in. Crusaders covered the main entrances and kept residents in place. Bishop Tannen stood on the large wooden platform they'd worked through the night to build. A large deck with a high frame. It wasn't just a stage, it was a gallows.

"That can't be good."

"Look," said Kyle, pointing to a podium in front of the bishop. The Eye of Orik sat neatly on a pillow, on display for all of Stronghold to witness.

"The bastard's taunting us."

"And he's not done, bro."

Two priests marched along the main walk leading a horse with a prisoner slumped over the saddle. Izzy wore a hood over her head and had her hands bound behind her back.

"What the?" I switched to party chat.

Talon: *Izzy!*
Talon: *Izzy!*

"She must be knocked out," said Kyle. "That's why she can't talk."

The priests led the horse up the platform steps and straight to one of three waiting hangman's nooses.

"No way," I muttered.

The door to Tannen's suite was forced open slightly. The guards yelled and stuck their arms through the opening, trying to push the statue away.

"What do we do?" asked Kyle.

I gritted my teeth and stepped onto the outdoor breezeway, holding my spear high above the unsuspecting army. "Kyle," I said plainly, "we're going to fuck shit up."

The door burst open. The brewmaster heaved a fire potion at the entryway. The knights shied away but they'd be inside in no time. I hopped onto the stone railing overlooking the Circus grounds and walked to a rope tied above. There were a bunch of them, with white flags along their length, running from the Circus walls to the central gallows. More of Tannen's flourish.

"Oh no," said Kyle. "You're not doing what I think you're doing."

"I totally am."

I hooked the dragonspear above the rope and leapt off the railing, zip-lining toward the center of the Circus. As I sped along, white flags ripped away one by one and fluttered down like leaves behind me. As I gained speed a buzzing sound, like a zipper, filled the stadium. People in the stands pointed my way.

Bishop Tannen stood in the center of the deck, hands raised mid speech, facing away from me. As I rocketed toward him, he felt the eyes of the crowd leave him. His speech faltered. He looked to his side. Then he turned around and widened his eyes at the death machine zipping toward him.

Too late. I unhooked my hold on the line and lined up the dragonspear. The poor bishop didn't have a chance. I crashed into him like a cannonball. We fired clear off the deck and landed on the dirt below.

Charge!
Surprise!
Savage!
You dealt 177 damage to [Bishop Tannen]

Agility Check...
Fail!

Fall damage!
22 damage

I tumbled and groaned. The fall damage was a small price to pay for the devastating hit on the bishop. I'd never even seen a savage notification before.

Crown Unlocked: **Human Cannonball**
Become one with the projectile.
1000 XP awarded

Amazingly, Tannen had somehow avoided a stun. As he struggled to his feet, I triggered dash and hit him again.

You dealt 42 damage to [Bishop Tannen]

Crusaders closed in from the walls. I spun in a circle, fending them off. Crossbow bolts warned a couple of them off. My head swiveled to Tannen's suite. Wow, Kyle had nailed two knights in the neck from the other side of the Circus. I wondered if the potion gave him an accuracy bonus. More black tunics advanced, wary of the sniper.

"Wait!" cried the bishop. He stood uncertainly, wiping blood from his mouth. "You wish to challenge me to one-on-one combat, Talon?"

I looked into his eyes and snickered. "Not really. I just want you dead." I activated deadshot and sank the dragonspear right into his heart.

Critical Hit!
You dealt 57 damage to [Bishop Tannen]

The proud man's eyes went wide again. Not fear this time. Not surprise. This was straight disbelief. The bishop couldn't fathom how a noob like me had gotten the better of him.

"Sorry, Tannen. I'm sending you back to Oakengard."

The crowd went quiet as I twisted the holy weapon from his chest.

[Bishop Tannen] is dead!

He folded to the ground.

The crusaders closed in fast. Kyle fired at them, but a rear guard held shields high and deflected the bolts. I was surrounded in seconds. Tornado spin kept them at bay, but I was cashing all my checks, one by one. Everything was in cooldown. I had nothing else to do. Instead, I saw the uncertainty in some of the crusaders' eyes and played off that.

"I am the Protector of Stronghold," I declared, loud enough to put on a show for the entire city. "I will not stand idle while Oakengard seizes our city!"

Mixed cheers came from the stands. Stronghold was a town divided, and not just because of the wave of Shorehome immigrants. While I'd been on my multi-day quest in the east, Tannen and the crusaders had been sweet-talking anyone who would listen. Who knew what he'd promised them.

I scanned the edges of the grounds. Men of the city watch were posted at various locations. They were here. They could help. I turned my head. Over the wall of crusaders and their flailing weapons, the Eye of Orik was nestled atop the podium. It needed to be returned to saintly control.

"Ready or not," yelled Kyle, "here I come!"

He slid down the same rope I'd used, hooked with his crossbow. I wondered why he'd abandon such a great sniper perch until crusaders stormed the breezeway behind him. They'd broken down the door. The knights paced the breezeway, afraid to follow on the zip line. The rope sagged under Kyle's weight, but it held. He was making a beeline to the deck. To Izzy and the soulstone.

Behind him, the knights sliced the rope away from the wall.

It went loose and Kyle careened to the ground, short of the platform by fifty feet. He took fall damage and scrambled to his feet as more crusaders converged on him.

Shit. My eyes snapped back to the Eye of Orik. We were surrounded by an army. That was the only thing that could save us now. Still waiting for my skills to cooldown, I charged the line of crusaders between me and the platform. Their swords pointed my way. I planted the spear and triggered vault. Flew right over their heads, their blades skimming a little too close for comfort, and landed on the deck. With a smooth roll, I shot to my feet and reached for the Eye of Orik.

The red gemstone glimmered and twitched. All by itself, it lifted off the pillow and rushed past me. I twirled around to see it land in the grip of Bishop Tannen's glove.

I froze in momentary panic. The gold cross atop the bishop's helmet glowed with shining light. Through the cross-shaped hole below, Tannen's eyes burned with rage.

"And now," he announced with menace, "Stronghold witnesses the true power of the White King. I cannot be killed. *I* am the protector the city deserves. Not a simple scoundrel like yourself."

I backed away on the platform. Kyle, unable to engage in close-range combat, was beaten and subdued by the army. Beside me, Izzy stirred awake, still bound and under guard.

Tannen's nasally voice rang out. "There is only one way out of this, Talon." My eyes met his. "You will hand over the dragonspear and your mantle."

"I won't."

"Yes, you will. It is a burden for one such as yourself." The bishop stepped closer. "Look at what it's made you do. Perhaps you've attempted good works, but you've only been met with failure. Hand over the dragonspear and I promise: you'll be absolved of your crimes."

I took another step away. I didn't get it. Cleric Vagram had shown amazing healing powers, but Bishop Tannen had been dead. I'd triple-checked the death notification. It was no trick, like Izzy's ice double. It was plain as day. I'd killed him. Yet here he stood.

Bishop Tannen was invincible.

"You're not getting the dragonspear," I growled.

Crusaders hurried to the platform steps but Tannen waved them off. The bishop stared at me for a long moment. Two knights dragged a bound Kyle to the deck.

"You and your friend will only find suffering if you go against us," warned Tannen.

"That's funny. I was gonna tell you the same thing."

His eyes hardened. "You think this is a game?" he snarled. "Hang them!"

Crusaders rushed up the steps. I plowed my boot forward and kicked one down. The guard watching Izzy came at my back. I swung my spear and landed a solid blow that forced him back. I followed with unrelenting swipes that put him on his heels. He accidentally backed off the edge of the platform. I grabbed Izzy's wrist.

"Izzy! Come with me! Get up!"

She was groggy and barely responded. Crusaders came at me with slashing blades. I twisted my spear into a crossblock. My skills recharged, I followed up with a deadshot that slammed one to the ground.

"Kyle! Break outta there. We need to go!"

He shoved against his captors. "I can't! It won't let me fight them."

I clenched my jaw as more swords flashed my way. Another crossblock. Another return swipe. But I had to back away. Knights swarmed the deck and flooded around Kyle and Izzy. The recharge time of tornado spin prevented reusing it any time soon.

"Get him!" snarled Tannen hungrily. "I want all of them wearing nooses!"

The wave of crusaders pressed forward. I slashed at another two but their blades finally found me. I took several quick hits as they threatened to surround me. Finally, my heels backed over the edge of the platform. I spread my arms to keep from falling.

Agility Check...
Pass!

Just as I regained my balance, a sturdy kick was planted into my stomach. I flew backward, right over a mosh pit of black tunics below. As I fell, I knew I couldn't beat them all. I'd led us to destruction.

Tumbling midair, I gazed skyward and caught a white flag billowing in the wind. The rope. Instead of crashing to the dirt or into the grasping arms of knights below, I activated dash and launched straight up. I caught the rope and looped around, slowing my momentum and planting my foot on the top. The line bounced wildly.

> Agility Check...
> Pass!

I ran up the rope, away from the platform and toward the stands.

"Cut the rope!" yelled the bishop. "Get him!"

They were already onto it. I stashed my spear and took only three more steps before I felt the tension release. As the rope slackened, I grabbed it with both hands. I was high enough now above the heads of the spectators that I held on tight and swung right into the stands. It was a hard landing but I didn't let up. The crusaders were chasing me. Still clutching the rope, I charged up the seats, weaving past aggressive and supportive residents alike. As I ran, I looped the rope around my forearm to pick up the slack.

"Talon!" boomed the bishop.

At the peak of the Circus' outer wall, I spun around. Knights clambered into the bottom of the stands, slowly moving to intercept me. On the central platform, Izzy and Kyle stood with nooses wrapped around their necks. Tannen climbed the platform steps and stood grandly in the center, placing the Eye of Orik back on display.

"You wouldn't leave before the main event, would you?"

> **Kyle:** *Get out of here, bro.*
> **Izzy:** *Do it. It's too late for us.*

I gritted my teeth, helpless to do anything.

The bishop smiled and swept his gaze over the crowd. "Let it be known that the catechists do not tolerate dissidents, whether they wear a mantle or not. As of this moment, the Protector of Stronghold is a fugitive. The drunkard and the mystic are sentenced to house arrest for their collusion. If any of the three are seen outside Dragonperch, they are to be killed on sight."

I scowled as his eyes landed on me. He smiled, genuinely this time.

```
Crusader Reputation -100
```

"Of course, reform does not come without punishment." Instead of turning to his men he kept his gaze on me. "Pass the sentence."

I grimaced. Trap doors beneath Izzy and Kyle swung open and their bodies snapped hard against the rope.

```
[Izzy] is dead
[Kyle] is dead
```

I shook with rage. The only thing keeping the bishop from breaking into laughter was the solemn countenance he wore for the crowd. I tuned out whatever morose words of absolution his lips blathered. That was a play for the audience. He spoke to them with his eyes entrenched on me.

"I'll kill you," I mouthed.

Again and again. As many times as it took.

Directly below, crusaders climbing the stands had nearly

reached the top. They'd been smart about it and had fanned out, flanking me, diminishing my options. My face soured and I turned away from my friends.

I stood on the precipice of a ninety-foot drop to the ground outside the Circus. Gripping the rope in my hand, I charged out and leapt clear of the building. I fell half the way before the jumble of slack in my arms slowed me down. After another twenty feet I caught hard and banged into the wall. From there I unlooped the rope and ran down the wall to the ground. The landing was jarring, but I'd avoided damage.

I had no time to rest. Hurting all over, I pressed to my feet and ran.

"Protector!" called a watchman from a side alley. "This way."

I didn't have time to think the offer over. I headed through the alley as more watchmen rushed past me. Crusaders spilled into the streets, but the city watch greeted them without reporting my presence. There were still some good people left in the city.

I sighed in relief and hurried away.

0940 Mount & Blade

Moving around in Stronghold, even in daylight, was easier than usual. Tannen's big production had attracted most of the residents and thus most of the crusader security. I passed through an alley on my way to Front Street, watching the road for the smallest signs of activity. I was ready for just about anything. Then a large mountain bongo trotted between the shops ahead and completely surprised me.

I paused and blinked, unsure if what I'd seen was real. "Bandit?" I called in a throttled whisper. There was no answer.

I advanced cautiously. I'd last seen the girl the morning before, right before we headed into Shorehome. But that didn't make sense. It had taken us two days to ride to the seaside city. She couldn't have made it back so quickly.

Then what did I just see?

I peeked around the corner as hooves disappeared past a fence in a shaded glade. Hesitation overtook me for a moment, but I felt pretty safe in the city. My dragonspear and skill combo were only a second away if I needed them. I took an anxious breath, looked up and down Front Street to ensure the way was clear, and rushed toward the glade.

I skirted the fence and Bandit stood there. She kicked the dirt and wiggled an ear. "Bandit! You're back." She practically bowled me over as I clasped my arms around her neck. "Good girl."

The mountain bongo snorted and drew away. Noting my confusion, she banked her head to the side. I followed the signal toward an open shed and spied a figure standing in the darkness within. My weapon was immediately in hand.

"Easy there, matey," he said, lifting his hands into the air. Errol Oates stepped out into the sunlight.

I lunged forward to protect Bandit and leveled my spear at the pirate. "What the fuck are you doing here?"

Errol grinned and wiggled his arms. "Ye might want t' be watchin' the point o' that weapon. These upraised hands be a universal gesture fer peace."

"And this is a universal gesture for 'Fuck off, pirate.' " I jabbed the spear closer to his face. He deftly hopped back. "You know," I warned, "you're lucky that scar through your eyebrow never made it down to your eye. I can correct that."

"Peace," he urged. "Parley."

"This isn't a friggin' Disney movie! There's no such thing as a pirate's code!"

"Aye, 'tis true. A man's ethics be his alone."

"Ethics? You're a turncoat pirate. You have no ethics."

Errol's eyes flared. "I be a pirate, all right. That's a badge o' honor, where I come from. But I ain't no turncoat. I'll not have you spread such lies."

"I don't believe this."

"Ye should, Talon. Why, yer the very reason I'm here. As

soon as ye fled Shorehome, I set sail to yer northern coast. Even found yer stray on the way an' figured I'd take her along as a peace offerin'."

"Peace?!?" I gagged. I couldn't even keep my temper down. I swiped the spear to the side, and as his eyes were on it I caught his chest with my hand and shoved him into the wall of the shed. I pressed my face close to his and held the spear to his neck. "Give me one reason I shouldn't open your throat right now."

He grimaced but didn't whimper. Errol showed his teeth and spoke bravely. "Fer one, if I were dead, who do ye think would've salvaged yer precious dragonspear or the pixie's snow staff?" I paused and considered him. His grin widened. "Not yer friend Lucifer, surely?"

My brow wrinkled. "You did that?"

"Course I did, boy."

He had a righteous tone so I shoved him into the wall again. He grumbled.

I remembered seeing a frigate on the water before confronting Lucifer. That must've been him. "Wait, you really *do* have a boat?"

He smiled cheekily. "They don't call me captain fer nothin'."

I blinked uncertainly. "I guess not. What happened out there?"

Errol grimaced, more than a little annoyed. "Like I said, I set sail. Saw the dragon on the Salt Sea. Ye were impossible t' miss, actually."

"With Vagram and Lucifer," I pressed. "What happened with them?"

"That's quite simple, boy. The cleric betrayed ye, as was always his plan. That devil on the dragon was already fleein' by then, but he sprayed one last blast o' acid on the island as a partin' gift. 'Twas more than the wounded cleric could handle. I docked aside the Salt Sea an' made my way across, searchin' fer survivors." His head took a smug lean. "Found naught but yer stuff. And I returned it, like a proper pirate."

My breath was laced with anger and adrenaline. It came heavy and filled the space that my words didn't. Bandit snorted. We followed her gaze and heard the marching soldier. I loosened my hold on Errol and we ducked into the shed. A single knight strode by, ignorant of our presence.

"She's a beautiful beast," noted Errol quietly. "Smart as a whip."

I gritted my teeth but nodded at the compliment. It was still hard to show the pirate any goodwill. It was one thing for movie pirates to constantly betray their friends, but that didn't fly in digital reality.

"You lured me to Shorehome under false pretenses," I muttered.

He nodded unapologetically. "That I did."

"You turned me over to the Brothers in Black. They were gonna sell me to the goblins."

"That much I tried t' prevent. My intention was to gather yer assistance, somethin' you freely willed t' the city. Ye heard me appeal t' Papa Brugo."

I scoffed. "Your appeal wasn't good enough. I could've been executed, like my friends just now."

Errol spat on the ground. "There's trouble, is there? Tell me,

Talon, is it these priests yer up against, or is it me?"

I ground my teeth and looked away.

"They be the enemy. You can be mine and I can be yers, but 'twould accomplish naught. The fight be with the priests an' the saints an' those that would control us." He leaned into me. "*That's* why I wanted ye in Shorehome. The Protector o' Stronghold. The defier o' saints. Ye are the one who can free us, as ye freed yerself."

I strolled outside again. "You have it backwards. The saints control this city. Or they did until the crusaders took it from them. Shorehome's the free one." He followed me out and we studied the road. "Is it true the saints abandoned you?"

"As far as I know," he said. "But our freedom runs like the tide. We swell with strength an' extend ourselves but will surely be met with equal resistance. Once this army is done with ye an' yers, it'll come fer me an' mine."

My face darkened. Errol was dead-on about that part. No way Tannen would rest while a bunch of goblins lived it up in a fishing village. Shorehome was a hard place to get by in. Men and goblins would have to work hard together, but that wouldn't be enough for the bishop. No matter how much they contributed, he'd see them as little more than an infestation.

"I never trusted them crusaders," growled the pirate. "I made that clear days ago. But I'm not one t' change a man's mind. I said me piece and let ye judge from their actions. I think the truth is now clear."

Truth. Damn that word. I'd known a lot of truths since establishing a permanent residence in Haven. Lucifer himself endlessly manipulated people with truth. Just because Errol made a good point now didn't mean he was suddenly trustworthy.

Then again, I was currently a fugitive. I didn't need trustworthy so much as I needed street savvy.

"So what do you want?" I asked. "Right here, right now, you're back. Is this all just to say sorry?"

He chuckled. "Pirates don't apologize, boy. We're men of action." He rapped the pommel of his rapier. "An' that's why I'm here. I saw what I saw when ye traveled with the cleric. I know yer heart, boy. I know ye'll fight fer me people. In return, I'll fight fer yers."

Swift action was better than being indecisive. "Fine, but if I get even a whiff of secret antics, you're answering for everything."

"This ain't about anythin' else but survival."

He strolled out to Front Street. I made sure it was clear and joined him, with Bandit following.

"Damn." I pointed across the river. A congregation of knights clumped around Dragonperch.

" 'Tis okay. Old Errol's a master smuggler. We can sneak in another way."

He led me under one of the Front Street pedestrian bridges. A small skiff was tied out of sight. The three of us hopped in and stayed low as he paddled down the brickwork river. It was broad daylight, but we hugged the wall close, below ground level. I gave it a decent shot we wouldn't be spotted. After all, Errol had done this before when he snuck into the grotto and made Kyle blow himself up.

On gentle water, we neared the tower. I held my breath and

watched the pirate work. He was a grizzled man. A survivor, no doubt about it. That made the poofy white shirt and flared collar more humorous. But his outfit was functional. Gloves, knee-high boots, leather pants. He moved silently and quickly, whether over water or dry land.

I was beginning to think we'd make it when a crusader taking a leak into the river jerked his pants closed. "Oi!" he yelled. "I've got him!"

"Piss all." Errol abandoned stealth and paddled faster. "Even the finest plans bend t' the mercy o' Mother Nature." We docked at the grotto and quickly hopped out. Errol moved to tie the boat down but the crusader was already navigating his way along the narrow precipice to intercept us.

"Leave it!" I said.

He did and hurried through the grotto gate just as I closed it. The lock clicked tight and we pulled away as the crusader punched a fist into the metal. "Fie! Open this bloody gate at once!"

"Ah ah ah," I scolded, wagging a finger in the air. "You wouldn't want the priests to hear that kind of language."

His face twisted and I laughed. Bandit, Errol, and I made our way down the tunnel and entered Dragonperch.

0950 Prisoners of War

We were safely inside, but our secret exit was burned. Besides covering the main door and the drawbridge, the crusaders posted a party outside the grotto gate.

"This is just great," I complained. "Some expert smuggler you are."

"Laugh it up," returned Errol. "But it's ye who put the screws t' me. Now I be trapped here an' guilty o' consortin' with the likes of ye. Me neck'll snap as easily as yers."

Izzy sat in the war room with her arms crossed, slight twitches the only thing marring her mask of hatred. Kyle appeared less outwardly homicidal, but he didn't have a beer or a snack so I knew it was serious. Errol stared out the window. A ring of catechist priests circled the tower. Crusaders backed them up two rows deep.

"You lose any good gear?" I asked.

"No," answered Kyle. "Apparently official executions within city limits are handled differently than normal deaths. No drops."

"Then what are you two stewing for?"

"Besides being prisoners in our own home?"

Izzy stared wordlessly at the table.

I leaned against the wall and pinched my nose to help me think. "Prisoners," I repeated. "Besides the twenty-four-hour lockdown, we're not allowed to leave Dragonperch anyway, under penalty of death."

"Pretty much."

"How could he do that?"

Errol chuckled. "It's about control, boy. Ye represent a threat t' the bishop. With ye disposed of, he's free t' exercise his will on the people."

I sneered. "Except I'm not disposed of."

"Ye are as long as ye remain in here."

I shook my head. Pinching my nose or rubbing my eyes wasn't working anymore. "What about you?" I asked Izzy. "You don't have anything to add? Not even a flurrg?"

Her lips slanted into a smirk. "We're way beyond flurrgs, Talon."

"Okay, the ball's in our court then. Talk to me."

She hiked her shoulders. "What do you want me to say?"

"I don't know. Anything. Whatever's on your mind."

She pouted for a moment. "Okay, well, I'm really struggling to answer why the crap you'd bring this asshole into our house."

Errol strolled by Izzy and bowed. "Me lady, the poetry that dances from yer lips be mesmerizin'." She grumbled as the pirate walked to the far end of the table, sat down, and unceremoniously kicked his feet up.

I sighed several times as I failed to properly explain the situation.

"I dunno," said Kyle. "I think it's a smart play. It doesn't matter that me and you are locked down. We're *players*. We can't fight back, but NPCs like Errol can, right? Honestly, he's more useful than we are right now."

My face brightened. Izzy didn't respond, but I thought just maybe there was a sparkle in her eye. I chided myself that, of the three of us, it was the frat boy who was thinking clearly.

"Is that true?" I asked Errol. "You can fight in the city?"

"Raise yer spear 'gainst me an' find out fer yerself," he said defiantly.

That gave me pause. I had done exactly that the first time we met.

"Yes," said Izzy plainly. "He can help us."

The pirate cinched his arms behind his head and leaned back.

"What about Lucifer?" asked Kyle. "You said he was kinda on our side."

"I have no idea whose side he's on besides his own," I answered truthfully, "but he's a no go. He's not addressable by email. As with the saints, even a direct reply to his own messages doesn't reach him. They must be trying to cut him out of the system."

"Or," speculated Izzy, "he purposefully disconnected himself as much as possible to stay hidden."

Kyle grumbled. "So it's just us then."

I nodded. "Unfortunately."

"Maybe not," said Izzy. "I mean, when has that ever stopped us before?" Something about the discourse had started to calm her down. She was becoming the cool and collected Izzy I knew. "I've been pissed because I screwed this whole thing up and got captured, but here we are. And my trip to the Great Library wasn't a waste. I didn't get a chance to swipe any books, but I discovered why Bishop Tannen wants the dragonspear."

I was the only one standing at this point, but she had my attention. I came over and sat at the head of the table. "We know why, don't we? With the dragonspear comes the mantle of Protector of Stronghold. Tannen doesn't just want to run the city, he wants to be its champion."

"Not to mention live in these sweet digs," added Kyle.

Izzy gave a measured nod. "Sure, of course he wants those things. But mantles come with something else. An ability we didn't know about."

I waited until she winked at me. "You're killing me," I said.

She chuckled. "Just wanna make sure you hear this. *Mantles* come with the ability to create new *factions*."

I pursed my lips and considered that. I leaned back and crossed my arms. "Interesting. The catechists already have a huge influence over crusader leadership, but apparently that's not enough. Tannen wants his own breakaway sect."

Kyle scoffed. "Dude probably wants to start his own new world order."

"That also might explain the wild king's situation."

Izzy nodded. "*And* why he wants the crown back so badly."

I was floored. A week ago, NPCs weren't even supposed to have the ability to wear mantles. But every day that passed was another day for Lucifer's hack to pivot the runtime away from expected outcomes. Every detour opened a whole new set of branching possibilities, further and further until the divergence appeared as completely different behavior.

NPC sapience had allowed the wild king to defy the goblin horde. Had bestowed the title of Protector upon Papa Brugo. The flip side of the same coin was the bishop himself. Despite recent buffs by the saints, Tannen had overthrown them. His hatred for the pagans was so strong that he'd rather become a dictator than fail at his holy mission. Rigidly applying his rule was the means to his end.

He wanted his own mantle. He was jealous of the dragonspear, the tower, the title. But that wasn't all.

Kyle grunted. "Not to be a total buzzkill, guys, but how does this info really help us? I mean, who cares if Tannen wants to be a crusader or something else? Who cares if the wild king wants to be a pagan or a wildkin? None of that knowledge kicks them out of our city."

Debbie Downer or no, I was happy to see Kyle giving a damn instead of just following along. Even Izzy was passionate in her cold, heartless way. I couldn't make it out yet, but it felt like we were on to something.

"There's something else I learned," offered Izzy. She turned to the mirror on the wall and the sanctum master panel activated. We all watched as she navigated to the socket manager. "We know Dragonperch has lots of locked features. Browsing the list of empty sockets, it doesn't take a genius to figure out how to upgrade this place."

My face brightened. "Don't tell me you found the sockets?"

"Nope," said Izzy, lips curling into a smirk. "You guys did."

I paused, not getting her joke.

"Read the names of the sockets," she instructed.

"Okay..." I frowned at the onscreen list, skeptical this would achieve anything it hadn't before. "Let's see. Feather, wind, water, earth—"

"That's the one. That last one."

"Earth?"

Izzy nodded. "What's another name for earth?"

I chewed my lip, still wondering how she thought I'd already found the socket. Then it came to me. I hurried to my inventory. "Dirt," I finished, producing the loot that the great sandworm had dropped.

The dirt pearl was a heavy palm-sized orb, like a snow globe without a stand. The glass-like surface was a darkened swirl of light and dark browns. Curious, though, was the faint translucent light it now emanated from within. It had definitely not done that before.

"You're kidding me," I said. "The dirt pearl fit into the earth socket the whole time?"

"Yes and no." Izzy watched as I hopped out of my seat and approached the master panel. I tried to apply the item to the earth socket but was greeted with an error sound. "And that's the problem," continued Izzy. "The library book mentioned something about a way to prep the pearl to plug into the socket, but it didn't go into details."

"What a tease," complained Kyle loudly. "I thought we were on to something."

I knew exactly how he felt. "But we have what we need. If it's just a matter of technique, there might be info on the wiki."

"You're forgetting that Dragonperch is quite possibly the only active sanctum in Haven," said Izzy. "You heard Lucifer. His black dragon unlocked it. I don't think that was supposed to happen for at least a couple of years."

"So no one knows dick about these things."

"It's more mysterious than that. Only *after* sanctums are inhabited do pearls present themselves, which makes them extremely rare. Those two pearls are probably the only ones in existence." Kyle and I stared at each other in awe. "But they're still random drops," she added. "Which means we don't always get what we need. Dragonperch doesn't have a socket for the bone pearl."

I grumbled. Haven, in general, wasn't the kind of place governed by rule books. The devs preferred an organic education that was less about instruction and more about experience. With a simulation so vast, it was a natural concession. The players did their best to keep up with the wiki, but that simply wasn't possible in a beta that hadn't revealed many of the game's features. That, combined with the branching genetic learning of the game and Lucifer's sentience hacks, meant Haven documentation would likely always be incomplete and out of date.

"If I can get back to the Great Library..." started Izzy, but even she realized the difficulty of the task. She was on lockdown and the crusaders had it in for us.

"We need to put a pin in it," I said. "As much as I want to get Dragonperch up and running, Bishop Tannen is the bigger problem."

"Actually," cut in Errol, standing and striding to the window, "the immediate problem be the circle o' priests at our door. Can they get in?"

"It shouldn't be possible," answered Izzy. "The tower may not be fully active, but the wards have held since the simulation started. Without the dragonspear, they shouldn't be able to enter."

"That be one blessing, at least. But so long as they stand vigil, we have no chance o' leaving here in one piece. Not with only Talon an' I to fight 'em."

"It all comes back to the city watch," I muttered. "They're on our side. I know that for a fact. But they can't act against Tannen while he's the boss. And grabbing the Eye of Orik won't be so easy with Tannen's magic ensnaring it. It seemed to be on a tether."

"I can't believe me ears," growled Errol. "*This* is the great Talon I hear whinin' 'bout the helpless city watch?"

I was taken aback by his choice of timing to mock me. "I—"

"Did ye twiddle yer thumbs an' complain when the goblin horde rushed yer gates?"

Kyle raised a finger. "Actually—"

"Don't answer that," I snapped.

Errol pressed forward. "Shorehome don't even have a full army, yet we get by fine. Tell me, it wasn't just the watch that defended yer town against the titan, was it?"

I gritted my teeth, finally seeing his point. "No. The players and NPCs banded together."

"Aye, they did. Against a common threat, the differences 'tween player an' NPC mattered not. An' here we find ourselves facin' a similar annihilation, do we not?"

"The difference," complained Kyle, "is that some people actually like that bishop bastard."

"Sure," I said, still thinking about how Stronghold had come together in a time of war, about how Shorehome had united in a time of abandonment. "But plenty of people don't. Errol's point stands. If we're gonna win this thing, we're gonna need help. And we're only gonna get that by thinking outside the box."

I went deep into my inventory and produced the satin sheath. My fingers dug inside and gripped the skull within.

"No!!!" cried Izzy and Errol in unison. They jumped on me and held my hand in place.

"What?"

Izzy glared. "You remember what happened the last few times we ran into the warden? We ran. Every. Single. Time."

"But—"

"He can't be beaten," spat Errol. "A cursed man spewing cursed damage. Don't invite that on us."

Even Kyle joined in. "At least not while we're stuck on lockdown."

I scoffed at them all. "Come on. It's not like Hood can get inside Dragonperch."

"If anyone can," said Izzy, "I'd put my money on him."

I stared at them like they were crazy.

"Look," she said, "Just wait. You remove that thing and you could be raining down hell. We need to think this through. Just... wait."

I frowned, nodded, and put the sack away. "Only 'cause you're cute."

Everyone breathed a sigh of relief, including me.

0960 Brain Assist

<hr>

The war room was the top floor of the tower. That meant it was a short flight of steps to zone outside to the roof. The sun was beginning to hang low in the sky, which I couldn't believe. Another day was passing since our betrayal at the Salt Sea and we weren't any closer to solving our problems. I was determined to take action today anyway, even if my companions couldn't.

Unfortunately, the roof was empty save for Bandit, who liked to nap out here. "Where are the saints when you need them?" I grumbled. The bongo flicked her ear sympathetically.

I waited around a bit to see if Saint Peter would show up. Heck, at this point I wouldn't have minded Loras. I zoned back inside and chatted and waited some more. After hitting the limits of my frustration, I realized I was missing the obvious. With everyone chilling in the war room, I went into my menu and ticked the green help button.

A man flashed into the room standing at attention sans salute. He wore shiny black boots and a British red coat adorned with large gold buttons. Blond hair, blue eyes, clean shaven except for a thin mustache, and he spoke with a thick Indian accent.

"Hello, sir. I am glad to make your acquaintance today."

My eyebrow twitched. I was only half surprised. "Varnu, Son of John. How is Texas this fine American day?"

"Oh, the jungle is sweltering."

"I—You're in a jungle?"

"Well, of course. It is a necessary component of tiger hunting."

"That doesn't sound legal, Varnu. And it definitely doesn't sound like you're in Texas."

"But this is a *killer* tiger, sir. The Ministry of Hunting has created a special exception."

I wasn't sure how to respond. Haven support technicians were clearly instructed not to reveal their nationality. No one wanted help outsourced from India. Poor Varnu constructed elaborate yet unbelievable lies about living in the USA. It was harmless enough.

"Listen, Varnu, we have a situation here and I think Saint Peter would want to talk about it. In fact, I'm kinda surprised he's not already here."

He nodded. "Yes. The saints send their regrets that they are unable to attend. This is due to the blockade, of course."

My eyes scrunched. "Blockade?"

He blinked patiently. "I am sure you have noticed, sir, that there is a ring of priests warding your accommodations with a circle."

"Yeah. The guards. They're casting a spell."

"Priests do not cast spells, but instead pray. This is basic information found in your Haven User Guide."

I waved the explanation off. "What I meant was, this circle of theirs can actually keep the saints from crossing?" Izzy and I traded a concerned glance.

"I do not have that information," answered Varnu, "except to send my regrets that the saints cannot come."

Kyle scratched the scruff on his chin. "At least it sounds like he actually talked to them. That's a step up, right?"

"It is," I agreed. "Varnu, does that mean you can deliver a message to them?" Staff members were unreachable by DM. The direct messaging system was generally limited to player communications.

"I am sorry," said Varnu Johnson. "It is impossible for me to relay player messages to Kablammy personnel."

I rolled my eyes. This was the not-so-harmless part of Varnu's script. "Dude, if there was ever a time to pass me up the chain, it's now."

"I do appreciate the gravity of the situation, sir, but my extensive two-hour training seminar was exceedingly clear."

"This is ridiculous!"

He clicked his tongue. "It is the truth. The handbook section entitled 'Handling Irate Residents' reads: As a resident companion, you are never, under any circumstances, supposed to refer anyone to a supervisor. Of course, they are not to be directly told this—" Varnu froze, realizing he had said way too much. I could see him scrambling for a save.

"We're way past that, Varnu. The saints have been usurped in Stronghold. The crusaders took over for the city watch. Criminals are running Shorehome. NPCs are downstairs keeping them from accessing my tower. Bishop Tannen is the new ruler now."

The eyes of the "resident companion" went wide. I wondered how up-to-date he kept with game events. Probably very little, if he'd been in the middle of a tiger hunt.

"The catechists are out of control," I told him plainly. "If they create their own faction, it'll only get worse."

Varnu's eyes lit up. "Ah! That is a bit of good news then. You see, creation of a faction requires saintly approval. It is impossible without it."

"That's something," I said, "but we still need to talk to them. Can't you have them open a line of communication with me?"

"They can't do it," interjected Izzy. "Don't you hear yourself? The saints lost their power. They can't even get in here to chat. What makes you think they could do anything to help us?"

"That's the whole trick," I explained. "The saints are still behind the scenes guiding things. They just can't directly interfere. But remember what happened last time there was a state of emergency in Stronghold?"

"Orik?" guessed Kyle.

"Right. A giant cyclops and thousands of pagans attacked the city. Like Errol said, it wasn't only the city watch who fought them off."

Izzy shook her head. "But that's because the runtime enabled combat for everyone in—" She paused, eyes wide, as it came to her. "You want the saints to declare some kind of martial law."

"Wartime measures, a state of emergency, whatever game system unlocks combat in town. Stronghold is a player city. If you ignore the guards, players outnumber NPCs four to one. If we let players fight, we just might be able to take Tannen down." I nodded to Errol for his idea. "Even if the city watch can't help."

The pirate strolled forward. "An' they only be out of it till we return yer soulstone t' the hands o' the saints." He nodded in satisfaction. " 'Tis a good plan. A suicide mission, mayhap, but as good a plan as any."

I laughed. I was starting to like the scoundrel. I turned back to Varnu, who was silently considering everything we said. "What do you think? The saints might not have the same control of Stronghold, but they might be able to tweak or trigger wartime measures? Can you get the word out?"

The resident companion pressed his lips together, unconcerned with masking his glum outlook. "I am not sure if they can accomplish what you say, but there is a problem."

"Oh, come on. You're from Texas, right?" I joked.

He half smiled. "I assure you, I am as American as lychee pie."

"Then give us that Southern attitude. Get 'er done, no matter what it takes."

He swallowed and cleared his throat. "That is the thing, sir. Resident companions don't actually, *technically*, have a method in place for contacting the saints."

The four of us stared blankly at Varnu.

"What do you mean?" asked Kyle. "Like, can't you just escalate a general support ticket or something?"

Varnu clenched his jaw. "No, sir. I mean that we have no form of communication whatsoever with anyone from Kablammy."

We blinked some more.

"But you're tech support!" I barked.

"And as such, we are a resident-facing support group. You

cannot possibly believe the development team actually cares about your day-to-day well-being, do you?"

Again, no one said anything for a moment. The curtain of corporate America was being thrust aside and no one wanted to believe the truth.

"BUT YOU'RE TECH SUPPORT!" I fumed. Maybe my brain runtime was stuck in a loop.

Kyle howled in laughter. It bordered on maniacal. "This is *so* jacked up. Tech support is a sham." He shook his head in disbelief.

"So the saints can't come inside," I said, about to join him in crazy town. "And we can't go outside." My hands hooked on my hips. "We're just supposed to sit on our asses for the rest of the afterlife?"

"Well, sir," offered Varnu helpfully, "that obviously would not happen. Eventually Bishop Tannen and the catechists would find a way to usurp you as well."

Izzy rolled her eyes and quoted him. "*Obviously.*"

He winced under her glare. "But that simply means, how do you say, the cricket ball is in your court." His forehead furrowed. "What is a court?"

"Varnu..." warned Izzy.

"No matter! What I mean to imply is that you must find an alternative exit from your tower."

"Aye," snapped the pirate. "And how do you propose we do that?"

"Obviously"—Varnu avoided Izzy's steaming gaze—"you must get your dirt pearl fitted for the earth socket so you can unlock the catacombs. Your artisan does engage in some craftwork, no?"

Kyle jumped under everyone's scrutiny. Except for mine. I was staring at Varnu with my jaw glued to the floor.

"What?" asked the resident companion. "Jewelry setting is a simple skill addition."

"He's right," said Kyle, dumbfounded. "With my existing glasswork skill set, it's trivial to pick up a jewelry setting skill." He turned to Varnu. "You're saying that's all we need to socket the pearl?"

Varnu nodded.

"Holy shit, Varnu!" I exclaimed. "You actually helped!"

He straightened his jacket. "I hate to point out the obvious, sir, but that is the stated purpose of my occupation. You should allow me to assist you once in a while instead of constantly asking to speak to the saints. It would be better for my self-esteem."

My apology got caught in my throat.

"And a favorable performance review once in a while would be nice as well."

I blinked. "Of course. I— Sorry."

Varnu snapped his head to the side and jerked into a defensive posture. "Shh. The tiger's back!"

I cocked my head. "You're in the jungle right now?"

"That is offensive, sir. I work in a twenty-two-story office building with central cooling." Varnu pulled out a rifle and scanned his surroundings, which of course were invisible to us. "I must deeply apologize, but I will not be able to complete the rest of my script until—"

A tiger audibly roared and the rifle went off. Not to be

outdone, Varnu let out a war cry and rolled to his side, spinning around and firing again. His hologram flickered away, leaving us with *so* many questions.

Izzy sidled up to me. "That just happened."

Errol picked his nails with a dagger. I wondered if he was programmed to ignore stuff like that.

"Okay," said Kyle, closing his skill menu. "Done. Kyle the Brewmaster is officially a jeweler." He held out his hand and I placed the dirt pearl in it. He did something that required a few minutes of concentration and presented us with a set dirt pearl. He walked to the master panel and applied it to the earth socket.

The screen lit up with a brown glow. A graphical line bled out from the image of the earth socket, pumping like an electrical current, or life's blood. Dragonperch shuddered ever so slightly. A cross-section map showed the brown current running deep to the basement door. A new label popped up.

Catacombs Entry: Locked

"This is so cool," said Kyle. "It's like our own ops center." We all watched as Kyle unlocked the entry.

"So this is our way out," I said. "If there are tunnels under Stronghold, we've gotta be able to sneak almost anywhere in the city." Kyle and Izzy accepted my party invites.

"It's very likely," agreed Izzy, "but we're still constrained by the lockdown."

Errol sauntered up. "Aren't ye forgettin' something, me hearty?"

I arched an inquisitive eyebrow.

"It's gonna be ye and me in those catacombs, boy. We'd make a better team if I was actually invited aboard."

I hesitated a second, but Kyle and Izzy nodded. I sent Errol an invite and for the first time we had a fourth party member. I frowned. I was sympathetic to Errol's cause, but I didn't exactly feel safe going on a solo mission with him.

"We'd better get going 'fore nightfall," said the pirate, hitting the staircase. "They say that's the worst time fer zombies."

"Zom—?" We all paused and turned to Errol.

He shrugged. "What other mobs do ye think wander catacombs? I hope ye can see in the dark, matey."

"Bad plan," I muttered. "Bad plan."

0970 Dead Rising

We didn't waste time. Gathering equipment was easy because it was already in our inventory. Kyle did gift me a couple of explosive vials in case we needed some undead crowd control. I also took the bone pearl on a gut feeling. Then we hurried through the door and they locked it behind us.

I took a slow breath as my eyes adjusted to the darkness. Errol stepped lightly down a set of shale stairs. He peeked both ways at the bottom and shook his head. I hastened to join him. The tunnel was mostly rock and damp soil. The river was very near. I compared what I saw with my map to utilize my dungeon skill combo. Given the downward slope of the passage, it was a good bet the catacombs ran clear beneath the water. We walked in the northerly direction.

"This isn't so bad," I hedged.

"Bah," growled the pirate. "It's unnatural bein' underground. Might as well be in a tomb."

I spotted half a skull protruding from a muddy wall. "Watch out what you wish for."

We inspected the bone. It was old. If it was paired with a skeleton then it was mostly buried within the wall formation—

not exactly a ceremonial grave.

"You familiar with the finer points of killin' zombies?" he asked.

"Besides a headshot with a double-barreled shotgun?"

He eyed me strangely. "I won't pretend t' know what that be, but there's no real trick t' it. The walkin' dead are enchanted with dogged determination. Hit 'em hard or don't hit at all. A scratch won't bother 'em and will likely open ye up t' attack."

"And if they bite you?"

"Then it fuckin' hurts, swabber. They won't be conscripting ye into undead service, if that's what ye mean. The only thing can do that is dark magic. Don't worry 'bout spells down here. Worry 'bout teeth an' nails an' weapons." The pommel of his rapier slammed into the skull and cracked it in half. He looked at me and shrugged. "Just in case."

We walked in silence a little more. The walls hummed with the river overhead. The tunnels were old, but very stable. At least that was something we didn't have to worry about.

"So," grunted Errol, "am I t' assume we have no real plan?"

I winced. "You noticed that?"

"Aye, it's hard not to. We've got one cunt over here calls himself a bishop an' wears a fancy helm. Comes into power an' all o' a sudden everyone's afraid o' him."

"You have to respect how powerful Cleric Vagram was on the way to Shorehome."

"I'll not be denyin' that. Still a shame, though. I expected nothin' more from the saints. They turned tail an' ran from Shorehome when they had the chance t' stand fer us. But yer city watch has its hands tied. Yer people can't draw their weapons.

This feels more like a game o' chess than a battle."

I chuckled bitterly. "Taking on Tannen will definitely require strategy."

"Yet we have none. No allies. No hidden gambits. Just a pirate an' a scout, wanderin' among the dead."

We came upon a thick bramble obstructing our path. Tree roots snaked through cracks in the ceiling and wound into the floor and walls. It must've taken years to grow. Errol sawed at it with his sword.

"We must be beneath the Foot," I concluded, separating the bramble from the floor. "This is a good sign. Doesn't look like anything large is walking around down here after all."

"That," said Errol, "or we're tearin' down the only natural barrier 'tween us an' them."

I suddenly became aware of just how much noise our chopping was making. We tore half the bramble to the side and ducked through the new opening. We were both cautious as we continued, but the catacombs were dead. In the good way.

It surprised me that I hadn't seen any exits yet. With the navigation and cartography skills, I figured I'd have seen something by now.

"What about this Lucifer fella?" asked Errol. "He seems a right rogue. Can he help us?"

"He might if it suited him. Although I'm beginning to think he abandoned Stronghold for Shorehome. He failed here but was successful over there."

Errol walked with a frown. "How so?"

"You must've noticed a difference. Lucifer gave NPCs and mobs free will. He saw to it that your city was stolen from the saints. He gave the Eye of Orik to the pagans and the Squid's Tooth to Papa Brugo."

The pirate snorted. "That's not the way I see things."

"No?"

Errol sighed as if the mere act of speaking politics was disgraceful. "I be the Papa's man, but only t' an extent. I never pledged my blood t' the Brothers in Black. I don't take orders, only advisement."

"You're a freelancer. A proper pirate."

"You said that right, boy. I'm a captain, on top o' that. But everything aside, Brugo and I go way back, an' if he's had dealings with Lucifer, I'd know about 'em."

"Listen to what you're saying. The devil moves to Shorehome and Brugo just so happens to be handed the keys to the city at the same time. That's a huge coincidence."

"Ain't no coincidences, an' ye ain't that daft. The saints abandoned Shorehome. Brugo was in place t' take command. Yer so-called devil likely just figured 'twas a good place t' hide from the saints once they lost eyes on the territory." He turned to me. "Maybe the whole world will be like that soon enough, an' Lucifer will move somewhere that suits him better."

My face darkened. Although I'd never consciously questioned it yet, Errol's affirmation touched on something that had been bothering me. Lucifer was a lot of things, but I believed he had a plan. And I didn't think he wanted me dead. He'd had his chances, and he always preferred words over combat. Back at the Salt Sea, he was appealing to me. He'd wanted to enlist my help, just as he had before.

Which wasn't to say Lucifer was a friend. The words had

come straight from his mouth: I was a cog and he was the grease. He had an endgame for us all, something beyond what we could yet see.

So if Papa Brugo had been Lucifer's disciple, or at least owed him a favor for retrieving the Squid's Tooth, then it stood to reason that our capture would've led to a meeting with Lucifer. Brugo would've led us to the devil if they were cohorts. Instead the Papa simply wished to sell us off to the goblin thirstiest for our blood. There was nothing shrewd or provident to it. Brugo was playing politics in Shorehome. Lucifer was playing on a completely different chess board.

"But if Lucifer didn't steal the Squid's Tooth..." I mumbled under my breath.

In my distracted state, my boot caught a stone and I tumbled forward. The damp soil hit my face. I pulled my foot under me, but it was caught.

"Avast!" shouted Errol.

He spun toward me with his rapier high in the air. My fingers scrambled in the dirt to recover my weapon. His slash came down as I threw the dragonspear up and triggered crossblock. Unfortunately, his blow was well under my guard. His blade hit the ground with a sickening crunch.

Suddenly my leg was loose.

I rolled to my feet, ankle aching. Something wiggled on the ground where I'd been. In horror, I turned my attention to my leg. Tightly gripping my ankle was a decomposing hand severed at the wrist.

Walking Dead
50 Health

Errol's rapier came down again and slashed the zombie clawing out from the ground. I clutched the undead hand, ripped it off my leg, and tossed it down the tunnel. It smacked into the face of another advancing zombie.

I flinched, but my instincts took over. I waved the dragonspear in a smooth arc and tore the zombie's head off. His body stuttered in place and fell to the floor.

More figures lurched in the shadows beyond him. It was strange. The zombies should've been easier to see with my darkvision, but it was almost like the algorithm ignored them. They blended right into the darkness and surprised us at point-blank.

"We're surrounded," I called out.

"Chop off their arms and they'll bite. Chop off their head an' it's lights out."

I jabbed forward a few times to keep the advancing mobs at bay. Anything with only 50 hit points wasn't a real concern anymore, but everyone knew zombies were a swarming mob. Kill one and three others follow. And in the narrow catacomb tunnels, my maneuverability was limited.

Bones crunched behind me as Errol swung into action. He had his own group to deal with, and in seconds we were back to back.

"How many have ye got?" he asked with a sideways glance.

"I can't tell. Three? Five?"

"That be better'n my ten. Punch a hole in 'em while I cover yer back. Then we run."

I pressed forward with well-timed horizontal slashes. My spear sliced open grayed flesh and exposed ribs.

```
You dealt 1 damage to [Walking Dead]
You dealt 1 damage to [Walking Dead]
```

Aw, great. Errol had warned me about this. Minor cuts and scrapes were all but ignored by these mobs. They closed in and I stabbed forward, impaling a figure of melted flesh in the stomach.

```
Impaled!
You dealt 1 damage to [Walking Dead]
```

Undeterred, the zombie gripped the shaft of my spear with both hands and pulled himself forward. Blood and guts oozed over my weapon as he drew closer. I tried to shake him off, but he had a death grip. To make matters worse, two others came at my flank.

I panicked. Call me a horror nut. I'd seen too much film and TV that had ingrained the raw instinct in me to not get bitten. Instead of taking minor damage, I doubled down and dashed straight ahead.

The two zombies at my sides grabbed each other as I skidded free, deeper into the catacombs. The one stuck to my spear pressed into me, disgusting juices splattering my face. I slugged him in the jaw. His neck snapped to the side but he instantly retargeted me. I pounded him again.

A swipe came from behind him. More zombies. A hand raked at my back.

12 damage

I grunted. That shit hurt, and I desperately hoped Haven devs didn't bother to simulate infection. I wasn't going out like Khal Drogo. But then, the zombies didn't have that in mind either. Their glazed-over eyes flashed as their jaws opened to chomp down on yours truly.

No.

I triggered tornado spin. It may have been nerfed but it was all about creating space. Gripping the spear tightly in both hands, I cut in frenzied circles. The zombie impaled on my spear was ripped in half and fell to the floor. The rest of the mob recoiled from the attack.

You dealt 37 damage to [Walking Dead]
You dealt 1 damage to [Walking Dead]
You dealt 1 damage to [Walking Dead]
You dealt 1 damage to [Walking Dead]

I came to a stop in a low stance, head on a swivel. The zombie on the floor had taken real damage because he'd been separated from his waist. The others had only superficial scrapes. The undead must've had serious damage resistance when it came to normal wounds.

"Let's go!" I yelled, waving Errol through the two-yard radius I'd cleared. I lopped off another head as he danced away from the oncoming horde. His swift blade had downed several of them, and he wasn't done. As he rushed past, he chopped another's leg off at the knee.

I tried to move but the one without legs grabbed me. My boot came down hard and crushed his skull. I leapt, but he'd slowed me down. The mob converged again. I hooked one's shoulder with the dragonspear and swung him into another, knocking them both to the dirt.

"Now yer gettin' it, boy!"

I hopped clear and equipped one of Kyle's arsonist specials. The horde moved like lightning but I slammed the glass down before them. Flames erupted and spilled out across the ground. Catacomb walls lit up with an endless orange glow. The fire coated everything in its path, and the zombies were too dumb to avoid it. Their emotionless faces burned as they stumbled over their dead comrades. They thrashed on the ground but eventually collapsed into heaps of charcoal.

Errol hissed out a curse and wiped his blade. "That was more intense than I thought it'd be."

"It's ironic, but we could really use a priest down here."

He guffawed and turned my warning back on me. "Watch what ye wish for."

We hurried down the passage. Errol wanted to light a torch, and for good reason. The firelight bounced off the shale and lit up our enemies, which was more than I could say for darkvision. Still, I convinced him to stay dark. We needed an exit and, for that, I prioritized awareness range. I swapped the map on and off until I noticed the depiction of what could've been a door in the ceiling. That knowledge kicked in my navigation display: a handy little pointer right on top of our exit.

"There," I called out, coming upon a pool of shadow on the ceiling. Short beams of wood were fitted into the dirt as a makeshift ladder, so covered with grime they were barely visible. I didn't even see the trapdoor at the top, but it had to be there.

Errol skidded to a stop at the ladder. "Where do ya suppose this leads to?"

A ghostly cry echoed through the tunnel.

"Does it matter?" I asked.

Errol shook his head. To get a grip on the old wood, he brushed away loose debris with his hands and feet. He started up the ladder.

I kept eyes on the tunnel in both directions, but it was hard to say how close the zombies were. Suddenly, a chunk of dirt sprayed into Errol's face. A skull erupted from the wall between ladder rungs. The pirate, without his sword in hand, reared back and nearly lost his grip. A deadshot hammered the brittle bone and crushed it into the wall. Errol took a calming breath.

"I'm getting real sick of things coming back to life," I confided.

He cocked his head thoughtfully. "That's what we all do here one way or another, isn't it?" He pushed up and zoned outside.

"Fucking Dr. Phil over here," I muttered. Then I stuffed my spear into my inventory and climbed the ladder.

0980 Gun

We found ourselves under a heap of straw in a cellar. The room was full of neatly stacked crates and supplies. We'd been lucky the trap door was just hidden, not blocked.

"Arr!" exclaimed Errol, hopping to his feet. "Look at all this booty. We've hit pay dirt, boy."

Boots rapped down a wooden staircase and an arquebus swiveled towards the pirate. "Wrong, rapscallion. No one steals from me and lives to tell about it."

Errol turned slowly, arms up, eyes wide.

I wiped hay from my face. "Trafford?" I asked with a smile.

He stared for a second before lowering his weapon. "Is that you, son? Now what in the sam hill are you doing in my cellar?"

I laughed as the stress left my body. "A better question would be why the hell do you have a trap door to the catacombs down here?" Errol's eyes shifted to Trafford.

"Oh, that." The shopkeeper scratched the back of his head. "Front Street's the oldest marketplace in Stronghold, you know. I've heard there was a time when things needed to be moved in secret."

Errol grinned. "If it would please the two of ye old chums,

can a fella put his hands down without getting shot?"

Trafford squinted his eyes suspiciously. "That depends entirely on who you are." Errol tensed.

"He's okay, Trafford. He's a smuggler from Shorehome," I explained. "He's gonna help me take down the bishop."

The shopkeeper's weathered face almost never betrayed surprise, but the eyebrow over his larger eye twitched. "Is that right?"

Errol lowered his arms. " 'Tis."

The arquebus vanished. "Well, if Talon says you're all right, you're all right."

The pirate showed his teeth and grunted. Trafford grunted in return. I couldn't be sure, but I suspected they were having some kind of gruff-off.

"Cut it out, you two." I climbed the stairs to the welcome shop's back room. "We don't have time for this." The two of them stomped up after me.

"No," muttered Trafford, "I suppose not. What's your plan?"

Errol grinned. "I've been asking fer a hint o' it, but there's nothin' there."

"That's not exactly true. I've been trying to get the various factions on our side. The watch can't do anything, but Gladius gave me his word. They'll move in as soon as I recover the Eye."

"That won't be easy, son." Trafford frowned as he mulled the situation over. "You talked to Grimwart?"

I blinked. "He's back?"

"He was in my shop not an hour ago. You know the bishop's been updating the pagan quests, tweaking things to snag more control. It's concerning quite a few grumpy veterans. Grimwart's one of them."

Errol spat. "That knight's heart is as black as his armor."

"I think you're pegging him wrong," returned the shopkeeper. "You know I have no love for the crusaders, Talon, but Grimwart seems a straightforward fellow to me."

I dipped my head. "I thought so too."

"Ye ain't listening t' this madness, are ye?" huffed Errol. He paced the back room. "Colonel Grimwart woulda turned on ye just as Vagram did, if only he hadn't been wounded."

"I disagree," said Trafford. "He's a knight with a sense of duty. A code of honor."

"I spit on his code."

"I'm sure he spits on yours," I pointed out. "But even a rogue like you has some semblance of honor. The question is if Grimwart's really on our side."

Trafford canted his head. "Since the bishop healed him up, the colonel's been finding he dislikes the changes in the city. The crusaders were never supposed to be parked in Stronghold this long. Tannen overthrew the saints without him."

Errol slapped the wall. "That's because Grimwart led an expedition t' get the Protector o' Stronghold as far away from Stronghold as possible."

"Cleric Vagram led the expedition," I said calmly. "What if they steered him away just like me?"

"What can he do? Grimwart follows their orders."

"If he's a good man, he might overrule them."

Errol scoffed. "Yer askin' a knight t' ignore the same sense o' duty ye praise him fer. Soldiers ain't like pirates. Soldier's do what they're told. When have ye ever seen someone so dedicated ignore their nature?"

I crossed my arms. "It's not so different from a grizzled pirate trying to save his city."

He scowled.

Trafford waited a moment before speaking. "These quest updates are a bit convoluted. I could request Grimwart's presence—get him over here within the hour—and nobody would bat an eye."

I looked from Trafford to Errol. I couldn't deny the risk, but my tank was nearly empty here. The city watch couldn't help. The players couldn't help. Even the saints were out of the picture.

"What about Saint Peter?" I asked.

"Bah," spat Errol. "Now yer pissin' me off."

"It's worth a—"

"It ain't worth a damn if ye get killed." Errol strode up and pounded a finger into my chest. "Yer a good kid, Talon, but ye have a trust problem. As in, ye trust everybody ye shouldn't."

My face tensed. "Including my pirate guide to Shorehome?"

"Bah!" He stormed to the other side of the room.

I ground my teeth and leaned against the opposite wall. "Listen, Errol. We can't do this alone. I'm the Protector of Stronghold, but it took the whole city to fight off the horde. Protection of the people without involving the people is meaningless." He shook his head in dismissal. "I'm not some stupid boy who's gonna blindly walk into danger. I don't trust the priests. I overthink every piece of intel the saints give me. And Lucifer is so far off the deep end he won't even make an appearance into this conversation. But that doesn't mean we don't have friends. Gladius and the city watch are pledged to us. Grimwart is the highest-ranking knight in the city. Can you imagine what would happen if he was on our team?"

The silvery pirate shook his head. "Yer words stir hope, Talon, but me gut says 'tis naive an' dangerous. I'll stand beside ya in a fight against our enemies, but when ye parley with them, I lose my stomach fer it. If ye meet with Grimwart, I'll be returning t' me boat on the river outside town."

"Aye," remarked Trafford. "A two-bit thief turning tail when things get personal. I'm not surprised."

Errol stepped to his face. "I've gutted men fer kinder words, shopkeep."

"Not surprised about that, neither."

Errol sneered. He turned to me and I could see it plastered all over his face. I was a lost cause. He hissed and stormed outside.

"Good riddance," snarled Trafford. "There's only room for one gruff asshole in my shop anyway."

I tried to laugh, but I kept second guessing if I was doing the right thing.

0990 Knights of the Old Republic

Trafford promised me an hour, but it was closer to two. Heavy boots pounded through the store as if on a mission, but they were alone. If Grimwart had come to arrest me, he'd have backup.

The knight entered the back room in full battle dress. Black plate vambraces, shoulder guards, and a full helm emblazoned with a white cross over the eye slit. A similar design was on the black tunic draped over his chain mail. A black cape covered his sword arm, but his weapon was sheathed.

"You made it back," I said.

"Aye, as did you. I regret that our quest was not a success. They told me the pirate scum betrayed us."

I hiked a shoulder. "It was a dick move, but he made a bad choice. He's not the one I'm worried about."

"No?"

I steadied myself. "Vagram was the one who betrayed us."

The colonel removed his helmet. He had a staunch face with a thick mustache. His loose black hair was striped with white, just like his tunic. "The hell you say?"

"It happened. After Lucifer killed Izzy and escaped, the cleric stabbed me in the back." Technically it was the chest, but the thought was the same.

Grimwart's eyes searched mine. His brow grew troubled. "There were rumors of you striking an alliance with the dark one."

"He was talking, I was listening. With a weapon to my throat."

"His lies can sway the best of men."

I hissed. "They didn't sway anyone. Lucifer's taken over two angels of the Golden Seven. He had us dead to rights, with a dragon to boot. You think I'd be on his side after he killed Izzy?"

Grimwart frowned. "No. No, I suppose not. But—"

"The priests had this whole thing planned," I said. "Trafford told me about your shared concerns. Every move the bishop makes is a snatch at power. My question is, where does *your* heart lie?"

The knight scoffed. "You don't think me a party to such scandal?"

"You tell me. Tannen couldn't have stormed the Pantheon without your crusaders. It's your army who's terrorizing the city."

"Those are strong words, Talon."

"They've arrested the head of the city watch!"

The knight scowled but swallowed back a reply. After some thought he said, "All my dealings with Gladius proved he was a good soldier and a trustworthy man."

"Damn straight," said Trafford. I nodded my agreement.

Grimwart clenched his jaw. "Then I'll make it a priority to

speak with him. I'm still a colonel, last I checked."

"That's great, Grim, but it's not enough. We need to oust Tannen from power, the sooner the better."

The knight's mouth widened in disbelief. "He's one of us!"

"He stopped being one of you the moment he moved on the saints."

He turned his head away from the hard truth.

"Have you spoken to them?" I asked. "The saints?"

He didn't answer immediately. "I am told they're dealing with other matters, but I suspect I'm being kept from them. Perhaps Gladius knows a way around that."

"No doubt. But the saints can't take direct action against Tannen. He holds the Eye so he controls the town. The priests are formidable, but it would be a trivial matter for your men to return the artifact to the proper owners."

Grimwart grumbled. "I am sorry, Talon. What the bishop is doing doesn't sit well with me."

"Then kick him out."

He shook his head firmly. "I will not bring arms against a fellow crusader."

"He doesn't stand for your cause. He stands for himself."

"Aye, that is likely true. This is why I must immediately bring this to the attention of the Trinity."

Trafford and I both wore our confusion plainly. Grimwart expounded.

"The crusader leadership in Oakengard is made up of three equal members: a devout bishop, a holy knight, and a wizened sage. Tannen is only one of three. If he is at fault, he'll be held accountable for his actions. I can dispatch a rider who'll return with orders."

"A rider? That'll take days each way. Why not just send an email?"

Grimwart chortled. "Direct messages. That's what players use to contact each other, is it not? NPCs work under a different rule set."

"Then let *me* send the email. I could send it to..."

He noted my pause. "There are no players in Oakengard. Besides that, the report would need to come from a trusted source. It really should be me."

The panic showed on my face. "You can't leave us in this position for a week."

He ruminated over the options. "Perhaps not. I have a man with a good reputation. I trust him to follow through. But I must remain steadfast in my conviction. If Bishop Tannen is acting against the Trinity, he will be excommunicated and we will remove him from power. Until I receive such orders, I cannot turn against him. I will not break the covenant of my faction."

"Damn it," I barked. I turned away from them and rubbed my eyes. Covenant of his faction. It was clear Errol was dead wrong about the knight. He was a good man who wanted to do the right thing just as he'd always represented. But, as with Gladius, he was prevented from acting by the contrivance of game systems.

The thing was, we couldn't wait a week while Tannen had free rein over Stronghold. And this gambit had just lost me the pirate as an ally. "You guys are starting to make me really desperate," I muttered.

Grimwart smiled and slid the helmet back on his head. "I

expect so. But desperation is not a stranger to great events. I am the colonel of the crusader army, and you are the Protector of Stronghold. I expect the world shall shudder at our influence. This is why it is imperative to only act when it is right to do so." The knight twirled his cape over his shoulder and marched from the welcome shop.

"Well," grumbled Trafford. "I'm just a shopkeeper. Where does that leave me?"

"In good company," I insisted. "You don't need a title to be a hero."

"Fuckin' A right," he snapped.

I studied him oddly. That was a strangely modern turn of phrase for the embittered old man. Maybe NPCs really were evolving after all.

"What are you gonna do about the ceremony?" he asked.

I casually scratched the side of my head. "What ceremony?"

He suddenly straightened. "Don't ya know? Bishop Tannen announced a grand ceremony at first light tomorrow. The whole town's invited."

I blinked, livid that I'd missed it.

"What?" asked the shopkeeper. "Did you not get sent an invite? Doesn't surprise me. The residents of Dragonperch just might be the only people in town not welcome to the bishop's little party."

"We'll see about that."

I worked my jaw. It was slightly after eleven at night. That meant in seven or eight hours, the bishop would throw another wrinkle at us. I was sure the abrupt notice and time were purposeful. Izzy and Kyle were still on lockdown and, as far as the priests knew, I was a victim of their blockade.

All the more reason to act now.

"Thanks for all your help, Trafford."

He contemplated me. "I know that look. You have a new plan, don't ya?"

I shrugged and headed to the exit. "You know what they say about desperate times."

The crusaders may have resumed patrolling the city since I was last out, but the darkness seemed to quell the neighborhood. Maybe everyone was calling it a night in order to get up bright and shiny for the ceremony. Either way, it made me a lot less worried about dodging random guards.

I wished I could be as confident about their refusal to arrest me, but Grimwart's moral character wasn't shared by all. I avoided the well-lit blocks of the Foot and snuck past my old neighborhood, Hillside. Soon enough I was at the meeting of the south wall and the river. I unceremoniously plunked into the water and waded to the river gate.

Before the siege of Stronghold, we'd once used the entrance to break into the city. During the rebuild the inner and outer gates were repaired with jumbo locks and shiny new keys. I'd made sure to keep copies.

Unknown to everyone else in the city, I snuck under the thick walls to the outer gate. I took a moment to reconsider before throwing caution to the wind and removing the crown of the wild king from its satin sheath. I tied it to the inside of the gate with a strip of leather. Then I heaved myself up onto a clump of land and settled in.

Desperate measures indeed.

1000 Quest for the Crown

I jerked my head at a snapping branch. I was cold and wet. My back ached.

Damn. I'd fallen asleep at the river gate.

My eyes darted to the stag skull. It dangled like bait on the strip of leather. I opened my menu to check the time: 4 a.m. I'd dozed off for the last four hours.

A slight movement caught my eye in the darkness. It was more of a void than anything else, a section where the star field in the sky didn't appear. But there were two stars, large and glowing, that seemed to shift in unison.

No, not stars at all. They were the eyes of the warden of the Blackwood.

I recoiled from the river gate. The eight-foot giant hunched over, half in the water, just outside my field of view.

"Is this a summons, mortal?" his deep voice beckoned. A black chain snaked along the wall.

I peeked around the gate before pulling away. The ogre was terrifying up close. Instead of giving in to fear, instead of succumbing to the natural fight-or-flight instincts, I spoke.

"I've... reconsidered my stance on certain topics these last few days."

Hood's slow, heavy breathing was my only answer.

"Perspectives are funny, aren't they?" I asked. Maybe it was the short nap. Maybe it was the liberation of making a decision and stating it aloud, but peace filled me. "Take yourself. Are you a monster or a guard dog?"

"I am no one's dog," he growled.

I shook off the misstep. "It's a figure of speech. A compliment, really. You're loyal to your cause. Steadfast in your conviction."

A chain rattled. "A warden must be ever vigilant, and an executioner resolute."

So he wasn't really one for conversation. People had worse faults. I frowned and asked, "Who is the wild king to you?"

That was met with a long silence. Maybe the warden was beginning to see the sway of the wind. When he answered, his tone was less threatening, if such a thing was possible from giant mutant ogres.

"The king," he uttered, "is a man who stands for his people. Better yet, he stands *with* his people. That can be said of precious few rulers."

I sighed and glanced toward the city. "I'm gonna be doing something really stupid tonight, Hood. To be honest, it probably won't work out. I don't know where that leaves me and my friends." I chewed my lip, one last bastion of hesitation niggling me. But I'd already come this far. "I have a duty to wield the dragonspear, to fight with it no matter the result. The stag crown, well, it's not part of my calling. I don't want to see it fall into the wrong hands. I wanna give it back."

Hood snorted in reply, almost in disbelief, but I leaned around the gate to give him a look at how serious I was. The giant's face was hidden behind his black hood, but his eyes, even of pure white, were adequately expressive. I saw a hint of what might have been respect.

"The decision is wise," he said. "I will take the crown and I will kill you."

My forehead knotted. "I know you're not the most diplomatic fella, but the point of this meeting is to hug it out. To avoid hostilities."

He grunted. "This meeting, this choice—you have saved some lives this day. You must know you cannot save your own. The wild king spake. He is owed one soul, and one soul he shall receive."

I clicked my tongue. "Can't it be someone else's?"

The warden's answer was steadfast and patient. "Perhaps there are worse pagan killers in all of Haven, but there isn't a more notorious resident of Stronghold. Your negative reputation is astounding. No one is more desirable to the wild king than you. You fought off the goblin horde. You defeated Orik. No one is more hated by the pagans."

"I thought the wildkins didn't align with them? You weren't part of the siege."

"The wild king desires not conquest or bloodletting. Our faction ties were thrust upon us, but they are there nonetheless. That is why you violated the Blackwood, broke into the Black Keep, and stole the crown of the wild king. To your kind, a pagan is a pagan. The die is cast. No other soul will suffice."

I hissed. How many times can a guy be rejected? Not a single thing had gone right today. "If you're gonna come for me anyway, what's the point of handing the crown over?" I snatched the stag skull from the gate. The executioner's axe clanged against it in warning.

"Metal and stone cannot keep me out," he boomed.

"You can't get into Stronghold," I scoffed. "You said it yourself. The pagan faction was thrust upon you. Pagans can't breach the city."

The warden seemed to smile beneath the hood. "That protection has been circumvented before."

I narrowed my eyes. After we'd first stolen the crown and entered the city, Hood had stayed out. He'd waited until the Shorehome expedition to ambush us. That was because the Eye of Orik protected Stronghold from pagan incursion.

But that protection *had* failed before, when Lucifer had stolen the soulstone for himself. The blessing against pagans only applied when the Eye of Orik was under saintly control. And now, with it in Tannen's possession, all bets were off.

Was there really just inches of steel between me and the warden of the Blackwood?

"You *can* come in, can't you?" I asked in awe, backing away from the gate.

"And when I do," he growled, "the lives that are cut down by my axe will be on your conscience."

My conscience. *Damn* my conscience. That's what had gotten me to expose the stag crown in the first place. Now Hood knew exactly where I was, and he didn't just want my blood, he wanted my *soul*.

"There's that dogged determination rearing its head," I snapped. "You want a fight, Hood? You've got one."

I stuffed the crown of the wild king back in the bag of satin. The ogre howled and leapt at the river gate. Even as tall as he was, he had to hang on or be submerged. I stuffed his king's crown into my inventory and hopped into the river myself.

"Sorry, big guy, but I've got a ceremony to attend. You and the wild king wanna clean up and throw on some duds? We could all crash the party. We'll be the guests of honor."

"This is a foolish mistake," he warned.

"And I don't like your attitude. I'll put the crown in the king's hand, no one else." I swam away and the warden bitterly howled.

"I'm coming for you, human. I'll not rest until you are mine!"

For all his talk, the upgraded steel bars were a fortification even he couldn't breach. I left him there, raging into the water and the wind.

1010 Dawn of War

I stood at the southern edge of Oldtown, surveying Dragonperch from a distance. The priests were fixed in constant prayer, holding a ring of torches. Eerie light danced around the holy men. I imagined I could see the answers to those prayers in the form of a reflective sheen around the tower. This blockade of theirs... I wasn't sure what it was doing but it wasn't good.

Not that it mattered. My friends were stuck inside, but I'd slipped the trap.

I opened party chat and saw previous messages attempting to reach me.

> **Kyle:** *What's the word, bro?*
> **Izzy:** *Any news?*
> **Izzy:** *Talon?*

At least the priest blockade didn't prevent player communication. Even though their messages were from hours ago, I tried them.

> **Talon:** *Sorry, guys. I fell asleep.*

Maybe they had too. It took a minute, but they answered.

> **Izzy:** *You what?*
> **Talon:** *I know it sounds crazy, but I'm sneaking around out here, huddled in the dark. I've tried enlisting help from literally everybody, but I don't know what else to do. Tannen's holding some kind of important ceremony at first light.*
> **Kyle:** *More hangings? Been there, done that.*
> **Talon:** *No idea, but this feels like something else. Something he doesn't want us around for. I have to be there.*
> **Izzy:** *We're still on lockdown until the afternoon.*
> **Talon:** *That's exactly why I have no choice. I have to go alone.*
> **Izzy:** *Talon...*
> **Talon:** *I'll keep in touch and give you updates. It's the only way.*

I stared at the blank chat prompt, but there wasn't much else to say. It did get me thinking about other players I'd neglected to touch base with. I swiped to my DMs and reread Dune's message. He'd been concerned about town events days ago, before trouble was even on my radar. I knew *he'd* be on my side, *if* he was still in the city. I fired off a quick email explaining the situation. I doubted he was awake now, but the whole town would be getting up within the hour for the big show.

That gave me some time to make final preparations. I checked in with Trafford. Sent a few members of the watch to coordinate with Gladius. Some of the players in Hillside were early risers, likely concerned with the day's events. I let them see me in the streets. Let them know I was going to fight for them.

Then I passed by the Pantheon. With all their machinations getting this whole shebang started, the saints had been conspicuously absent of late. The priest blockade only explained part of it, because even Grimwart hadn't seen them. If I was gonna get the players to fight with me, I needed Saint Peter to lift the citywide combat ban. If that didn't happen I was dead in the water.

I grimaced at what I encountered. The Pantheon was under heavy guard—a contingent of knights and priests that rivaled the showing at Dragonperch. No prayer circle, but plenty of might to keep the saints in and me out.

There was nothing I could do. My eyes ran up the impressive Corinthian columns to the golden angels frozen at their summits. The in-game security system was meant only to prevent players from unbalancing the game. When they were designed years ago, the devs had never expected Tannen and his crew of NPCs to be doing just that. Of course, Kablammy hadn't counted on Lucifer giving the otherwise well-behaving NPCs free will.

My gaze lingered on the two columns with missing angels. Lucifer's new pack. Much of this was the fallen one's doing. It scared me to think of what use he was putting them to.

I grunted as the sun peeked through the alley. First light. I was out of time. I cursed and turned my back on the Pantheon.

This was bound to be a difficult morning.

As I headed along the main thoroughfare, thick lines filed into the entrance of the Circus. Players, NPCs. Priests, crusaders. Stronghold and Shorehome residents alike. I saw some friendly faces but there were enough threatening ones that I stayed out of sight.

Then, like a snap, the streets were empty. The grand event was about to start. Everyone was in place. Past the Circus, I spotted the guards at the west gate and atop the wall. The gate was open, of course. Stronghold wasn't locked down by default, and the city watch never shirked their duties. Their number was bolstered by crusaders, of course—Tannen wasn't stupid enough to leave the watch with sole control of the gates—but there were enough good guys around for me to work.

From across the road, I flagged down a watchman. He hid his surprise and casually checked if the crusaders had noticed. Seeing they hadn't, he marched over. I gave him a warning of what to expect. He tensed nervously but nodded and returned to his post.

I smiled. It was almost as if we had a chance.

The sun fully broke over the city. Morning was here. Inside the Circus, the audience's eagerness transitioned to hoots and hollers and roars as Tannen no doubt showed himself. I could practically feel his smug grandeur from the other side of the wall. After the crowd quieted he confirmed his presence by addressing them.

I twisted my lips thinking of the gallows within. No part of this confrontation wasn't risky. Sometimes the first step was the hardest.

I set my dragonspear against the ground and strolled down the empty thoroughfare, in full view of any onlookers. The crusaders at the Circus entrance turned their heads lazily.

"You're late, citizen. The bishop's—" He stiffened as he realized who he was addressing.

I smirked. "Stand aside, knight. I'm wanted within."

"Yer wanted, all right," said the second one, hand tightening around his sword.

I lifted the dragonspear to his neck, poking the tip just under his helmet. He froze.

"I assume you know what this weapon is?" I asked.

He nodded nervously.

"Then you know what I can do with it. And you also know the bishop wants it. Do you *really* want to stop me from going in there?"

His helmet swiveled to his companion.

I sighed and drew the spear away, planting it in the dirt. The crusaders weren't sure if they could move. I spoke solemnly.

"The dragonspear isn't just a deadly weapon. It bestows on me a mantle. A duty. What has Colonel Grimwart taught you about duty, knights?"

The two men traded another glance. Their weapon hands relaxed. Their helmets sagged.

I nodded confidently. "Then stand aside and watch the Protector of Stronghold work." I brushed past them and emerged into the Circus to wild cheers.

1020 Royal Rumble

Take your best shot. That's what people say. It doesn't need to be a fight. Talk, subterfuge, truce—there are many ways to achieve victory. But if it comes to it, if you need to get dirty and risk life and limb, if you need to *fight*—take your best shot.

I had a bunch of shots. Various gambits that might swing the tide in my favor or end with disastrous consequences. The thing was, I wasn't free to take any of those shots yet. The city watch was under orders. The saints were under guard. I was marked for death by the warden of the Blackwood. The crusaders wouldn't turn on their own. And players were unable to engage in town combat. It was all a delicate house of cards, the foundation for Tannen's supremacy. I just needed to figure out how to budge one of them to get everything tumbling down.

So yeah, I had a plan. I had lots of plans, actually. I'd schemed and planned as much as could be expected in an occupied city. Now was the time to get the cogs turning. To start knocking some heads—knocking some cards—loose.

Now was the time to act.

Bishop Tannen stood triumphantly on the gallows stage, hands raised magnanimously as he gave a rehearsed speech.

"The sun shines on a new day in Stronghold. A new era of leadership."

Gasps from the crowd announced my presence. Tannen caught sight of the lone figure intruding on his show. A line of crusaders at the base of the platform tensed.

"You're no leader," I called out. "You're a dictator."

Tannen's eyes went wide behind the crosscut helmet. He was a regal figure. Plate armor with flowing white robes. The gold cross on his tunic was more ornamental than others. It had sweeping lines that glittered with genuine specks of gold. A small gold cape rested on his shoulders. The star of the show, however, was the golden cross affixed to the top of his full helm. If there was ever an artifact that gave Tannen his power, it was that.

Of course, his *political* power came from the Eye of Orik, the soulstone the city was founded upon. That had to be on his person because it was nowhere in sight.

Behind the propriety of his regal dress, the bishop's face twisted in rage. He mocked me in his nasally voice. "Talon, the Betrayer of Stronghold. How thoughtful of you to join these proceedings. After all, new heroes can only be born after the old ones are hung out to dry."

"I'm giving you one last chance," I proclaimed loudly. "Gather your people and go back to Oakengard. If you refuse, you'll fall, along with your twisted cause."

The bishop snorted. It must be easy to act brave on an elevated platform behind a line of crusaders. There was a crowd of men, too, sharing the stage. Priests and crusaders standing together in a huddle. I sidestepped to get a glimpse of Saint

Peter among them.

"My *cause*," spouted the bishop, "is to protect the people of Oakengard, Stronghold, and soon, Shorehome, from all manner of cursed ilk. Pagans, devils, and those they collude with." He sneered gleefully at me with his last words.

I swallowed, wondering what exactly he had planned.

> **Kyle:** *What a total douchebag.*
> **Talon:** *What? You guys can see this?*
> **Kyle:** *You're on the flat-screen, bro. I guess the bishop didn't want anyone to miss this.*

I scanned the setting for cameras, but I realized I wouldn't see them. This was a simulation. Game cameras didn't need to be rendered. They didn't need to be physical objects at all, for that matter. I refocused on Tannen and his accusations.

"I am no champion of Lucifer," I announced, "but he has freed the minds of every NPC in Haven. Do you not understand that your very actions—your very choices—are only possible because of him?"

Tannen spat through the vertical opening of his helmet.

I chortled derisively. "The irony is doubled when you consider that you would never dream of freeing those who serve you. You're worse than the devil you slander."

Audible gasps broke the tension, but were they directed at me or Tannen? Was I really defending Lucifer? In my haste to cast Tannen in a bad light, I wasn't exactly coming off sympathetically. Against as charismatic a speaker as the bishop,

I needed to appeal to the people's more primal emotions. Tannen used fear and panache, but I preferred heart.

"What are you doing with the saints?" I demanded.

Tannen crossed his arms over his belt and pressed his lips together in thought. "You've spoiled my surprise." He nodded at the cluster of soldiers on stage. They stepped aside to reveal a handful of men wearing the iconic white robes of the saints. Peter and Loras, among others. "You didn't presume to be the guest of honor at this function, did you?"

My jaw tightened as I saw the setup. Six saints lined up beside three nooses. It was like Tannen had said: out with the old, in with the new. The audience was stunned.

"Release them at once," I ordered.

"I have a better idea," he answered. "How about you join them?" He motioned for me and the troop of black tunics on the ground advanced.

I twirled the dragonspear casually in my hand. "Any man that comes for me forfeits his life."

"And women too?"

I spun to see Lash advancing with a slew of priests. Her party members, Glinda and Conan, waited by the wall.

Izzy: *What a traitorous bitch.*

"Lash," I snapped in surprise. I quickly confirmed she was still level 8.

"Halfway to level 9," she pointed out, guessing my thoughts. The white knight was a head taller than her company. "I warned you to stay out of this, Talon."

"No." I shook my head. "You're not one of them."

Her black tunic said otherwise. The black-on-white color scheme was a perfect fit for her. But the crusaders were warmongers and zealots. Lash wasn't the same, was she?

"You can't fight," I said flatly. "It's not wartime. I'm the only player who can fight in the city."

"That much is true." With the cleaver still hanging on her back, Lash cast a rallying spell. A yellow glow washed over the localized priests and crusaders.

Bolstered Legion!
Allies within the active radius are granted 20% physical damage resistance.

The white knight shook her head in grim determination. "Don't make this any harder than it has to be."

I gritted my teeth. "My mom always said I was hardheaded."

She shrugged as the NPCs advanced. I spun my weapon to the oncoming soldiers. This was madness. One of Stronghold's own, fighting for the bishop. If he had significant player and NPC support, this would turn into a civil war.

I feinted a few times to keep them at bay, but I couldn't dance forever. They came from all sides, forcing me to take action. I scored a headshot on one, a deadshot on another. Slashed a few more before dashing out of the scrum and hitting them from behind. They kept coming. A sword found my back. Another, my leg. I killed a knight in return, but there was a whole force of them.

"You can't win, Talon. You can still give up."

I fought back harder. When a few of them cut me at once, I triggered tornado spin and pushed them back. With the nerfed damage, it was just a stalling tactic.

Suddenly a white aura overtook me.

Greater Holy Light!
For the next 30 seconds, you have the ability of Greater Regeneration.

Lash and I scanned the rows of seating. Caduceus saluted from on high as her buff completed. A few rows back, Dune huddled under his bright green cloak. I turned back to the white knight.

"It looks like I have friends too."

I wasn't sure how Caduceus was able to manage the healing spell, but the buff was on par with some of the stronger healing I'd seen of the priests. My health bar maxed out in seconds and would continue to regenerate within the time limit. I struck out with renewed vigor, allowing myself to sustain hits where it translated to greater damage-dealing potential. Priests and knights fell before me, the home protection bonus of my legendary weapon overpowering Lash's damage resistance.

But as several priests fell, Bishop Tannen's cross flared with golden light and they crawled back to their feet.

"You guys are worse than zombies," I muttered.

A gatehouse swung open and another contingent of

crusaders swarmed in. Banging came from the opposite side of the Circus. Stigg's red robes fluttered as he slotted a beam across the second gate, effectively locking it. The knights behind that door pressed their weight against it. Stigg did too, to buy me time.

Time would only help me so long. It was numbers I truly needed. And right now, Tannen's numbers were bearing down on me hard.

"Ahoy, ya scurvy landlubbers!" cried Errol from the audience. He stood on the edge of the barrier wall, holding one of the ropes tied to the scaffolding. He leapt forward and swung right into the action, planting his boot against an onslaught of knights. They toppled over themselves and made easy targets for my spear. When the rope swung around again, Errol landed lightly beside me. "Figured ye could use a hand," he drawled.

"A sword, more like."

"Arr."

The pirate's rapier flew from his waist and slashed oncoming enemies. His weapon was much faster than mine. Together, we fought off another wave, back to back.

"How'd you know I was in trouble?" I shouted.

Errol: *Ye do fuckin' realize I'm still a member of yer party, don't ya?*

I rattled a knight's helmet with my boot and chuckled.

> **Talon:** *You know, I'm not so sure your pirate speak is internally consistent.*

"Duck!" he yelled.

I did and he tossed a small blade over me into a knight's eyehole. "You too!"

He dipped low as I swung up and returned the favor by tearing a priest's head off. Errol rolled under my guard and impaled a crusader at my back. Lash shouted and began casting another buff. A loud explosion rocked her forward. She pitched to her hands and knees.

Trafford strode into the main entry holding a giant smoking hand cannon, much larger than the one I'd previously seen him with. As he marched, he poured a horn of powder into the weapon and bit off a length of wick.

"You asshats don't think I'm gonna leave all the fun to you, do ya?"

Everyone turned, fearful of his unpredictable weapon. It sure packed a punch, but Lash wasn't down for the count. A crater in her armor smoked, but she regained her feet.

Trafford joined our side. It was funny. The NPCs I'd been trying to recruit were the watchmen, but Errol alone doubled my fighting power. With Trafford it was beginning to look like we had an outside chance of success.

Unfortunately, seconds make all the difference in combat. At about the time my regeneration buff elapsed, Stigg lost his battle with the second closed gate. The wooden doors splintered open and another legion of crusaders flooded into the Circus.

The three of us cleared our backs and stepped away from the new wave of soldiers.

"Stop," shouted Grimwart, annoyed. "Stop this at once." The colonel brushed away an escort of priests and forced his way through the main entrance. "Leave me be! I will not be kept away from these proceedings." He turned to face the arena and paused in shock.

The crusaders slowed their advance. One priestess didn't notice the lack of backup and moved in. Errol and I simultaneously stabbed her through.

Grimwart marched up to Lash, his black armor contrasting her white. "What is the meaning of this, soldier?"

Both knights were impressive specimens. Lash was a player and stood taller. Then again, Grimwart was technically her superior.

"Ask the bishop," she squealed under her breath.

His helmet swiveled to Tannen. To the saints at the gallows. "This is not what we are here for. We're inciting violence. The very evil we're sworn to stamp out."

Tannen glared at the priests who'd failed to keep Grimwart occupied. "This does not concern you, Colonel."

"The hell it doesn't."

"Watch your language."

"Fuck my language," he boomed. "You presume to hold the saints prisoner now?"

Tannen stepped forward. "And you presume to question your superior?" The bishop snubbed his nose in the air. "I am aware of your midnight antics. Do not forget, Grimwart, that the only reason you have not succumbed to your curse was because of my healing hand."

"That matters not, Bishop."

"It is *all* that matters. This is a criminal prosecution. Now order your men to capture the dissidents."

The priests surrounding us looked to their knight counterparts. The crusaders appeared divided.

"I will not," announced Grimwart. "The crusaders will not be responsible for murdering the Protector of Stronghold."

Tannen scowled at the soldier. "I will reward the *dutiful* knights who bring me his head!"

The men shuffled. Some closed in.

"Stand down!" commanded Grimwart. He drew his bastard sword in both hands and slammed it so hard on the ground we all shook. "Do not forget who your colonel is! Do not forget who has traveled with you, bled with you, and died with you." He swept his gaze over his soldiers and lowered his voice in stern sincerity. "Do not forget your honor."

The crusaders began backing away. Uncertainly, at first, but once the momentum shifted it was easier for the army to follow along. They were soldiers, after all.

Still, Grimwart's ranks were not without dissenters. Some of the knights, perhaps seeking favor with the bishop, remained in place clutching their swords. Many others backed away but shuffled listlessly, waiting to see which direction the wind blew. The three of us weren't exactly in immediate danger, but I wouldn't call this a truce. It was more like the eye of a hurricane.

Bishop Tannen stood straight up in a good show, hands clasped behind his back, but he was livid. He clicked his tongue a few times in annoyance.

Grimwart approached the stage. "We cannot mimic the lawlessness of Shorehome in the holy city. This is the seat of the saints in Haven."

"Well said, Colonel. And it is here that I aim to make the same statement against lawlessness." Tannen sneered at me. "Your refusal to arrest Talon will be noted, but it is inconsequential. If the Betrayer of Stronghold wishes to have front-row seats at the trial, let him have his wish."

The priests retreated to the base of the stage. Outnumbered by the wavering crusaders, they unified to protect their leader.

Temporarily sated, the bishop turned to the crowd and boomed. "All of you have heard me warn of the evils of the fallen one. A great foe, he is, indeed. My latest reports confirm his hijacking of two golden angels."

The audience listened in earnest. The stalled combat, the saints imprisoned—it was a lot to process.

"But in this isolated case, the cause of our ills was not the devil. It was not Lucifer who handed the city of Shorehome over to the enemy. The saints detonated the Great Well and abandoned their people. The saints left them to the mindless goblins and savages."

Grimwart stepped closer to his leader. "No one is denying mistakes have been made."

"A mistake is an accident, dear knight." Tannen smiled pitifully. "Robbing the Great Well of the Squid's Tooth. Unleashing the dreaded kraken upon the city and handing it over to criminals. These were the conniving actions of the so-called father of Shorehome, Saint Loras."

Everyone gasped. I have to admit, I did too. But only 'cause my heart stopped for a second there. The arena turned to the broken saint, already fitted with a tight noose. The guilt splayed across his face made the truth clear. Even the saints beside him displayed shock.

Bishop Tannen flashed a grim smile. "As we all know, reform does not come without punishment." He turned to the gallows. "Pass the sentence."

A single trapdoor swung out and Loras snapped down. I jumped forward but he was dead instantly. I clenched my jaw, unsure what was happening.

The bishop held his head low in mock reverence. "Next is the man who nearly destroyed the holy city. The man who empowered a false Protector, and allowed the Eye of Orik to be reunited with the cyclops." He signaled and the priests on stage shoved Saint Peter forward. A knight hooked a noose over his neck and pulled it tight.

"No!" I yelled. "He wasn't at fault!"

"You're welcome to take the blame and stand for him on the gallows, Talon."

I grumbled. I'd expected a fight, but with Izzy and Kyle safe in Dragonperch, I hadn't expected Tannen to hold leverage against me. I had no choice but to go full crazy.

"Wait!"

The bishop arched an eyebrow as I removed an object from my inventory and strode toward the platform. The priests massed ahead of me but I growled at them and they backed away until I stood at the base of the stage, under the bishop's feet.

"I know what you want, Tannen. You'll never get the

dragonspear, but you can make do with this." I held the object high. Tannen cocked his head and fixated on it. "I'll make you a deal," I said. "I offer this to you, a gift, in return for releasing the saints. If Loras did indeed sin, no other saints need to be punished for it."

The bishop was frozen with indecision and hunger. His lips curled back as he salivated. His eyes flashed to Saint Peter and back to the red satin sack in my hand. Finally, he gave a quick nod. I tossed the bag to the stage. It tumbled at his feet and he scooped it up like a dog finding a bone. Tannen reached long fingers into the sack and pulled out the crown of the wild king.

"This is a pagan artifact," he said. The priests and crusaders looked on with distaste.

"It is, but it gives you what you want. What you *truly* want."

"The mantle of Ruler of the Blackwood?" he sniggered.

"The mantle provides the power to create a new faction." I leaned closer. "That's your goal, isn't it? Strike out on your own. Forsake the Trinity. Make your mark on the world. You can do it with the stag crown. But only if you let the saints live."

His eyes flicked to me.

"Faction creation requires the approval of the saints. Only they can do it for you. Let the others go. Release them, and Saint Peter will approve your request."

The crosscut helm turned to Peter. I wasn't sure how to prove the truth to Tannen. I wasn't sure what gauge NPCs had against lies, or what handle they had on game mechanics. But, as far as Varnu had reported, this was how it worked. And when Saint Peter gave his nod of confirmation, the bishop realized, for the first time, that he needed the saints. Or one of them, at least.

"The White King is not cruel," Tannen announced to the crowd. "The saint who betrayed us has been dealt with. Release the others." The priests seemed to be disappointed, but they followed the order unquestioningly.

Grimwart motioned to a few trusted knights. "Make sure the saints are returned to the Pantheon without harassment." The men nodded and led the saints, sans Peter, away. The developers didn't appear especially reassured by their escort, and I didn't blame them. But Grimwart had already proven his moral fiber. The world might not be black and white, but his beliefs were as stark as the colors he wore. There'd be no subterfuge with him.

And now I swallowed uncomfortably as the proverbial cat was out of the bag. Not only did the crown expose us, but I'd just given Bishop Tannen *exactly* what he wanted.

1030 Guild Wars: Factions

"The sun shines on a new day in Stronghold," blared the bishop, mimicking the opening words of the ceremony. This time, however, his eyes stared hungrily at the skull in his grip. "A new era of leadership." Tannen held the crown of the wild king for all in the stands to witness. "I do not take the mantle of Ruler of the Blackwood for my benefit. It is a burden, in truth. But any power of the pagans held by *me* is one withheld from *them*."

His priests nodded, but it was obvious many in the crowd could see his zealotry. This was a man of shifting morals, one who saw the right thing as the one which coincided with personal gain.

"Today I use an object of evil as a force for good. A day for all to see that the pious in the world have a new home." Tannen turned to Saint Peter with an alligator smile. "Would you do the honors, dear friend?"

Saint Peter frowned and contemplated all the people in attendance, all the people he'd sworn to guide. Every second of this decision was a miserable one for him. But he had already saved his fellow saints, whatever the in-game ramifications of doing so were. I wondered why they hadn't just logged off. I wondered if they were incapable. Peter stretched his neck against the uncomfortable noose, no doubt still in place as an incentive to comply. Eventually, his gaze landed on me, and I nodded. Peter turned to the bishop and gave his blessing.

"Then it is a glorious day indeed!" gleamed Tannen. A global notification popped up.

Global Haven Alert:
Bishop Tannen has formed a new faction: the Catechists.
This is a branched faction of the Crusaders.
Various faction attributes will carry over.

The bishop erupted in boisterous laughter. "Yes!" he shrieked. "It is done! I am supreme!" He fanned his arms toward the sky and basked in his achievement.

I'm not sure if Tannen thought he'd ascend into the heavens right then and there, but no holy spotlights consumed him or lifted him to grace. He just kinda stood there, surrounded by his groupies. After an awkward moment, he realized he was the center of attention and addressed the onlookers.

"Come to me, my men. Welcome to a new world. A new order." Notifications popped up in front of everybody.

> **Faction Invite**
> Stronghold residents are hereby invited to join the Catechists.
>
> ***Join Catechists?***

I swiped the dialog away and muttered, "You've got to be shitting me." The priests gobbled up the invites. Grimwart canceled the request and commanded the crusaders to do the same. The order received a mixed reaction.

> **Izzy:** *Did Tannen just win?*

I forced a brave face even as my stomach turned.

> **Talon:** *Magic 8 Ball says too early to tell.*
> **Kyle:** *I had one of those!*
> **Izzy:** *I did too. I don't think that was one of the possible answers.*

"Colonel!" bellowed the bishop as he spun to his subordinate. The crosscut helmet lowered and his face darkened, two golden eyes the only visible feature. "I understand your duty to the crusaders. We are one and the same in the fight against evil. You must, however, understand that the righteous are often tested. I now ask for your faith, Colonel Grimwart. Listen to your bishop and corral the violators. Do your part toward the unification of Stronghold. Bring them to me at once."

The staunch military commander weighed his sword in one hand. He twirled his off hand in the air to gather his troops to him. They snapped into disciplined lines.

"You speak the truth," he replied to his superior. "We are indeed one and the same when it comes to faction lines. But our minds are wholly different."

The bishop's eyes narrowed. "Do not act in a way you might regret," he warned.

"If I turned on the very people I was sworn to protect, I'd regret it the rest of my life. I will not assist in your quest for power."

"I do not ask for assistance," snapped Tannen. "I demand compliance."

"I am the colonel of the crusader army. I answer to the Trinity. Last night I sent a rider to Oakengard. They are to be notified of your treachery."

Tannen grumbled. "The good knight and the wise lady." He spat. "I care not for their edicts."

"Then you will be dealt with."

Soldiers on both sides of the line tensed. Several quietly drew weapons. The bishop, however, wasn't concerned. He stood over the crusaders and goaded them on.

"Dealt with?" he guffawed. "By you? It is blasphemy to attack me without their word. Tell me, are the leaders you choose to prefer in attendance? Are they supporting this mutiny?"

Grimwart stood defiantly against the catechist inquisition.

The bishop hissed and appealed directly to the knights in black. "*He* is your colonel, but *I* am your bishop. Your holy compass. My word supersedes his. Arrest him."

I'd never seen so many full helms swivel in unison. Armored feet shuffled listlessly in the arena dirt.

"You've outdone yourself," returned Grimwart, emboldened. "Upon the founding of your own faction. Granted, our objectives may still be aligned. My oaths still stand. You are well aware that my men and I are barred from personally ousting you. But you're a catechist now, *Bishop*. I will not bow to your orders, and neither will my men. I am still their colonel. Our original charge, handed down by the Trinity, was to recruit and fight the war against the pagans." Grimwart made a show of looking around. "I see not a goblin or imp in sight. I declare Stronghold free from danger. The crusaders are no longer needed here."

Tannen's helmet visibly shook as he stewed underneath. "This is high treason."

The colonel ignored the catechist and barked orders. "Men! Round up. Gear up. Saddle the horses. We ride out of Stronghold forthwith!"

The bulk of the black tunics snapped into action. I think they were just excited at the prospect of getting the hell out of here. But jabs were traded among fellow soldiers. Some swords were brandished. Tannen and Grimwart snapped orders at the men who hesitated, getting them to second-guess their actions even more. Both leaders were resolute in their stances and left little room for consideration.

"If you refute my order," announced Grimwart, "you are no crusader. March out or abandon your vows. *That* is your choice."

The army began exiting in a line, but it was clear they were leaving some behind. Black tunics planted their feet and joined the catechists. Black cloaks blinked to white. Crosses filled with gold. It was demoralizing to witness, but I tried to focus on the fact that the majority of the army was abandoning Tannen.

Colonel Grimwart stepped to me as his soldiers marched past. "I'm sorry I can't fight the bishop with you, but I sure as hell won't help him. I hope that, by pulling out the crusaders, I'm preventing all-out war."

The growing number of catechists watched as the colonel fell in with his army and exited the Circus. A void was left behind them, trampled dirt and other remnants, like the circus had just packed up and left town. Bishop Tannen's forces were crippled by the sudden departure.

At the same time, members of the crowd slowly rose to their feet. Cloaks fell away to reveal the olive-green tunics of the city watch and the banded armor of the centurions.

The exodus of the crusaders meant the Pantheon was now only guarded by priests and stragglers. The city watch made up the larger force now.

If only they were free to move in.

Tannen's influence over Grimwart had failed, but his hold over the city watch was less tenuous. As long as he possessed the Eye of Orik, they couldn't act.

In the ensuing confusion of shifting threats, I signaled to Saint Peter. He still stood at the gallows wearing a noose, but the rope was slack enough for him to move around. I slipped closer between a few priests and huddled at the edge of the stage.

"We need the players," I whispered.

He focused overburdened eyes on me. "What?"

I reached up and worked to untie his wrists. "Look around you. The stands are full of players who want to join this fight, one way or another. If the saints enact wartime procedures, the players can join our cause. Fight off the bishop. Retake the Pantheon."

The defeated saint shook his head.

"You have to do it now. Tannen's weaker than he's been in days. The longer we allow him to re-establish his power—"

"You don't understand, Talon. We can't turn on town combat. That logic is handled by the Haven runtime."

"But you've got to be able to override it? Make a special case?"

He gave a tempered nod. "Usually, we can. But the catechists hold the Pantheon. Without access to the Oculus, our abilities to direct the sim are inhibited."

I stared at him, the grim reality splayed across my face. We couldn't get the Pantheon without the players, but we couldn't get the players without the Pantheon. "So we're stuck?!?"

Before he could answer, Saint Peter was jerked backward by the noose. The rope I was untying slipped from my grasp. I tried to reach out but the nearby priests converged on me. I had to dash backward out of harm's way.

"What's this?" demanded Bishop Tannen. "Conspiring against the crown?" His eyes glazed over in anger. "Pass the sentence!"

"No!"

The hangman's slack yanked tight as Peter was dragged back to the trapdoor. He desperately worked to cast off the loosened bindings. He slipped a wrist free and brought his hands around to throw off the noose. He was a step too late. The floor sprang open and he popped downward. If it wasn't for his hands bracing the rope, his neck would've snapped.

But he wasn't out of the woods. Peter wasn't strong enough to resist the tug of gravity against his throat. The Kablammy employee kicked his legs and widened his eyes as the simulation he'd helped bring to life slowly strangled him.

I snapped my spear at the closest priest and feinted at another. Instead of striking, I slammed the dragonspear into the ground and used my vault skill to carry me up and over the men. My boots were inches from the platform before Tannen blasted me with a cone of golden power. My skin burned and the force sent me tumbling backward into the dirt.

I shook my head, feeling more stunned than I actually was. "Save the saint!" I yelled.

Errol whipped into action, slicing at white tunics left and right. Trafford scrambled for a clear shot and I pushed to my feet.

Tannen wasted no time. Another golden cone engulfed me, this time while I was a standing target. It was a crushing blow.

> 72 damage
>
> Withering Light!
> For the next 20 seconds, you are enfeebled and cannot partake in combat or skill use.

I choked down the pain. It felt like I was suffocating myself, but Peter was the one who was turning blue. He attempted to gasp under his own crushing weight. I couldn't even find the strength to stand.

Trafford took careful aim at the bishop. A newly anointed catechist with an axe ran at me to take off my head. I couldn't fight back, but at least I would see Tannen get blasted.

Trafford spun and fired my way. The knight collapsed at my feet, a bloody mess.

No. Not me. Save the saint.

Through blurry eyes, I watched Peter heave in panic as Errol and Trafford struggled to get to the stage. All around us, the audience burst into rioting. It was madness.

We needed more. It was the players who would turn the tide. We needed the players. We needed them on our side. We needed wartime measures enacted.

Then it clicked.

I planted the dragonspear in the ground and pulled myself up, fueled only by sheer determination. "I hereby invoke my mantle as Protector of Haven," I shouted, "to found my own faction."

A dialog presented itself.

```
Faction: (Unnamed)
Cause: (Unspecified)
Founder: Talon, Protector of Stronghold
Membership: (Awaiting Approval)
```

I didn't have time for the details. I locked eyes with Saint Peter. He was struggling mightily and failing. Slowly suffocating whenever he failed to take a breath. He was completely exhausted now, unable to ease the pressure against his neck. At a distance and with a melee between us, my gaze implored him to intercede.

Peter nodded. That was it, and I had his blessing. I felt a whoosh as the faction was founded. Immediately I had access to a special faction menu. In the membership section, I mimicked Tannen and invited the whole city. Windows everywhere sprouted into view.

Faction Invite
Stronghold residents are hereby invited to join the (Unnamed) (Talon, Protector of Stronghold).
Join (Unnamed)?

Kyle: *First!*
Izzy: *Rolls eyes.* *I'm in, too, obviously.*

Acceptances flooded in all around me. Bishop Tannen assessed the stands and turned to me in rage.

I smiled and opened the special faction commands.

Players, you see, can't engage in town combat. Lucifer had hacked an exception into my runtime, but everyone else in Stronghold was forced to comply with Haven's original design. There were times, however, that residents were freely allowed to take up arms, and that was in defense of the city. Barring a saintly override, the threat of Lucifer's black dragon and the goblin horde had both enacted wartime measures. Here I'd been trying to go for the wrong thing. I hadn't seen the forest for the trees.

We didn't need wartime *measures*. What we needed was *a war*.

I clicked over the faction commands: Declare Alliance. Declare Armistice. I settled on the final option: Declare War.

With the catechists as my target, I was now technically an invading force in Stronghold. And not just me. Me and every other person continuing to enlist in my faction.

> **City Alert:**
> The (Unnamed) have invaded Stronghold! *Stronghold is under threat. All residents may engage in combat. While within the walls, all watchmen and residents are immune to friendly fire.*

Suddenly, a rush of swords scraped from their scabbards everywhere. The catechists whirled in panic.

The city watch was still relegated to the sidelines. They could've chosen to fight off the intruders, of course, but they stayed their ground. That was Gladius and his good men supporting me.

Every single player in the city, however, was suddenly free, whether they were on my side or not. Sure, that equated me with the goblin horde from almost two weeks ago, but at least it meant the battle for the city was on.

1040 Total War

Energy renewed, I immediately focused on Saint Peter. He sagged limply in the noose, one arm falling to his side. Out of nowhere, a silver arrow sliced through the rope and the saint crumpled to the ground with a gasp. Deep in the stands Dune now held his spent longbow. He tipped the bow to his head in salute before nocking another arrow and applying his expert aim elsewhere.

Scraps of fighting broke out in the stands—players choosing sides—but the unrest was dying out. Anybody with sense wanted Tannen out of Stronghold, but the urge to "defend the town" needed to be overcome first. The city watch's inaction really helped me on that score. It was inspiring others to wait and see. Preferable to being enemies, even if I'd rather they fought for my side.

Unfortunately, not every player had common sense.

I dove to the floor as a cleaver swooped over me. I rolled aside and swiped my spear at Lash, but she threw a heavy black shield in the way.

"What are you doing?" I yelled.

"You're ruining everything!" she snarled. She caught me with a backhanded swing and I tumbled again.

42 damage

Damn. Over the last several days, I'd been having a moral crisis and was stuck in lockdown, but Lash had been doing nothing but leveling. She was level 8 but, more importantly, she was a soldier class. The white knight had more power and combat proficiencies than I did.

She swung down and I crossblocked. I followed that up with a dead-center deadshot, but she'd been waiting on that one. Her shield spun in a full three-sixty as she triggered her own block skill. She'd avoided all damage.

What she didn't account for was the rascally pirate who somersaulted to her back. Errol's rapier glazed her hard and the white knight spun away. We had her flanked now.

"Wow," remarked an awestruck Errol. "Ye be a *lot* o' woman!"

"You got that right," she snapped, clanging his sword away with her cleaver. It looked like he was holding a car antenna compared to her monstrosity.

"What are you doing?" I repeated, noticing she still wore the black tunic of the crusaders and not the catechist uniform. That meant she hadn't joined Tannen yet.

She swiped at me. "I'd found an army to belong to, and you took that from me." Another slash and parry. "I didn't want them to leave. I couldn't—"

Errol attempted to dance past her guard but she kneed him

in the stomach. The pirate fell back with a grunt.

I engaged her to protect him, but I lightened my attack. Lash was laughably like her namesake, lashing out whenever angry.

"You're not mad at me," I told her. "You're mad at yourself. You couldn't make a decision."

"Shut up, Talon."

"But not deciding was the right decision," I assured her. "Don't you see? The crusaders abandoned the city. You couldn't do that. You also didn't join the catechists. Doesn't that tell you everything you need to know about what side you're fighting for?"

She crossed her arms to her chest and exploded in a yellow flash. Behind her, Glinda and Conan also received whatever buff it was. They rushed up to join her.

"Shut. Up." Lash boomed her sword at me. I triggered crossblock, but this time the damage spilled through.

23 damage

"Don't do it, Lash," screamed Glinda. The elderly healer was a non-affiliated priest. She chanted and a will-o-wisp of light flew into me and healed some damage.

Conan ripped his black sash off. It drifted to the floor and he readied his axe. "They left us here instead of fighting," he spat. "How could we ever side with someone like that?" A catechist priest charged Trafford and Conan sank his axe head into his chest. "Yes!" boomed Conan. "This feels *right*."

> **Izzy:** *Heads up, Talon. The catechists abandoned their blockade of Dragonperch. They're gathering whatever reinforcements remain in town and heading your way.*

The catechists, discovering players turning on them left and right, charged us. Lash backpedaled. Conan fought back. A rush of rabid knights and priests came at me.

"Batter up," I shouted, tossing Kyle's fire vial into the air above me. As it fell, I spun out of the way and swung the dragonspear, shattering glass into enemy faces. They fell, awash with fire. A cone of flames lined the ground. Errol and Trafford moved closer to the wall. It was one less point of attack for the catechists.

On the platform, silver arrows veered away from the bishop, each time the cross on his helmet flaring like a beacon. Stigg yelled wildly and charged up the steps to meet him, gnarled wooden staff swinging violently. Bishop Tannen's hands flashed as I'd seen Vagram's do, but instead of weapons appearing in them, he equipped thick bronze gauntlets. As Stigg swung, the skinnier bishop didn't shy away. His gauntlets smacked the heavy blows away without effort.

Stigg's party member, Caduceus, ran to the base of the platform to support him. She tweaked her physicker talents to debuff the priest. Whatever she did, it hurt him. Her medical poison began sapping his health.

Priests and knights in shiny white tunics spilled into the entrance. It couldn't have been everyone in town. I figured the catechists were reserving enough soldiers to guard the Pantheon. Still, the added numbers were daunting. But the skirmishes in the stands had mostly settled down. The players in the Circus flooded to the ground in a unified force. The opposing sides crashed against each other like rival waves.

"They're being overwhelmed," I told the others. "I'm heading to the platform. This only matters if we put down Tannen."

I cut through a knight but a priest swarmed in. He folded his hands into a hook and I practically froze in place. I struggled against the spell, but it was a strong one. At least, it was until a giant blazing cleaver cut the priest in half lengthwise.

"Get up there, Protector," growled Lash. "I'll keep them off the gallows." Her arms crossed and all nearby players flashed a pale yellow.

Morale Boost!
All players in affected radius receive +10% damage bonus.

Another flash, this one scarlet, followed.

Advanced Training!
All players in affected radius receive +10% chance of crits.

The white knight hefted her cleaver and turned to the catechists without another word.

I shook my head. "Someone's a bit bipolar today," I muttered under my breath.

On the platform, Stigg was driven to his knees with a body blow. His staff clattered to the ground. A nearby priest on the ground took a bellyful of gunpowder from Trafford and keeled over. I planted my boot on his back and vaulted. This time I lined up my spear for a deadshot and triggered dash to make sure I didn't fail to reach the platform.

Tannen barely saw me in time. He raised his gauntlets but the combo attack broke through. He yelped and stumbled away as I slammed onto the stage. Caduceus threw a heal at Stigg as he chugged a spirit vial. It was a close recovery.

Two priests and a knight already onstage charged me. A silver arrow caught one in the middle of a prayer. I twirled my weapon and swept the knight's legs from under him. The priest and Stigg cast offensive spells at each other, but Caduceus came up behind and slipped a surgical blade into the catechist's neck. At the same time, the dragonspear crashed down and severed the knight's helmet from his body. All three were dead.

The bishop threw his golden cape over his shoulders and paced along the platform with a sneer. The ground below was rife with the tides of combat. Up here, it was just him against me, Caduceus, and Stigg.

"You must know," said Tannen with an evil gleam in his eyes, "that the White King is not so easily defeated."

He raised a bronze hand as the helmet cross exploded in a beautiful aurora. We braced for impact, but the golden light ignored us. Instead, men on the ground stirred. The priests we had just killed convulsed and shook off their deathly slumber. All over the arena, men wearing white and gold stirred from the great beyond and once again took up arms.

"Oh, yeah," I muttered. "*That.*"

A high-pitched chuckle escaped the bishop's lips as the men we'd just killed came at us again.

Stigg's black beard shook as he widened wild eyes. "That just means we do this the hard way," he boomed. A wave of the red robe's hand hit me with a buff.

Berserker's Frenzy!
For the next 30 seconds, your physical skills do not require cooldown.

I smiled. You couple the dragonspear with an upgraded deadshot and you have a killer combination on your hands. I still have to spend the skill points, but if you take away the need for a cooldown—well, let's just say those reanimated priests didn't stand a chance.

The entire platform ripped into action. Stigg recovered his staff and swung toward the priests. I fended Tannen off to prevent him getting a cheap shot in. His gauntlets crashed against my crossblock and I slid back a couple of feet. My arms jarred from the impact, but the damage was minor. I counterpunched away from him, killing a priest with a deadshot before reengaging Tannen.

"I think I can keep them down for good," said Caduceus. She pulled a small vial from her medical bag and stabbed it into a catechist's chest. The injector reminded me of one of Kyle's crossbow bolts. The physicker repeated the shots into the other two as they fell.

Meanwhile, Stigg turned on the bishop. The gnarled staff caught Tannen on the back of the helmet, twisting it around. Tannen spun a fist and banged the staff to the floor. Before he could hit the berserker, I stabbed the back of the bishop's leg. He whirled on me but I dashed away. Then I lined up another deadshot and hit him again. Tannen swung but I was fast. Caduceus ran by and slashed his back.

Enraged, the bishop screamed. Light danced up his body like a candle flame as he powered himself up. I attempted another strike but Tannen beat me this time. He batted the spear away, almost jerking it from my hands. Stigg moved in, pounding the catechist's chest several times, knocking him toward the platform edge. Off balance. With a last desperate maneuver, Stigg leaned in, grabbed the golden cross, and ripped Tannen's helmet from his head.

It wasn't without cost, though. The berserker's hand immediately erupted into red fire. He screamed and flung the helmet clear of the platform. Tannen was livid now. He raised both gauntlets together and a rush of power fired out and consumed the berserker.

Caduceus moved in to save him but it was too late. The light cleared and Stigg was a blackened heap.

> [Stigg] is dead!

"Piece of shit!" snapped Caduceus.

Tannen raised his gauntlets to her and her eyes widened. Suddenly, Trafford's shot pegged the bishop in the back. Instead of falling backward off the platform edge, he pitched forward awkwardly. Without the magical protection of the helmet, a silver arrow caught him in the neck. He choked and clutched his throat. Caduceus wasted no time in burying her scalpel into one of Tannen's golden eyes.

I likewise lined up the dragonspear and activated dash and deadshot at the same time. The legendary weapon punched through the bishop's breastplate and knocked him backward. This time he did fly off the stage. Tannen's dead body crashed into the dirt amid the priests fighting to protect him.

The localized crowd around us stopped fighting. I panted on the edge of the platform, staring at the bishop's body, waiting for the loot to drop. Behind me, Caduceus went to assist Stigg, but he was long gone. She then made sure to inject Tannen's body with her poison. Errol weaved through the combat in the distance to recover the bishop's cross helmet. He heaved it over his head triumphantly before stuffing it safely in his inventory. With the artifact in our possession, victory was guaranteed.

I surveyed the Circus grounds. It sure didn't look like a guarantee, though. Despite our numbers, Tannen had been making the most out of his. Some of the same catechists that had been killed two or three times were still fighting. Many of the good guys were spent. Conan was trampled on the floor. Glinda got a last healing push to Lash before succumbing to her injuries. Even the white knight was being overwhelmed.

Blaring horns announced a new arrival. Instead of coming from the city gates, they came from just outside the Circus. Combatants on both sides turned their heads to see where momentum would swing next.

I drained spirit and health flasks down my throat and wiped

my lips. "Dandy timing," I muttered, and turned to the new threat.

The city watch marched to both sides of the Circus entrance and left a path for the distinguished guests, just as I'd instructed them to. Without needing to fight his way into Stronghold, the warden of the Blackwood strolled into the Circus grounds, hefting his axe.

1050 Breath of the Wild

The eight-foot brute plodded forward like a siege engine. He wore mismatched armor and strips of blackened leather in patchwork protection. The executioner's axe was worn and tinged with rust, but had a bright edge where it had recently been sharpened. It was an intimidating weapon, though not his only one. Dark chains hung from his body and snaked along the ground like living entities.

Most striking atop an overbearing persona, though, was the simple black hood masking his identity. Two white eyes glowed from the eye holes.

"Pagan abomination!" swore a priest in white. He charged Hood, white fire on his fists. The executioner's axe swung like a blur. The catechist's head flew high into the stands, leaving the body sprinting several more yards before it had the sense to fall. The seething crowd was silenced.

"Talon," growled the man in black. "It is time for you to surrender your soul."

I stood defiantly above the skirmish as Errol and Trafford

climbed the steps to join me. The pirate leaned close.

"Why do ye have that look on yer face as if ye knew this was happenin'?"

Trafford chuckled. "He's savvy for a pirate, I'll give him that."

Behind the warden, a line of Blackwood prisoners followed. They were a ragtag band of goblins, humans, and otherwise. Stripped of both their independence and individuality, the only thing they shared in common were their black hoods with missing eyeholes.

I'd expected as much. The warden always had some prisoners on hand. What caught me completely off guard was the lean bare-chested figure with ropy muscles who followed. He wore a mask of dried leaves that resembled a domino mask, tan hair clipped short behind. A tattoo of a black deer skull dominated his chest, antlers stretching from shoulder to shoulder.

I stretched my jaw. "I need to watch who I invite to these things."

"Why?" asked Errol. "Who be that one?"

"It's the wild king."

Wildkins without hoods marched behind him. The free people of the Blackwood. They looked like humans wearing wild clothes. Nothing more, nothing less. And there were a lot of them. I hadn't expected the whole nation to answer my summons.

The king stopped and surveyed the crowd. "Tiding, tidings to the white city."

> **Izzy:** *Talon, what the hell is he doing here?*

Players and NPCs rustled on either side of the procession. The city watch remained at the entry gates, but one man rushed in. Gladius wore steel-banded armor with a gold helmet and a red cape.

"The wild king is a guest in Stronghold," he decreed. "Freely allowed through the gates on the word of the Protector of Stronghold."

"A debt, a debt," recited the king. "Payment is due."

I gritted my teeth. Of all my stupid plans, this one took the cake. I cleared my throat and stepped forward.

"No one else has to die," I announced. "The bishop is dead. I'm gifting the wild king his crown back. I'm abandoning the quest, null and void."

I opened my menu to the quest status, trying to angle my screen so others could see.

Dethrone the Wild King
Abandon quest?

I killed it and turned to Trafford.

"Aye," he agreed. "We won't be used as catechist pawns anymore."

The wild king watched, amused, then turned to his bodyguard. "What say thee, warden?"

The giant grunted. "All that remains is a crown and a soul."

I grimaced. This was a long time coming. I patted my friends on the shoulder and descended the platform. The crowd gave way, forming a path between Hood and me. I approached him, dragging the dragonspear in the dirt.

Errol and Trafford were on me like glue. The shopkeeper raised his arquebus. Black chains reached along the ground and lashed out, knocking the weapon from his hands. Before the pirate jumped into action, I held them both back.

"No," I urged. "This is a fight I started days ago. It doesn't concern either of you. I need to take it on alone."

They stared hard, but they listened. When I turned to the executioner, they didn't follow.

Izzy: *Talon! What are you doing?*
Talon: *I'm sorry, Izzy. The truth is I don't know half the time.*
Izzy: *Come back to Dragonperch. You'll be safe.*
Izzy: *There's gotta be a hot tub upgrade or something in here, right?*

I worked my jaw. That sounded real good right about now. It really did.

Talon: *I wish I could.*

I lifted the spear and faced the warden of the Blackwood. "It's about time we did this, huh?"

His white eyes narrowed.

Cackling came from the mass behind me. A flurry of priests fanned away from the bishop's body, now alight with golden fire. He raised gauntleted fists to the air, lifted by invisible hands to a standing position. His jaw gaped, revealing a row of small teeth.

> **Kyle:** *WHOA! He did NOT just do that. Hold up. Don't do anything till I get more popcorn.*

I looked at Errol quizzically, who still had the crosscut helm in his inventory. He shrugged like it wasn't his fault.

Tannen was a sight without his helmet. His head was unnaturally bald, his face lined with veins. Skin stretched thin against sharp cheekbones as his eyes shone ever bright. "My power," he boasted, "comes not from an artifact, but from the White King himself." He regarded the parade of wildkins with a snort. "So, you're in collusion with a bunch of savages as well."

All around us, dead priests and knights scurried to their feet. Hood growled under his breath.

Tannen chuckled. "The warden of the Blackwood. Quite a specimen you are. You must be pleased to see your new ruler."

The wild king's eyes narrowed.

Tannen feigned surprise. "Why, do you not see before you the man who wears the mantle? *I* am the Ruler of the Blackwood, not this pagan pretender. But worry not, you can have Talon's soul. I just need his weapon."

The bishop marched toward me with a contingent of priests. The wildkins watched without objection. Trafford scrambled for his arquebus. Errol swiped at the nearest priest. Tannen fired a golden beam from his bronze gauntlet and battered the pirate to the ground.

Catechists bearing down on us, I swung the spear, high then

low. I swept heads and feet clear, but I couldn't stop the golden light. It washed over me too. I stumbled. A knight wearing catechist colors impaled Trafford clean through his heart. The old man fell to the floor, dead. Tannen's eyes lit up as he brought his hands together.

Lash swooped in with her cleaver, bringing it down like a sledgehammer. It snapped his collarbone clean through and dug deep into his shoulder, forcing him to his knees. He screamed in agony but fought through it, clutching the white knight with both bronze gauntlets. A surge of hot electricity ran through them, steam and smoke and searing pain. I shook off my own hurt and clawed to my feet against battering swords. A small explosion stalled our combat.

Lash lay on the ground, smoking. She'd sacrificed her experience points—halfway to level 9—just to buy me some time. I didn't have a good shot, but I had to take it. I dashed ahead, a sword biting into my knee as I did, and hefted the spear toward the bishop.

His good arm battered my deadshot to the side. Tannen tried to yank the spear away, but I held it with both arms. Instead he released it and kicked me to the floor. I rolled from a follow-up punch but only partially avoided it. I hit the dirt, still clutching my legendary weapon.

Tannen laughed, held a hand high, and washed himself with healing energy. Full health again. Shoulder good as new.

Caduceus lunged. He battered her down. Silver arrows clanged off his armor. One punched into his arm. A bronze hand slapped a headshot from the air. The gauntlet turned on the distant ranger. Dune's green cloak weaved between spectators but the energy blast connected and tripped him up. Errol was up again. His rapier flew under the bishop's guard and connected, but bronze clamped around his neck. I charged and Tannen threw Errol into me. The collision took us both down.

Amid our struggles just to regain our feet, Tannen screeched a battle cry. Familiar golden energy erupted outward from his body. It hit everyone and everything, friend and foe alike, and blasted us all to the ground with impressive efficiency. I rolled in searing pain within a large crater. Errol had just enough life to chug a health potion, but I had already spent my one for the day.

This was crazy. Tannen was superpowered now. Whether due to repeatedly dying or finally acquiring his faction, something had clicked loose in his head. Not only was he insane —he was taking us all down.

The warden's heavy leather boots stomped close. His shadow fell over me. Once again I forced myself to my feet, wincing through the pain.

"That is my kill, warden," interrupted Tannen. He had the gall to place a bronze hand on the giant's chest. "You will learn to serve your new ruler faithfully. Witness what happens to those who don't."

I grunted. "Witness it yourself." I summoned the last of my energy and raised the dragonspear.

Tannen snorted and batted the legendary weapon to the side. He decked me. "Don't embarrass yourself. You're—"

A black chain clinked around the bishop's neck. His upraised arm was tied up in another. Tannen whirled on Hood, swung a heavy fist, but the giant leaned away from the blow. The warden swatted Tannen's punches away with the axe as the chains lifted the bishop off the ground. Their faces met inches from each other.

Hood growled. "He is mine."

Tannen clutched the chain with his free hand, eyes going wide. It reminded me of Saint Peter at the noose. He strained against the wildkin's strength, but it was too much. "Yes," he conceded. "Fine. Take him."

The black chains snapped away and the bishop landed on his feet. The executioner turned to me on the ground and said, "You see, Talon. There is no need for others to die."

"Feel free to make an exception for him," I muttered. I tried to tug the dragonspear to me. Tannen clamped a metal boot on it. He had it pinned.

"You are the one," grumbled the warden, eyes on me. "Pagans hate you more than any other in Stronghold." He stepped closer.

I wanted to crawl backward, but I couldn't leave the dragonspear. Tannen showed his teeth as his men surrounded Errol, now disarmed. "It's over, Talon."

"No," I hurried. "I'm not an enemy of the pagans."

The warden didn't relent. "Your notoriety says otherwise."

I shook my head in desperation, denial more than anything pragmatic. "You're wildkins, not pagans. Your king told me himself."

Tannen scoffed. "Open your eyes, Talon. Pagans are pagans. They are what they are."

The executioner lifted his axe.

"You can think for yourself," I blurted out. "Lucifer's hack gave NPCs and mobs free will. That's why your king broke away from the horde. He no longer wanted to be governed by numbers."

Hood's voice scraped. "Your numbers are the accumulation of bad deeds."

He had me there. I hadn't glanced at my reputation score in forever—it stopped mattering a long time ago—but I did now.

Pagan Reputation: -950

It wasn't bottomed out at -1000 anymore.

I threw a hand up. "Wait! What about the good I've done?" I displayed my reputation score for others to see, though Hood must've known it already. "While visiting Shorehome I defended a helpless mother and child. Goblins. I was awarded reputation for the good I did. My eyes are open now. There's more yet to come." I swept my gaze across the players, NPCs, and mobs in attendance. "There's what the game wants us to do, and what we actually do. We don't need to be at war. We're in control. We can be our own change."

Tannen smiled cruelly. "Haven has seen enough of your deeds, Talon."

I sneered upwards, refusing to release the spear from my grip. "And what of yours, Bishop? When we first met, you bragged about killing pagans for years. You displaced them, tortured them, hunted them. What's your pagan rep?"

"Indeed." The warden cocked his hooded head. "Curious..."

"No," snapped Tannen. "He's the one you want."

I studied the bishop anew. NPCs didn't have visible levels,

but now that we were in opposing factions, I could see his reputation.

Pagan Reputation: -1000

"No," he repeated. "He's the one who stole your crown."

"You're the one who holds it," Hood countered.

"Take it." Tannen produced the stag skull. "Give me the dragonspear and I'll hand you the crown." His eyes scrunched cruelly as he conspired with the warden. "*You* can hold the crown. *You* can be the king."

I sat up, head clearing as the two men faced off. But they faded to the background when I focused on the true power here.

"Theoderic," I called out, addressing the wild king by his true name. "You've entered Stronghold in peace. The city watch welcomed you. *I* welcome you."

Everyone's eyes turned to the lean ruler. He didn't grace us with a reply, but he watched on with half a smile.

I cleared my throat. "I have more good deeds to accomplish. Starting with this one." I scrolled through the faction menu and selected an armistice with the pagans. "I am Stronghold's Protector, but I can't speak for its people. I can, however, speak for my faction. We'll withdraw hostilities against peaceful pagans."

"A useless gesture," Tannen snickered. "That won't last more than a week."

"We'll try," I assured. "You have my word."

"The word of a thief."

The wild king laughed lightly. "Withdraw, withdraw."

Pagan Reputation +100

Tannen spun to Hood. "Don't listen to him. *I* am your Ruler." The warden didn't move.

Tannen read the crowd. Saw the eyes of the wildkins turn on him. The bishop lifted a bronze gauntlet above to strike me down.

An axe cleaved his arm off.

Tannen spun around in shock. The executioner attempted to reverse his swing for a finishing blow, but the bishop still had one good arm. The bronze gauntlet slammed into Hood's chest with cataclysmic force. The impact battered him backward into a stumble.

Tannen still stood on my dragonspear. I considered prying it out from under him, but I realized the bishop was entirely occupied with the warden. Perfect opportunity for a surprise.

"If I can't kill you..." I muttered. I sprang to my feet and triggered subdue.

I wrapped the bishop in a headlock and squeezed. My intent wasn't to do damage, but I hadn't bothered to think through exactly what would happen. Surely if the skill hadn't been an automatic knockout against a random guard, it didn't stand a chance against Tannen. But I held on tight and the bishop's knees wobbled.

The second he dropped to his knees, I jumped off his back and scooped up the dragonspear. As he turned, I dashed along the ground and plunged the object he so earnestly desired right into his chest. The bronze gauntlet clamped onto the dragonspear, preventing me from driving it deeper.

Hood stepped close and released a throaty growl, this time targeted at Tannen. "Bishop, I follow my king not because of a crown. My oath is more than a symbol." He glanced at me. "More than a number." He heaved his axe high.

The bishop's mouth opened in a boisterous cackle, spittle dribbling down his lips. "Fools. You cannot kill me."

The axe fell hard on Tannen's head and he slumped to the ground.

[Bishop Tannen] is dead!

The entirety of the Circus couldn't drown out my heavy breathing. That's how quiet it was. We stared on as a faint glow built over the bishop's body.

"He's right," I said. "He doesn't die."

"I do not seek death," said the warden. "I seek compliance."

From a sack on his waist, the executioner withdrew a black hood. As Tannen's head healed and reformed, the executioner slipped a prisoner hood over it. The golden light exploded and the bishop hopped up, good as new. Then he lowered his head and humbly joined the ranks of the rest of the hooded prisoners.

"His soul belongs to the Blackwood."

All the present catechists fled from the Circus. The city watch followed to make sure they left the city.

"Wait," I said, using the shaft of the dragonspear to prop myself up. I trudged over to what remained of the bishop. The blank hood faced me expectantly. He was alive, but I wasn't so sure Tannen was in there anymore. "I need the soulstone."

Since none of the prisoner hoods had eyeholes, Tannen's golden eyes were impossible to read. But the head swiveled to the warden. The big man in turn did the same toward another. King Theoderic pressed his lips together and nodded. The prisoner complied by handing over the Eye of Orik.

Gladius was helping Saint Peter out from underneath the gallows platform. The old man looked like hell, but he was alive. I strode to them and handed over the blood-red gemstone. A surge of power rushed over the city.

The head of the city watch wasted no time barking orders. "The Circus is secure. Watch, form up. It's time to take back the Pantheon." The guards and legionnaires, now free to act against the wishes of the bishop, rushed from the stands and formed disciplined lines. They marched from the Circus in double time. Gladius himself remained at Saint Peter's side and supported his weight.

"You did it, Talon," said the commander.

I shrugged halfheartedly. "It got done, at any rate."

"Nonsense. Your duties as Protector were upheld. It's a proud day for the city."

The two of them moved toward the line of wildkins. Before them, the stag crown rested in the dirt where Tannen had fallen. I hurried to pick it up, but Hood growled in warning. I turned to the big monster cautiously.

"Let him be," called the wild king.

The warden simply grumbled. It wasn't the cleanest gesture of peace, but I felt confident enough in his loyalty to the king that I picked up the crown. I reverently brushed dirt off the skull and limped to its owner.

"I believe this is yours," I said. "It was a mistake to ever think otherwise."

The king's dark eyes were unrelenting voids, but he flashed a smile. He took the crown and fitted it over his head. "So it is a friendship thou art proposing?" he asked slyly.

"I'm not so sure I deserve it. But I'm a friend if you'll have me."

The Ruler of the Blackwood took in the post-chaotic arena. "Thy bishop was correct about the armistice not lasting. I am a king among the errant folk, but we have many kings. I've accepted thy terms, but I do not speak for all pagans. A unified faction it is not."

I cleared my throat. "Why don't we fix that then?" I snatched Saint Peter before Gladius could take him away. "The founding of a true faction requires saintly approval."

The skull of the stag turned to Peter in quiet surprise. The saint studied the king before turning to me and trying to speak. His voice was hoarse from the noose, and barely a whisper.

"You have my blessing."

> **Global Haven Alert:**
> The wild king has formed a new faction: the Wildkins.
> *This is a branched faction of the Pagans.*
> *Various faction attributes will carry over.*

I pulled one more item from my inventory. "You have a new faction, but an old home. As a gesture of goodwill, I'm thinking it's time you upgrade the Black Keep." I handed the king the bone pearl. "A creepy place like that, I'm sure you can socket this thing."

Theoderic released a light chuckle that flowed on the breeze. "Now I see, I see how thou hast accomplished so much in so little time, Talon. Thou art a man who can accomplish much."

"As are you, wild king. You rule your own people now. What do you say? You up for a faction alliance?"

I opened the menu and offered the alliance to the wildkins. The Ruler of the Blackwood took an extra moment to survey the grounds. The destruction.

"The fates, the fates are watching this day," he said in his jovial manner. "Alas, my kind are indecisive and fickle." He canceled the alliance request. "This is a good thing," he assured, noting my disappointment. "Fate is not yet clear whether thou deservest an alliance"—his face darkened—"or a war."

I swallowed. Hood lumbered past me with a growl. The line of Blackwood prisoners filed out, Tannen in tow. His catechists still existed somewhere, but he was no longer their leader. He wouldn't be shrugging off his yoke with golden power or respawning in Oakengard any time soon. He was the warden's now, in a place between life and death. I didn't envy him that.

The wild king motioned for the exit. His people led the way. The tension in the Circus eased as we watched the wildkins leaving Stronghold.

"Fear not, Protector of the white city," said the king in farewell. "The wildkins shall honor the pagan armistice as long as it lasts. It will be broken, but not by us."

"And afterward?"

He snickered. "No doubt, no doubt fate shall draw us hither once more. We will settle the matter of our grievances anew, be it through diplomacy or conquest. Take heed, take heed the path thou choosest."

Wildkin Reputation: 0

1060 Black Flag

Happy endings belong in storybooks and TV.

I had initially hoped retaking the city would restore everything to normal, but I quickly realized there was no such thing. Life wasn't a sitcom. Neither was the afterlife, for that matter. Everything we did here—through progression, genetic algorithms, even hacks and exploits—it all summed up to evolution.

The simple truth was we could never go back to how things were before. Seeing the vulnerability of the saints, the rise of the NPCs and mobs—it all contributed to a collective consciousness. Was it community? Kinship? Self-preservation? Maybe it didn't matter. We lived in this reality now, something not quite what it was meant to be. Something we needed to protect and nurture because of that fact.

"You did it," exclaimed Izzy as I returned to the tower. "Without us. You were all alone and you did it."

I shook my head. "Not alone. Not by a long shot. There was a whole city of people out there. Players who wanted to fight but couldn't. A city watch who faded into the background until they could act. Dune fought. Lash fought. Errol and Trafford and other NPCs. Everyone and everything came together to combat Tannen's oppression."

Kyle punched me in the side. "So you got lucky."

"I wouldn't swing the pendulum *that* far in the opposite direction. Lucifer claimed he acted as the grease to a bunch of cogs. I like to think I did the same. I touched base with Gladius and the city watch. I lured the warden here. I coordinated with the saints and the players and tried every damn thing I could to overthrow the bishop."

He nodded. "Sure, I get it. You're basically saying you threw a whole lotta shit at the wall to see what stuck."

Izzy rolled her eyes and spun me away from his teasing. "If it's any consolation, *I* believe in you." She popped me with a kiss. I blinked back disbelief. She wasn't being vindictive or ironic or bossy. She was just being... nice. Izzy flashed a demure smile.

"Get a room, bro."

I turned to Kyle. "You're still here?"

"Aye," drawled Errol. "An' me an' Trafford as well."

Kyle pulled everyone close in a huddle. "Just the OG crew of the baddest new faction around."

The shopkeeper nodded. "Of course, we might strike more fear into people's hearts if we weren't fucking called (Unnamed)."

I chortled. "Everyone's a critic."

My faction menu opened and everyone peered over my shoulder. "Well, let's see here. I'm the Betrayer of Stronghold with a stolen weapon living in a stolen tower. Kyle's a drunkard. Izzy's a blaspheming mystic. We've got the Scar of the Six Seas over here beside a foul-mouthed questkeeper. We're occasional acquaintances of Lucifer, the Brothers in Black, and the wildkins of the Black Keep. Let's face it: we're black hats. We might as well embrace it."

Everyone nodded their approval. It was, after all, the black hats that had saved the white city.

> **Global Haven Alert:**
> Talon has named a new faction: the Black Hats.

We all tried out the new moniker. It rolled off our tongues. None of us were true villains, of course, but constantly fighting against a predetermined rule set had a way of casting one in a bad light. What was that saying? If you really wanted to make enemies, try to change something.

I laughed at the ridiculousness of it. After everything—the raid on the Black Keep, the quest to Shorehome, the battles with Lucifer and the catechists—the party had been killed. We'd lost all our XP. Killing town guards, or those acting in their stead, doesn't award experience. Not until the official war, anyway. That meant we were technically behind from where this whole thing had started. Not a level up in sight.

But stats didn't tell the whole story. We'd gained a completely different kind of experience. One that wasn't wiped by a spawn penalty or a debuff. Experience that told me Haven would never be quite the same as it was before. It would be stronger. It was a simulation in flux, and it all started in Stronghold.

The Oldtown refugees were a shining example. We did our best to restore order and calm. To impress in those displaced that their city soldiers on. Some welcomed the chance to return home. Some looked forward to braving a new life past the frontier of saintly influence.

But others no longer felt safe without the high walls of Stronghold or the guiding hands of the developers. Goblins living in a city run by criminals? It was an experiment by even the most optimistic measures. Many immigrants, having forever lost the home they remembered, focused on the future instead of trying to recapture the past.

There were other changes brewing, too. Talk of a new patch. A way to allow city residents to always defend themselves. Awakened NPCs could initiate town combat on a whim, so to restore equality, players will be given that functionality as well. It was power to the people. Something that would've prevented Bishop Tannen's rise and stranglehold on the city.

But the downsides were harsh. The change would essentially turn Haven into a PvP server. The city watch would still have the advantage of being protected from friendly fire, but they'd need to work three times as hard to maintain order in the city. Many saw it as a worthy sacrifice in the pursuit of true freedom from tyranny.

But it was a process, not a solution.

Lucifer was still out there, and his intentions were as clouded as ever. There were other inconsistencies, too. Saint Loras had worked against Kablammy's interests and handed over the keys to Shorehome. Vagram and the catechists would persist, perhaps as a rogue faction. The hostility between the holy and the pagans—and more primally, the humans and the goblins— was still a hot button. Despite everything we'd accomplished, coming events were uncertain.

That future was something I was thinking about a lot lately. Oldtown was a mess of ruins. Dragonperch was full of budding potential. Building plans were drawn up. New accommodations to handle the influx of NPCs and faction members. I foresaw a great black hat hall. A tavern and meeting place where the people could debate, safe from the prying eyes of the capital. Hell, anything was possible.

But, as with all plans, there was no quick fix. We had to carry through our convictions and see where they led us, even when the destination wasn't so pleasant.

It was a journey I was heartily looking forward to.

-Finn

Character Sheets

Talon		Level	9
Class	Explorer	XP	53428
Kit	Scout	Next	74950

Strength	17	Strike	337
Agility	24	Dodge	400
Craft	6	Health	261 / 261
Essence	10	Spirit	227 / 227

Coin	
Silver	103
Plates	89

Skills	2
Spear	3
Crossblock	3
Deadshot	3
Tornado Spin	1
Awareness	
Darkvision	
Survival	
Navigation	
Cartography	
Traversal	
Dash	
Vault	
Scale	
Stealth	
Sneak	
Subdue	

Proficiencies	
Expert	
Searcher	
Skilled	
Tracker	

Reputation	
Pagan	-850
Crusader	50
Wildkin	0

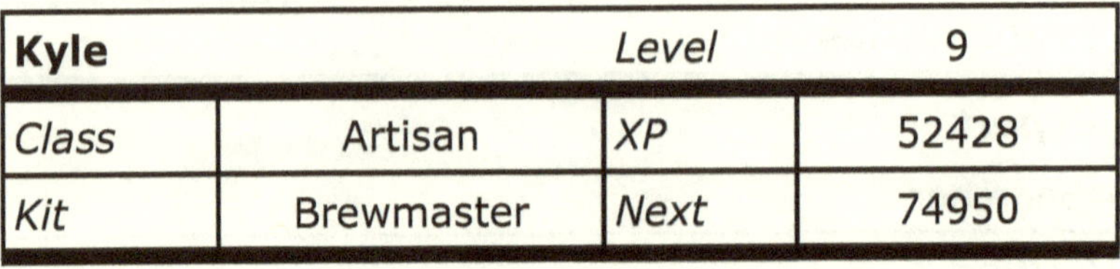

Kyle		Level	9
Class	Artisan	XP	52428
Kit	Brewmaster	Next	74950

Strength	22	Strike	319
Agility	5	Dodge	166
Craft	19	Health	220 / 220
Essence	10	Spirit	195 / 195

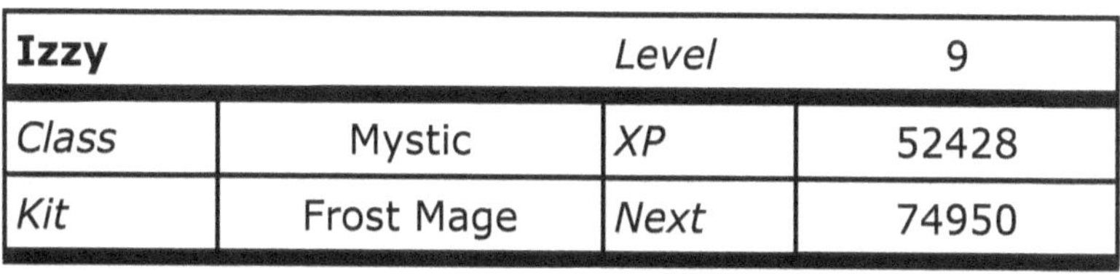

Izzy		Level	9
Class	Mystic	XP	52428
Kit	Frost Mage	Next	74950

Strength	8	Strike	184
Agility	17	Dodge	265
Craft	6	Health	148 / 148
Essence	25	Spirit	393 / 393

Town Wiki

STRONGHOLD   *"Strength in Unity."*

The bastion of all civilization in Haven, Stronghold rests in the center of the Midlands. Ninety-foot walls protect this teeming Roman metropolis from outside invaders. The petrified carcass of the titan Orik, kneeling but unfallen, is a daily reminder of the city's victory... and vulnerability.

Nicknames
The holy city, the jewel of haven, the core city, the white city

Population 800
200 (city watch, centurions, legionnaires)
400 (players)
200 (general NPCs)

Leadership
Stronghold is the main seat of power for the saints in Haven. Their control is tenuous after a couple of challenges to their rule, but a competent city watch and standing army keep the peace. Saintly leadership confers player protection and access to the hub.

SHOREHOME

"Alls we need be some silver and mead."

To some a den of villainy, to others a pinnacle of independence, Shorehome is defined by its outlaw attitude. It's a working-class port city where hard labor is often outshined by shady pursuits. Humans and goblins and more eke out livings in close proximity, and they wouldn't have it any other way.

Population 850

50 (players)

300 (general NPCs)

500 (goblins, imps, ogres, boggarts)

Leadership

Shorehome is run by eight criminal enterprises led by one Papa Brugo, head of the Brothers in Black. His iron grip translates to an efficient rule, but it is power obtained through fear, including the threat of the kraken. The lack of saintly presence means surviving in the city is a free-for-all, and there is no hub access.

OAKENGARD

"Without light there is not darkness; there is nothing."

A super fortress atop mountain terrain, Oakengard is a training station for crusaders of all stripes: knight, priest, and sage. Not much is known about the mysterious town as no players have ever been within its walls.

Population 500 (estimated)
200 (sage NPCs)
150 (knight NPCs)
150 (priest NPCs)

Leadership

Ruled by a devout bishop, a holy knight, and a wizened sage. The Trinity was fractured when Bishop Tannen broke away to form the catechists. Crusader leaders are rumored to be fighting wars from within and without, but their zealotry and discipline provide a unifying front.

Faction Wiki

Pagans

Members: 2858
Leader: None
Base: None

The largest and most disparate of all factions, pagans represent those following the call of the wild. Originally created as the quintessential enemy order in Haven, deviations in AI routines have muddied their role. Pagans are dominated by humanoid but animalistic creatures who use guerrilla warfare tactics against better-armed enemies. Most serve the Nine, but many merely seek disorder and survival of the fittest.

Wildkins

Members: 223

Leader: Theoderic, the Wild King

Base: Black Keep

An offshoot of the pagans who favor sanctuary over warmongering, wildkins reside in the Blackwood and fervently follow their king. Other than that, their motivations are a mystery.

Crusaders

Members: 522

Leader: Fractured Trinity

Base: Oakengard

A lawful sect of humans fighting for order and control, crusaders diametrically oppose the pagans. They raze forests and build roads, continually breaking ground in their thirst for greatness. Most serve the White King, but many merely desire a civilized society.

Catechists

Members: 100

Leader: Cleric Vagram

Base: None

An offshoot of the crusaders aimed at holy purity, catechists proved too zealous to establish a stable home. Without their bishop, Cleric Vagram leads their rogue numbers in exile.

Black Hats

Members: 48

Leader: Talon

Base: Dragonperch

Seated in Stronghold, black hats are the youngest and smallest of all factions, but the first run by a player. Their appeal lies in their apparent outlaw behavior while sticking to the mantra: don't be a dick, dude.

About the Author

I'm Domino Finn: game-developer-turned-fantasy-author, media rebel, and product of my generation. (SE-GA!)

Afterlife Online will be back. Join my reader group (http://dominofinn.com/newsletter/) to get the first word on sequels, cover reveals, and other DLC.

QUEST NOTIFICATION: Review Black Hat
DESCRIPTION: Post a book review online.
REWARD: 100 XP. And my eternal gratitude.

Finally, don't forget to keep in touch. You can contact me, connect on social media, and see my complete book catalog at DominoFinn.com.

Also, word on the street is the *really* cool kids are joining my Facebook group (https://www.facebook.com/groups/dominofinnfans/). No pressure. Just sayin'.